ASYLUM FOR THE QUEEN

Asylum

FOR THE

Queen

BY

MILDRED JORDAN

19 48

NEW YORK: ALFRED A. KNOPF

TO MY TWO FATHERS:

Charles William Jordan

who nurtured my first little-girl efforts with the pen,
and has never failed to help and encourage me;

AND

Solon Daniel Bausher

who, all his life, gave me deeply of his love and
understanding.

ACKNOWLEDGMENT

❀❀❀❀❀❀❀❀❀❀❀❀❀❀❀❀❀❀❀❀❀

IN THE FOUR YEARS spent on *Asylum for the Queen* I have fully realized how important are the help and courtesy of other people. Many have been tireless in obtaining research books for me, especially Mr. Richard L. Brown, Librarian of the Reading Public Library, Mr. Ellsworth H. Brininger, Reference Librarian, and Mr. George E. Pettengill, former Reference Librarian. Dr. Alfred D. Keator, Director of the Pennsylvania State Library, has been most co-operative, as well as Miss Grace Estes and Miss Josephine Pedigo of the Osterhout Free Library at Wilkes-Barre. Mr. Gilbert S. McClintock of Wilkes-Barre very cordially put at my disposal the wide list of books on Pennsylvania in his private library.

Others have been gracious in different ways. Mrs. Mark C. Hagerman, who lives on the site of the Grande Maison on the Susquehanna, answered a hundred questions; Dorothy Welder, Florine Lesher, Lavinia Keffer, Mrs. Rita Eberl, and my daughter Phyllis Bausher typed frantically to meet publisher's deadlines; Mlle Germaine Benoit arduously checked on my illicit French.

To these, and to many others who have given me their time and interest, go my deep appreciation for making the publication of this novel possible.

PART *One*

❀❀❀❀❀❀❀❀❀❀❀❀❀❀❀❀

CHAPTER I

May 1789

"Green walnuts! Green walnuts!"
"The list of the winners in the lottery!"
"*Carpe vive!*"
"Death to the rats!"

The cries of all Paris were in Pierre's ears. But he heard only the cooing of an absent dove. He was in love again.

The Pont-Neuf was a screaming Hydra. The bridge teemed with hundreds of venders; knife grinders, well cleaners, vinegar merchants, ink and parasol sellers. Did these venders ever leave the bridge? Had they eaten and slept here between cries and begot their filthy little urchins of a night in the squalid stalls since Henry IV?

"Rabbit skins!"
"Who'll buy spoons and larding pins?"

Tall, squat; swarthy Savoyard, ruddy Norman; the blind and the halt; the fashionable horseman; the fresh young milkmaid in her red jacket; the wily crone in her dismal rags; the gendarme, the pickpocket; the worn housewife, the lush grisette; farmers' carts, gentlemen's coaches; sulking cats, sniffling dogs; spies, fortunetellers; rag pickers; street singers—quavering voices lost in the babel.

Pierre was buffeted brutally from one to the other, his goal, the Palais-Royal where Mlle Hyacinthe lived. Ah, what a rosy little unplucked flower! Was it the balmy Maytime that gave such a gnawing sweetness to his rapture, or Mlle Hyacinthe's tiny silk ankles that enhanced the balmy Maytime, he wondered? But that was a problem for philosophers like Helvetius and Diderot. It was enough to feel that the swelling chestnut buds, and the touch of the little ballet dancer's alabaster hand on his arm added up to a total of bliss. And her lashes, quivering like dragonfly wings. . . .

His mind consumed with the delicate cream of her neck, Pierre roved into an ancient flower vender and upset her basket of nosegays, most of which were promptly trod into the mud by a pair of carriage horses.

"*Cochon! Imbécile!*" she screeched, striking him with her fist.

"*Dieu me pardonne!*" exclaimed Pierre, fumbling for a gold louis, which he thrust into her hand. He rescued one of the bouquets.

"*Ah, mon ange!*" screamed the hag in adulation now. "*Mon petit chou!*"

The perfume of crushed pinks drugged his senses once more and crowded out the low-hanging odors of fish, horse dung, river water, lemonade, human sweat. . . . Mlle Hyacinthe was fragrant as a pink, her waist thin as the stem of its flower. . . .

"Baked apples!"

"*La vie! La vie!*"

"*Portugaises, portugaises.*" (Oranges.)

"*A la barque!* Sea-fresh! *A l'écaille.*"

The men screamed with the falsetto of women; the women bawled with the hoarseness of men. Church and convent bells mingled all the sharps and flats of the scale. Suddenly through the rumble of carts there was the sharp clack of horses' hoofs on the cobblestones. A coachman shouted "*Gare!*" and his nobleman's carriage cut the throng as a knife cuts bread.

"*Dieu!*" cursed a broom merchant, seizing Pierre's red velvet arm and tossing him among the brooms. "Are you a suicide? I've saved you from the Châtelet and purgatory, fool!"

"He's only another aristocrat!" cried a fishwoman shrilly. "Let them kill each other off!"

Pierre turned angrily in the direction of the voice. But it had become disembodied.

Collecting his wits nimbly, he brushed himself off and picked up his malacca sword cane and the bruised nosegay.

Who was it had said Paris was a "hell for horses, purgatory for men, and paradise for women"?

He had been a fool to go abroad on foot. There was seldom a day on the Paris streets that one did not see a child killed or a pedestrian tossed into the gutter like an old rag. It would be news at the court of Versailles, indeed, if Pierre Louis Bertrand Marie de Michelait, son of the Marquis de Bussac, were mangled by the horses of a water cart or of a mere bourgeois lawyer. Would his friends light a candle to his soul, he wondered? Would his Queen, Marie Antoinette, grieve for him just a little?

He picked his way more carefully toward the Quai de l'École, dodging skillfully into doorways as each new carriage flashed up and away with the arrogance of a Ben Hur. His mood today urged him to be of the pulse of Paris, to drink in closely the odors of herring and coffee and herbs and grime. He wanted to crouch in the doorways of these dirty, dilapidated houses to save his life, wanted to be close to the twittering bird cages at every window, to the rustling skirts of the grisette; close to the venders, shouting, shouting—

"Japan your shoes?"

"Brick dust today!" (For cleaning knives.)

"Ladies, take your pleasure!" (Only almond biscuits, these!)

And most of all he wanted to be close to the colored billposters which said that Mlle Hyacinthe would be dancing tonight in the *Ballet de Psyché* at the Opéra.

Pierre beckoned a brusher-down and four came running to him, jamming their footrests against his legs. He chose his man, who began work assiduously on the mud of his white silk stockings with the remnant of an old wig. A moment later Pierre's shoes were resplendent with a mixture of oil and soot and he was none the worse for his trifling accident.

He paid the fellow his two liards, returned the parasol that had sheltered him from the sun, and recalled how many women had told him there was no handsomer gallant at court. How could Mlle Hyacinthe help but succumb to his charms?

He had watched her casually from the family box at the Opéra throughout the winter. She had fluttered, and frisked, pirouetted, and twinkled like so many butterflies, harlequins, and fairies. He watched her absently, his mind dawdling on the caresses stolen from the Comtesse de Frivouac while the court had been at St. Cloud. And then, one night, just as usual, Mlle Hyacinthe had raised her exquisite little foot to touch her alabaster hand, and just as quickly Pierre was enslaved. The following night he had met her in the Green Room of the theater, the melting pot of noblemen, authors, musicians, actors. Pierre at twenty was well acquainted with the Green Room, the rendezvous where danseuses became rich courtesans as noblemen became poor pensioners. The Duc de Choiseul had often wittily called the Green Room the Exchange.

But up to this time Pierre's amours had been strictly limited to the court. Being librarian-in-ordinary to the ten-year-old Dauphiness, Marie-Thérèse Charlotte, known as Mme Royale, he had an apartment in the palace at Versailles. And how was a man to find time for everything? Moreover, he had never really been in love with anyone but the Queen, he mused.

Born in the Hôtel Michelait, the mansion of his parents in the rue de Grenelle of the faubourg St. Germain, he had been sent into the countryside of Touraine to live with a wet nurse after his christening. This was not because his parents were indifferent to him. It was because Rousseau had published *Émile,* and infants must now have sweet, untainted air, à la Jean Jacques.

Catherine de Michelait, the Marquise de Bussac, had been an affectionate mother however. Beautiful, lily-graceful, pure, Catherine, raised by her aunt, the Abbess at Fontrevault, had early become pious. A chance meeting with the dashing Grégoire had decided her not to become a nun. Infatuated with the handsome young agnostic, she married him only to very soon regret her carnal sin. Although Grégoire turned Catholic for her, at heart he would not be reformed and had no use for Jesuitism. He came of a long line of Huguenots on his father's side—Jansenists on the distaff side. His religion was a hybrid of the two, liberally tinged with the ideas of recent philosophers.

After bearing him three sons Catherine had retired again within her spiritual life. In Paris she kept an apartment in a convent, often going into retreat for weeks. It was her joy to make summer pilgrimages to Argenteuil or St. Geneviève-aux-Bois or other little villages when fêtes were given in honor of their patron saints. Of late years she had been deeply concerned with the prisons and hospitals of the city, aiding Mme Necker with large sums of money for reform. Catherine's charity, unlike that of so many French, was not merely a religious duty but a passion.

When Pierre was six he had been torn from his foster mother and had been brought back to Paris. He had found he had older brothers, Gilbert and Maurice. He did not like them as much as his brothers and sisters in the country. He kicked and screamed and insisted on going back to Touraine. But his new governor, the Abbé Blafond, took him sternly in hand and said it was high time that a little aristocrat like Pierre become a good Jesuit. Monsieur l'Abbé was a distant cousin of Catherine's.

Until he was twelve Pierre studied with the Abbé Blafond, attended lectures at the University, and traveled in England and Europe. Secretly he envied Gilbert, who would go to Louis-le-Grand Collège in Paris and then to military school. Gilbert, being the oldest, was destined for a career of military glory. But Pierre was very pleased about not being Maurice, who would have to go into the Church and pray even when he was hungry. It was very, very nice just being himself, for his father had secured for him an appointment as one of the twelve pages of the Queen's chamber. This was a great honor, the Marquis had impressed upon him. One's family had to be of the nobility since 1550, of the Nobility of the Sword. There was no remuneration. The reward came in serving their majesties Louis XVI and Marie Antoinette and in learning dancing, fencing, and horsemanship to perfection. These would be preparation for a military career, if he wanted one, or for subsequent duties at court. And there had always been important de Michelaits at court. (Pierre's father was a descendant of the bastard line of Henry IV.)

Those early years at Versailles had been very happy. What could be more exciting than to be dressed in a crimson velvet and gold lace suit costing 1,500 livres, and escorting the Queen to mass or offering ices to her ladies at the Queen's balls?

It was his first day of duty as page that Pierre had fallen in love with Marie Antoinette. Those were the early years of her motherhood, when she had been proud to show a critical people that the *Autrichienne* could bear heirs to the throne; that she was not all frivolity and extravagance, a Mme Déficit, as some called her; that her inimitable grace and her fresh blond beauty could win the love of her husband after his early years of indifference.

Pierre lived in the intimate circle of the Queen. He had watched her play the harp and sing out of tune; ride horseback with elegant boldness; gamble away eighty thousand francs a night; embroider a waistcoat for the King; flirt innocently with the Comte d'Artois, her brother-in-law; pamper Mme de Polignac. He had had his ear twitched by Léonard, the Queen's hairdresser, because he'd laughed at a four-foot *coiffe* and had said it looked like a mountain of garbage; he had had his cheek patted by Mlle Bertin, the Queen's dressmaker, because he told her she made Marie Antoinette the most beautiful woman in the world. He had seen the Queen make her toilette a thousand times, rouging and dressing before those of the court privileged to see her perform the banalities. He had seen her impatience with the French formality when Mme Campan had handed a handkerchief (to be in turn handed to Her Majesty) to the wrong person and political wrangling had ensued. He had watched Marie Antoinette weep because

France did not understand her, and stamp her foot because some minister presumed that he did.

As Pierre hurried to the Palais-Royal he compared the little Mlle Hyacinthe to his Queen. What he felt now so suddenly for the exquisite danseuse was a thing apart from his lasting and growing adoration of the Queen. Mlle Hyacinthe belonged to the province of the material: she was of his senses like the heavy musk and candlelit beauty of the Opéra, the swaying of boats on the Seine, the ripening of a plum on its bough, a fritter flavored with acacia flower, the headiness of a masquerade, the soft velvet of moss in the wood. Mlle Hyacinthe, like others before her, was a fever of which he knew some day he would be cured. For a while it would burn in his black eyes, flush his cheeks to a new crimson, pound in his fingertips as he touched her, dry his lips with insatiable desire. For a while he would live in delicious agitation. . . . What if one minister after another threatened the collapse of the banking system? What if bread riots and political dissension had come to such a pass that the amiable Louis had recalled the States-General after its one hundred and seventy-five years of extinction? What if this national representative body was being elected by fifteen million voters —a body without precedent in the history of France? A proud little instep made one oblivious of government and of the snowstorm of anonymous pamphlets showering down on Paris! Even if one should go to the King's hunt some brisk autumn morning and find the world cold and clear again and the fever gone. . . .

Pierre left the rue St. Honoré and entered the gardens of the Palais-Royal. The Duc d'Orléans, who owned this mad confusion of palace and shops and promenades, loathed the Queen, it was said, because she had spurned his advances. If only France knew Marie Antoinette as he knew her, thought Pierre sadly, could even one man condemn her?

He remembered his wide-eyed, twelve-year-old wonder at her regal beauty—the liveliness of her oval face, the high forehead, the delicate aquiline nose, the fine blue eyes, the full, passionate Austrian lips, and the striking dignity and elegance of her bearing.

"You are my new chevalier, M. de Michelait?" she had asked him gaily his first day of duty.

And then her smile had struck him shy and dumb. Its alluring curves were filled with so many things—sweetness and pride, generosity, frankness. It drew Pierre to her with an irresistible fascination. And fumbling with the lace on his new velvet hat, he had been smitten with eternal love for his Queen.

Once before, he recalled, in Normandy a little peasant girl had smiled at him just like that. Although she had not been magnificent in gold brocade and plumes and diamonds of state, she had smiled at him . . . just like that. It had been at a country fair. The child was fresh in starched white, with a sky-blue sash. Dark brown ringlets escaped from the frills of her cap, which was trimmed with crisp cherry ribbons. He thought she was prettier than any flower he had ever seen. In fact she was the first little girl he had ever really noticed. An apple slipped from her hand as she stared at him, and it tumbled away on the green, but he recovered it and handed it to her. Then she looked into his eyes, and smiled. He was conscious of being a new, a very glad Pierre. For a few seconds time had stood still in her smile. After that he had begun to look at all little girls—to look for their smiles.

Yes, thought Pierre, Marie Antoinette was of his blood, of the core of his being. He had heard her ridiculed; he had seen her swollen with child; he had watched her retire haughtily to the Petit Trianon, where she held a simple milkmaid's court in defiance of her growing unpopularity. And always she had stirred in him a sense of chivalry, of innate fineness, a consciousness of the hundreds of years of nobility that flowed through his veins. She embodied the legends of chevalier and martyr from the time of Charlemagne; the vision of a Joan of Arc; a sense of indestructible might moving down through the ages—a might of feudal lords and cardinals and kings, a continuity of the life of France, over and above its lowly peasant and its lofty domes.

Though Austrian by birth, thought Pierre, Marie Antoinette *was* France!

CHAPTER II

Pierre glanced at one of the two watches he wore; the chain between them hung with handsome fobs, like fancy lingerie on a line. Mlle

Hyacinthe had promised to meet him here at three. He was fifteen minutes early. This was puerile indeed. It would have been far more politic to be seen hurrying toward Mlle Hyacinthe a moment late, offering the nosegay as an apology. He must not seem too anxious at this first rendezvous for it was said that M. Fleury of the Théâtre Français was her hotheaded lover. Yet was there a danseuse so witless that she would prefer an actor, even a good one, to the son of a marquis?

Pierre paid a sou to lounge in one of the chairs near the circus in the center of the garden. His hair was curled and powdered to immaculateness. The detail of his dress bespoke wealth and discrimination —the gold buckles of his shoes, the clocked hose, the rich lace at his cuffs, the fine embroidery of his azure vest, and the smart flare of his cravat. No flower in the parterre could rival his musk. Conscious of his perfection, he relaxed to the plash of the fountain and began to compose a mental poem to his new love:

> "*Oh Cyprian Queen, willowy as the tendril of a flower,*
> *Soft, coaxing lips. . . .*"

A jaunty spaniel with a pink bow lifted its leg against the rung of his chair and escaped toward the shrubs and flowers with a dainty yelp. His mistress gave a solicitous squeal, and trotted after him, her roguish hat *à l'anglaise* shockingly awry.

Pierre was annoyed, distracted. The Palais-Royal garden was alive with activity at this hour of the day, shimmering with rich reds, blues, and purples. The promenades were as thronged as the halls of Versailles when the King dined in public on Sunday: coquettes, coxcombs, abbés, clerks, soldiers, simpering old men with rouged wrinkles, tittering grisettes, elegant footmen with perfumed billets-doux, "whitings," ghostly with flour, running to madame's coiffure; venders, poets, poodles, *marchandes des journaux,* crying pamphlets on chemistry, languages, physics, literature, politics—the whole jabbering lot of them seeming to exhale perfume and fresh roasted coffee.

But now he had only ten minutes to wait!

His eyes lifted above the throng to the palace. Somewhere in the Palais-Royal were the alluring rooms where Mlle Hyacinthe lived.

The garden was bounded on three sides by uniform buildings, ornate with bas-relief, fluted pilasters, and festoons, crowned with balustrades and vases. The fourth side had a double row of galleries, with no upper apartments. Under its colonnade—for here were some of the one hundred and eighty shops of the palace—swarmed buyers, pickpockets, and buxom *filles de joie*.

Shop after shop displayed its ware seductively for three or four times the price of any other in Paris: the bookseller's print, the baker's wafer-cake, the pawnbroker's gewgaw; the armorer's gleaming cutlasses and swords. Rouge pots and ribands, laces and feathers, herbs, surgical knives, wigs, bonbons, shining liqueurs, snuff, astronomical instruments, artists' oils, bonnets and taffetas, baubles, jewels and toys—only a few steps apart. Pierre knew every corner and trick of every shop. All offering glass for crystal at the price of diamonds.

He looked at his other watch, a repeater given him by the Princess de Lamballe, the Queen's superintendent, that paragon of virtue, of whom, nevertheless, he was very fond. Seven minutes to wait. The poem was doing poorly in this box of Pandora, as someone had justly called the gardens. A man could be born and die here without ever seeing a chestnut tree beyond this little Paris within Paris, it was said.

"Soft, coaxing lips, nectar-sweet and pure—"

His pulse began to quicken with desire, and he jumped up and paced with the parade under the chestnut trees.

The poem ebbed from his mind. On this soft spring day the windows of the buildings were open. One could hear the confusion of the gaming-rooms, musical instruments, the hubbub of voices and the clatter of dishes from the various cafés. . . . He was not only lovesick, he thought, amused, but starved. And it took a strong will to pass the lemonade boy shouting his wares of biscuits and iced fruits and sweetmeats. But he was to take the little danseuse to dinner. . . .

He looked at his first watch again. Three minutes to wait. That is, of course, if she were as eager as he.

A procuress gave him a languishing smile and said: *"Bon jour, Monsieur!* What a lovely little Japanese *fille, voilà* . . . (softly) and so well trained in the arts that please. . . ."

Pierre returned half a growl. He was reminded of various letters on Paris he had read of visiting Persians, Indians, and Englishmen. There was no den of vice so great in the world, they said, as the Palais-Royal where no decent woman might raise her eyes from the path. Rooms above the galleries let out to lovers by the single minute. Bawdy songs in the beer cellars, and pornographic scenes on the walls; abbés flaunting their mistresses at Astley's Circus; "matrons" soliciting the honest wives of the bourgeoisie, dangling before them the bait of a bauble for an hour of "natural pleasure" with a nobleman at a house of ill fame. And then, amenable police, filthy ballads, tumbling like rain on the populace, mad *modes du jour*—literally lasting from sunup to sunset.

The French people were a giddy race, said the Persians and Indians and English. "A lively nation who loves to read and hates to think." No law, no morals, no religion. Pleasure mad, witty but witless, inconstant, ostentatious, fickle, seldom noticing the good but going into ecstasies over the beautiful, polished, heartless, elegant, serious about little things, light and indecent about the grave, unresourceful, insatiably curious, faithless. Certainly doomed to spiritual destruction. This was what the Persians and Indians and English said, writing their memoirs, partaking of French hospitality.

Much of their indictment was true. Although Louis XVI had never had a Madame du Barry, or Marie Antoinette an acknowledged lover, the court had never been more depraved, and Pierre knew it. Even the clergy was profligate. There were bishops who had never visited their sees. What Pierre did not know about the court at Versailles was insignificant, for at fifteen, too old to be a page, he had become an assistant to the porter of the Queen's wardrobe. Now in his new capacity he conceded without shame that his pension of thirty thousand francs was little more than a gratuity. He was young for the position of librarian, but he was as well qualified as many an abbé for he had read avidly. And it was necessary to read to know if *Manon Lescaut* or *Gil Blas* were suitable for the innocence of a ten-year Dauphiness. Yes, he was probably better qualified. His father before him was a thinking man, who had once frequented the *bureaux d'esprit* of Mme Geoffrin and Mme du Deffand, who knew d'Alembert, Diderot, Holbach, and Saint-Pierre, and was intimate with members of the Académie française. With this influence was Pierre himself then one of the worst offenders of his age, he wondered, submitting to the tide of debauchery that swept him so pleasantly forward?

For in spite of the Persians and Indians and English he knew people that were good. He thought of his mother, kneeling at her *prie-dieu* in the family chapel; the sweet, pious Mme Elisabeth, sister of Louis; the virtuous Princess de Lamballe; the Sisters of Charity; Dominique, his valet; Julie, the daughter of his tailor; and all of the simple, hardworking peasants of the Vendée who sweated for bread. He even knew of a few husbands and wives who loved each other. He felt reassured and his spirits soared again with the perfume of May and the pinks he carried.

When he actually came upon Mlle Hyacinthe it was a surprise and for long minutes he had forgotten to look at his watch.

She was slight but her skirts of blue and violet *glacé* taffeta billowed about her. Tight sleeves flared at the elbow in soft ruffles of silk and lace, hiding the crinkled tops of her blue kid gloves. Her hair was powdered and curled and crowned by a masterpiece of yellow straw and white satin, a blue feather around the crown, and a panache of blue feathers at the side. Long streamers tied beneath a determined little chin. Mlle Hyacinthe was fashionable to the finishing touches of black lace shawl, web handkerchief, satin-bowed slippers, and lilac sunshade.

But as for the alabaster hand, the thick lashes, the ivory skin—these were largely of Pierre's romantic dreaming. She had, rather, a pallor of undernourishment emphasized by large eyes and delicate features— eyes not so heavenly blue as tantalizing. The small mouth had a childish, questioning curve. Her natural elegance of manner was so light, so exquisite that it gave her an air of floating rather than of walking.

Pierre stood entranced before her, kissing her hand, offering her the nosegay of pinks. And then he noticed a woman in black beside her, a simple creature of about thirty, her black hair natural under a cap, and a demure apron about her waist. His heart sank. A matron! A duenna to chaperone them! To assure a world which knew so much better that Mlle Hyacinthe, a young woman alone in this perilous Garden of Eden, was a virgin!

Pierre cursed his luck as he whispered: *"Mais vous êtes belle!"* and drew the blue-gloved fingers over his arm. Mme Bouquet walked half a step behind them, sedately.

He took them to the Café de mille colonnes in the Palais-Royal, which sparkled with the best society. Little Mlle Hyacinthe was the most exotic woman there, thought Pierre triumphantly, his arm burning from the touch of her blue-gloved hand. What feathered and jeweled marquise or duchess could compare with her? Her adorable eyes, her delicate little ruby mouth, the ravishing ivory of her neck and hands. . . . His appetite for food was quite gone as he lost himself in her charms.

But not so the appetites of Mlle Hyacinthe and Mme Bouquet. With dainty perseverance, they despoiled the orders of *potage en tortue, anchois à l'huile, fricassée de poulets garnie, côtelette de mouton, artichauts à la sauce, biscuit à la crème*—and all the accompanying wines. At tables beside them, at tables all around them, women of the beau monde who drank vinegar water at home to stay thin were trifling with a morsel of fish or cheese. Pierre himself sat before an untasted entrée of fresh salmon, sipping Rhine wine, hopeful that he would at last catch Mlle Hyacinthe's hand idle upon her knee. And that Mme Bouquet, a creature growing uglier by the minute, would have the grace to look away.

"What a shy little thing you are!" said Pierre at last. "And yet there's as much ginger in your eyes as in your toes."

"You would not like it on my tongue," she retaliated, and he thought her voice was sweet as the tinkling of silver on glass. "And I do love to hear you talk of court, M. de Michelait!"

He found her hand at last beneath the shining damask and pressed her fingers warmly in his palm. She gave him a roguish smile.

"Mon Dieu!" she laughed softly. "A man of your courage should wear the Cross of St. Louis."

"Ah, that's for my brother, Gilbert. He's a colonel in the army."

"Your only brother, Monsieur?"

"No, no, no. There's Maurice—appointed Bishop of Agen seven years ago, when he was only sixteen." (The fact that Maurice was a bishop meant, of course, that he had four quarterings and that his family was in favor at court.)

"Ah, and your father?" she inquired innocently, hoping his answer would last through the *biscuit à la crème*. (As if everyone at the Opéra did not know that the Marquis de Bussac and his mistress, Madame de Chenault, the plain, lame but fascinating woman who had a ten-year-old son remarkably like Pierre.)

While he talked about his father, Mlle Hyacinthe nibbled at a few remaining raisins.

Mme Bouquet tried to stifle a belch. Her face, which had been vulgarly florid a moment before, was the alarming gray green of a hurricane sky. Mlle Hyacinthe hurried with her raisins.

In another ten minutes the storm would break, she thought. Poor Javotte! A pint pitcher cannot hold a quart of milk . . . and she giggled to herself. What a beautiful, beautiful feast! How was she ever to dance in a couple of hours? Would her toes be leaden with *côtelette*, or sparkling with claret? But M. de Michelait, in his box, would be too dazzled by love to observe.

Her heart gave a foolish flutter as she considered him: black eyes restless and ardent, brows dark and heavy, arrogant, thin nose, and thin, proud lips. It gave her a queer feeling of victory to see the proud lips melt into tenderness for her. And his purse! . . . *Nom du criel,* how the francs must flow in and out of his purse! She had felt from the first that M. Fleury was a bit too old for a girl of eighteen. A bit demanding . . . a bit poor. . . .

Mlle Hyacinthe gave one more look at Javotte, asked Pierre the time, and hurried the party toward the garden again and its entrance to her room. For she would be late to the Opéra, she said. (How thoughtless of Javotte to turn bilious, the *gourmande,* with Pierre brimming with passion and the shops in the arcade eager to help him express it! But that set of turquoise buttons would likely be in the window tomorrow. And it was just as well that M. de Michelait should not misjudge her in the beginning and think her avaricious. . . . Ah, she was certain she had acted the Comtesse to perfection every moment —if only Javotte did not suddenly taint the atmosphere of refinement! . . .)

"Je suis désolé!" exclaimed Pierre as she drew her hand from his arm. "And to have to watch you from beyond the footlights after having had your hand in mine, *chérie*—to have known heaven for one instant and be wrenched from it . . . *ah, mademoiselle, je suis bien désolé!"*

Mlle Hyacinthe gave Javotte a sly nudge with her toe. "Hurry, Mme Bouquet," she said. "Lay out my Turkish dress of striped moiré. I am having supper after the Opéra with the Comte de Vogeur."

Javotte disappeared, holding her handkerchief to her mouth.

Mlle Hyacinthe sighed with relief. *"Ah, mon ami,"* she whispered, "it is sweet to be alone, *n'est-ce pas?* . . . I, too, am *affligé*. But tomorrow after the Opéra I have invited a small party here to supper and to play. Friends of the theater . . . M. Molé, Mme Bellecourt, M. Sebastien Mercier—he is droll, you know, and makes fun of us in his writing. We should be so honored, M. de Michelait, if you should condescend. . . ."

Pierre kissed her hand. There was nothing in the world he desired so much. But tomorrow afternoon he must go to a fête at the château of the Comte de Varionnet at Passy. The Queen wished him to attend so that he might report to her the trend of the conversation on the eve of the States-General. It was a matter of diplomacy. A pressing matter. Ah, to think the fates could so contrive against him—to make him the most agonized of men! Three days at Passy in utter darkness, torn from the starlight of her eyes . . . from the exquisite pain of touching her glove with his lips. . . .

But surely he could challenge the fates, thought Pierre, the next noon after Dominique had handed him his cane. He might have a glimpse of Mlle Hyacinthe before the trip to Passy. He drove in his carriage to the Palais-Royal and bought a fan of tortoise incrusted with topaz, its ivory silk painted with an autumn scene.

Hurrying through the corridors of the palace, Pierre thought the interior had a definite air of deshabille at this hour. The floors of the lofty corridors were untidy with papers, and tradesmen and occupants bickered and fumed. Clerks were yawning in the ground-floor shops; on the entresol, the shopkeepers' wives were wielding a broom or scolding a cat; the exhibition portraits on the first floor, deserted, had a sulky air; billiard and gaming tables were not so green without sparkling white bosoms behind them; and the galleries and restaurants seemed to smell of fish and soap.

On the second story were the more ample furnished and unfurnished lodgings, but Mlle Hyacinthe's flat was not here. Number 89 was above, under the *mansardes,* where lived the thrifty bachelors, musicians, poor noblemen, artists. M. Fleury might have done better for the little Hyacinthe, thought Pierre, with a certain satisfaction, after his success this year at the Comédie Française in *Frederick the Great.*

Pierre found Number 89 and paused. What if Mlle Hyacinthe might actually be alone? What if her tantalizing eyes had meant their invitation? Ah, the soft, youthful curve of her cheek and neck after one had found ennui in the aging bosom of a Comtesse de Frivouac!

There was a scuffling sound beyond the door, a sort of irregular beat he had heard above the cries and bells of the city and the disorder of the Palais-Royal. He knocked.

"Entrez!" called the crystal-silver voice of Mlle Hyacinthe, and he opened the door to a new stage scene in his *affaire de cœur.* For a moment he stood transfixed as if Marie Antoinette had slapped him.

Mlle Hyacinthe, who did not turn around, was in pink tights and a chemise, violently doing her routine at a bar improvised from an old bed post. Her curls, pinned carelessly atop her head and bound with a gold ribbon Greek fashion, were a curious compromise between silver and gold, for last night's powder had worn thin.

A flute's wailing of Mozart came from the open window, at which was a jungle of flower boxes, bird cages, and plants. The parquet floor was bare and the scant furniture disarranged as if it might be playing tag. A muslin corset hung boldly across a gilt chair back; crumpled lingerie sagged over pillows and stools; sheets of an unmade couch trailed onto the floor with conscious abandon; here were books and pamphlets dripping from the marble mantel, along with brilliant feathers and fans, stubs of candles, china, billets-doux, ballet slippers. In a foot bath, soap floated milkily. A pair of silk stockings and Javotte's handkerchief from yesterday were drying suspended from an ornate Venetian glass luster in the center of the lofty room.

Obviously breakfast was over. A tray on a low marble table was untidy with broken bits of roll and empty chocolate cups—like nice little boys with dirty faces.

Mademoiselle's frilly toilet table near the windows was filled with a thousand little bottles and jars, mirrors, scents, ribbons. The sun streaming in seemed to embrace it, to render it glorious and hallowed— the throne of the danseuse! Behind the throne in the corner were muff and hatboxes piled to the ceiling at a staggering slant, dripping their contents. Last night's Turkish gown of striped moiré hung from the open door of the wardrobe, seeming to stand alone stiffly, bewitched.

Close to Pierre was a large table strewn with artificial roses in varying stages of bloom, pastepot, scissors, scraps of paper and silk, wanton leaves and petals of rose, peach, and red.

For a moment Pierre was bewildered. He wanted only to run away, as the night a certain Baron had discovered him loosening the corsets of his Baroness in a game of blindman's buff near the orangerie. But it was the Baron who had subtly pretended to night blindness. The amusing recollection brought back Pierre's poise. Let Mlle Hyacinthe do the running away!

The Mozart tune wailed on, Mlle Hyacinthe kicking arduously in rhythm and the finches singing out their tiny hearts with the music and the sunshine. Only the parrot on its perch near a gilt bidet looked a trifle skeptical.

Pierre watched, fascinated, as Mlle Hyacinthe went through the last of her squatting *pliés;* now she melted into a *développé,* reaching out slowly for something invisible, and he could see the muscles of her thigh tauten. How long would this go on? Wasn't he worse than an eavesdropper? . . . Now she began a *fouetté,* her one leg whipping her around in a furious whirl, once, twice. . . . Suddenly, Mlle Hyacinthe settled on the soles of both feet with a little scream. Snatching up a blue peignoir dripping with ribbons, she swished it about her shoulders, but the effect was that of a court jester and she knew it.

"Nom de Dieu!" she exclaimed, panting from the dance. "I thought you were Javotte! *Eh bien, me voilà!"*

The beautiful M. de Michelait was lost then before he was altogether won, she lamented. And yesterday her decorum might have put the stately Mme Etiquette to shame. Now, in the second that Pierre was lost to her, Silvie Hyacinthe totally forgot his purse bulging with louis d'or and remembered only the passion his dark, feverish eyes had offered her over the footlights. *Sacre-bleu!* . . . even the bidet had not been emptied! . . . She could faint beautifully, of course, and if she fainted he would have to pick her up and carry her to the couch. But then, Javotte would be coming back any moment. . . . Ah, the angel, he even had a love offering for her in his hand, and how he must wish he had never spent a sou on such a sloven. . . . Well, if his eyes were no longer burning, at least he might like her to dance in exchange for the gift!

She gave an hysterical laugh. Pierre laughed also, and she felt much better and tiptoed over to him in a mincing gavotte.

"But, M. de Michelait, I am that honored! Come, sit here. *Ah—pour moi?"* As she tore open the package with childish rapture, the peignoir slipped, leaving a naked expanse of pink, perspiring shoulder and breathless bosom. *"Dieu, quelle exquise!"*

Pierre jumped up to assist her but she had disappeared behind a Japanese screen.

Ah, to think that she had been naïve enough to believe that a man's desire could be quelled with stockings hung wet on a luster! . . . But in a moment she could be *really* entrancing!

Pierre watched the screen as a cat watches a mouse hole, and found his lips were dry.

"I am going to dance for you, Monsieur—very special! . . ." She leaned close to the window and pulled a cord that dangled from the *mansarde* room above. "Romain . . . *hé!* Romain! *Chut!* I shall tell you when to commence." The music stopped. She chattered on to Pierre as she changed to a costume of blue, spangled gauze. "He is my orchestra—Romain. He is a *tapissier par excellence!* That seat of the chair you are sitting on . . . (Pierre was pacing the floor). He plays for me by the hour and when I am gone, comes to sigh about me to Javotte. . . . There is one bad thing though, about Romain . . . he is antiroyalist."

"What do you mean?" asked Pierre, stopping to examine a dusty Dresden shepherdess with half a crook.

"He is very bitter about the fat King and says there are many more who will not give another centime of tax to buy jewels for the *Autrichienne* while they starve!"

"We have not had such a cold winter as this for many years, *c'est vrai.*"

"And the court sleighing in dragons and sirens, with drivers dressed up like Cossacks and Monjiks! Romain says he even saw coachmen with long, false beards like the Russians. If one is shivering, Monsieur, it is hard to see the *noblesse* wrapped in furlined velvet cloaks laughing and singing!"

"But the royal family have not adopted this silly custom! And often they make excursions about Versailles to aid the poor. The Queen gives generously from her own purse!"

"I know, Monsieur. I adore the Queen. But Romain—he is like touchwood. He belongs to a club that meets in the Café des aveugles, and sometimes his talk frightens me."

"The coming States-General will pacify them," said Pierre. (A representative assembly of the people would give them confidence.) But he was disturbed nevertheless. "What takes you so long, my little heart?"

The door burst open and Javotte entered; she and Pierre stared at one another with amazement.

Here was no formidable Mme Bouquet, a matron, but a grisette of five and twenty, powdered and beribboned, with a bold eye and a bolder ankle. A gendarme or a pork butcher might have thought her ripely pretty in her scarlet morning dress and starched white fichu.

Pierre bowed, and she curtsied, grinning broadly, and dropped an armful of bundles on a chair.

"Javotte? Ah, Javotte, do you mind going out again? Some sunflower seed for the parrot, *ma chère* . . . and some pins! I have lost my last pin!"

"I met M. Fleury below," answered Javotte, tossing another smile at Pierre, "separating some friends who were fighting over Piccinni and Gluck. He was going to take a short stroll in the gardens then. A very short stroll—*first!*"

"*Bien!*" called Mlle Hyacinthe as Javotte left, slamming the door. And to herself she said, *"Diable!"*

She emerged from behind the screen, sparkling in the sunshine.

"Come, Monsieur, bring me a few roses for my hair. And help me to place them, so. . . ." She glanced at Pierre through the mirror of her dressing-table. His fingers fumbled as he arranged the pink rose-buds on her hair and she felt a bounding joy. With a deft twist she wound the roses into her curls with a turquoise ribbon.

"You must not mind Javotte," she said frankly. For since there was nothing to conceal from M. de Michelait now, she might as well amuse him. "She was a *pierreuse,* Monsieur. Very poor. She was sent to La Force prison because she had a passion for roses and she stole some. They were good to her—the other prisoners—and made her roses of silk and paper. Her cell was transformed into a bower. *Incroyable, n'est-ce pas?* . . . She regained her reason by making roses from morning till night. When her term was finished I brought her here. She is my matron—or my *femme-de-chambre. N'importe.* But she is my slave, Javotte. And she is no longer wicked on the street. She is very faithful to a poor Vicomte who is a poet and lives in a garret in the Louvre. One hundred and sixty steps she climbs to his room! And she says his cabin stinks odiously from the treasures of the ages!"

Mlle Hyacinthe darted away to the open window, pulled the cord, and the wheedling of the flute began almost at once, along with the mad competition of the birds.

Pierre thought he had never seen her dance so superbly. The *soubresauts* reminded him of a hummingbird loath to alight. At last she sank before Pierre's eyes—the languishing swan, golden curls and rosebuds escaping from their ribbon.

He pulled her up to her toes, an armful of fluff and breathlessness, and embraced her fervidly. No lips of any countess had ever been so honey-sweet as these, no lips of any poem. . . . He wanted to be lost in their soft clinging forever.

"Ah, Monsieur . . ." she sighed at last, and her eyes were misty. "But this time you must go."

To the devil with M. Fleury! thought Pierre rashly. What of the ignominy of being caught crouching behind a screen? What of a possible duel in the Bois de Boulogne tomorrow? . . . He caught her passionately in his arms again.

But Mlle Hyacinthe was urging him toward the door. She knew M. Fleury only too well. And she was feeling the first sweet exultation of love and wanted to preserve it.

"But do come back to me, Monsieur de Michelait . . ." she whispered with pleading. "Do come back. . . ."

Pierre found himself staggering down the gallery of the palace. It was an enchanted palace.

CHAPTER III

"BRAVO!" cried the Marquis de Bussac as the curtain went down on the last scene of *Figaro*.

It had just been skillfully performed by Mme de Staël, the Vicomte de Noailles, and other guests in the château theater of the Comte and Comtesse de Varionnet. The little playhouse was exquisite, sparkling with luster light on gold leaf and richly brocaded wall.

But Pierre was irritated.

In the first place, he had not wanted to come to Passy. To the devil with the trend of thought on the eve of the States-General! In the second place, footlights brought to him only the image of Mlle Hyacinthe, nebulous as a hummingbird, and the earthy little room where she lived in a hedonistic whirl of joy and innocent sin. No wonder he could not concentrate on the spirited acting of Madame de Staël, or that of Madame Condorcet although she was a famous beauty.

Moreover, the newly built Louis XV Château de Varionnet stifled him in spite of its expansive elegance. The ceilings and moldings, sensuous with cupids entangled with vegetables and flowers, were a large replica of the breathless Comtesse (what were all those gadgets bobbing on her head as she chatted now with that green-faced nonentity—was it Robespierre they called him?) And why were the *nouveaux riches* surrounded by even more mirrors than royalty, Pierre wondered. Was it to reflect the symbols of their hard-won glory?— the most costly Aubusson on the sofas, the most costly Sèvres clock on the mantel? How flagrantly new were the ornate chairs of his bedchamber—the bulging chiffonier, the bright moquette carpet the exact shade of the wine damask drapes! Did he just fancy that the Comtesse flaunted her fabulous gems and her bejeweled young abbé the way the guest chamber wore its bric-à-brac? Treasures without sentiment, arrived perfect from the shops? No yellowed ivory snuffbox, no china inkwell nicked by the haste of one's great-great aunt. . . .

Yes, the château stifled him. And he was counting the hours until

he might escape to Paris. But there was something else, some vague
dissatisfaction which had come with his father's crying, "Bravo!"

Of course the play was well done. Mme de Staël could act as well
as her father, M. Necker, could handle money. One began to see now
why the King had forbidden the play to be produced publicly when
first it was written. That was eleven years ago. Caron de Beaumarchais,
the author, had at last obtained permission from Louis to have it
performed at the country house of M. Vaudreuil with the understanding that he would suppress all parts of his work obnoxious to the
government. But the contents of the satire had leaked out to a public
that felt the repression was an attack upon its liberty. People demanded
Figaro. The play was at last scheduled for the Théâtre Français and
was the sensation of all Paris. Pierre remembered that the *noblesse* had
taken a box lunch to the theater hours in advance of opening time in
order to avoid the astounding crush. And simply to see a satire on
the court, on themselves!

Pierre had seen *The Marriage of Figaro* dozens of times. Why should
this particular performance annoy him, he wondered? It was not the
first time he realized that the revelations of *Figaro* were being accepted
too lightly by the very people ridiculed, that a court long dissolute was
openly admitting its intrigue, its profligacy. Yes, the court needed a
house cleaning. He and his valet, Dominique, had often agreed on that.
But one had to have brooms and mops for house cleaning. Who was
there who really minded the filth enough to attack it? And when there
had not been a house cleaning for so long, in what corner did one
begin?

Perhaps *The Marriage of Figaro* made him restless today because
M. Romain, who played the flute, belonged to a club in the Café des
aveugles. What did Romain and his friends discuss that his talk frightened the little Hyacinthe? Antiroyalist. . . . Were there many of
these antiroyalists? Ah, the court might admit its sin, thought Pierre,
but who was Romain, a *tapissier,* to sit in judgment on the court? And
now he felt only a quick and senseless anger as he helped his father's
mistress, Mme de Chenault, recover her fan.

The hundred or more guests began to draw together in little groups,
some sauntering out to the terrace, others to the salons. Fans began to
shimmer, snuffboxes to click. Perfumed powder and wax mingled;
satins and jewels flashed alive; voices rose in shrewd competition like
outbidding at the bourse.

Those who had been sitting near Pierre drew together: his father, the Marquis de Bussac, the limping Mme de Chenault, the Marquis de Lafayette, and a little and young black-taffeta widow from Passy.

"Mme de Chenault claims that free speech is the first *droit de l'homme*," said the Marquis de Lafayette. "Free speech like that of *Figaro*. I do not agree. Surely *representation* is the most divine right of man . . . the freedom of America!"

He was pale, had a fatuous expression, and wore enormous epaulets like the Americans. His hair, without powder and ill arranged, and his large nose, reminded Pierre of the American savage. Pierre did not like him. What made him so adored by the French, this conceited pouter pigeon? He and his soldiers who had fought for the freedom of America and had never ceased rhapsodizing?

"What has representation ever brought to France," Pierre challenged, his black eyes glowing, "but greature rupture between the monarch and the people?"

The Marquis de Bussac smiled leniently at his son. The iron-gray eyes carried that particular warmth they held only for Pierre, Mme de Chenault, and her son. It was the warmth of a mother watching a child struggling with a knot.

He was tall, erect with the dignity of a general, yet with the geniality of a huntsman. His hair, of a natural, pure white, needed no powdering; heavy eyebrows, black as Pierre's, were a shocking contrast. At Pierre's age the Marquis de Bussac had been merely handsome; at fifty he was also distinguished.

Today he wore a white Maltese cross decorated in gold, suspended from a riband of blue watered silk. Its gold lilies of France and white dove sparkled proudly. The Marquis de Bussac was a *cordon bleu,* or Knight of the Royal Order of the Holy Ghost, one of the privileged hundred of France. The order had been founded by Henry III in 1578 because the order of St. Michel had fallen to low esteem, had become too common.

Pierre's remark about rupture between the monarch and people was the very cue the Marquis de Lafayette waited for.

"*Oui, oui, oui,*" he exclaimed, offering snuff to the little black-taffeta widow, "but you are talking of representation under autocracy, not democracy. With the example of America, my dear M. de Michelait, what a constitution the Frenchman might have! What a future of order and individual rights!"

"*Ma foi!*" cried Pierre, "the American and French temperament are not one! Monarchy is the very soul of France."

"But a monarchial constitution is what I allude to, *mon ami*. I was scarce speaking of a blood revolution!" The Marquis de Lafayette waved his hands impatiently. "Ah, the purpose of kingship in the times of Hugh Capet was to hold before the people a symbol of all that was good and powerful in man. The king was a being next to God. Now, what do we find our King? A guide to huntsmen and a locksmith! He no longer leads us. The philosophers lead us. *Oui*, M. de Michelait, if you do not like the example of America, without a king, let us take the example of England—with both a constitution and a king. Surely—"

"Monsieur de Michelait," interrupted Mme de Chenault, "don't tell me that our Anglomaniac Duc de La Rochefoucauld has not convinced you that England's Rev—"

"England's revolution was not bloodless," cried Pierre hotly.

The Marquis de Lafayette shrugged his shoulders.

"My son would die for his sovereigns and their feudal rights," said the Marquis de Bussac, his heavy dark brows drawn together.

A potential note of regret in his voice caused the Marquis de Lafayette to turn to him and say: "But you, Monsieur le Marquis, of all people, should understand democracy. You—a student, a bosom friend of the glorious Diderot. A man who was forever preaching 'the greatest good of the greatest number.'"

The Marquis de Bussac made the Marquis de Lafayette a silent bow.

"*Dieu*, if it were not for our help to America our own debt would not be so staggering!" Pierre went on stubbornly.

"And a M. Calonne would not have the colossal nerve to suggest taxing the rich the same as the poor," interceded the little black-taffeta widow from Passy. "*Eh bien*—he deserved his dismissal and M. de Brienne was even a worse minister after him. *Dieu*, it has come to a pretty pass when we nobility must not only furnish the King's army but fill his coffers. Ah, France is very ill—*très, très malade!*"

Mme de Chenault's live blue eyes had followed one conversationalist after the other. Now her words came tumbling. It was as if her lameness had given wings to her speech.

"An old woman usually does not die from one cause alone!" she exclaimed, and there was something commanding in her very homeliness. "She dies because there are many ills—one of the heart, one of the liver, a nervous affection, a gout of the stomach. *N'est-ce pas?* France is old. And she has many ills . . . Voltaire was an ill. *Candide* made us think, and to think is not good for the health! Ah, and the

Church! With the coming of printing three hundred years ago we
began to read our Bibles and found ourselves abused by the clergy—"

"*Mais oui!*" agreed Pierre warmly. "And do not forget the Calvinists,
Madame, in your list of ills. They were among the first to be imbued
with the Marquis de Lafayette's 'democratic spirit'. . . . And the Jansenists—"

"But the greatest wound of *La Belle France* is Versailles!" declared
the Marquis de Lafayette, returning Pierre's enmity. "The Americans
would not conceive the truth when we told them! A palace costing
a hundred million francs; sixteen thousand men attached to the personal service of the King, and two thousand courtiers! A ménage
costing forty-five million francs a year! There are some two hundred
carriages, *n'est-ce pas?*" he asked Pierre. "And close to three thousand
horses? The Queen's—"

"Tell me, M. de Michelait," gurgled the little black-taffeta widow
from Passy. "Is it true the Queen has four pairs of new shoes a week
and that her ladies-in-waiting buy fine wardrobes through selling the
candles that have only been lighted once in her apartments?"

"Madame," replied Pierre, bowing deferentially, "the Queen has four
new pairs of shoes a *day* and deserves six, her instep is so elegant. As
for the ladies-in-waiting, they not only buy furs and gowns from the
candle stubs, but ancient châteaux and tiaras!"

The group laughed at his irony and began to move away toward
the music in the salons, chatting amiably. But if Pierre had been
irritated a few moments before, he was now burning with a slow,
implacable anger. Here were men and women whose every benefit
had derived from the ancient form of government biting the hand
that fed them! He had resented the fact that M. Romain and his ilk
presumed to pass judgment. What could be expected of the bourgeoisie
if they were encouraged by men like the Marquis de Lafayette and the
Duc de La Rochefoucauld? These men were undoubtedly thinkers, but
weren't they a little too radical to wield the broom in a general house
cleaning?

"People are ingrates!" Pierre snarled to his father, as they sauntered
along together.

"Because they find the worm in the apple and want to bite it out?"
asked Grégoire. "*Dieu,* you are not blind, Pierre. You admitted to me
not long ago that France is *très malade,* as our little widow says. And
I have never found you too orthodox in your thinking."

"Not too orthodox, perhaps, in some things. But always loyal to the throne."

"Ah," exclaimed Grégoire, with a fervent warmth in the gray eyes that rested on Pierre. "How Marie Antoinette has bewitched you!"

"C'est que je m'ennuie beaucoup ici!" Pierre answered curtly, "I think I shall go back to Paris."

"Come, if you are bored and vexed I know the very thing to beguile you." (Grégoire's voice had often sounded mellow like this when he had said to the child Pierre: "Come, I shall show you my etchings.") "The Vicomtesse du Luvin has agreed to read palms in the Salon de Mercury. And she is very, very shrewd, they say—and amusing."

The Vicomtesse du Luvin had been a devotee of a long string of mystic adventurers in Paris. She had learned to make beauty pastes from Casanova the astrologer. Mesmer had healed her with his magic touch. But the elixir of life sold to her by Cagliostro had not preserved her youth. She was a wrinkled old hag with flecks of snuff about her moist, rouged mouth, a heaving bosom, and a falcon's eye. Pierre knew that she held séances at midnight in the black bowels of her *hôtel,* when she and an African protegé, naked, pleaded with the departed spirits to return to them.

The Vicomtesse examined Pierre with a gold-rimmed spyglass.

"Place your hand upon my knee, M. de Michelait," she said. "It is *comme il faut* . . . do not cringe, *mon cher.* Ah, it is sweet to have a palm so young, so strong. . . ."

A little group had gathered round them and tonight Pierre resented the attention he usually enjoyed.

"Ah, I see that you will be married twice, M. de Michelait, and that at this very moment you are burning with passion—"

Mme de Staël, still in her stage garb of Suzanne, tapped his shoulder with her fan. "All feminine hearts are aflutter, Monsieur," she said with the vivacity and impulse that caused men to think her coarse features beautiful.

"If they flutter too fast they may fan the passion cool!" Pierre retorted.

The coterie laughed.

"Par Dieu," the Vicomtesse went on, sniffing loudly. "You will come close to losing your life more than once. I see much blood flowing. But do not let them bleed you, Monsieur. It is now the fashion to bleed and bleed one. The fashion will be growing. . . . Do not let them bleed you, Monsieur, I implore. . . . You are going on a long journey.

Not at once—but I see water. . . . But you prefer knowing what will happen *de bonne heure*. Youth is impatient! . . . Well, then, on the very morrow you will meet the woman of your fate. . . ."

There was a gay applause and Pierre drew his palm away from the thorny hand of the Vicomtesse.

"A thousand thanks, Madame!" he exclaimed, bowing himself away. "I am indebted to you for life—and perhaps for life itself!"

Escaping from the group that closed in on the prophetess, he felt like a worm escaping a hook. He caught the twinkling eye of his father and scowled at him.

It was reassuring to know, at least, that tomorrow he would get back to Paris to see the little danseuse. The woman of his fate! . . . Well, he would hardly have called her that: was there, indeed, such a thing in the life of a courtier of France?

CHAPTER IV

THE FOLLOWING NOON Pierre lay staring up at his bed curtains of gay flowered silk, a neglected copy of Richardson's *Clarissa* beside him.

He was still in a bad mood, with the thought of Mlle Hyacinthe and the moist, inviting pink of her skin more tormenting at every moment. But his father was right: Marie Antoinette had bewitched him. Now that he had actually dragged himself to the fête he felt that he must fulfill the mission the Queen had given him. Marie Antoinette wanted him to talk with Lady Atherton, in whose honor this distinguished and varied company had assembled, for William Pitt's aunt might reflect in her conversation the prime minister's policies with regard to France. However, it seemed to Pierre after *Figaro* that the convictions of the radical French nobility were of a far more exigent nature. Like Romain and his "club," they were the worm in the apple. . . .

Oh, he had tried to find Lady Atherton alone for a moment. But it was as if she had been Windsor Castle surrounded by an ever changing guard. There had been an ancient tournament in one of the courtyards, *Figaro,* a bacchanalian supper, whist, and rouge et noir. Today, he must make the opportunity of talking with her, if it meant kidnapping!

Without ringing for Dominique, Pierre began to dress, nibbling at a date from the Levant. To a man of the world it was a novelty to have one's appetite curtailed by love, and he smiled at the sight of his *déjeuner* practically untouched on the marquetry table beside the fire: oysters chilled in ice, compote in cupids' arms, red partridge from Guercy broiled autumn-leaf brown, gold omelet of pheasants' eggs, and a decanter of claret. (Not so neglected as the food, the decanter of claret!) All the cold things warm, all the warm things cold. . . .

He had not joined his father and others of the party this morning in a tour of the Comte's hunting boxes for two reasons: his head ached and the Comte's braggadocio was repulsive to him.

"Over one hundred acres of park!" . . . "Five coach houses!" . . . "Stables that lodge eighty horses!" . . . "A modern dovecot second to none!" . . . "Seven hundred and fifty acres of vineyards!" . . . "Cellars vast and equipped with wines numerous and venerable as the French army!"

There was a motive in the Comte's bombast, Pierre knew, for Mlle Victoire de Varionnet, now in a convent, would soon be eighteen, when she would be presented at court. And then she would be in the market for a husband. A husband on whom she would shower a stupendous dot provided he give her in exchange a title of the older nobility.

Pierre glanced at his naked strength in the cheval glass. His arms were those of a soldier, he thought proudly, not of a court dandy— muscles that came of hard riding, fencing, and tennis. Pleased as a little boy, he doubled his fist and watched the muscle run up his forearm and ripple down again. Even when he was fifteen the Queen's tirewoman, who first seduced him, had whispered that he was more beautiful by far than Adonis. . . . Ah, but he and Mlle Hyacinthe would give one another ineffable pleasure—if he could ever get back to Paris! Perhaps during the masquerade ball tonight he could sneak off to the Palais-Royal in his carriage, to embrace the "woman of his fate!"

Pierre found his father half an hour later in the billiard room, performing some complicated shots for an admiring group.

The Marquis de Bussac was in good spirits. He had had chocolate with Mme de Chenault during her footbath, and had just discoursed on politics and literature with Mme de Staël in her boudoir during the tedium of her hairdressing. The latter had revealed that Mme Vigée-Lebrun was painting a portrait here at the château. Would Pierre care to pay his respects to Mme Lebrun?

Of course, Pierre yawned, why not? He had known the artist for a long time. She had painted twenty portraits of Marie Antoinette in the last ten years, singing to the Queen as she painted; last season, her *Royal Family* had won great acclaim at the Paris Salon. Now and then Pierre had even accompanied his father to one of her small concerts or suppers, so popular that a duc often had to sit on the floor.

A liveried footman escorted them through florid galleries to a remote apartment of the château and a *femme de chambre* admitted them. Several small lap dogs scrambled to the door with yelps. In the boudoir, sparkling with grandeur like the rest of the château, Mme Lebrun was painting a young girl who sat on a chaise longue in a window of bird cages. The girl held in her lap a billowing straw hat of rosebuds.

Without waiting for them to be announced, Mme Lebrun deserted her palette and welcomed them with enthusiasm. Her beauty was fresh as her simple white gown and her curls tumbled naturally from a gauze cap.

"*Ah, vous êtes trop bons!* The Comtesse has told me you were of the company and has begged me to appear at supper. But as you know, I seldom indulge myself—not since that fatal night I took a last dab at a portrait and sat on my palette in my best white satin! . . . But surely you have been presented to Mlle Victoire de Varionnet?"

As the tall young woman made them a deep curtsy several flowers from the billowing hat tumbled among the yelping little dogs, which had returned to her. The de Michelaits, who had bowed with one accord, retrieved the rosebuds.

Mme Lebrun, who always saw everything, noticed the swift-passing frown of the young woman.

"You have sat surprisingly still this morning, Mlle de Varionnet, and deserve a recess," said the artist. "Come, my dear Monsieur le Marquis, tell me, what do you think of David's latest picture?"

Pierre followed Mlle de Varionnet, who moved with a firm haste away from the sunlight to a sofa near the embers of a fire. Chaste in white muslin with blue ribbons, she continued to hold the straw hat in her lap, painfully erect as if she had not forgotten her backboard.

She lowered her eyes automatically to the hearth and did not raise them, for she was still of the convent.

Pierre observed her with indifference.

Her hands held the straw hat with the grace of a thousand portraits but it was not a grace that belonged to her. Pierre had a feeling that behind scenes Mme Lebrun had arranged the long fingers that caressed the roses. Well, her complexion was not so bad now that she was out of the sunlight. But what stubborn hair! The brown curls, garlanded with flowers, fell rigidly over her shoulders. And what a wide mouth she had, too wide and full-lipped for the long equine face. There was a curve of smugness about it that somehow belied the virginity of muslins and ribbons. . . .

"You are studying with the sisters?" he asked, swallowing a yawn and sitting down at a respectful distance.

"I am at the Convent of Panthemont, rue de Bellechasse," she answered. There was a surprising quality of vigor in her voice.

Pierre knew that the Convent of Panthemont admitted only young women of the highest families, with a maid of honor and several attendants. He wondered if Mlle de Varionnet had the privilege of a daily cover at the table of the Abbess. It was said that the latter was no ascetic and that she turned out products finished in the arts of conversation, deportment, and worldly wisdom.

If Mlle de Varionnet were benefiting by the traditions of St. Cyr and Mme de Maintenon she would be a devout Catholic well fitted for the part she would soon be playing in society. He could scarcely imagine this ugly duckling assisting the Comtesse de Varionnet in the honors of the salon or joining the coterie of the Duchesse de Provence or the Duchesse d'Artois at court. . . . How dull she must be in her convent habit, sans rosebuds and azure ribbons!

"You take lessons in music, Mademoiselle, in dancing?" inquired Pierre, and the word "dancing" reminded him again of the Opéra and made him inattentive to her answer.

"*Oui,* M. de Michelait, with drawing and mathematics, the history of France and the Church, and translation of literature."

Pierre swallowed another yawn. He wondered vaguely if Mlle de Varionnet washed her feet. Wasn't it considered shameful in the convents to wash one's feet, and wasn't it needful to cover them from sight if one washed? . . . He would begin to feel like a leper if she didn't raise her eyes just once. He could almost hear the admonition of the Abbess. "*Baissez les yeux, Mademoiselle. Il y a du monde!*"

"What a vivid portrait!" he said then, glancing at the bold-eyed woman above the mantel.

"It is my grandmother, Mme de Varionnet," she answered, and Pierre thought he noted a quickening of interest in her voice. "She died at thirty—a victim of the pox."

He studied the portrait with new curiosity. Here, indeed, were the same features as Mlle Victoire's: the full lips, the high brows. But there was an eagerness, a vitality about the expression which was enhanced by the sumptuous court gown and the powdered hair towering *à la mode*. Ah, he remembered now . . . the woman was a notorious courtesan. And he recalled the details of Victoire's ancestry related to him yesterday from behind Mme de Chenault's fan.

Her great-grandfather Felix Fleuriez had been born of a bourgeois family in Marseilles, a distant relative of the burlesque poet Scarron, husband of Mme de Maintenon. It was through Maintenon's influence later as wife of Louis XIV that Felix Fleuriez had bought a title. His exorbitant wealth, derived from a family that had exported tapestries, enabled him to marry his daughter into the older nobility. She was Victoire's grandmother Mme de Varionnet. Tiny, dynamic, ambitious, she had had the reputation of beating her husband and pampering to excess her one son, the present Comte de Varionnet. The gambling house she had sustained in her *hôtel* was infamous and her lovers, including the Régent, had been legion. *Hélas* for the courtesan (so Mme de Chenault had whispered), her grave, learned, defeated husband had contracted smallpox and it was her duty as his wife to retire from court life and nurse him. "And what tricks the fates do play!" Mme de Chenault had chuckled. "It was Mme de Varionnet who succumbed to the pox a few weeks later and her husband who lived to become celebrated as the lover of one of the Mlles de Nesle, a crumb tossed to him by Louis XV."

The green eyes of Mme de Varionnet gazed down at Pierre with an impudent challenge and he thought: "I'll wager Mme de Varionnet sold her kisses dear! And on the contrary, Mlle Victoire will buy her kisses dear!"

"*Allons,* Pierre!" called the Marquis de Bussac. "We have interrupted the sitting long enough. Madame Vigée-Lebrun loves us, *sûrement,* but she loves her painting more!"

As Mlle Victoire made Pierre an extravagant curtsy her green eyes flashed on him for a moment in bold appraisal. Pierre, involved in a bow himself, failed to notice.

He and his father sauntered down the gallery, Pierre whistling a minuet softly.

"Charming young woman, the Mlle de Varionnet," observed the Marquis casually, a jeweled hand on Pierre's shoulder.

"A mouse," said Pierre shortly. "Caught in a trap."

❀❀❀❀❀❀❀❀❀❀❀❀❀❀❀❀❀❀❀❀❀❀❀❀❀❀

CHAPTER V

PIERRE left the masquerade ball after the opening minuet, settling back into the red velvet cushions of his carriage with the prankish delight of a small boy who has just run his fingers over the fresh icing of a cake. The little black-taffeta widow would be so busy all evening trying to discover him!

The drive from Passy to Paris would take well over an hour but he had given his coachman orders to let the horses foam. It was important to reach the Opéra before *Télémaque* was finished so that Mlle Hyacinthe should not escape him. He had determined that he would kidnap her from either supper engagement or rendezvous with M. Fleury— though how, he was not quite certain. His ardor would find a solution, Pierre thought, if he must resort to a rope ladder from the Palais-Royal window, or a dose of laudanum in M. Fleury's wine.

Ah, the days to come would be so sweet with love-making that he would wish to cling to the little Hyacinthe like a bee to a flower! He would keep her in a boudoir of a thousand mirrors so that their joys might be a thousandfold enhanced; he would bathe her lovely body in cologne to further satiate them in their hours of rapture; he would cover her beauty with flowers on some moss bank of a silent wood— only to unveil it!

And throughout months of bliss they would wander about Paris together; see the view from Mont Valérien or from the Dôme des Invalides, intoxicated with height; drink to some actor of the hour in the old Café Procope; drive to the bridge of Neuilly or to the potteries at Sèvres; laugh at Martin the bear in the Jardin des Plantes. How Mlle Hyacinthe would brighten the boulevards, with their coaches and chaises gaily colliding at five o'clock of a summer's day! Perhaps she would tuck her arm through his and saunter along the sanded sidewalks to bargain with the venders of oranges, nougat, and flowers. Had she ever been to a waxworks, this dainty little waxen doll? Did she like the puppets and the tightrope walkers and guitar players? Oh, there was an aura of enchantment about Silvie Hyacinthe!

And how he would shower her with the finery of Paris! Bonnets and laces from the establishment of Mlle Bertin, dressmaker to the Queen; sweetmeats from the Convent of Gervais; toys from the Petit-Dunkerque, the shop that furnished *brimborions* to the elite.

Pierre's blood pounded faster than the feet of his horses over the aged stones of the road. And cottages and acacias and shrines flew past him without notice.

Ordinarily he might have stopped at one of the *ginguettes* with its squeaky orchestra of violin and flute. Many a time he had sat at a rough deal table under a tent, drinking white wine, or had joined in the wild farandole with several hundred people, whirling as fast as the best of them and surviving with the fittest.

Yes, life had been anything but dull and he intended that it should remain so. There was only one disturbing element in the contemplation of his utopia. Pierre had a presentiment that Grégoire de Bussac and the Comte de Varionnet were conniving. Recently Grégoire had hinted to Pierre that it was time he should marry. The de Michelait estates were deteriorating; the family fortune had been ebbing away in extravagant living. Pierre wondered if Grégoire, *cordon bleu,* would actually stoop to "manure his lands" by an alliance with nobility of the robe. (The court was not delicate when it referred to a marriage with inferiors.)

Certainly tonight Pierre was in no mood to think of a marriage contract in spite of the de Varionnet gold plate, jeweled billiard cues, and ubiquitous footmen. Even if his infatuation for the little danseuse had not obsessed him he could not imagine marrying the trapped mouse of Mme Lebrun's portrait. And having Mlle Hyacinthe for his mistress could never entirely compensate for having a dull wife and a nursery of bourgeois children.

The Comtesse de Varionnet, he knew, had a background even more ordinary than her husband's. The mother of the Comtesse had been involved in a disgraceful affair with her steward and it was known that Mme de Varionnet was their illegitimate child. Mme de Varionnet's mother, admitting her disgrace, had devoted herself and her household to the Virgin for six months, all of them appearing in white from head to foot, much to the amusement of Paris. Mme de Varionnet's legal father had been a farmer-general, one of the sixty tax collectors of the government. If he produced a million francs for the King each year he was not questioned as to the surplus the taxes on salt, tobacco, and the land brought to him personally; his was a post easily worth one hundred thousand annually. As a result Mme de Varionnet had been accustomed from childhood to more ornaments on her head than she could gracefully balance. The farmer-general had not minded about the steward too much, it seemed. . . .

Now Pierre was coming to the outskirts of Paris. Solitary farms were giving way to dye works and tanneries and houses whispering together in twos and threes. It was a comfortable time of day, six o'clock, with the angelus ringing and the early summer sun growing moody. Throughout France thousands of simple farm people were on their knees reciting the Ave Maria.

His mother too, thought Pierre, would be at her *prie-dieu*. He felt guilty. Since he was small he had never tasted life to the full without being mildly conscious of her sanctity. But it was virtue he could not comprehend, try as he would. Far better could he understand the frank *joie de vivre* that had turned his father to the vigorous Mme de Chenault and had tempted Marie Antoinette to give her love to the handsome young Swede, Comte Axel de Fersen.

The sound of the angelus was suddenly depressing—and the thought of Catherine on her knees. Ah, how narrowing, how crushing to sacrifice one's precious years to the end of spiritual perfection! Cold, dank, lonely, like the snowy steppes of Russia. . . .

One has been born to live fully, thought Pierre, as they approached the city gates. One has been born to follow the dictates of the heart whether it be pursuing the grape or the ballet dancer.

Pierre regaled himself with a pinch of snuff and ordered his footman to drive to the Opéra.

Backstage he encountered one of Silvie's friends hurrying off to her dressing-room. She was in the process of unhooking her bodice but stopped before him with a devastating smile.

"Ah, M. de Michelait . . . you were looking for me, perhaps?"

"I am looking for Mlle Hyacinthe!"

The smile thinned out. "You have not heard then? . . . Mlle Hyacinthe sprained her ankle last night in a *pas de deux*. She was in great
pain when they took her home, Monsieur. And today she has gone into
the country to stay with an aunt."

"Where in the country?" Pierre demanded urgently.

The ballerina shrugged.

A little group gathered about them, including the manager who was
flattered at M. de Michelait's presence.

"Where has Mlle Hyacinthe gone?" asked Pierre pettishly now,
more concerned with his immediate disappointment than Mlle Hyacinthe's career.

"*Je ne sais pas,*" returned the manager, shouting above the music.
"Near Rheims perhaps? She was very fond of the cathedral at
Rheims."

"Silvie used to talk a lot of boating on the Loire," offered one of the
dancers helpfully.

"Fooh!" cried Suzanne. "I don't think it was an aunt at all! . . .
That artist in St. André has been in love with her for years!"

It was really shocking, of course, deplored a little danseuse, that none
of them knew where she was! But Silvie had been whisked off so fast
while the chorus was dancing. . . . Following the Opéra they all had
suppers and the usual duties. And today Mimi had gone to see her—
where was Mimi now?—but Silvie had left by coach. Ah, if they only
knew where Silvie was they could write to her by the next post, the
poor darling, to cheer her!

Pierre rushed to the Palais-Royal then to tear Romain the *tapissier*
from his mournful fluting. Romain was thin as a reed, with a purple
birthmark on one cheek and the pouting mouth of a fish that blows
bubbles. Pierre hated him on sight.

"*Mais oui,* she was in great pain," Romain informed him. "I bound
her foot myself with surgeon's lint while Javotte gave her orange-flower
water."

"But where did she *go?*" insisted Pierre.

"*Je ne sais pas.* She and Javotte left by early morning coach."

"You do not know? *Incroyable!*"

"*Incroyable? Mais pourquoi?* I am not Mlle Hyacinthe's keeper!"
Romain said nastily. "Unless it might be near Alençon. She has mentioned an aunt there, a Mme Clot, who is a lace worker."

"She left no message for me at all? . . . For M. de Michelait?"
urged Pierre.

"Mlle Hyacinthe is a coquette," said Romain sullenly, and turned his back to Pierre and began to wheedle his flute.

The next day Pierre went to Alençon and searched the countryside. No one had ever heard of Mme Clot.

Of course M. Fleury would know Mlle Hyacinthe's whereabouts, thought Pierre, but could he be bold enough to approach him? Pierre tried various little strategies. He bought a bonnet for Mlle Hyacinthe and had it delivered to M. Fleury's lodging, the wide-eyed errand girl asking where she might forward Mlle Hyacinthe's order. M. Fleury said the ballerina would not need the monstrosity now, as she was confined to her bed in the country. Dominique struck up an acquaintance with M. Fleury's concierge. M. Fleury had not left the city of late but the concierge would be happy to spy on him for fifty francs if he should leave it. Pierre confided in Marie Antoinette, who was romantically sympathetic and who sent a request that Mlle Hyacinthe come to Versailles to dance. But even the Queen's seal did not penetrate the mystery. Mlle Hyacinthe was not *chez elle* anywhere, reported the royal footman. And M. Fleury had impudently shrugged his shoulders and said that if the Queen *should* unearth her he would appreciate being informed of her cachette.

"The damned little hypocrite!" thought Pierre miserably. She did not deserve the attentions of a marquis's son. He would forget her. He would make her suffer for not sending him an explanation.

"Please, my dear St. Anthony," pleaded Pierre a moment later, "make me find Mlle Hyacinthe and I will light a candle in your honor . . . any number of candles, St. Anthony!"

CHAPTER VI

IT WAS the end of May and Pierre was attending a service in the palace chapel of Versailles. In spite of the pomp and frills of a feast day he was feeling morose.

If his own linen clung to him like a tenacious beggar and his cravat seemed to have a strangle hold on his neck, how unbearable the plight of the women, he thought. In their stiff court silks they were fluttering and restless, moths stirring to break through their cocoons. There was Mme de Frivouac, his mistress, unable to resist a very wee, graceful scratch at her scalp through her itching coiffure. He wondered how Marie Antoinette could keep her gracious smile. Certainly Louis made no pretense as he mopped his moist red face with a crumpled handkerchief.

And, *grand Dieu!*—but he was thirsty! For days now he had either been thirsty or he had been drinking. And no one to blame for his thirst and dehydration but that little witch of a dancer!

A young baron beside him nudged him to rise. The court descended from the tribune to the ground floor of the chapel. Louis and Marie Antoinette ensconced themselves in armchairs placed on the sumptuous carpet, surrounded by chaplains and guards. Pierre was among the officers and ladies of the court who ranged themselves behind the sovereigns.

Dieu, but the riot of color and incense was stifling when one's head was a plum pudding! And now it was time to collect the alms and that was a rite eternal. There was a clink of gold collected on this feast day for the curés of Versailles.

Pierre wondered vaguely, running his finger under his limp cravat, who would collect the alms today. It would be some young thing who had recently been presented to the King in his cabinet after Sunday vespers. On other feast days Pierre had always been actively curious, for frequently it had meant the debut of a beauty.

His eyes followed the young woman in her yellow brocade court dress with its enormous panniers and long train. It was difficult to see her beyond the high, feathered coiffures. She was tall and carried the enormous hoop with a certain hasty arrogance. Two long lappets of black lace hung from her headdress, and her bosom and arms sparkled with a wealth of family diamonds. There was something familiar about her restless manner, he thought, as she curtsied before each prince in the proper order. Curtsy-clink, curtsy-clink.

"With her bold eyes Mlle de Varionnet should collect more than a hundred louis for the vultures," whispered the young baron beside him, and Pierre was stupefied.

So—it was Mlle de Varionnet! The little mouse of Mme Lebrun's portrait, whose muslins and rosebuds of a few weeks ago had fallen from her like the simple chrysalis of a butterfly, gaudy satins and hard gleaming gems in their place. It was only her name that remained the same, he mused. Her brown stubborn curls were a powdered masterpiece and the poor complexion was disguised with rouge and powder. Mlle de Varionnet's full scarlet lips and large green eyes combined a dashing challenge to a stingy purse. Pierre had an uncanny feeling that the first Mme de Varionnet had stepped out of her portrait and had come back to Versailles to regale the jaded courtiers. He watched her every movement, still incredulous. When she stopped before him he thought he detected a second's pause before she curtsied and held out the gold salver. Then she flashed him a robust smile. Curtsy-clink. Somehow he wanted to slap her face for she was obviously enjoying the bewilderment he could not hide.

"Dieu!" whispered the young baron after she had passed, *"mais elle a du ton! . . .* And a dowry of eight hundred thousand francs!"

On the fourth of June, the Dauphin died of rickets. For a long time he had been puny and querulous. The court mourned, with black mortcloth on its buildings and carriages, and after the burial the cortege moved dolefully to Marly. But it was only Louis and Marie Antoinette who mourned deeply, for Louis Charles, the second son, was a far more promising Dauphin, with his bubbling spirits, his beautiful heart-shaped face, and dimpled chin.

As an excursion to Marly was always at the King's expense it was not actually courteous to be bored here, thought Pierre. However, though Lansquenet and faro were played each evening in the Queen's card room in the Pavilion of the Sun, the black of the court mourning was depressing. Instead of the sparkle of balls there were small gatherings at which was read a discourse on some social or moral problem and always a eulogy of the late little Prince. Women yawned and during the vacant hours trained their canary birds to sing to the harp, formed an herbarium of the province, or translated some Italian romance. It was even rumored that Mlle Victoire de Varionnet, attached now to the service of the Comtesse d'Artois, had a *marcassin* as a pet. The small, wild boar played happily with her dogs but made a rush at strangers with its large tusks and shaggy square head, causing much screaming and amusement.

"Some day he will gore you to death!" Pierre warned Mlle de Varionnet as he met her walking in the gardens with her pet.

Mlle de Varionnet smiled broadly and her green eyes twinkled. Pierre sensed that she was ready with a witty answer that was not *de rigueur* for a young girl so fresh from a convent. She curtsied to him, gave a jerk to the gold braid leash that restrained the bucking boar, and merely replied, *"Si fait, si fait, M. de Michelait!"*

Gentlemen, tired of battledore and shuttlecock, began to sneak off to the races at Vincennes or Sablons, and more than one stomach became deranged and suddenly required the water of Le Mont d'Or in Auvergne, or some other spa.

Pierre, still unable to find Mlle Hyacinthe, languished with ennui and desire to her. He had been trying to buoy himself up with a romantic correspondence with Mme de Frivouac (although he saw her every day) and with an attempt to get a lock of Marie Antoinette's hair through one of her *femmes de chambres*. But after a week at Marly, Mme de Frivouac, her aging bosom a little haggard in black, found Pierre's caresses more truculent than tender.

"How long does it take a sprained ankle to heal, *chérie?*" Pierre asked her one night after they had effaced their boredom in the moonlight.

"Eh bien! C'est ce que je pensais! You have been trying to maim me! Of late I have wondered if this was a liaison or rape!" exclaimed Mme de Frivouac with gushing tears. *"Par Dieu! . . . c'est de quoi faire perdre la tête!"*

For two days Mme de Frivouac had a nervous affection and had to be soothed with ether. The thought of her began to affect Pierre biliously, like a third praline. He would never touch her odious person again! The restlessness, the *tristesse* that had been burgeoning in court life for the last six or eight years had come to a climax in his own person. *Dieu,* but he would like to escape from it all! To fight a War of the Roses or go to the Holy Land on a Crusade!

For it was folly not to admit the crisis in France. There was a sharpness in the discussion of politics that would have been considered bad taste six months ago. The States-General, which had opened a month before at Versailles, had produced constant wrangling. The Tiers-État, or Third Estate, composed of the bourgeois deputies, fought to be united with the clergy and the nobility in a common voting body. The Third Estate's representatives far outnumbered those of the two other groups, and a union would be a distinct voting advantage. The Marquis de Lafayette, the Vicomte de Noailles, and others of the nobility ardently espoused the cause of the bourgeoisie.

One afternoon Pierre was startled to come upon Marie Antoinette alone in a small library adjoining the Dauphiness's boudoir. At first he did not see her. It was the hour when he usually read to the Princess, who had not returned from her ride, an hour in which his lips repeated the words on the printed page and the fancies of the Dauphiness and himself wandered to separate greener pastures.

So unusual was it to find Marie Antoinette unattended that when Pierre saw her, he could scarcely stammer his apologies for intruding. Moreover, he noticed that the blue eyes, famed for their vivacity and sparkle, were dull with tears. She had been looking out of the open window, and as her hand slipped from the gold brocade of the drape she was left in shadow. In her simple black with a plain white fichu she looked like any other mother who has lost a son. Pierre noticed also that she wore a brooch of the Dauphin's hair. And this was the woman that France accused of intriguing for a diamond necklace worth one million, six hundred thousand livres!

"Do not apologize, M. de Michelait," she said with the toss of her head that her enemies called arrogance. Pierre had never found in it anything but dignity tempered with sweetness. "It is I who intrude. I have only come to hear you read to Mme Royale. Ah, I see that my tears distress you, my devoted friend!"

She held out her hand to him and there was a warm stir of rose scent; Pierre felt giddy and accepted the honor of kissing her hand with confused rapture.

"I cannot bear to see Madame suffer!"

"You have always been my devoted friend, M. de Michelait," she repeated with confidence. "And I have need of friends. . . . My ill fortune began when I lost my little Sophie a year ago. And now it seems to me an ill omen that my son should be buried in the last vacant tomb of the kings of France at St. Denis. . . ."

"Your Majesty is overcome with sorrow."

"Sorrow for the plight of France."

His eyes adored the transparent whiteness of her skin, the fine high forehead, the soft oval of her face. But its radiant color had vanished. He felt a sharp pain at her pallor.

Pierre knew that Marie Antoinette was superstitious. She had been born at the time of the Lisbon earthquake. At her marriage nuptials, fireworks had caused the death of hundreds of people in the place de Louis XV. She had never ceased grieving at this catastrophe. Only a few days ago, it was rumored, four wax tapers freshly lighted on her toilette table had gone out of their own accord. The Queen had shuddered at this strange occurrence and considered it sinister although Mme Campan assured her that the four tapers had no doubt been run in the same mold, all of them having a defective wick at the same point.

"Come, M. de Michelait, let us sit here at the table and wait for Mme Campan who has gone to fetch my needlework. . . . Do not feel ill at ease, I beg of you. You have helped me milk cows too often at the Petit Trianon for that. . . ." She smiled at him with the peculiar warmth and charm that had held him prisoner since he was twelve.

He felt that in this rare moment Marie Antoinette wished only to be a woman talking with a friend, that she was lonely. The intimacy of her words was unbearably sweet but he continued to stand, fumbling for the book he had planned to read to the Dauphiness.

There flashed into his mind the last humiliating scene of Marie Antoinette in public—the day the States-General had opened in Versailles. She had appeared in the procession in regal grandeur (who would suppose it was for the last time?). And on seeing her a rabble of low women had cried out hoarsely: *"Vive le Duc d'Orléans!"*—her sworn enemy. At the memory of it Pierre's blood raged with anger.

"Do take care what you read to Mme Royale," said Marie Antoinette. "She is young and she dreams!"

"I do my best to keep her away from the nightmares!" he reassured her. "I realize full well that France is only too full of them."

He thought guiltily of the philosophers and pamphlets that he read and weighed in his own leisure. The dynamite set at the foot of royalty. . . .

"I trust you, my friend," she said simply.

He was deeply touched.

"I've had but one purpose since I first laid eyes on Versailles," said Pierre. "To serve you, Madame, and my Sire, and all your loved ones!"

"I may have need of you," she answered gratefully, and she held out her hand to him once more as she rose, for she heard Mme Campan approaching.

His lips pressed her fingers passionately.

M. de Michelait—the little boy Pierre—did not wish her to be quite human, she thought, amused. He wished only to worship the goddess. A tryst, perhaps, with the idealism of his childhood. So be it. . . . And she would see that he got his lock of stolen hair. . . .

CHAPTER VII

AFTER SHE had listened an hour to the life of Gregory the Great the Dauphiness was wriggling although she thought M. de Michelait's voice like honey. Marie Antoinette had not stayed after all (she was always changing her mind), and an undergoverness, who sat near the window of the closet doing needlepoint, was distracted by the strollers below.

Mme Royale secretly counted the volumes that had red binding in the bookcase; she tried to braid a few locks of loose brown hair; she sniffled; she recalled the delicious thrill which ran through her body when her horse nibbled sugar from her palm. For a while she watched a fly washing his legs. Running her fingers under the table, she was pleased to find it quite dirty, and a moment later transferred the smudge to her moist little face. Then she remembered three jujube lozenges in her pocket and wondered if she could slip them into her mouth without anybody's seeing her. It must be nice to be Papa King, she thought, and not have to read but simply color maps or make locks.

It was a happy surprise when the undergoverness was called from the room. Pierre closed the book with a plop and Mme Royale seemed to become hinged together again.

"M. de Michelait, I see something brown. Guess what it is!"

"The dirt on your face! . . . But it is too hot to think, Mme Royale!"

"Let us play drafts then."

"I'm afraid you'll win. I have a conundrum: When is a cat not a cat?" proposed Pierre, relaxing with a pinch of snuff.

"*Je ne sais pas.* . . . Tell me, M. de Michelait!" Mme Royale shoved one of her jujube lozenges over to Pierre's side of the table. Then on second thought she relinquished another. Her mother was firm about her not being selfish.

"Not until you tell me what you heard about me yesterday when you visited your aunt, the Comtesse d'Artois," he said between sneezes.

"A cat is not a cat when he is a copycat?"

"No, no, no. But not bad!—Who was it said what yesterday?"

"Eh bien. It was that young lady with the *marcassin*. She said you were the handsomest man at court. And she couldn't understand why someone hadn't married you!"

"Mlle de Varionnet?" Pierre curtailed his last sneeze.

"*Oui*. I told her it was because you are waiting for me. You *are* waiting till I grow up, aren't you, my dear M. de Michelait?"

"A cat is not a cat when he is a catfish!"

Mme Royale laughed gaily and ate the three lozenges, unthinking.

At that moment there was a great commotion at the door and the Comtesse de Polignac appeared with the Dauphin Louis Charles, who was four and a half years old. He dashed over to Pierre.

"Draw me a picture of a berline, M. de Michelait," he demanded, his large wide blue eyes coaxing, "with a funny man looking from the window. And make one for Mme Royale too."

The little heart-shaped face and high color and full lips were so like Marie Antoinette's that Pierre had always adored the child. His eyebrows were dark and delicately arched and the high cheekbones were prominent. The nose, already straight and pointed, was not a Bourbon nose. The Dauphin was nearly all Hapsburg, thought Pierre, with satisfaction, even to his erect carriage, his lively grace, his warm, beguiling smile. Louis Charles had been born gay, said his mother.

Pierre wondered how the King had dared to have this beautiful child inoculated against the smallpox, for the new practice was considered very dangerous. The inoculation had occurred the year before at Saint Cloud in the presence of the royal family, Madame de Polignac, his governess, and all of the doctors. The punctures on both arms had been successful although indelible scars remained. It seemed sacrilege to mar the child's beauty in any way, thought Pierre. The boy had been born, of course, with one slight deformity; the lobe of the right ear was much too large and ill-shaped, but the hairdresser always concealed the disfigurement and very few people knew of it.

Now, as Louis Charles hung affectionately over Pierre and the embryo berline, his pale yellow curls tumbled forward exposing the blemish. Mme de Polignac, beside him, hastened to straighten his hair and exchanged a glance of embarrassment with Pierre.

It was at this moment that two dogs in the garden below began to snarl and fight. The little Dauphin cried out in terror and clung to Mme de Polignac. Sudden noises always startled him. Mme de Polignac put her arm about the child and drew him from the room, and Mme Royale ran after her brother to console him.

Pierre crumpled up the picture of the berline he had started and sat for a moment gazing out of the window. His encounter with Marie Antoinette had left him feeling more restless and melancholy than usual. If only he could forget the gloom of the court and be gay! It occurred to him that there was a fair on the outskirts of Marly. Why not go? Obviously there would be no more reading today. And he might wear a provincial suit of Dominique's and lose himself in the hilarity of the crowd. . . .

It was the hottest part of the day but Pierre left his carriage and wandered among the fairgoers with a feeling of rejuvenation. His pulse, which had been sluggish for weeks, began to quicken. Ah, some day he would like to be a tightrope walker (it was no wonder that the Comte d'Artois had sneaked by night to the Petit Trianon to practice this fascinating art!). Or perhaps he would learn to be a ventriloquist. How the young lady beside him was appalled to find the meowing of a cat coming from her own modest bosom! Pierre laughed heartily along with the others and sauntered along the path lined by two rows of illuminated stalls. There were puppet shows and performing dogs, dwarfs and giants, rabbits with four ears, half man and half woman.

Pierre was jostled by sturdy peasants, squawling children, dapper pickpockets. He bought tartlets for the trollops who ogled him, and then dodged them, enjoying the chagrin on their faces. It was good seeing children with running noses, babies at pink blobby breasts, dogs at large—finding mates. Here was a detached voice bawling lemonade, ices, snails, brandied cherries! There was the wail of a lost child, the squeal of a coquette with ticklish ribs, the cacophony of strolling players. Beauty, deformity, perfumes, and stinks—all broiled in the cauldron of July sun-glare. Was that his own voice hissing the vaudeville team singing its bawdy couplets, applauding the marionette players?

His spirits continued to soar like a balloon with the charivari and he felt as he had weeks ago when he wandered along the Pont-Neuf on his way to meet the little Silvie Hyacinthe. At Marly the hands of the clock had been stopped and one could scent the mold of the tomb. Here in the garish life of the midway life was immortal.

"Your palm read?" cackled an old gypsy crone in bright rags and beads.

Pierre hesitated. Perhaps she would be able to tell him where to find Mlle Hyacinthe. Strange that he thought he saw Silvie in every pretty face that approached him. . . . But he would come back later when the dancing on the green was over. He passed a group of hilarious bowlers going onto a small field that was merry with flags and music. Dozens of bourgeoisie were dancing the *gaillarde* or *tricotet,* the young girls flaunting their pink ribbons. (In two adjacent fields the *paysanne* in her simple cap was doing the Picardy Jig, and the provincial belle in her sash and plumes, a polka.)

Pierre watched the dizzy pace of the dancers and the flying reds, greens, and blues of skirts, his hands stuffed into his pockets. It was only the old who looked on, sipping their beer or cider and nibbling at gingerbread with toothless enjoyment. The laughter, the frolic of the fiddles, the smell of grass fresh crushed by flying feet, the whirling of pretty legs, all coursed through his blood like a frothy wine and he snatched the hand of a plump wench and began to twirl her about in the throng. What did it matter that he didn't know the steps, so long as his soul was dancing? . . . The girl was expert (many who couldn't read paid a fancy price for dancing lessons) and she pushed and prodded him at the right moments and flew into his arms and out again, and by the time he was breathless the Picardy Jig had just reached its stride.

It was in his most abandoned moment, when he refused to let go of the plump waist of his partner and had just planted a wild kiss on her willing lips, that his eyes met those of the astounded Mlle Hyacinthe. Leaning on a cane with a devoted swain beside her, she was watching the frolic.

Pierre's senses began to lurch with his feet. He tried to stop dancing but his partner continued to bandy him about like a tennis ball. Mlle Hyacinthe flew in and out of his vision; he smiled at her ardently to reassure her that he was indeed Pierre de Michelait, that he would be at her side the first moment he could break away from this demon. She returned a nasty little frown and mentioning something to her escort, leaned on his arm and turned from the dancing.

"*Par Dieu!*" exclaimed Pierre to his partner, frantic lest Silvie should escape him again, "you must help me. . . . You see the young man with the lady in the shell-pink dress with scallops of rose and green? . . . If you engage him to dance as I engaged you I shall give you enough francs to keep you in gala for a year!" He fished in his pockets but his purse was gone. The girl began to laugh at him, her arms akimbo. Pierre flushed angrily.

"*Diable!* Here's my watch then. . . ." And he made sure it was there before he offered it. He jammed it into her hand. "Give it to your lover as an *étrenne.*"

"I have no lover."

"Then you will have a lover on New Year's Day. Come, *vitement, ma chatte,* or they will be gone."

The girl, wide-eyed, dropped the watch into her bosom and kidnapped Mlle Hyacinthe's swain without compunction.

"Chérie!" whispered Pierre, at Mlle Hyacinthe's side. "I have been insane trying to find you."

"A likely story when you did not even bother to answer my letter!"

Her lips were in a sorry pout and her eyes refused to look above the buttons on his coat. He gripped her hands so tightly that they pained her.

"What letter, *mignonne?* I swear by all the saints I had no letter!"

"Romain promised—"

"Romain! . . . I pleaded with him for news of you. He sent me goose chasing to Alençon! The liar!"

"And I thought you had forgotten me, M. de Michelait! Oh, if you please, Monsieur, do not let go of my hand again, ever!"

Her tantalizing blue eyes and her lips broke into a smile of confession. And he led her like an obedient lap dog down the field to the edge of the fair where he hailed a limping fiacre and lifted her gently into it. They jogged along the country road, their lips pressed together. Neither of them heard the taunts of the youths that passed them.

Pierre felt that he wanted to swoop through the air like a drunken swallow; to roar like a stormy tide; to leap like a tongue of fire; to intoxicate himself with the sweetness of Mlle Hyacinthe as a bear intoxicates himself with a find of honey.

Hours later in a small wood beyond the house where Mlle Hyacinthe stayed with her aunt he lay beside the little danseuse on a carpet of moss. They had been so silent, so content, that the squirrels were chattering in the oak branches above them and a small hare had come quite close, peeking at them through the thousands of dried lilies of the valley and periwinkles of the grove. Mlle Hyacinthe's bonnet hung on her cane, standing upright in the moss like a sentry. Her hair, tousled and entwined with a blue, orchidlike flower, swept the moss like a late-afternoon sunbeam, and her head lay in the curve of Pierre's arm.

She could hear the beating of his heart, swift thuds of a horse's hoof on the ground. And her own heart was no laggard. She knew instinctively that what had come to her with the proud Pierre was something tragic as well as beautiful. She had not meant to really love him. Nor had she ever known what it meant to really love until now. Lying in the curve of his arm, listening to the hard beating of their hearts, she was frightened.

Through an opening in the trees they watched the flash of fireworks that rose from the fairgrounds. At first it had startled them. Then he had drawn her close and they lay gazing at the shower of stars that sprinkled the twilight, bursting greens and reds and blues, deepening the dark of the summer sky as they vanished. Finally there was a transparent triumphal arch, the palace of Pluto, cupids lolling on columns, dodging stanzas of verses and flowers.

They sighed with delight over the exotic brilliance like two little children. It was sad to see Pluto's iridescent palace crumble away into darkness. Pierre drew the small cambric figure closer to him again, and his fingers and lips fondled the flowered hair, the soft honey lips, the white bosom.

"Je vous aime," he whispered, "little Silvie—little elf."

There was a sweetness in her submission that was new and mellowing, he thought. He no longer wanted to roar like a jungle lion. He wanted to float like an aimless lily on a pond, to drift like a wanton milkweed in the meadow. . . .

CHAPTER VIII

SEVERAL WEEKS LATER Pierre spent a few days at his father's home in the rue de Grenelle as Silvie wanted to do some shopping in Paris.

He returned one afternoon after a horseback ride in the Champ de Mars with the Comte de Ségur. He was in no mood to see his mother. Her solemn world of the spirit was in mean harmony with the gossamer floating of himself and Silvie. But it was necessary to pass her apartments to reach his own.

Catherine and the Abbé Blafond were sitting in the ante-chamber of her boudoir and the hall door was open. Catherine sewed on some linen for the poor and sick at the Hôtel Dieu, the hospital of Notre Dame. It grieved her to see them herded together like beasts, forced to sleep on their sides in crowded beds regardless of contagion.

The Abbé napped in his *bergère* and the floor about him was littered with pages from the *Journal de Paris* and the *Petites Affiches*. Although he was a Jesuit, he wore the distinctive dress of an *abbé commendataire,* a short, dark-violet coat with a narrow collar.

Twenty-five years ago at the time the Jansenists had been influential in having the Jesuits expelled from France, the Abbé Blafond had been a young man and subsuperior of a Jesuit college. Many of his colleagues had withdrawn then to free-thinking Russia or to the protection of Catherine II. But there was nothing to prevent the Abbé's early return to become secular tutor of the three de Michelait sons.

"Pierre!" said Catherine with quiet warmth, and held out her hand to him. Pierre kissed the long slim fingers, cool and unjeweled.

The two of them talked of the family for a few moments, softly so as not to disturb the Abbé.

Finally the Abbé's tonsured head rolled like a bottle on a wave and then snapped upright.

"Resting my eyes," he explained, and yawned. His eyes had always been bloodshot and Pierre wondered if that was from too much reading, too much rest, or too much Kirschewasser, his favorite beverage. There was a half-full liqueur glass beside him now. The Abbé squinted the sleep out of his pudgy face, smoothed the wrinkles out of his black gown, like a little girl at a party, and began again on the Kirschewasser. The Marquise smiled at her cousin leniently. She never touched strong spirits herself but she thought the Abbé who had been her confessor all these years was faultless.

Pierre, resigned, dropped into another *bergère* for a dutiful moment and it occurred to him for the first time how much the little salon suited his mother. It was like a small Greek temple, with cool white pilasters, ebony furniture touched with gold, and draperies of emerald green. No cabinet filled with curios marred the simplicity of the room, no collection of china cane tops, or mother-of-pearl incense boxes. The only ornament, hung above the mantel, was a Fra Lippo Lippi of Christ on the cross. And tonight on a table beside Catherine, a glass of white violets the Abbé had brought from the woods. This room, of all the salons in the mansion, had the restraint and the exquisite refinement of his mother, thought Pierre. Cornelia, mother of the Gracchi. . . .

"We have just been discussing the salvation of the soul," said the Abbé, who glanced at the Marquise as much as to say that their own immediate problem had been solved. *"Dites-moi,* Pierre, how much time do you spend considering the salvation of your soul?"

"Not so much time as I spend in damning it, Monsieur l'Abbé," Pierre answered, squirming at the thought of serious talk. In five minutes he must excuse himself. . . .

Moreover, of late Pierre did not want to consider his soul. And what was his soul, anyway? A muddy thing, Protestant and of Jansenist sympathy on his father's side, Jesuit on his mother's. . . . It was better not to think at all when thinking only increased his confusion.

The very books his father had given him to read and had discussed with him the last five years were the books his mother had burned: Voltaires' *Philosophic Letters on the English;* the volumes of Locke and Descartes; d'Alembert's *Geneva,* a stinging reproach to the clergy of Versailles; Helvetius's *De L'Esprit.*

The fact that many of these books had been burned in public by the hangman or were published outside of France had only increased Pierre's interest in them. If his tutor the Abbé Blafond had brought him up with the strict Jesuit doctrine of obedience and conformity to the age-old tenets of the church, his father had encouraged his independent thinking. Grégoire was a Christian, ostensibly a Catholic, but the philosophies of the radicals had come within the Marquis's serious scrutiny and consideration. And although Pierre had prayed too often beside his mother in Mass to accept these new ideas, neither could he reject them.

Actually, what was this fuss between Jesuit and Jansenist all about, thought Pierre? They were all Catholics, even if Jansen's doctrines did smack of Calvin.

The Abbé Blafond was shuffling in his chair now like a little boy who suddenly has to go to the toilet. Pierre smiled to himself. This meant the Abbé was preparing another question. How well Pierre knew the Abbé!

The boys had wandered with the Abbé through Europe, from town to town, from palace to palace. Along with mathematics and expurgated editions of Virgil and Horace, had gone St. Ignatius's *Spiritual Exercises.* It was only Maurice who had made all the exercises. The meditations on sin and hell terrified Gilbert after a day or two so that he would throw a convulsion. Pierre could not stand the silence and isolation. The Abbé desponded. The boys were too young, perhaps, for this instruction. He must teach them fear and the will of God through another channel.

He kept them under the strictest surveillance, directing their lives as if they were novices. They learned to move the head gravely, use a moderate gait in public, hold the lips not too much closed or too much open. He taught them that a Jesuit must grow cold to all things worldly: a love of friends, the beauty of Nature, a romp on the sand, the thrilling dead aim of an arrow.

But the Abbé had had a hard time of it regimenting them, thought Pierre. Maurice was the only one amenable. Solemn from childhood, he had been an ascetic at twelve, even to self-castigation. Gilbert, who pretended to accept Jesuitism with the obedience of the novice, broke blithely into epicurean dance and song when he was alone. And Pierre, always his father's son, was not above stealing from the Abbé's mattress a risqué novel.

Perhaps the Abbé was justified in never trusting them to a thought or action of their own. He even watched them carefully when they bathed or urinated, wary of masturbation. Gilbert and Pierre were interested in his motive. Sex hunger, of which the Abbé spoke so disparagingly, was certainly worthy of exploration. And it soon became an exciting game to deceive the Abbé. Gilbert was caught one day admiring his anatomy behind some rocks at the seashore, for the Abbé watched him from his hotel window with a spyglass. Gilbert spent a week on a hermit's diet while he copied the *Directorium* over and over. Maurice caught him eating smuggled sweetmeats and found favor with the Abbé for tattling. From then on the two other boys began to torment him.

Ah, thought Pierre, the failure of their education was that on holidays when they returned to Paris, Grégoire, the agnostic, again became their father!

Pierre watched the Abbé straighten and take a sip of cordial. Even in the old days of travel, the Abbé had loved his Kirschewasser, had claimed that he needed it as a heart stimulant. While he dozed, the boys had giggled over illustrations in library books or a mutilated Venus. Pierre remembered suddenly the sketch Gilbert had once made of the Abbé asleep. Gilbert had given him the ears and whiskers of a cat and instead of the glass in his hand the Abbé had been dangling a large rat with the features of Maurice. That was the time the Abbé had punished Pierre for his lusty laughing. Pierre had had to transcribe some ancient inscriptions come upon in a crumbling building. Everywhere they went, everything they did, thought Pierre, it had been the past that was important. And now today France was stirring in her sleep and stretching. And if she wakened, thought Pierre, he knew nothing but dusty words except the little his father had taught him.

"Have you been regular at Mass, my son?" inquired the Abbé, and Pierre knew that Catherine and the Abbé had been discussing him. Hang it all, why couldn't they let him alone? He was only twenty and there was plenty of time for salvation! If they should cause him to reach the Palais-Royal too late to see Silvie he would turn atheist!

"When I don't want to go to Mass I think of what Jansen said," answered Pierre. "That no amount of churchgoing will save a man unless the love of God is in him. And yet I'm not sure I believe with Jansen that I can't give this capacity of God-love to myself. And that whether God converts me or not depends on his own good pleasure."

He did not like to make his mother wince but he felt rebellious. This was the way he argued against Jansenism when his father attacked Jesuitism.

"Surely you could not believe in predestination!" exclaimed Catherine with a melancholy vigor. She laid her sewing on her lap and her large, black eyes clung to Pierre.

She was really the most beautiful woman he had ever known, thought Pierre, her white skin untouched by powder, her face lighted with a constant spiritual glow, soft and radiant as a faithful altar candle. When a child, he had pictured the angels as wearing the white gown and simple cap of Catherine.

The Abbé coughed nervously and his cheek twitched. It was only of late that Pierre had openly dared to question his early training, to show initiative and independence.

"Pierre," said the Abbé in the voice perpetually husky from Kirschewasser, "you will go to Hell if you believe this fantastic idea of predestination!"

"I didn't say I believed it," Pierre fumed. "I am merely quoting Jansen. It would be much simpler to believe as I was taught, that no matter how I sin, you, Father, can easily absolve me, without actually knowing if I mean to repeat my sins on the morrow."

"You know well that your confessions to me have always brought you release and a love of God!" the Abbé said evasively.

"I am not so sure. Now and then I have sinned during my very confession. Wondering what you were really thinking with your hands before your face. Wondering if my hour with you was not merely a formula, a mincing devotion. Often it's seemed to me that Jansen's indictment against us Jesuits might be true: that our society is everything, the individual nothing; that we're intolerant of all that does not stem from St. Ignatius; that if we dare to listen to anyone but Aristotle or St. Thomas Aquinas we think we are damned. . . . I have a dreadful longing to be myself, to be somebody different!"

"If enough others think like you," exclaimed the Abbé, "the tie between the Church and State will snap. And then—the deluge! Believe me, my son, France can only keep her equilibrium by submission to the Church. This is no time to be different. The Church is tottering. The Church needs you."

Catherine rose and her sewing dropped to the floor; her eyes were dimmed with tears.

"Oh, my child, how my heart bleeds for you! You were too young, too sensitive, too weak to be sent into the pitfalls of life at court! I pleaded with your father to give you to the Church, along with Maurice—pleaded on my bended knee!"

"But I wasn't meant to be a priest, Mother!"

"As a little child you were devout!"

"I'm sorry I've wounded you!" cried Pierre, deeply touched at his mother's distress. "I don't know what possesses me at times . . . forgive me."

"Come then," said Catherine softly. "Let us pray for your soul, my Pierre. . . . Let us pray to the Holy Virgin to make you childlike and trusting again—as you once were when you prayed at my knee."

Pierre had a mad desire to look at his watch. Even religion could not keep Mlle Hyacinthe out of focus. And yet there was Catherine before him, with her eyes pleading, pleading. . . . Had someone told her about Mlle Hyacinthe? He followed her sheepishly across the twilight of the antechamber. *Dieu,* here he was, a small child again being chastened because he had been saucy!

Pierre knelt at the *prie-dieu* of the little oratory with Catherine and clasped the hard gold of a crucifix. With closed eyes he could vision the walls and ceilings richly painted, the bas-relief of the altar, the silver statuette of St. Anthony, the exquisite woodwork of black carved oak, the bronze cross under the miniature rose window. The mysticism of the oratory had never failed to bring him the beauty of chastity, if only for a moment. From childhood he had been soothed by the singular sweetness of Catherine's voice giving him a sense of humility. But to-night he did not want to feel humble.

Catherine's fingers, dipped in holy water, caressed his forehead with the sign of the cross. He told the beads of his rosary. In spite of the debonaire ballet ankles, he began to feel the hushed peace of the tiny room and the old throbbing sense of penitence. When Catherine's voice had ceased Pierre found he had an ache in his throat. He hated himself for his weakness.

They rose slowly to their feet. The whiteness of Catherine's gown faded into candlelight, making her nebulous, part human, part shadow. Ah, but she was a saint and he adored her!

"Since you were little," she confessed to him softly, "I wanted life to hold everything for you, every beauty! You were my baby, Pierre. The last symbol of a love which had been beautiful!"

"Mother, I'll never torture you again," he answered fervently, holding the softness of her hand to his cheek.

And he believed what he told her.

At any rate, for a little moment. . . .

CHAPTER IX

IT WAS MONDAY, the fifth of October. The dripping gloom of the day annoyed Pierre though a ruddy fire lighted his Versailles apartment.

The suite consisted of two miserable rooms, in one of which was a sleeping alcove for Dominique. After one had passed the smell of latrines in the corridor he entered the dark, narrow passage that gave onto the sleeping-chamber.

It never occurred to Pierre that he wasn't well established. Being in the service of the royal family, and in constant waiting upon the King's lever, the Queen's Mass, and the Dauphiness's whims, was a privilege one couldn't forego. And how could one live away from the court and get a coveted post before one's rival, or remind the minister that one was a prodigy—or even pander to the man who might be the new minister tomorrow?

Pierre sat at his escritoire writing to Holland for some French books that had recently been banned in France. He was not concentrating well, for the past months had been a medley of political and romantic outburst.

Throughout the summer idyl with Silvie Hyacinthe the furor of politics seemed subordinate somehow. The Third Estate had finally won its victory and the three orders had assembled in June as one body, calling itself the National Assembly. This union had given the bourgeois representatives a predominance of votes over the nobility and clergy, and heaven knew what sort of constitution would result from their power! Then the storming of the Bastille on the fourteenth of July had shaken the very roots of France. Pierre smiled now as he recalled Silvie trying to understand the "Rights of Man." Women were so much more interested in the fashions that came from England than in the principles. He had taken her once to the Tennis Court where the Assembly was in session, and they had sat in the gallery thronged with beautiful noblewomen watching history in the making. Fashionable it was for gleaming jewels to look down on sweating law.

Silvie, of the magic toes. . . . Nothing was really important to an artist but his art, thought Pierre. The world might crumble about her and she would never know so long as she might dance, and love, and be merry. Was her outlook infectious, perhaps? . . . He realized that he, too, had looked upon France's raging as a threatening gale outside of a cozy cottage fireside. If he and Silvie heard Camille Desmoulins ranting in the Palais-Royal gardens, surrounded with red, white, and blue cockades, and were pelted with fiery pamphlets—what did it really matter when they were about to walk together in the Bois de Boulogne or the Luxembourg Gardens? It grieved them both to see the queues of hungry people before the bakers' shops, or to hear that châteaux were being burned by peasants who could not subsist on boiled grass. Yet, behind their pity was an even greater hunger, fed but never appeased.

That had been an unforgettable day when he and Silvie had gone to visit the actor Talma and had met in the street the dripping red head of Foulon on a pike, its mouth stuffed with grass. Foulon the grain speculator had made the mistake of condemning the criminal views of the Duc d'Orléans and had advised Louis not to part with his Paris army until order was restored in the streets. Besides, he had once said: "Let the people eat grass." Following the head had been paraded Foulon's crimson, pulpy heart in the middle of a bunch of white carnations. On that day the gale had rattled the cottage windows.

It was no wonder that there had been an exodus of nobility from France, thought Pierre. The very day after the storming of the Bastille, the Comte d'Artois and Mme de Polignac the royal governess, among others, had hurriedly left Versailles. This turmoil would soon come to a climax and blow over, of course, but in the meanwhile the palace was grim. Marie Antoinette was solemn. Louis had been forced to accept the new cockade and a National Guard was established under Lafayette. There were rumors abroad that Louis, his family, and ministers intended to flee to the troops at Metz and the populace guarded his moves jealously.

But these things were too disturbing to dwell on, thought Pierre, as his pen scrawled the address of the publisher. Better remember the nights after the Opéra when he and Silvie sat at a little table in the Café Foy of the Palais-Royal, treason rampant and noisy about them, and absently munched wafer cakes and drank beer or cider. Or their comforting patriotism when the clergy had melted down the church plate for the national coffers, and he had given his gold shoe buckles and diamond buttons, and Silvie had sacrificed her grandmother's bracelet. . . . Ah, how happy they had been browsing about the aged Henry IV houses and windmills of the Montmartre; discarding Silvie's finery from the old-clothes shops in the rue Tirechappe in favor of the rue St. Honoré; singing "Gloria in Excelsis" at Le Sacré-Cœur, thinking not of God but of each other's touch! But it was the woods of Meudon they loved the most. Often they plodded up the steep paths beyond lofty groves and pine vistas and solitary ponds, dining at a little lodge or picnicking. And in the heart of the woods with spotted fern and gay woodbine they revived the ecstasy of that early summer twilight. If they were living in a misty world of their own, it was because little Silvie Hyacinthe had come to idolize her Pierre de Michelait, and because it was the first time he had ever been really loved.

He could not tell which was a greater emotion, Pierre mused, the joy of possessing Mlle Hyacinthe or the pain he felt at the fear of losing her. For their liaison was in defiance of the fiery M. Fleury, who refused to be tossed aside like an apple peel. Pierre wondered if M. Fleury would simply shoot him sometime without benefit of duel in the Bois de Boulogne. And he even went so far as to wonder if Mlle

Hyacinthe's embrace would be quite so sweet if each time it were not potentially the last.

It irritated him that his father still pursued the subject of marriage. And now Grégoire openly named Victoire de Varionnet as his choice. At the flight of the Comte and Comtesse d'Artois to the border Victoire had left their service and returned to Paris. She had consistently refused her family's pleas to fly with them to the border. Why shouldn't they all remain in Paris and see the fun, she had said. . . . Ugh! There was nothing more repulsive than an intrepid woman, thought Pierre.

He sanded his letter, then yawned and stretched. Tonight he would lie with Silvie. But tonight was too many hours away. . . .

Dominique knocked quickly and entered.

He was more than a valet, thought Pierre warmly. He was an old friend.

"There is news, Monsieur," said Dominique, his voice tense.

Pierre raised his eyebrows inquiringly. Dominique's news would relate to the ball the bodyguards had given the new Flanders regiment a few nights before at the palace. The royal family had made an impromptu appearance, gloriously greeted with *"O Richard, O mon Roi!"* The Queen's health had been drunk, National cockades trampled, and white Bourbon cockades cheered. It had been an hour of great reassurance to the court; but what would seething Paris say?

"They say Paris marches on us," exclaimed Dominique.

"Dieu!" cried Pierre, and he felt an ugly twisting of his vitals. "Who says this?"

"Messengers to the King. Paris is wild with fear of Louis's army stationed there. Thousands of fishwomen, they say, have attacked the Hôtel de Ville at dawn and are coming this way with cannon and shot, led by Maillard, hero of the Bastille."

"Diable! What could they want here?"

"Du pain et parler au Roi. . . ."

"It's only a threat of course. What good would it do to march upon Versailles?"

Pierre began to pace nervously up and down before the fire although Dominique was the one person in the world with whom he felt utterly at ease.

When Pierre was eight Dominique, a young widower, had come to the de Michelaits as steward. He had spoiled Pierre shamefully and had become a court footman to follow him to Versailles. Dominique had often visited Pierre in his quarters in the Great Stable, coaching the boys at billiards or cheering them on at "prisoner's base." It was Dominique who was close at hand when hazing by the senior pages became too severe, and Dominique who brought special pastries or reconciled Pierre to the tutors who complained that he "dreamed" or dawdled. Dominique had always been mysteriously close at hand to mop up Pierre's wounds in interpage duels, or to supply him with a few extra sous for the pit of the public theater.

It was when Pierre became a porter of the Queen's wardrobe that Dominique turned valet. When he was young Dominique had given up his own yearning for education to become an engraver so that he might send his two brothers to college. Of the bourgeoisie, they were nevertheless far better educated in a formal way than Pierre. One was now a lawyer, another a wealthy silk merchant. Dominique had never ceased to be hurt at their social inferiority.

"What do the nobility have that you do not have?" he had often exclaimed to them angrily. "They do not have your education, your ability, nor even your money. They do not come close to having your good character. . . . You are fond of your families, and your wives are industrious. And yet you are excluded from the higher clergy or a commission in the army. You are even barred from the higher magistracy. What is your reward for your privation? You bear the burden of the bulk of taxation, and how good are your investments in the Compagnie des Eaux and the national debt? St. Gris! I am sick of all of them but Monsieur Pierre and his sainted mother."

His small myopic eyes would squint then almost to closing and his thick, sensitive lips would tremble. When Dominique was angry a heavy red flush spread over his olive skin and aquiline nose, and even his hands became a mottled pink.

His brothers had always laughed at him when he turned virulent, and retorted: "What do the nobility have that we want?" But Dominique knew that class distinction rankled in their breasts also.

Pierre paused in his pacing and faced Dominique squarely.

"Dominique, what is it actually that the *poissardes* want?"

"Food, Monsieur—and security."

"But the crops this year were good."

"Then you do not believe that the Orléans faction has bought up all possible corn to send out of the country to reduce the people to famine?"

"I've heard the rumor. Also that Orléans's agents have appeared in the Queen's livery to make people think the court is monopolizing the corn. The rat! The filthy rat! He no sooner robs the people secretly than he spreads his gold among them to win their support. Do you think the reports are true that the Orléans league is scheming to kill the royal family and proclaim him constitutional king? *Dieu,* I couldn't bear it!"

Pierre began pacing up and down again. He remembered suddenly a conversation among the family at dinner not long ago in Paris when the same subject was under discussion.

"But of course events will never get that far," Grégoire had reassured the family. "The most radical thing that can happen will be that young Louis Charles might be proclaimed regent with a governing democratic council."

Catherine, straight and pale, had added quietly: "Perhaps monarchy by divine right is really ended. It can only be maintained along with the old faith in the Church. There is no longer the old faith in the Church."

Pierre flushed.

The Abbé paused in his wine drinking long enough to say: *"Oui, oui, oui,* those who undermine Catholicism undermine France's devotion to the old ideals and symbols. *Madame la Marquise* is right."

"You believe then that men like myself are dethroning the Queen!" Pierre ejaculated. "But how can I have faith in a faith which has offered a cardinal's hat to Voltaire—to buy him off—to divert his satire against the Church?"

The Abbé spluttered, or was he merely choking on a piece of bone?"

Grégoire said hastily: "If hereditary monarchy goes, Monsieur l'Abbé, it is not because of religion. It is because the royal government is a jellyfish. It has no consistent policy of reform at this critical time. There's no minister, no genius to lead us, with the great men of the Assembly being barred from the ministry. So we must be led by a vast number of crude, local politicians. Little men from little places in the provinces—including the Marquis de Bussac, of course."

Grégoire was an ardent representative of the Gironde. The family had smiled at his self-deprecation that night at dinner and returned to its turbot with seeming amicability.

Pierre stopped before the fire now and kicked a charred log. Yes, the nobility always returned to its turbot, he thought, while the people kept moving on and starving. . . .

"Dominique," he said, "I grant you that the stories of Orléans are likely true. But are twenty-five millions actually in danger of starvation? Aren't the farmers in the provinces hoarding, perhaps, frightened by the talk of famine? . . . And isn't much of the fear due to Prussian propaganda? Frederick the Great was jealous for years of our alliance with Austria. We were too strong and he had to weaken us with his secret agents and Freemasonry lodges—trying to set one class against the other."

Dominique rubbed his mottled hands together in agitation. "When there is no work starvation comes easily, Monsieur . . . and two hundred thousand nobility have left France since the Bastille. That means many servants thrown out of work—and many goods unsold in the Paris shops."

"There are peasants who feel a quarter million aristocrats is too many aristocrats," laughed Pierre. "They should be glad to see us emigrate!"

"Ah, et pourquoi, Monsieur Pierre?" demanded Dominique hotly, his eyes a thin, watery line. "My Émilie was a peasant, as you know. I have seen how they slave. What is there left when the land tax is paid, and the poll tax, and the gabelle—the tithe to the Church? *Dieu,* if one has his own press or mill he must still pay the *banalité* for use of his lord's, and then there are more rents and fees. And if he is starving is he allowed to hunt? No, Monsieur. Though his own land is over-ridden with his lord's game, and his children cry with swollen bellies. He must watch his crops trampled by noble hunters, and does not dare even weed or mow in breeding time lest he disturb the partridge's eggs. But you are well aware of all this."

"Oui," admitted Pierre, disturbed, "these are ancient evils. But my father and others are amending them in the new constitution."

"Which Louis refuses to accept," added Dominique dryly.

"Dominique, order my carriage. I am going to the Palais-Royal."

(The nobility always returned to its turbot.)

Dominique felt the rebuke and left, wordless. But his face was flushed and his hands were a mottled pink.

Pierre was troubled, however. He had always had a sympathy for the peasant, he thought, as he continued to pace the floor. His mother at her châteaux had nursed them, had taken them food, had been their confidante. His father, although firm in his rights, had treated them with understanding. When the Marquis or his wife passed on horse-back or in the carriage the peasants sank on their knees before them. Yes, the vassals of the de Michelaits were protected children. . . .

But since Pierre was an impudent page Dominique had continually told him new tales to make him indignant: noblemen harnessed the poor to a cart and drove them like oxen; noblemen kept the peasants in their grounds all night to quiet the frogs so nobility could sleep.

Pierre believed that Dominique's stories were medieval legends. . . . But there were the taxes. There was the hunger. All very real. . . .

Pierre hesitated, thinking he heard a distant roar. It was a tongue of fire leaping up the fireplace, he concluded. Or the wild wind pursuing the rain through the woods of Satory. And yet it persisted! He stalked to the window that faced the avenue de Versailles with its four rows of elms. It was a gray, shimmering mass of rain and people.

So it had come, he thought! The thing they called the Revolution. Like a tidal wave Paris was overflowing Versailles. With trembling fingers he snatched his spying glass from the mantelpiece and knelt at the window. The esplanade was covered with women, seething like worms. There were cart horses drawing guns and cannon. He could see the bodyguards in their wet buckskins in front of the palace gates. The Flanders regiment bristled with weapons. Within the gates the red-coated Swiss under arms stood alert.

Pierre threw open the window and a shower of rain ushered in the growing roar of drums, the piercing tocsin. But surely there were shouts of *"Vive le Roi"* and the strains of *Henri Quatre*. Unconscious of the gusts of wind and rain, hypnotized by the constant din, he was motionless.

There would be shooting soon: women killed, women enraged, heads on pikes! Thousands of hearts within these golden walls stricken with terror, for the present, for the future. . . . What future? A future of blood? . . . Had the émigrés, then, been the wise ones? Or had they been the cowards? Would the future take unbounded courage? Thank God Marie Antoinette had courage! And thank God even more that she was safe at Trianon!

Pierre continued to watch the nest of worms before the palace, his thoughts flying, his blood running fast. Challenge was like a spice . . . one grew alive. . . .

It was an hour before Dominique returned. He was pale, and wore a heavy dark cloak over his livery. The rain seeped from it in a tiny puddle on the Aubusson rug.

"The King has been rushed back from his shooting at Meudon," he said tensely. "The Queen has been driven here from Trianon in ten minutes. . . ."

"Will they be safe?" demanded Pierre.

"The gates of the Orangerie are closed . . . all the gates are closed. And there's a National Guard picket. . . ." Dominique's voice dropped.

"It is said the royal carriages are being yoked for Metz."

"Metz!"

"You will have the grippe, Monsieur, standing in the cold. . . ."

"What else do they say?"

"They say the ministers are in conference and a deputation of women has gone to the National Assembly to demand an interview with the King . . . that he has seen them . . . that he has promised them help, and has promised provision shall be sent to Paris."

"You have not told me all!" cried Pierre, for Dominique's squinting eyes were averted.

"*Eh bien,* they say the National Guard is short of ammunition."

"Give me your cloak—so I'll not be killed for an aristocrat! And my English pistol. . . ."

"But you can't go out, Monsieur! You'll be killed!"

"*Sacrée bête,* don't coddle me!"

CHAPTER X

PIERRE was quickly absorbed by the throng. Drunkards, with butcher knives and rusty muskets; fishwomen, hair wet and straggling, rain dripping from their smudged faces, armed with axes and billhooks. Smells hung low and foul: garlic, sweat, gunpowder, vermin, firewood, fish, the cheap musk of the prostitute. Soon there was the tang of roasted horseflesh, the bloody carcass of M. de Moucheton's war horse.

Hands which had torn off gateposts for the funeral pyre gnawed at the stinking flesh, gnawed even at the roasted vitals. Bits of raw meat were snatched from one to another; singed, bristling hair spat out.

A great hulk of a woman, swinging part of the bloody, matted mane, bellowed out in an Indian warhoop: *"Du pain!"*

Pierre lunged through the drenched crowd, ducking pikes, ragged umbrellas, men dressed lewdly as women, harlots with powdered hair and white festival gowns. He had no idea where he was going.

"*A la lanterne!*" the shout rose as a slim young flowergirl, Louison Chabry, returned with others from an interview with the King crying: "Life to the King and his house!"

"*A la lanterne!*" "She lay in the King's arms!" "She has only brought us words!" "Promises, not bread!" "*Courtisane!*" "The King'll give us provision in Paris? *Dieu,* we want food *now.*" "Millers shall grind again? Fooh! One can't eat the future!" "*Du pain!*" "*A la lanterne!*"

Pierre's heart beat rapidly as he watched Louison Chabry being tossed from shrew to shrew. She was delicate as a wax doll, with tiny features that reminded him of Mlle Hyacinthe. As she was lifted screaming to a lamp post, a garter thrust about her neck, he was filled with violent emotion.

"Stop!" he shouted, forcing his way among gross, wet bodies. But two of the French guards had already released her, and she dropped fainting into their arms.

The crowd was screaming in bafflement. Pierre was seized with a sense of injustice, a loathing of this roaring mass that was a fever. He thought: "This is how Gilbert feels in battle!"

"We want an answer from the King in writing!" cried a woman the size of an elephant with a voice like a foghorn. The cry skipped from one to another like a pebble on water.

The guards brandished their sabers; growls and shrieks and bellowings blew askant with the rain. A few shots were fired. The great cannon of St. Antoine was rolled forward, shining wet. Astride it still was Demoiselle Théroigne de Mèricourt, the prostitute leader of the insurrection. Her rich brown locks were gummed together with rain, her helmet askew, her pretty lips blue and chattering, her manner triumphant. She carried pistol and sword—a disheveled Joan of Arc.

A dirty, bulging woman applied her flambeau to the touchholes of the cannon. A savage scream of jubilant expectation arose. But the touchholes were wet.

"Stop! It is not yet time!" Théroigne de Mèricourt warned them hoarsely.

"You will get two shots for one!" threatened Pierre, but his voice was lost in the uproar.

A buck-toothed harpy, enraged with disappointment, picked up a tattered white cockade from the muck and lunged at him, smearing his face with it. For a moment he was completely blinded. When he wildly wiped the mud from his eyes she was gone and a sniffling, grimy girl in rags clutched him like a fury.

"Blindman's buff!" she laughed, her words brittle.

Her wet clothes pressed close to his body. He tried to shake her off but she writhed in a shameless orgasm, hoarse with laughter, pressing closer to him with the strength of a demon.

"No charge, my young lovely! . . . all free! You don't like me? I am too thin? . . . give me bread then and I shall suit you better! *Cochon!* . . . Oh!" she screamed. "He is raping me!" And as Pierre finally pushed her into the mud she spat at him. A crooked pike shot toward him but he dodged it and slipped away, wondering if the girl had been ground to a pulp on the cobblestones by the raging *poissardes*. He could die in a better cause, he thought, contemptuously.

Hours of confusion passed feverishly like minutes. Bonfires appeared with the muddled twilight. They were fed with palings and bench rungs and wagon wheels and pike handles. Struggling fires, quelled by the downpour and whipped by the wind.

The windows of the palace were inviting, glowing softly. It was a comfort to know that over there in the left wing Louis and Necker and the ministers were conferring; that soon there would be a solution to this bedlam; that Marie Antoinette would be smuggled safely to Metz. Pierre did not pause to ask himself why he did not return to the palace. Within there was warmth and food. He had had no dinner. There was an insistent gnawing in his stomach. The cries of *"Du pain!"* seemed to have a meaning now. Bread sounded as sweet to him as *poulet à la tartare*. It was not good being hungry, even for a little while. It left one short of reason. . . .

But the excitement gripped him like quicksand . . . pikes, gleaming in the firelight like spikes of wheat in the sun; the thirsty clack of sabots; the oily smell of dank hair; a beautiful girl in brocade crying: *"Scélérat!"*; a crucifix held aloft and kissed; a bleeding arm; the sweetness of a single voice singing like an angel. . . .

Bits of talk hit Pierre like stinging hail—just words, sometimes, or phrases. He tried to put the jumble together. Maillard had returned to Paris with Louis's decree concerning grains. Twelve crawling miles in the seeping mud! And couriers had said Lafayette was coming soon with thirty thousand National Guards. *Dieu merci,* let Lafayette come soon for the Swiss could not prevent bloodshed much longer! . . . The fishwomen had got into the Assembly again, sprawling over benches and conducting mock debates. They had demanded food *now*. Bread! Bread! Bread! A hundred voices took up the chant. A thousand voices, drenched with rain. The rain that persisted, ruthless like the zeal of these wantons. *Dieu!* It had taken less rain to wash away Noah's Ark.

The damp and the rain seemed to penetrate to Pierre's marrow. And the night was coming on. Faces leered up suddenly now in the light of the torches, upon him and gone again, masks in a nightmare.

Suddenly Pierre's ears were filled with the hideous howling of a wench as her cap took fire from a swirling flambeau. She was close behind him. Her screams were almost lost in the babel. She might have been alone on a desert. The straggling hair quickly lapped up the blaze. Pierre snatched a woman's scarf and bound the girl's head in it, quickly, tightly. The girl clawed at him in pain, cursing, struggling, her eyes insane and red with firelight. She collapsed then in his arms; there was not room to fall. The stench of her burning flesh sickened him. He gave the senseless mass over to a shivering hag, trying to scream above the din what had happened.

"So you want to burn us and strangle us!" the hag cackled shrilly. "Burn us away to ashes!"

Dominique's coat had availed him nothing. Aristocracy and pride and contempt were written on Pierre's face, in his manner—written in his well-fed look.

"He wants to burn us all to ashes!" The cry leaped from one to another like the licking of a flame.

"*A bas les aristocrates!*" shouted a drummer.

"Long live Marie Antoinette!" shouted Pierre mightily in return.

A fishwoman who was supporting a suckling baby with one arm brandished a jagged garden rake at him with the other.

"Give us Marie Antoinette!" she screamed. "My apron's big enough to hold her bowels!"

"*Oui,*" raged a sans-culotte with a tile-red beard, a great hulk of a fellow. "We'll make cockades from the Austrian's bowels!"

Pierre, livid, swung madly at the fellow with his fist, but he was jostled as he aimed. The sans-culotte lowered his pike and shot it toward Pierre with a swift vengeance. Pierre had not fenced for years in vain and evaded the man with cunning. Now he lunged at him with success, mashing his jaw. It was not much to do for Marie Antoinette, the thought swept him sharply.

The red-bearded brute shrank into a soggy mass on the ground, spitting blood, and Pierre felt himself suddenly whipped into the air, tossed from one brawny arm to another, like a coin.

"*A la lanterne! A bas les aristocrates!*" rang in his ears. The words were caught up like the plague.

He kicked and raged and pounded the heads below him. Although he knew it would be suicide to touch his pistol, he struggled to wrench it from his belt, mad with desire to shoot blindly among the mob. He wouldn't die! He would tear himself with fiendish strength from the noose. His arms would have the iron force of a cobra. . . . The burning stabs of pikes pelted his flesh and drove him to greater madness.

"*Vive Marie Antoinette!*" he cried again, and now he felt his arms nailed to his side, his head dangling back of him with a painful rush of blood. The skies poured a dark rain of ink into his eyes, his mouth. But the words rushed from his lips again: "*Vive Marie Antoinette!*"

The lash of a whip drew blood from his lips. He could feel it oozing in a soft bubble down his neck. A sabot tossed at him lingered on his chest and toppled away. The rain seeped through his stock, drenched his hair, for his hat was following him on a pike, blithely swinging.

With every lunge he made, his hands were bound more closely to his sides. And something within him, a demon possessed, kept crying out: "*Vive Marie Antoinette!*" and speeding him to the *lanterne*.

He was dumped at last to his feet and he reeled dizzily. The iron post reached out to him with an ominous arm. A dozen hands eagerly looped a filthy torn petticoat around his neck. . . .

It was only then that he thought of what it meant to die; that the easy, drifting years of his youth, and the image of Catherine at her *prie-dieu,* stumbled through his enraged mind. Hyacinthe, white with horror; Grégoire, tight-lipped and drawn . . . And Marie Antoinette —his France!—knowing he had died for her, knowing at last how he had worshiped her every smile and little gesture . . . But he wanted to live! *Dieu,* how he wanted to live. . . . He could feel his eyes starting from his head as the noose tightened . . . and he tried to cry again: "*Vive Marie Antoinette!*" But his tongue had become a separate thing and he could not move it. And his breath was suddenly the whole of him, his gasping, labored breath fighting like God to be loose of Satan.

But now in the swollen burning of his ears he heard other cries mingling with his death knell. "*Du pain! . . . A la lanterne! . . . Voici, du pain! . . . Du vin, des saucisses! . . . A la lanterne! . . . du pain! . . .*"

The new cry superseded the old one. The stinking rags about his neck, deserted, slipped loose; an overpowering sweep of pain pierced his head and he retched. He was dropped ignominiously into the mud. Half conscious, staggering, unable to get his footing, he crashed through a deserted drum with melodramatic impact. A young vixen, arms akimbo, shrieked with glee at his plight but no one else even noticed him.

The throng was struggling toward a wagon, bruising and buffeting him in the scramble for food. For food was indeed arrived, sent by a harassed Assembly. Here it was in bags and wheelbarrows, carts and baskets. From the pastry cooks', bakers', vintners' and butchers'.

And now the cry *"Du pain!"* filled the night like the merciless rain.

Pierre, reeling like a drunkard against the lamppost, was in the midst of the carnival.

Loaves were torn to fragments by a sea of hands; sausages stuffed into an infant's mouth; dainty puffs of pastry tossed into cavernous jaws. Cheese, mighty one moment, were crumbled to fragments the next. Bottles, emptied at a quaff, sailed into a bonfire to explode. Fowl, racked limb from golden brown limb, were snatched from one ghoul to another. Cakes and hams, trampled into the mud, were recovered by the vultures and consumed. Buns, soggy with rain, were the more filling.

There was laughter now, hard laughter—but laughter, nevertheless, and rejoicing.

Pierre's power of thinking began to return in spasms . . . *Grand Dieu,* life was sweet! . . . Even life with a throbbing neck. Even life in the black rain, with his clothes half ripped from him and sopping. His stomach seemed to roll over like a lazy porpoise. And blood from his nose dripped onto his ragged jabot. . . . He had been an ass. A purple ass dangling from a noose would have done Marie Antoinette no good. . . . "The Revolution began," history would have said, "because an ass of an aristocrat enraged the crowd!" . . . The thing to do now was to get back into the palace. It would be impossible to pass the guards at the gate . . . he would have to go the long way. . . .

As he tried to move he realized that he had no shoes and that Dominique's coat was gone. He pushed his way through the cold, slippery ooze, colliding with baskets and people. His teeth began to chatter, the pike wounds burned over his body like a thousand fires . . . but it was good to be alive. . . .

He groped his way through the place d'Armes toward the boulevard

de la Reine of the town. The street was almost deserted. The last of
the *poissardes,* running, jubilant, toward the food, was left behind.
A dog growled at him, nipping at his legs as he passed. And a man
swathed in black nearly tripped him up as he seemed to leap out of
the darkness into the darkness again. At intervals a feeble haze of
lantern light guided him past the astonished blue-blood houses, from
which an occasional wary eye watched the holocaust. But now his
strength was returning a little . . . he could think of nothing but
steaming punch, a joint of fowl, and the warmth of a fire. Yes, it was
understandable that one came at last to horseflesh . . . but he had only
been hungry one day . . . St. Antoine had been hungry for months.
. . . It flashed through his mind that he had lived as a puppet, that he
really did not know what it meant to live; that in spite of his hard,
beautiful muscles he was soft. For a second he hated himself even more
than these wretched human beings. . . .

At the Basin of Neptune, he turned up the allé d'Eau of the palace
grounds. The bestiality was no more than a murmur now, deadened
with food and distance. Perhaps he had only been dreaming! . . . But
he still wanted to kill. There had been born in him the frenzied joy of
killing, the fierce mob fury that possessed one like a virulent poison. . . .

A sentry stopped him, and it took long to convince him that this
wreck was Pierre de Michelait, librarian-in-ordinary to the Dauphiness.
Pierre knew every step of the graveled paths, every curve of the invisible Neptune and Tritons, the giant bronzes that had watched his
stolen amours. The marble nymphs and goddesses were dripping, even
as the fishwomen; groves and dainty paths saturated; the velvet carpet
of grass a black, muggy sea. . . . When he was a page he had tried to
hit with pebbles the richly carved leaden vases on the wall which shot
their jets of water to the heavens. But there was no plashing of fountains now; only the plop of rain on water. *Dieu,* but he was tired of
water! Rain in his face, in his stinging eyes.

He passed other sentries with increasing difficulty. But fortunately,
the guard at the door of the Hall of Mirrors was one he knew. The
warmth, the welcoming smell of tallow, made him almost faint. A
strange premonition gripped him. The gilded, tapered salon, magnificent with mirrors, was empty, even the footmen gone. The château was
like a waxen corpse, beautiful, deserted in its last repose: pale, cold,
without the glitter of brocade and jewels.

CHAPTER XI

THREE O'CLOCK came to Versailles, and deep exhaustion. The gourmands had seeped into churches, offices, coffee houses, sentry boxes, drying their rags before a fire. Lafayette had arrived with fanfare "to offer his head for the safety of his Majesty's," and had settled the watches and retired.

Four o'clock came. The palace drowsed. Pierre lay on his bed, half dressed in fresh linens and breeches. Beside him were his sword and pistol. The powder on his black damp hair was washed into streaks, and his face was scratched and swollen with welts. His body felt like a beanbag but an angry fire surged through his veins. Somehow it seemed ignoble to have escaped death on the *lanterne*.

His thoughts drifted like the shadows from the hearth, for the hot grog had made him languid. . . .

Lafayette had brought requests from the city, but none so brazen as that *His Majesty should come and live in Paris!* Paris! The moldering Tuileries, thought Pierre. But he would follow Louis and Marie Antoinette anywhere, to Paris, to Metz, to Rambouillet. . . . No, he mustn't sleep. The royal family would not be sleeping, although Necker had urged them to make no attempt to escape tonight. Marie Antoinette would be wakeful but dry-eyed—a woman who only wept over the little things that did not matter. Today she had been calm, courageous, it was whispered on the stairways . . . she alone held her head high. . . . No, he mustn't sleep. . . .

He dozed a little, dreaming of her smile, and now she became the little peasant girl with the apple, and now she danced with the magic toes of Mlle Hyacinthe. He had forgotten his rendezvous with Silvie. But she was beside him now and they filled one another with warmth . . . There was something wrong though. Her voice was hard, insistent. She was flinging a white cockade in his face. Pierre opened his eyes angrily. Dominique hung above him, holding a candle, his eyes narrowed to red slits, his face mottled pink and white.

"They're invading the palace!" he exclaimed. "They're pouring up the Queen's staircase! *Tout de suite,* Monsieur, your clothes and your sword!"

Pierre's apartment was in the south wing, on the same side of the château as Marie Antoinette's. He flew along the innumerable galleries toward the marble stairway, encountering a confusion of servants and nobility. Some doors were opened to disheveled rooms; other doors were locked and barricaded with furniture. Barons and chevaliers appeared in nightcaps, half clothed. Women cried hysterically as they packed. Passing Mme de Frivouac's apartment, Pierre heard her swearing shrilly at the Comte. Lighted candles appeared everywhere; once there was a cry of "Fire!" as a few bodyguards ran past a footman who was jostled, candelabra and all, into a drapery. Lap dogs yelled with fright. There was the smell of ether held to fainting noses, the strong scent of tallow, a whiff of incense, the aroma from a broken punch bowl. There were stray swords, angoras, billets-doux, garters, earrings. Pierre, running, knocked over a small boy who stood in his nightgown calmly picking his nose. There were barons emerging sheepishly from the rooms of countesses, and a frightened canary fluttering about a chandelier. Only the ancient portraits were placid, half amused at the scurrying and deshabille that a hundred years from now would not matter.

Pierre, his strength returned, ran deafly past the warnings of a bodyguard at the end of a gallery. There was a narrow stairway here that led to the lower floor, opening into a reception chamber close to the Marble Stairway. (He had been playing hide-and-seek here once with another page and had bolted head-on into Her Majesty! *Dieu!* How his knees had melted! But she had only said: *"Eh, bien,* soon enough it will be blindman's buff, M. de Michelait.")

Now as he stumbled through the dark reception room there burst upon him again the roar of the mob invading the palace. Like a tidal wave, St. Antoine poured up the stairs, screaming, swaying, brandishing flambeaux, crying for the Queen.

Once more Pierre was among them, carried along by force, his body almost crushed by bleary-eyed fishwomen flooding toward the Hall of the Queen's Guards. A dozen sentinels, their backs to bolted doors, aimed their muskets at the onrush. Pierre's fists struck out at the demons beside him. A moment later and the doors had been smashed in by frenzied pikes and clubs, and splinters flew and the mob began to pour into the great Hall of Guards.

Terror struck Pierre, a sharper terror than he had felt a few hours

ago when he thought he would be hanged. He rushed to the door of
the antechamber, his back against its gilded flowers, his sword alert.
He cried to the ladies-in-attendance on the other side: "Save the Queen
—they've come to kill her. For the love of God, save her!"

The distinctive blue and red uniforms of the guards had been a
target for the mob. Two dripping severed heads were hoisted on pikes;
the mashed features of de Varicourt were swung aloft to a chandelier,
smearing the jangling crystals with blood while a thousand voices
cheered. Wall paintings were slashed open with thirsty pikes, taborets
tossed into the air and ripped apart for weapons. Marbles and bric-a-
brac were mashed to bits. The room was black except for waving
flambeaux and candles snatched from sconces. A sea of faces leered
at Pierre, a blur of apish grins and snarls and cursing lips. And the
ceiling of clouds and cupids swam as pikes lunged at him and rent
his flesh.

"The Queen!—the Queen! . . ." came the cries above the shots of
musket.

But three guards had joined him now, fiercely fighting. Every moment of delay might save the Queen, thought Pierre wildly . . . every
moment of agonizing pain. . . .

A great ax swung above him, but he escaped it and the door behind
him was bashed in with the swoop. Losing his balance, Pierre fell
back into the cavity, his head clawed by the jagged stalactites of wood.
He swore like a guttersnipe, enraged and writhing with pain. Muddied
shoes trampled over him, bandied him about like a marble. He could
see only a stampede of legs. The mob cared nothing for him now—
not even enough to murder him. All they wanted was the Queen.

"*La Reine! . . . La Reine! . . .*" As the legs poured past him into
the small antechamber the shout became deafening. Pierre tumbled
to his knees, his hands braced against something soft. It was a small
dead infant, blue and suffocated. As he stared at it, sickened, a large
sabot crushed in the puffy face and the soft skull spurted blood like
a geyser.

Pierre forced himself to his feet, and now he was hurtled to the
door of the Queen's bedchamber. There was one last rare chance to
save her, he thought, if she had not fled. . . .

He hoisted himself for a moment above the shoulders of two sans-
culottes long enough to scream: "She's gone . . . the Queen's gone
. . . to Trianon. . . ."

The man into whose face he spat the words shouted them again, and the words ricocheted like bullets, until the room was thunderous with the cry: "Gone—the Queen's gone! To Trianon!"

The crushing eased a little . . . only a few madmen leaped on the door of the bedchamber trying to pound it in.

Pierre, gasping for breath, faced yesterday's giant of the tile-red beard. His jaw was like a slab of uncooked beef. The man roared with triumph at the sight of Pierre and reached out like a boa constrictor to crush him with his naked arms. Pierre, kicked and jostled, tried to lunge at him with his sword. The blade made its mark swiftly. The man gave the death cry of an animal and swayed. A woman attacked Pierre now with a butcher knife. He felt the hot steel sink into his shoulder and the noise of the furor dissolved slowly into a cold silence. . . .

When he regained consciousness he lay on the floor of the Queen's bedchamber. He was alone in the room. It was quiet. He was supposed to be dead, he thought. The excruciating pain carried him off with sharp waves and then carried him back to the room again, like the caprice of ether.

But something struggled within him great as a fetus's will for birth. . . . Marie Antoinette—was she safe? He tried to move and gave a savage cry. . . . But he must live long enought to know. He couldn't die without knowing.

His eyes, dim as the ashes on the hearth, shifted slowly, painfully, from the lions and Austrian eagles of the ceiling to the details of the room he knew so well. On the wall royalty hung in ribbons from their oval frames. Armchairs were overturned like helpless bugs, mirrors were pulverized, draperies gashed. The tall clock with the dragon feet had been deboweled, the pendulum used, very likely, to smash the Sèvres bowls and Venetian vases dribbling flowers and water. Ink dripped lazily, drop by drop, from the elaborate marquetry of the escritoire. Over a folding screen was slung a ragged vest. On the carpet mashed crystals from the chandelier caught an occasional flicker of light from the embers and glittered like dew in the sun. Rigidly against the wall were the abandoned folding stools of the duchesses. But it was the mutilation of the royal nef before which the Queen's ladies had curtsied—that hurt Pierre the most. The exquisite little ship was a pulp of gold, its diamonds and rubies gouged out; the jeweled crown, once supported by two angels, was gone. (On the lousy head of some sans-culotte, no doubt.) The enamel arms of France and Navarre lay in the symbolic wreck of the ship and its pedestal of white enamel shells. Dolphins and cupids, Tritons, sirens, and turtles lay pinned to their destiny like the victims of old Pompeii.

The room was utterly quiet except for the tapers of a forgotten candelabrum on the rosewood chest; they sputtered angrily with the draught from the broken windows and clung to their flame tenaciously.

It was when Pierre's eyes met the ravages of the bed that his hope shriveled and died. The gilt balustrade that surrounded it was twisted and uprooted. Tossed into the cupids and lily garlands of the canopy was a rakish National cockade. The royal blue hangings sagged drunkenly over the sculpt footboard; the silken coverlets were slashed; pillows, slit with butcher knives, oozed a soft down over the stairs of the dais. The mattress gushed hair.

In a soft fluff on the floor was Marie Antoinette's nightgown; within a few inches of his fingertips lay a small gold mule. He tried to reach out and touch it. If he could touch the mule, he thought, it would give him hope, like a fetish. But his arm refused to move. Now it was dead weight attached to him; again, it was a miracle of pain. . . .

Marie Antoinette! Oh, God, he must live long enough to know if his dying had saved her! If he could only crawl through that door to the little passage that led to the Œil-de-Bœuf, surely someone must find him. If the Queen were safe, and there were no pools of blood in the bed, she must have fled through that very passage, through the Œil-de-Bœuf to the King's bedchamber. . . . Strange, she had never loved Louis; but danger would send her to his thick, comforting bulk!

"A lamb governing tigers," someone had called Louis. Gentle in his strength. Timid. Surprised by the revolt of his people, as a lamb in the field, assaulted by wolves. Why hadn't Louis been born a simple peasant, to live content, working with his hands? What freak of fate had made this homely, waddling man a monarch instead of a hermit at peace with his books and a life in the woods? Even when he dined in public at the Grand Couvert every Sunday he spilled his soup and ate like a wood chopper. But Pierre thought of the kindly, near-sighted eyes, and Louis's patience over little things, and loved him. . . . Useless thoughts for a dying man, he mused, when he should be taking the extreme unction. Tomorrow little Silvie would be sprinkling holy water at his feet and he would not be able to reach out and touch her. And soon her delicious softness, her gay freedom of spirit, her infectious joy of living, would belong to another. . . .

A soft rose scent moved with the guttering of the candles, and the room was filled again with the image of Marie Antoinette, gossiping flunkeys, ushers, valets, honorary ladies, train bearers. How poignant this last communion with Marie Antoinette and the past! . . . There was the day she had caught him stealing pounded sugar from her night table—he was only twelve and so hungry!—and she had tweaked his ears. That was where she sat, arrogant, the day that the Abbé Vermond, her confessor, chided her for wearing an aigrette that had been in the hat of the Duc de Lauzun. And the morning she had been fitting a violet gown, surrounded by scissors and pins, and had first called Madame de Noailles "Madame Étiquette." How everybody had laughed as the straight-laced old lady turned pallid! Once Pierre had picked up the Queen's glove, and she had tapped him on the shoulder with her riding crop and said: "Arise, Sir Arthur!" For weeks he'd had an imaginary court of his own. Nor would he ever forget the time she had allowed him to play her *glascorde,* presented to her by Benjamin Franklin. "Come, Monsieur, more verve!" she had said as he tinkered shyly. Then he had pounded so hard with the little hammer that one of the glasses had broken! She had dried his terrified tears with her *point d'esprit* handkerchief and afterwards had tucked it into his pocket.

Those were the old days when she had shone like the Holy Grail in her court dress and diamonds. And when she had coquetted with the Comte d'Artois and the many other men who adored her. The days when she had led the women of the court a merry pace with her new styles, fickle as a weather vane. Sneaking to masquerades without her sire, acting stealthily in comedies, making her toilette before innumerable sycophants, losing thousands of francs every night at play. Louis had always paid, of course, from his private purse as patiently as he would have recovered her fallen muff. Those were the days of glory and excitement; those were the days her entrancing smile was more roguish than wistful.

But the newer memories were even more precious—the Queen established at last in the heart of France as the mother of its princes; not so frivolous now, more simple in her tastes and pleasures. Strange, France had only begun to hate her as her interest in affairs of state increased, as she began to show her real stature. How contemptuous she was of public criticism, of the swarm of scandalous, scurrilous verses about her! How stubbornly she clung to the confidence of the Princess de Lamballe and the ambitious Mme de Polignac, not caring if she wounded the older nobility! The true daughter of Maria Theresa —head always high, whether she conferred a purse of gold on a pauper or interviewed Necker! . . .

He remembered the day she had solemnly danced a minuet in her closet with the tiny Dauphin; the day she had warned Mme Royale that if she did not have patience with her needlepoint, she would never have patience with her subjects.

The bright blue eyes, the transparent skin, the sensitive lips, the quick, bewildering smile: these were the things he had worshiped instead of God as he had consulted her on the day's wardrobe. These were the images that were his saints. And now he was going to die here alone, unconfessed—alone, in the dark. This was his punishment for listening to the philosophers, he mused. . . . The Abbé Blafond and his Kirschewasser would be avenged. . . . *Dieu,* it was terrifying to die! In his gravest moments of danger it had not occurred to him that he would die. Others, yes. All about him. But his own consciousness was the world, wasn't it? The universe. When he died there he would be a nothingness. . . . It was black, dying, and it was anguish with no faith to hold his hand—neither the Jesuit piety of his mother nor the calm agnosticism of his father. A shallow skiff, beaten about the sea. . . . He groped for words of prayer, words of his own mingled with words of the creed. He wanted to pray that his soul might live on. Through the blur of doubts and fears he wanted so much to reach God. . . .

Suddenly he longed for Catherine: her cool hands, the purity of her spirit—taking from her more strength than he had ever given. That was the relationship of mother and son, he thought, a giving and taking of strength in varying forms and intensities. But an ebb and flow. Always constant. Like sap leaving a tree, going down to the roots, rising again to the leaves in the spring. Sap. Life energy that can never be destroyed but must find an outlet, restless, infinite. . . . Now, at this moment, his strength would go back to Catherine, giving her courage to bear her loss. As she was giving him strength to die alone . . . *Dieu,* but he was muddled! . . . He would like to confess himself. Now, without a priest, he was trying to confess himself directly to God. . . . Perhaps God would understand. Oh, he had never meant to hurt Catherine. He had always meant some day to fulfill her noblest hopes. . . .

How cold the draught from the shattered doors and the window— and how warm and wet the pulp of his shirt! A salamander, he was . . . rotting in the mud. . . .

Pierre gave a slow groan of pain and defeat and closed his eyes in a shroud of bittersweet memories.

❀❀❀❀❀❀❀❀❀❀❀❀❀❀❀❀❀❀❀❀❀❀

CHAPTER XII

March 1791

SYLVIE HYACINTHE sat at the toilet table in the boudoir of her doll's house. The *mansardes* were covered with snow and a blur of large flakes scurried toward her and piled up on the window panes. She felt the joy of a little girl and her heart sang along with the chorus of canaries. Even her toes would not be still, although she was puttering with mirrors and bottles. Somehow the snow seemed to purify the frightening events of the year and a half during which she had been Pierre's mistress. She could still hardly bear to have him out of her sight. So it had not been too ill a wind, she thought, that had forced the court to move from Versailles to the Tuileries in Paris. And today there was not only snow. There was Pierre whistling softly in the bathroom as he shaved, and chocolate steaming before a ruddy fire. Was it wrong to be so happy, she wondered, with the rest of the world upside down?

If the house had been created with a magic wand it could scarcely be more perfect. Her boudoir was a tiny replica of Marie Antoinette's bedchamber at Trianon. The upholstery was of pale blue silk (blue added seductive shadows to the blue of her eyes, Pierre said). The bed was covered with white lace (not as expensive lace, of course; but then Pierre was not Louis, was he?). Thin silk scarves fringed with pearls drew back the white gauze curtains so one could see the lovely snow and look down on the fashionable throng in the rue d'Anjou. On the walls doves and Cupid's arrows, alternating with bunches of poppies and other field flowers, were fastened by thin gold links.

Javotte, of course, had made the flowers, which were a very satisfactory substitute for the fresh ones plucked from the Queen's gardens. Javotte was very busy these days, for she was really a *femme de chambre* now with a dainty uniform and so many duties to keep Hyacinthe as entrancing as the Queen! In the corners of the room, fat-bellied Sèvres cupids bore horns overflowing with fruit and flowers. (And of course there was always that overflowing of the room which accompanied Silvie whether she lived in the Palais-Royal or the rue d'Anjou: ballet slippers and bills and sweetmeats, discarded ribbons, programs, soiled gloves, and birdseed.)

Who would ever have thought Silvie would have footmen? Or a little row of orange and lime trees in her salon? (At Trianon, of course, Marie Antoinette had brilliant butterflies especially bred for her garden; but here they would only drift away into other gardens of the rue d'Anjou and mix with the *hoi polloi!*) Certainly Marie Antoinette had no small practice room of her own with a chased silver bar and a music box to supplant M. Romain.

No, it wasn't wrong to be so happy, even if she did have a new amethyst necklace for her New Year's day gift while the people went hungry. And it was weeks since Pierre had mentioned that his father was urging him to marry. The Marquis would be much too busy with his *cahiers* in the Assembly to think of matrimony again for months. . . . It would be unbearable to have to share Pierre with a wife!

Love was no less sweet because the arms on Pierre's coach had to be hidden from the rabble with a blue cloud. He was the same gallant Pierre, although the law had abolished titles and he was now just Pierre Michelait instead of Pierre de Michelait. He *was* the same, wasn't he? His hair was still powdered and gathered into a club in spite of the Jacobins. The black suit the Royalists wore now was not so smart as the old brocades, but Pierre was handsome even as a *"noir."* Thank goodness he had not adopted the general negligence of the Tuileries: morning costume, English coats, muddy boots, neglected lace! And of course everybody had to wear the tricolor cockade! . . . It was quite natural, Silvie thought, that Pierre should spend less time telling her how beautiful she was, and more time fencing at the Academy and reading about that plodding leader of the Assembly, Robespierre—the dyspeptic lawyer who was already so powerful that he had become the target of pamphlets.

Silvie tied a blue ribbon around the gold hair. (Pierre said she looked like a naiad with her hair flowing.) Some of the sparkle of the

snow seemed to shine in her eyes this morning, she thought. Vestris
the dancer had told her that she had just come alive, that she was like
a new heifer heady with the breath of life, and when her legs grew
steady he wished to dance with her. A *pas de deux* with Marie-Auguste
Vestris! The ambition of every ballerina in Europe! But who could
not dance, possessed, with the love of Pierre awaiting her?

His tongue would be in one cheek now that he had stopped whistling,
and his lips screwed into a knot, his eyes squinting at the white jaw
in the mirror.

She danced over to pour out the chocolate, and at last he came in,
smelling of fresh, sweet soap and orange-flower water. As he sank
contentedly into the armchair before the fire she alighted on his knee
and her fingers lingered on his cheek and neck. The long, jagged scar
that ran deep below the collar of his silk dressing-gown made her
shudder.

"You know, sometimes I am jealous of Marie Antoinette," she
pouted.

"*Pourquoi, mon petit chou?*" he asked, tweaking her hair. "She's
old enough to be my mother!"

"Even so, I am jealous! The scar belongs to her."

"I like to think I helped to save her life. . . . Look, my sweet," said
Pierre, and he picked up the white alabaster fingers and placed them
on his left wrist. "This one belongs to you!"

She smiled and caressed the scar that had closed the bargain between
M. Fleury and Pierre in a duel.

Pierre felt a sharp pang at recollection of the famous fifth of October.
For over a year he had succeeded in tossing the insurrection out of his
mind by day. But now and then it invaded his dreams by night: the
grilling moment he had thought he would be hanged; his own fierce
struggle with the sans-culotte at the Queen's door; the harrowing
certainty that he would die and never know if she were safe!

Then the regaining of consciousness in the King's bedchamber and
the dressing of his wound by Louis's doctor. Pierre had been too weak
to move at once and he had lain there on a couch, content because he
knew that Marie Antoinette was near him. His eyes closed, he had confused the murmur of bodyguards and the waiting-women in the apartment with the swelling thunder of the mob below in the Court of
Marble.

The apartment, dull with the mingling of dawn and candlelight,
had been cold—cold with the fear that clutched at every heart, fear

and despair and humiliation. Marie Antoinette sat before the fire with the little Louis Charles drowsing on her lap like a puppy; Louis, with his ungainly bulk, waddled back and forth, up and down, a hurt, puzzled look in his eyes. On a stool beside Pierre sat Mme Royale, sniffling, replacing the coverlet when he tossed with pain and trying to hold a towel beneath his shoulder so that blood would not seep from his bandage onto the brocade.

Consciousness had drifted in and out like the sun toying with a cloud. Now the news that Lafayette had come and reconciled the National Guards with the King's bodyguards; shouts of "Long live the King!" as Lafayette and Louis and Marie Antoinette appeared on the balcony. "Long live the General!" "Long live the Queen!" . . . Oh, thank God for that sound: "Long live the Queen!" . . . What did it matter if the cry changed? "To Paris—to Paris!" . . . Marie Antoinette was safe for a little while longer. . . .

And then the clink of china, and Marie Antoinette holding hot broth to his lips. The white fingers close to his mouth were trembling. He tried to tell her with his eyes that he adored her—that one life was too small a sacrifice for anyone so exquisite. And she had seemed to know what his eyes said, and had answered softly: "You must follow us to the Tuileries, M. de Michelait, where we can nurse you back to health. I owe you my life, poor a thing as it is. I am eternally grateful. No, no, no . . . do not try to speak—just sleep."

The firing of cannon at one o'clock the next day had announced that the long period of Bourbon residence at Versailles was at an end. There followed the humiliating procession to Paris, snail-like through the rain and mud, the royal family riding silent, protected by the National Guard. Marie Antoinette's chin was high as insults were hurled at her carriage and the heads of her butchered guards bobbed within sight, drooling blood. Wagons of grain covered with foliage; voices raised in triumphant singing: "We are bringing you the Baker, the Baker's wife, and the Baker's boy."

The pain of Pierre's wound had never been as sharp as the pain in his heart when they entered the draughty, desolate Tuileries, and when the little Dauphin had said: "Mama, everything is very ugly here." Marie Antoinette had replied: "My son, Louis XIV lived here and found himself very comfortable. We should not be more difficult to please than he was!"

But life at the Tuileries had proved far from comfortable, thought Pierre, as he stared into the fire and stroked Silvie's hair. The Tuileries was an old hag of a palace, cold with decrepit age, garish with soiled, outmoded finery, tainted with a decaying breath. For eighty years it had been invaded by the dregs of society: actors, artists, courtesans, pensioners. They had hacked the palace into shops and theaters to suit them, adding mezzanines, adding staircases, cutting through partitions.

And then of a sudden out must go the whole rabble, with a few hours' warning, to make place for the court and royal family. Carpenters, painters, and locksmiths had been frantic, trying to give the old hag the semblance of a lady.

There had not even been furniture enough for everybody. And the cold was so piercing that Pierre's wound had only begun to heal when he had succumbed to the grippe. His mother and Dominique had nursed him as he lay ill for weeks in a chill *mansarde* apartment, too weak to be moved. And there had been Silvie, who had come every day to hold his hand and amuse him with gossip of the Green Room.

As there were constant rumors that the royal family was planning an escape, Louis was guarded strictly by half a dozen grenadiers. When he walked in the gardens the gates were barred and no one was admitted without a ticket. The Dauphin played with rake and hoe in a small enclosure like a little caged rabbit. Tutored to be obsequious now, the golden-haired Prince, no matter how great the insult . . . and always, the grenadiers.

Pierre saw Marie Antoinette frequently. She often plied her needle while he read to Mme Royale. Not that the Queen really listened. Much as he adored her, Pierre had to admit that she was not intellectual. And now of course there were the most critical affairs of state on her mind. Louis had been forced to sign the Assembly decree compelling the clergy to take oath to support the new constitution. (It had been a blow to the devout Louis as well as to many of his pious subjects, like Catherine de Michelait!) If only Louis could be made to take a stand with the Assembly! Marie Antoinette, it seemed, acquired vigor and decision as he became more irresolute.

Pierre knew that she was trying to enlist the help of Austria with whom she was in secret correspondence. She stood in equal dread of the Revolutionists and the *émigrés*. He had heard her whisper to the Comte de Fersen that to yield to the former was ruin, to the latter, degradation. For some months, the Comte de Fersen had been warily visiting foreign courts trying to induce them to coalesce in an invasion of France.

Marie Antoinette still received the court twice a week before going to Mass, then dined in public with the King. But she had no concert or play. Her only diversion had been attending the parties in the Princess de Lamballe's salon. Pierre, who was invited also, saw that the presence of the Duchesse d'Orléans and her two sons was embarrassing to the Queen, for the Duc, who had been exiled to England, was now returned and active in the Assembly. And the talk was almost entirely of the Revolution. Of late Marie Antoinette went seldom to the parties. She had few friends left and felt keenly the reluctant presence of her women who had once been ecstatic to wait upon the Queen.

No, life at the Tuileries was not comfortable. Not nearly so comfortable as days and nights stolen with Silvie Hyacinthe in the doll's house that had mortgaged him to the hilt!

Pierre began to leaf through fresh copies of *Le Moniteur, Patriote Français, Ami du Roi,* and other papers that lay on a fireside table. Everybody in Paris now published a paper. His one hand toyed with Silvie's hair and he did not notice that she had slipped off his knee and was drinking her chocolate from a stool at his feet. He read the headlines of Marat's *Ami du Peuple* avidly.

"What is the news?" asked Silvie. Why could a man be so passionate over a woman one minute and so passionate over print the next?

"Mirabeau is accused again of selling his services to the King."

"Hm," said Silvie, "everybody knows how rich he has grown of late. And who else could have paid all his huge debts but Louis? I'm sure it's true that he's two-faced and playing along with both the King and Assembly!"

Pierre smiled down at her. She was such a lovely little wanton, so like a milky white hyacinth that overwhelmed him at night with her sweetness. He knew she had no more interest in politics than in a plough, and that her knowledge came from the butcher, the baker, and the candlestick maker. He himself was finding it constantly more difficult not to divulge with a word or an eyebrow the whirlpool affairs of the court.

"Mirabeau's a dissolute Italian pig," said Pierre indifferently. "That's common knowledge. But he's also a dynamo and a genius—and he's tried hard enough to bring the King and Assembly together, to balance the power."

For months Mirabeau had urged the King to go to the provinces, gather a great convention there, and show the people that he recognized that feudalism and absolutism had passed forever. But Louis was stubborn. (Grégoire said he was just not bright enough.) And Marie Antoinette would never accept such positive humiliation.

"I heard M. Vestris say that any day the royal family will escape to the border," said Silvie. "That there've been plans afoot for months. Pierre, sometimes I am afraid for you—afraid that they will suspect you because you are close to the Queen—that you might even be involved—"

"Nonsense!" Pierre glanced at her quickly and shrewdly from beneath his black brows as he picked up his chocolate. His heart was pounding like a brass knocker. "These rumors of escape only feed the Revolution! Let's not repeat them, *mignonne.* . . . What would you like to do before the Opéra?"

While Pierre dressed and read his papers Javotte massaged the calluses of Silvie's feet. She would wear her orange velvet, thought Hyacinthe, with the marten fur border and her English hat of chocolate beaver with the fruit trimming. This was such a special day, somehow, with the flying snow. And Pierre had been so specially sweet last night, far outrivaling the lover of the woods of Meudon. If only she were not a woman of the theater who could not even be buried with a Christian ritual! If only she had been born a rich baroness or even a destitute duchess so that she and Pierre might marry! What hopeless folly it was to fall in love with one's lover! . . .

They went out in the carriage with its clouded coat of arms. Hyacinthe suggested that they stop at the Academy of Painting to see a new portrait of Lafayette, father of the "Constitutional Monarchy." But they did not stay long. The salons were filled with pictures of the Revolution and Pierre was depressed. *The Opening of the States-General, The Oath at the Tennis Court, The Taking of the Bastille, The Hôtel de Ville on the Fifth of October*. Portraits of Necker and Lafayette abounded. At last, as Silvie stopped horrified before David's *Les Deux Fils de Brutus* with its bleeding heads and torsos Pierre could stand the carnage no longer. He pulled her small gloved hand into his muff and trotted her toward the entrance.

Ah, she had been tactless, she thought, after what Pierre had suffered! She would divert him with laces and brocades. . . . Really, she needed a lot of clothes; there would soon be Holy Week and the races at Vincennes (after one had dispensed with hearing the office of *Ténèbres.*) And there was that divine ground of white gros de Naples, embroidered with *reines-marguerites* in silk. Just the thing for Easter!

She coaxed him to the fashionable little shop in the rue de Richelieu, aglitter with gilt and mirrors, warm and yellow with candlelight after the blue-white chill of the snow.

The shopkeeper, M. Moulard, displayed the brocade lovingly, caressing it with lingering fingers, draping it lushly over his shoulder.

"Ah, mais c'est exquis!" exclaimed Silvie, clapping her hands in delight.

"Fit for the Queen, Monsieur," cajoled M. Moulard, tinkering with his sausage curls, "or the glistening shoulders of a beauty like Madame . . . Only one length left. And so cheap! *Incroyable! Absurde!"*

There was a moment of silence as Silvie and the draper seemed lost in a deep reverence.

Pierre had never been able to resist the desire of those tantalizing blue eyes! That was indeed why he had come to a financial impasse. This very day he had meant to make another loan. . . .

He beckoned the shopkeeper aside with a raised eyebrow and they retired to a love seat.

"How much for the length?" asked Pierre.

"A thousand francs, Monsieur. Very cheap! *Incroyable!* Fit for the Queen!" M. Moulard offered Pierre a pinch of snuff.

Pierre was adept at hiding a shock. *"Bien.* I shall establish credit with you."

The draper's unctuous tone dissolved. *"Mon Dieu,* I should like to do this, Monsieur. But I no longer give credit since the first of the year. Monsieur knows how the *assignat* drops from day to day like mercury in the winter."

Pierre was humiliated. It was true; a pocketful of the paper government money issued on usurped church and crown lands in 1789 was no longer worth two clinks of gold. He was beaten. He had five hundred francs in his pocket—his worldly wealth. His, of course, if one did not consider that even this was part of a loan. He shrugged and rose.

It was at this moment that the street door opened with a blast of fresh air. A few fugitive flakes ushered in Mlle Victoire and the Comtesse de Varionnet, whose breath steamed like a teakettle. The footman shook snow from an umbrella onto the parquet floor.

As Mme de Varionnet, a mountain of fur pelisse, collapsed breathless on a delicate Louis XIV chair, the shopkeeper winced. Victoire, mouselike in a puce-colored velvet, began to examine materials laid out on the tables. With a quick flash her green eyes had encountered Pierre.

But by mutual consent Pierre and the women did not exchange a greeting. He was with his mistress, a woman of the theater.

Silvie drew herself up so that her pouter-pigeon fichu gave her the bosom of a Greek goddess. She cordially hated Victoire. She had seen her at the Champ-de-Mars the July before, at the fête in celebration of the Bastille. She had seen her on the boulevards with her nuzzling *marcassin*. She had seen her sitting between the dozing Comte and festooned Comtesse in their box at the Opéra. And Victoire's green eyes had always held a subtle note of challenge.

The girl looked like a loaf of half-baked bread, she thought, pale and doughy. No wonder she wandered away from the daylight of the window, with that pasty skin. And from the shape of her face, one expected her to whinny. Silvie giggled behind her muff at the thought.

Mlle Victoire sauntered to the daisy material, which lay crinkled in white and gold folds rich and inviting in the candlelight.

"Oh, Mama, here is the very thing for you!" she exclaimed with a mild convent enthusiasm. "Simply perfect with your canary diamonds!"

The Comtesse de Varionnet nodded. She was very busy breathing.

Silvie laid a restraining brown glove on the material. "Pardon, Mademoiselle, but the brocade is sold."

M. Moulard advanced, fawning on the asthmatic Comtesse as Pierre drew Silvie's arm through his own and whispered the bad news in her ear. Her blue eyes filled with mortified tears.

"Fit for the Queen!" coaxed M. Moulard, ogling Victoire now, his back turned to Silvie. "A mistake, Madame—the piece is not sold. And so cheap! *Incroyable! Absurde!* Ridic—"

"But the piece *is sold!*" Pierre said suddenly, finding the crisis intolerable. "I am leaving five hundred francs with you as deposit, M. Moulard, and shall return in an hour with the balance!"

"*Ah, certainement, Monsieur. Mille pardons!* . . . I did not understand. . . ." His hands were wildly apologetic.

Victoire's green eyes, raised to the blue-blurred tears, had become tawny. Now she turned them to Pierre. Men had looked at him with challenging eyes like that when they had crossed swords . . . but women, never.

It was not so much that he could not disappoint Silvie as that he *must* humiliate Mlle Victoire. . . . And it was at that moment that Pierre decided to marry Victoire. Yes, Silvie would have her brocade and Victoire would pay for it. He felt a sense of triumph, a relief in having decided on the marriage at last. But at the same time it was as if Mlle Victoire had whisked a thousand-year-old de Michelait treasure to the floor and to ruin. . . .

Pierre and Silvie hurried to the waiting coach and snuggled under the fur robe.

Silvie began to laugh a little hysterically. In her muff was one of Victoire's virgin gloves that had been dropped especially for Pierre when she had entered the shop, and that he had failed to see. It would do nicely for Javotte when she cleaned the silver *bibelots* of the dressing-table!

Oh, it was such a special day after all, with the sleigh bells, and the brocade, and Pierre's thrilling defiance of that tiger-eyed mouse! How she would dance tonight, light as the swirling flakes!

She nestled close to Pierre. His lips closed over hers with a sudden passion.

"Don't laugh, you little fool!" he exclaimed, and she saw that his eyes were narrowed to black angry slits. Her heart contracted with fear, quick as the lash of a whip as he went on: "How would you like a coach of your own and a *petite maison* in the country?"

CHAPTER XIII

April 1791

IT WAS the middle of April when Pierre announced to his father that he was ready to marry. The Marquis de Bussac was gratified. Pierre's wild oats were beyond his income; the château at Avignon had been razed by the peasants; inflation was swelling like a toy balloon.

"You are of an' age when you should be considering a wife and family before a mistress," Grégoire told him.

Pierre found himself more often in the company of his father, sometimes at the home of Grégoire's mistress. He had never known his father could be so witty, so débonair. Mme Chenault, her small eyes gleaming like sapphires, her words tumbling like a tower of blocks when an idea obsessed her, discussed with them the recent death of the smoldering Mirabeau or the proletarian outbreak at Vincennes which the people felt was being converted into another Bastille.

With his father Pierre attended some of the salons of the Rolands, which were held four times a week. M. Roland had lately come to Paris to arrange with Assembly committees the affairs of Lyons. (He had been an inspector of manufactures there.) Their apartment was at once a rendezvous for reformers—Brissot, Pétion, Buzot, Robespierre. Many of these were Grégoire's compatriots from the Gironde. Most of them were educated and cultured men, and their eloquence was convincing. They were the extreme party, declaring themselves for a republican form of government (while the Cordeliers and Jacobins hesitated). Why couldn't France have something as ideal as More's Utopia, Sidney's Arcadia? With their high learning and classical education, they loved the freedom of the ancient world based on slavery.

Mme Roland—beautiful, witty and chaste—fascinated Pierre as well as all who met her. Sewing or writing letters, never entering into discussions of the men, nevertheless she imbued them with her passionate Revolutionary enthusiasm and a thirst for self-sacrifice that lighted her deep blue eyes and sensitive features. In her company Pierre began to wonder if he was as much Royalist at heart as he had been a month before. He was young enough to be stirred by radicalism, to give half credence to her ideas not because he was convinced but because they were new.

He visited the Roland salons as well as the Jacobin Club and Assembly with a sense of guilt, but he told himself it was so he could be better informed on the exigencies of the day. Moreover, he would still lay down his life for Marie Antoinette whom Mme Roland reviled and despised. Attending the meetings too had been of practical benefit; it made him realize the crucial state of finance and made him resolve that his marriage was not a matter of choice but necessity.

The Comte de Varionnet was eager for the alliance. His oldest son had died of smallpox after entering the army. With his second son in the priesthood, he depended on Victoire to unite the fabulous family wealth with an old and venerated name. And Victoire, it seemed, in the purity of her girlish hopes had already anticipated the marriage.

Pierre appeared at the town mansion of the Comte de Varionnet the night after the contract had been agreed upon, and formally asked the hand of Mlle de Varionnet. Her relatives were assembled, heavy with family diamonds and importance. In these days of political combustion what did four quarters avail? Tables were turning, weren't they?

Victoire, in virgin white, prim and artless, flitted among the family like a whitecap at sea; a restless, prancing whitecap with the undertow beneath. A white mouse now, thought Pierre. And, already annoyed with the maternal unctuousness of the Comtesse, he waited only till the contract was read and signed, and left them to their celebration. His first duty was the consolation of Mlle Hyacinthe, wasn't it?

The King approved the alliance and the banns were published the following Sunday.

Catherine had not been averse to the union. She knew a great deal more about Pierre than he supposed, and felt that marriage might give him balance. Also the family fortune was tottering and this was the customary way of replenishment. Victoire seemed a modest young girl, with flawless conventual manners. And although money had literally gone to the head of the heaving old Comtesse, the daughter seemed to resemble her stolid father. The girl, moreover, was in love with Pierre (so Grégoire had reported) and would likely guide him over his youthful amours and agnosticism.

It was a crushing blow to Catherine when the subject of the wedding was discussed. The de Varionnets, it seemed, insisted on having the ceremony performed by Talleyrand the Bishop of Autun, under whom their son Guillaume served as *vicaire*. The Bishop had already consented and Guillaume was to assist in the service. Talleyrand and Guillaume de Varionnet were juring priests. To Catherine a juring priest who had denied the authority of Pope Pius VI in favor of the new Constitutional State was no better than a heathen.

The news, carelessly announced by Pierre at the dinner table in the rue de Grenelle one night, caused a heavy silence. Catherine laid her knife and fork across her plate; the Abbé Blafond, whose appetite nothing could defeat, ate resolutely to his last crumb of Ziegen cheese—but without his usual prattle; Grégoire attempted to chat about the flight to Italy of Mesdames the King's aunts. The old *Béguines* had been accused of trying to smuggle off gold with them, as well as the Dauphin, for whom, it was said, they had substituted a changeling. Their exodus was considered by the people a prelude to the King's escape.

No one seemed to be listening to Grégoire. Pierre sipped his wine and wondered when the storm would break, for the problem of the juring and nonjuring priests was a vital one. But one no longer discussed anything more serious than Bologna sausages or whalebone corsets before the servants, since half of them were Patriot spies.

After dinner Grégoire led the way to his library. It was a room seldom used by the family, a room mellow with old furniture and a thousand volumes—books worn and fingered and loved. There were the two small heads done by Rembrandt, the canvas cracked, the dark, aged faces ageless; the cabinet of rare German porcelain; engravings, pastels of three small boys; a microscope (how beautiful had seemed the stamens of a rose when he was seven! thought Pierre); a portrait of Catherine above the mantel—Catherine with the sweet, fervid hope of youth; busts of Plato and Henry IV; the rosewood chest of Assyrian coins (Gilbert had loved filling his pockets with them, pretending he was Midas, while Maurice puffed at the silver flute!). How the room had seemed to include the five continents within its four walls in those early days, the red drapes barring blizzards in the winter, the doors opening to the redolence of flowers in June! How many times Pierre had lain flat on his belly before the fire while the firm, persuasive voice of Grégoire gave him Plutarch or Shakespeare: "To thine own self be true, and it must follow, as the night the day, thou canst not then be false to any man." Oh, the mysteries of one small room when one is little, thought Pierre. The magic of maps and shipmodels. Turkish scimitars, the aroma of brandy! Before he went to court that room had been his world—except for Catherine's *prie-dieu,* where God lived and judged him!

Catherine sat down, her hands folded quietly in her lap. Behind her was a *torchère,* casting an aura of gold and blue on her straight black hair. She looked soft and ethereal, but her eyes were adamant and her voice was low and controlled as she said: "Pierre, I can never consent to your marriage by a juring priest!"

Pierre glanced instinctively at his father for support. Grégoire, he knew, was secretly exultant at the overthrow of papal rule, feeling a sweet revenge for the persecution of Huguenot ancestors. Grégoire was examining a handsome calf-bound book that the Abbé Blafond had illuminated.

"But the arrangement of the ceremony is in the hands of the bride's family," Pierre answered uncomfortably.

"You would consent to such heresy?" Catherine asked, a note of horror in her voice.

"The Bishop of Autun is an ordained priest. What has the state of the Pope to do with marriage in the eyes of God?" Pierre picked up a letter opener and tapped it nervously against the desk.

"The Bishop of Autun is an infidel. Any day he will be excommunicated by the Pope."

"He has already made his break with the Pope voluntarily. Mother, you know as well as I do that marriages are being performed every day by juring priests, the same as—"

"Pierre, my child," said the Abbé hoarsely. (Kirschewasser had already appeared mysteriously at his elbow.) "Madame la Marquise is right. It *is* heresy. And M. Talleyrand is a thorn in God's side—profligate to boot. All true Christian priests are nonjuring since the Pope has condemned the Constitution and the whole Revolution. Your brother, Maurice, is a nonjuring priest. And I . . ." He paused and took an emphatic sip of his liqueur. "I, myself, shall be nailed to a cross before I swear allegiance to a revolutionary state in defiance of the Pope!"

The Abbé twiddled the amethyst cross that the Marquise de Bussac had given him when Gilbert came of age, and the tic of his cheek seemed clownish. It was a very handsome cross. Pierre wondered how much longer the Abbé would dare wear it in public. A nonjuring priest and a Jesuit besides!

"I think M. Talleyrand's ideas on education will outlive his profligacy!" said Pierre stubbornly.

"Education!—is this our fetish then?" cried the Abbé. "Education in lieu of religion? The Pope's appointments may not always have been discerning. But the Church run by the Assembly! . . . Holy mother of God—what a debacle!"

"One must decide these things for himself," said Pierre, and he began to feel angry.

"You have risked your life for Louis and Marie Antoinette. Louis has the courage to hear Mass by a nonjuring priest," Catherine pleaded, and Pierre thought her hands looked bloodless, folded like the hands of a marble effigy on a tomb. This was not the same Marquise de Bussac who made lint for the military hospitals, worked in the soup kitchens of the convents, or kept a huge fire burning in the courtyard of her mansion in the winter for the paupers. She was not the same soft woman who had ordered *truffes au vin* for dinner to humor him, who had read him Gilbert's letters with affectionate warmth.

"Louis even had the courage to attempt a flight to St. Cloud at Easter

for that purpose." The Abbé was pointing the amethyst cross at Pierre
now. *"He* is willing to risk his life for his religion. Then you—"

"I risked my life for Louis and Marie Antoinette because I love
them."

"And because your faith is the same, *mon Pierre!"*

Pierre's eyes were resting on the second shelf of the library, on a
small Chinese incense burner. It was there that had stood the books
Catherine burned: works of Diderot, Saint-Lambert, Marmontel, La
Harpe, Montesquieu's *Persian Letters;* Voltaire's *Philosophic Letters
on the English;* Holbach's *Christianity Revealed;* Helvetius's *De
L'Esprit*—which had been burned in public also by the hangman.
The empty spaces had never been filled by Grégoire. They were like
the vacant dinner chair of one deceased. They remained a vivid testi-
mony to the schism between Catherine and himself. Pierre glanced
again at Grégoire. The black, heavy brows under the white hair were
drawn in concentration on his book; the deep-gray eyes, riveted on the
illumination. He might have been alone in the room meditating on art.

"I don't know what my faith is," Pierre admitted bluntly, in a flood
of feeling.

St. Anthony or Voltaire, both of the church. Voltaire had been a
Catholic, even a Jesuit: had had the extreme unction when his end
came, and a Catholic burial.

"Is it so wrong then to think for one's self?" he exclaimed. "To follow reason? What goes on under the mitre? . . . days of intercession,
the Feast of the Holy Innocents, Masses to bring dead sinners to God.
Litanies on the lips and adultery in the heart! What am I to believe
when I see abbés ogling *filles* while they say their paternosters? *Dieu,*
what does it all mean? What am I to think? What are millions of
others to think—those who wish to think?"

Grégoire's strong, gray eyes were fastened now on Pierre's, and his
lips moved but no sound came from them. Catherine seemed to have
turned entirely to marble. The Abbé's pudgy elbow upset his glass, and
the last few red drops seeped from the table, like blood dripping from
the wounds of Christ in a painting.

"Can they all be wrong—these priests who have sworn to the State?"
Pierre went on hotly, and his letter opener scuffed the desk. "It is only
the discipline they want reformed—not the doctrines of worship.
Hasn't the Civil Constitution only brought the church back to the
early ages? For twelve hundred years the bishops received their power
from the metropolitans. You, *M. l'Abbé,* taught me this history your-

self. Are the first twelve centuries of Christianity to be condemned then? . . . What is right, Catholicism now or then? The rankling jealousy between Franciscans and Dominicans, monk and friar—which is the real faith? Faith is something one believes in—it's not rote. It's not the Protestantism or Catholicism of one's heritage!"

"You have no faith then?" asked Catherine, and Pierre knew her grief was too deep for tears.

"Marie Antoinette is his faith!" condemned the husky voice of the Abbé. "Idolatry . . . graven image!"

"Better than no faith," cried Pierre. "Why can't you let me alone—all of you? . . ."

Catherine laid one cold hand on his, and he shoved it away in a brooding ugliness.

"I'm old enough to be married by a Jewish rabbi, if I wish, or a Mohammedan imam. A juring or a nonjuring priest! And it doesn't matter, I tell you."

"You love Mlle de Varionnet so much then?" Catherine asked in a whisper.

"I loathe her."

"*Dieu!* . . ." she whispered. "Marriage without love; religion without love; life without love . . . Holy Mother, what is there left?"

"Freedom . . . I love my freedom."

"You are a Republican!" challenged the Abbé, stammering in his excitement.

"I am neither Republican nor Royalist!" exclaimed Pierre passionately to his own amazement. "I am not Catholic or Protestant. I am neither good nor bad. But I am an individual . . . and I want my freedom."

"Pierre," said Catherine, wringing her hands, "I beg of you, think of what this marriage will mean. A loveless marriage—without the sanction of God. It will be a curse to you. It will be a curse on the children your wife bears to you. It—"

"You think my son will be born lame—be a Talleyrand, perhaps. I loathe superstition. It's the religion of weak minds."

"Pierre!" Catherine's voice was like a hot coal detached from her frozen beauty.

"God forgive me! I always hurt you so. And I never mean to hurt you. . . ." Pierre was in an agony of remorse.

What was it Burke had said? The pain in Catherine's voice brought it back in vibrant phrases: "Superstition which builds is more tolerable than that which demolishes . . . that which adorns a country better than that which deforms it . . . that which endows better than that which plunders . . . that which disposes to mistaken beneficence, better than that which stimulates to real injustice . . . Such is nearly the state of question between the ancient founders of monkish superstition and the superstition of the pretended philosophers of the hour . . . Wise men are not violently attached to these things, nor do they violently hate them."

Wise men . . . thought Pierre, and he looked at his father, who was able to keep his iron-gray eyes on the colored filigree of the illumination. Grégoire: Philosopher-Christian; Republican-Monarchist; Sentimentalist-Politician; Hedonist-Crusader. Neither violently attached to these things nor violently hating them. Wisdom, or weakness and lack of faith? What was it Grégoire had?

"Grégoire," murmured Catherine, "in God's name—help this boy. Do not sit there and watch his perdition." She rose, standing before the Marquis with her tortured soul on her lips and eyes.

Grégoire closed the book. He rose too; his eyes were filled with a keen pity. He had loved Catherine. He touched her shoulder gently with his jeweled fingers.

"Catherine," he said, "I watched his physical birth, anxious, helpless; again, I watch his spiritual birth, anxious—even more helpless."

She turned away from him then and the tears overflowed at last.

Pierre had a strange feeling that he saw his parents objectively for the first time in his life. There was Grégoire, a man whose faith was in many faiths, a man too broad in his sympathies to be a strong man. The revelation shocked Pierre, left him floundering. And there was Catherine the fanatic. He would never kneel beside her at the *prie-dieu* again. She and the *prie-dieu* were apart from him now, like his hoop and stick under the eaves in the attic. He recalled his childhood—the unthinking days—with a dreadful nostalgia. Grégoire had seemed so wise, so understanding. Catherine had seemed so perfect. . . .

Spiritual birth—it was anything but joyous. If he could turn neither to Grégoire nor to Catherine now he must turn to Descartes, he reasoned grimly. Descartes would have said that Pierre was in that state of uncertainty and doubt essential in the search for truth, wouldn't he? Descartes, truth, freedom! This was it, this doubt and uncertainty. This was Freedom.

But there was a pain so great in his new-won freedom, a gall so bitter in his proud triumph that he longed for the childish moments of hypocritical penitence, the absolution of those gentle hands, the anodyne of Catherine's blessing. There she stood, but tonight he was unable to reach out and touch her.

He covered his face with his hands. He wanted to shut out all of them, all of these vultures at his soul. He wanted to shut out the smug ticking of the clock, the false pedantry of a thousand books, the stifling twilight of a dying world.

Stumbling from the library, he went off to be alone.

❀❀❀❀❀❀❀❀❀❀❀❀❀❀❀❀❀❀❀❀❀❀❀

CHAPTER XIV

VICTOIRE, a matron, was an earthworm transmuted to a butterfly.

The Comte de Varionnet had established the newly married couple in an elegant house on the rue St. Germain. There was a Swiss porter, a thieving maître d'hôtel, a neurotic housekeeper, and numerous *femmes de chambre*. Also there were such indispensables as a cellar man, a confectioner, a pastry cook. Two footmen delivered Pierre's billets-doux; two others collected Victoire's. A private courier was retained for mutual errands. The thieving maître d'hôtel, richly clad, wearing a sword, a diamond ring, and a gold snuff box, had his own lackey.

It was an impressive staff, although the chef wore a blue, white, and red cockade (boulevard or bouillabaisse) and the chambermaids wore patriotic garters and visited the Jacobin Club. But who could be more loyal to an old master than Dominique, who also frequented the Jacobin Club? Wasn't it the *ton?*

The carriage, a fat sky-blue creation that bounced along the cobblestones like a soap bubble, was the special wedding gift of Victoire's mother. It was filled with so many elaborate gadgets of crystal and gold and enamel that Pierre said one could be born or die in it with equal convenience and luxury. Two coachmen and a postillion glowered down on the shabby rabble. The stable housed several spirited

riding horses; each morning Pierre snatched Volante from the curry-
ing of the groom, rode to the Champ-de-Mars, where he cantered with
gentlemen of the court and then breakfasted with Silvie.

Victoire seemed unaware of Silvie. While Pierre roamed she was
receiving poets and abbés and incipient statesmen in her milk-clouded
bath. Although Victoire was no Diane de Poitiers her admirers were
legion. They played whist with her at her bedside, worked with her
on translations, exchanged with her little gifts of *amitié,* usually china.
One aspiring lover presented her with a Newfoundland dog, which at
once cavorted through the house upsetting the morale of the love birds
and cats: the *marcassin,* which might have given him some competition, had become fierce, and had had to be killed.

In this day of political tumult, Victoire's salons defied all presentiment of civil war. Her tapestry frame before her at the fireplace, she
received her court like a duchess. There was variety in her entertaining: one night, a strong punch party to hear a popular harmonica
artist; the next night, an elite gathering to watch the blindfolded
François-Andre Philidor the famous chess player. Again, the bacchanalian dinners were followed by a general melee, the drawing-rooms
disposed with cards and refreshments and newspapers like a café.

Victoire was never alone. Whether she sat for her portrait in crayons
or had her profile taken by the *physionotrace,* someone languished beside her. Pierre, who had sedulously avoided her and her parties, was
mystified. What did Victoire talk about as she applied the rouge on its
cotton stick, as she tinkled out notes on the harpischord? What pro-
voked such gales of laughter? At last he was curious enough to seek
out her company, and in spite of himself he was amused. Her wit was
quick and caustic and her precise convent learning was twisted by her
fancy like a finger of dull dough into a brioche.

There were a great many rich bourgeoisie who came to Victoire's
salons. Pierre resented their confident bearing as well as a new resignation in the noble scions who accepted them. After the formality of the
court he had known, the lax etiquette of Victoire's coterie was disturbing. However ribald a gentleman's tastes, he should always keep up a
proper appearance, thought Pierre.

In spite of the gay camaraderie Victoire offered him, the gleam of
challenge never left her green eyes. He had been shocked and gratified
to find that she was no timid mouse, that she was capable of a passion
Louis XV might have relished. There was a strange attraction between
them, born of an old antagonism, making intercourse purely physical

and gross. It was with Victoire that he felt himself the adulterer. Compared with her pagan ardor, Silvie's love-making was innocent and seraphic. Pierre felt that Victoire was craftily moving pawns; that whatever the length or strategy of her game, she intended to win it.

Pierre was fundamentally unhappy. He seemed to be living feverishly from hour to hour.

Catherine welcomed him whenever he visited the rue de Grenelle. "Gilbert has written for more linen," she would begin. Or: "I read to the most charming little boy in the School for the Blind today."

But their eyes wavered when they met. There was Catherine's wound between them. The Marquise was courteous to the de Varionnets. Her frugal habits, her frequent retreats to a convent, explained the fact that she seldom saw them. Pierre craved the old feeling of trust between him and his mother; it was something he seemed to have lost irrevocably, like a pearl dropped into a sewer. However, there was nothing in the declaration he had made that formidable night that he could honestly revoke.

He went to Mass often—but to confession, never. Was he so inured to his own sins, he wondered, that he felt no need for confession? When he went to the Hôtel Michelait, the Abbé Blafond was so solicitous over his soul that he seemed to Pierre as nauseating as too much whipped cream.

"Madame la Marquise is right!" he admonished Pierre constantly. "Your marriage will never have God's blessing without the sanction of the Pope. You must have a second ceremony by a nonjuring priest, my son. Is it too much to ask, to give your mother this comfort?"

His own purpose accomplished, Pierre was not unwilling to gratify his mother. But when he approached Victoire on the subject she pursed her wide red lips together and said: *"Parbleu!* What would you have that you do not have now, *mon cher*—love, or . . . money?"

When at last he suggested a ceremony by Maurice, Victoire turned upon him angrily. "You talk as if we were living together in sin! Is the Marquise de Bussac the only one to heed? My own mother is highly incensed that you should not consider the marriage legal! That you are so narrow that you think the benediction of Talleyrand and Guillaume a mockery."

Pierre's pride prevented another conflict. But it was far from the last time that the Abbé Blafond plagued him.

Marie Antoinette herself had shown a slight apathy in her manner toward him since his marriage. He often assured her that he was no less loyal because of a civil ceremony—that he would finally win Victoire over to the orthodox rote. He knew also that the Queen was suspicious of his attendance at Republican meetings when he had been involved for many weeks in the plans of the royal family for escape.

"The more I am seen at the Jacobin Club, the less I shall be suspected," he convinced Marie Antoinette. And daily he avowed his loyalty to her in impassioned words and deeds that gradually dispersed her doubts. When she remembered his bravery of the fifth of October she felt resigned and ashamed.

He maintained his apartment at the Tuileries and kept on with his duties of librarian as usual. But he was constantly risking his neck in secret scheming with the Comte de Fersen over details of the flight. They met in some cellar hole of the Montmartre or some attic cell of the rue de Noyers.

The intrigue made him nervous and irritable. Silvie annoyed him often. She was forever losing things, casual if she mislaid a five-hundred-franc *assignat,* desperate if she couldn't find a ballet tie. Even Victoire's banter gave him more sense of stability than Silvie's endless cavorting. And certainly more diversion.

What was it he wanted? The safety of the Queen, of course, but then what? . . . He refused to think of the months ahead. He would only think of the immediate future. Faith in Marie Antoinette: that was enough for any one man, he told himself as he accompanied Victoire to Notre-Dame, a footman carrying her white-satin prayer book. A short time ago on their knees under a canopy of white moiré, in the heady smoke of the censer, they had vowed eternal loyalty to one another.

Was she really the prototype of Mme Lebrun's portrait—this sophisticated woman who dandled on her knee a black elf-jokei, fondling his kinky hair and childish thick features; a woman who had proved such a slave to fashion?

It was the end of May when Victoire gave her notorious *fête champêtre* at the château of her father at Passy. Because the spring had been perfect in Paris, and the boulevards crowded, society longed for the dulcet music of the uncaged bird.

Victoire and Pierre had been entertaining a score of their friends for several days. The grand ball followed a day teeming with activities: fencing; battledore and shuttlecock; a scientific séance; *Tartuffe,* with Victoire playing the lead; a reading of his own poems by the Abbé Delille; and countless little strolls in the woods. The young man of the

Newfoundland dog, the Chevalier de Tuite, was the life of the party. He had put salt in coffee, pepper in snuff, frogs and crickets in chairs, essence of bitter cucumber on the water tumblers. Pierre found his riding shirt smeared with resin, in spite of Dominique's surveillance; the Comte de Noailles' bedclothes were sprinkled with finely chopped horsehair. M. Tuite and his abettor appeared at the ball in the guise of fashionable ladies, zealously applauded.

There was a quadrille in the old French costume; a second, in Tyrolean garb; an Indian exhibition; and a group of mountebanks, dancing comedians.

Pierre felt that the lavish display was in bad taste, with the King and Queen virtually prisoners at the Tuileries. He wondered if suddenly he had become a prude. But he was too anxious over state affairs, over his share in the imminent escape of the royal family, to enjoy buffoonery. Nor could he forget the red eyes of Marie Antoinette as she toyed with her sewing.

The climax of the evening was to be a professional dance in a sylvan setting, hidden by green brocade curtains dividing the ballroom in half. The guests were seated now at the opposite end, waiting.

On one side of Pierre were Victoire, the Chevalier de Tuite (in his flowing taffeta) and the Comte Axel de Fersen, the Queen's favorite. On the other was Mme de Staël, the brilliant, vain, and impulsive Germaine Necker whom he despised. He had purposely urged Victoire to invite her because Mme de Staël had an absorbing passion for liberty and the cause of the Roland salon, and he felt that her presence might be an antidote for that of the Comte de Fersen. It had been indiscreet of Fersen to come. Their business together was too grave, too momentous for them to take the chance of rousing suspicion. But doubtless the Comte de Fersen had his own reasons for accepting, thought Pierre.

Small wonder the Queen had loved the handsome Swede from the time that she was Dauphiness. He was tall and robust, with a supple grace the women adored, a man of the world who had only quit its four corners for the French court because Marie Antoinette was of it. He spoke French with a slight Swedish accent that was charming. But smaller wonder, thought Pierre, that the purchaser of the Royal Swedish Regiment had loved the Queen. . . .

Pierre felt mellow with a pleasant exhaustion from tennis and the wine of the evening.

"Mme Michelait has a penchant for unique entertainment!" Madame de Staël whispered to him, her coarse features lighted with anticipation.

He felt a momentary glow of satisfaction. It was not the first time he had heard spirited praise of Victoire. Perhaps he was becoming a prude after all. . . . That would be really amusing. He must try to be more tolerant of Victoire.

Certainly she was efficient, a manager. The supper table in the adjoining room was a *chef-d'œuvre*. Designers, statuaries, painters, sandworkers had been on hand all day to produce an English landscape on the long lace banquet cloth. There were cottages, fields, flocks of sheep, churches, and bridges of colored paste and spun sugar. A *surtout* of crystal and gold branched into innumerable vases and salvers of flowers and sweetmeats. The gold of service plate glittered in the light of myriad tapers. Dozens of footmen in orange velvet moved slowly, arranging chairs, passing punch, carrying in platters.

There was enough food to feed the hungry faubourg of St. Antoine: cooked hams from Bayonne and tongues from Vierson; ortolans embalmed in pastry; lobsters and oysters and ruffles of truffles; Bologna sausage, eel pasties, crayfish; a turtle of twenty pounds; poor little legs of frogs, poor little pickled feet of pigs; surrounded with pastel sauces and trimmings so exquisite that it seemed sacrilege to despoil the whole —a slashing of a Rembrandt oil.

And then delicate ices tinted with hothouse berries; wines of every hue; fruits from Montreuil shining like spun glass. What a pity that no one was ever hungry for more than a mouthful of cheese with such an assortment of rare cheeses!

Yes, Victoire was a superb hostess. And tonight, in white muslin and blue ribbons, her crook garnished with hyacinths and narcissuses, she was really almost lovely. What could she be saying to the Comte de Fersen which made him laugh so inopportunely in the growing quiet of the room?

"Dieu, Mme de Michelait, how you exaggerate!" he heard the Comte de Fersen say. And Victoire's large red mouth was gay with laughter. Her sudden outburst made him unaccountably angry. She was common and wounding as thistle, and yet a few hours from now her full red lips would be covered with his, and she would be giving herself to him with a sort of fierce mockery, knowing that in his very passion, he despised her. . . .

"And you—you naughty thing," Victoire said, turning to M. de Tuite, who hovered close like a lap dog, "you have been the life of the party!"

He simpered, rearranging his skirts. (He made an enchanting

woman!) "I'm afraid the Vicomte de Noailles will never speak to me again!"

"Nonsense! You know he'd only have been yawning without the horsehair!"

"What we need is more originality like yours!" exclaimed the little black-taffeta widow from Passy, tapping M. de Tuite's shoulder with her fan. "Really, what is there new to think about? . . . Haven't we eaten oysters in every possible stage of dress and undress?"

M. de Tuite basked in the compliment as the others laughed. Even Mme de Staël laughed, but there was lightning in her laughter.

"*C'est vrai,* Madame, there is nothing new in the world . . . even a Revolution is an old story!" she exclaimed.

The little black-taffeta widow quailed before the flashing of the black eyes

"Don't let Mme de Staël frighten you," M. de Tuite assuaged the little widow. "Revolutions come now and then . . . but what to do with the oyster! That is a daily problem, an eternal problem."

Pierre met the glance of the Comte de Fersen. He knew the Comte was sharing his thoughts. To how many people was the oyster more absorbing at this moment than the Revolution? How many aristocrats actually cared about the fate of France, provided a new cloak for the oyster furnished a new flavor? Was it the little black-taffeta widow and M. de Tuite frolicking in petticoats that he was willing to risk his life for? He was sick with the same confusion that came to him sometimes after an evening at the Rolands'.

There was a hushed expectancy as the tapers near the guests were extinguished. Footmen drew the curtains aside, disclosing a breathtaking rural scene behind a thin sheet of glass. Oaks and shrubs in profusion were painted on the walls; orange and lemon trees grew from the floor; in winding paths and beds of flowers there wandered forty shepherdesses (ballerinas from the Opéra); and in the background a real cascade of water plashed and gleamed in the light of a thousand candles.

The applause was deafening. Pierre, startled by the unique beauty of the spectacle, forgot his disillusionment of a moment before.

Victoire glanced at Pierre quickly. He condescended to be pleased at last. It was not too dark to see his black eyes shining with approval and his thin proud lips curved into a smile. She had had no idea it would be so hard to make him fall in love with her. He wasn't jealous; he never seemed to notice whether she wore cloth of gold or sackcloth;

and he only tolerated the bons mots that sent other men into convulsions.

No, she simply would not have it. Although she hated everything about him but his reckless embraces, she would make him fall in love with her. All that occupied his thoughts was that wanton of the Opéra, that little what-do-you-call-her. The heiress of the de Varionnet millions deserved something better. But how to break his pride, how to humble him in the eyes of a world that knew he despised everything about her except her money?

Perhaps if she made an effort to be genteel. . . . Other men liked the snap and vinegar of her talk; yes, other men with the same damned four quarters; But Pierre was different. Even at court he had been attracted by the Mmes de Frivouac, with their twittering insect manners. The maternal influence of a Marquise de Bussac, no doubt, thought Victoire. An ivory icon, the Marquise, and bloodless. . . . Yes, perhaps he would fall in love with a genteel Victoire. Or, perhaps if she had a baby. . . .

She slipped the hand with its forget-me-not bracelet onto his knee; he pressed it and smiled his congratulations. Her heart began to skip in triumph.

Now the ballerinas were commencing to dance behind the sheet of glass, the music luring them into nymphean pose. A few willowy steps —an exotic tableau—then a Boucher painting come alive again! From the shrubs a fawn skipped to the fore, joined by a water nymph from the sparkling pool. Her blond hair was drifting gold; her lithe body, silver moonlight . . . Mlle Hyacinthe. . . .

There was a surprised murmur. Pierre felt a hot flush of anger. The impudence, the presumption, the arrogance of Victoire to engage his mistress for an affair like this! He thanked God he was sitting in the dark. Perhaps he would lose the scarlet of his humiliation before the dance was over.

But humiliation was to be the keynote of the evening. Following the solo a flock of sheep, a shepherd's dog, and a young heifer were to be led across the greensward behind the glass curtain. The first half-dozen sheep followed their shepherd dutifully. Then suddenly a sulky heifer bolted onto the scene from the rear. In a second all was chaos. Agitated sheep tumbled into uprooted shrubs; the distraught shepherd tried to save a lamb from the cascade with his crook, only to slip on the wet moss and land with a comic splash into the pool. The dog barked fiercely. There was a conglomeration of legs and arms and toppling lime trees as the heifer rammed his horns into the sheet of glass; shattered fragments flew onto the ballroom floor like sparkling, iridescent rain. Through the breach rushed the liberated sheep, the dog, the dripping herdsman, and the frantic ballerinas.

Guests laughed hysterically or screamed. The women seemed to have turned to centipedes. They scrambled in a tangle of petticoats to stand on their chairs, clutching their supper partners, while sheep gamboled in and about the company, impartially spreading manure. The Chevalier de Tuite, privileged by his skirts, squealed and ran for shelter behind a screen. The Comtesse de Varionnet, her headdress toppled askew, was having an attack of asthma. Snuffboxes, fans, boutonnieres—all were on holiday. The astounded Mme de Staël gripped Pierre's neatly pomaded hair for support, and he felt himself anchored by her avoirdupois. He steadied her fat gartered knees with disgust. Velvet footmen tumbled about the company like so many juggled oranges. Tapers! . . . The sheep were bolting into the tapers! Save the drapes from fire! . . . Here was the little black-taffeta widow from Passy, fainting. What to do with her?

The stampede went on brashly, completely, while the guests huddled together and waited for the servants to restore order. Pierre, wrenching himself at last from Mme de Staël's drowning grip, ran to the supper room, giving one ornery sheep a kick in the ribs.

The shepherd dog yanked at the banquet cloth so that he could pull from its platter a colossal trout rushed by special courier from the Lake of Geneva. The great *surtout* began to writhe like an angry python. A shower of sweetmeats and crocuses garnished the woodcock and oysters and quail as the Comte de Narbonne tried to steady the *surtout* with his sword. The villages of sugar, spent by the hurricane, collapsed.

Screams and barks and footmen rushing after the gleeful sheep only encouraged the frolic. But at last each lamb was shackled by a lady's scarf or napkin and dragged back to its fold.

Pierre returned to his disheveled guests. The tapers were being lighted again, the ladies assisted down from their chairs. Victoire, clinging to the arm of the Comte de Fersen, actually seemed to be enjoying the debacle. They were both laughing. As Pierre gave his hand to the buxom Mme de Staël, Victoire's voice rang out above the babel.

"*Nom de Dieu!*" she exclaimed. "You and the Comte de Fersen

were wonderful, *mon Pierre.* Such spirit! As if you were helping the
Queen to escape France and the Revolution!"

Pierre's blood turned to ice. The Comte's laugh ended as if he had
been pest-struck. Neither dared to look at the shrewd Mme de Staël
or at one another. Neither could summon to his tongue a bit of
persiflage. Mme de Staël's black eyes were calculating, keen.

Pierre's control lasted throughout the riotous supper. If Victoire had
planned the chaos it would not have proved more stimulating to a
jaded company, for the oysters were garnished with bonbons.

But at last he was alone with her in the same sitting-room in which
Mme Lebrun had painted her portrait.

"The most vulgar fiasco I've ever seen!" he raged.

"But it was a huge success—like some banquet of Claudius."

"Claudius—the ascetic?"

"Well, Nero then . . . *n'importe. Dieu,* it was marvelous fun! Did
you hear M. de Tuite's mock menu? . . . 'Candle-grease soup; thumb
nails *au naturel;* fricandeau of lamb's wool au crocus sauce; cote—' "

"*Victoire!*" He grabbed her by the arm and shook her, and her flowered crook with its bedraggled flowers clattered to the floor. "Fun, you
fool! Your fun will likely send me to prison!"

"*Morbleu!* What have I done now? . . . God sends meat and the
devil cooks!"

"To suggest that I might be implicated with the Comte de Fersen
in the escape of the Queen!"

"*Enfin—are* you, that you are so green with terror?" She pulled away
from him defiantly.

"No, of course not! . . . But the walls have ears these days. And—"

"Everyone knows the Queen would like to escape!"

"The more reason not to suggest it. *Dieu!*" . . . He knew he should
never have made an issue of her remark, but his wrath had need of
explosion. He thought of Mme de Staël's brooding eyes and turned
cold again. "Forget it now. It was a joke. But a dangerous joke. Keep
the Queen off your lips!"

"I won't be treated like a child!" she threatened, and stamped her
foot.

"Child! . . . Only an infant, a *cretine* would be so crude as to have
my mistress dancing here before my friends!"

Victoire raised her green eyes to his, and her voice faltered.

"Your mistress? Mlle Violette your mistress? *Oh, mon Dieu, je suis
désolé . . . je meure de chagrin!* Mlle Violette. . . ."

"Mlle Hyacinthe—s'il vous plait!"

She flung herself onto the flowered chaise longue and burst into wild tears, her face hidden in her hands. The canaries under their satin night covers began to rustle and twitter.

Pierre paced the floor. It was inconceivable that she hadn't known about Silvie. Simply inconceivable! Yet more incredible that she knew and could be so gauche. It must be that she was just learning the truth about Silvie. Well, he was glad he had hurt her. He continually wanted to hurt her, even when he took her in his arms. But it was her own fault. Her eyes were always flinging the gauntlet. . . .

"It was that Mlle Violette who tripped the heifer," sobbed Victoire. "That's how the trouble began—the stampede. . . ."

"That's a lie. His horn was tangled in a rose bush."

"Ask D-Dominique if you d-don't believe me! . . . Well, she won't ruin my marriage, I tell you! She won't come to my own ball and make a laughingstock of me! . . . Oh, I wanted you to be so proud of the fête. . . . And I thought if you were p-proud of the fête maybe you would love me just a l-little. . . ."

Pierre stopped and stared down at her, completely nonplused. Her hauteur, her pose, her challenge were broken down into little molecules before his very eyes. He felt less triumphant, less hateful. Was it possible she was in love with him?

Victoire peeked at the strong, hard figure with his coat slung over his shoulder. It was going well, she thought. The genteel suffering of a wronged, a loving wife. . . . How men did love tears and humility! What did it matter if she won humility with its like? His vanity was expanding like a bloated bullfrog. . . .

She sat up and mopped her eyes, which were not too red because there had been more sobbing than tears. She thought she must look very young and defenseless because her hair had tumbled about her shoulders and the blue satin sash was crumpled.

Dieu, if only she were beautiful, how she would make him suffer! But it was dark here in the corner and she had struck the right chord. Eyes full of hurt melancholy . . . breath quick and passionate. . . .

Pierre snatched her into his arms. He could never understand what happened between them. It was always a violent emotion, like the clash of the wills of two devils. Or the meeting of two wayward winds at sea. . . . Ravishment without beauty. Burning flesh without spirit. Her eyes, turned tawny, gave out dark sparks as her lips closed on his. *Dieu*—how strange was this woman, and how she had begun to possess him! . . . He pulled the thin muslin gown from her shoulders so that her breasts were naked and crushed her to him. She would have what she wanted—more than she wanted. . . . Soft red mouth, starved white breasts—were they bruised? Let the horror of rape flood her eyes . . . let her blood run wild to bursting! Let her know the savage strength of him—more than she wanted!

❁❁❁❁❁❁❁❁❁❁❁❁❁❁❁❁❁❁❁❁❁❁

CHAPTER XV

June 20, 1791

IT WAS after three o'clock on that fateful June morning. The escape of the royal family was materializing at last. Pierre, riding Volante before the huge coach, thought he had never known such a mingling of fear and joyful anticipation. In a few hours all Paris would be bursting with the news. And Victoire would instinctively know that his story about going on business to Touraine was a ruse.

Now in the cool quiet of the midsummer night he had time to think rather than feel. Everything had gone according to plan—almost. Louis, Marie Antoinette, the two children, Mme Elisabeth, Mme de Tourzel, and two ladies-in-waiting had fled during the night from the palace; gathering at the barrier of Saint Martin, they had started in a berline and cabriolet for Metz where they would meet General Bouillé.

Comte de Fersen had accompanied them as far as Bondy. Pierre's heart had given a sharp leap when the Comte said good-bye, for now the safety of the royal family was relegated to him. He was dressed in the livery of a courier. Bodyguard, he was. Pierre Louis Bertrand Marie de Michelait, bodyguard—courier. Coachmen, lackeys, all in the retinue were of royal blood, whether they knew anything of the road or not. No one else could be trusted.

Dieu, how the sleepy croak of a frog sent his pulse flying, like that of a small boy stepping on a twig in the dark. But what could go wrong? Who would ever suspect as *émigrés* the party of the Baroness de Korff (Mme de Tourzel), going to Frankfurt with her two children, her companion, Mme Rochet (Marie Antoinette), and her steward (Louis in his bottle-green suit, roughly made wig and lackey's hat). Beyond Châlons at different points along the road they would be met by faithful units of the French army; each unit would accompany them as they proceeded northeastward until finally with their impressive escort they would reach Montmédy and be joined by fifteen thousand Austrians. There could be no suspicion of the troops in the countryside for General Bouillé had spread the report that a considerable payment of money was being transported to the army along these roads and must be guarded. Once at the border, the King would order the dissolution of the Assembly; the nation, already wearied of the drastic moves of the Revolution, would throw itself at his feet; there would be a triumphal return to Versailles. And life would go on again, the storm clouds dissipated. It was all very simple. Pierre wondered why the subterfuge had given him so many months of worry and irritability.

They had been two or more hours late in getting started, of course, but what if they were behind schedule? All the more certain then, that the troops would be at their appointed places awaiting them.

How pure was the early morning dawn, the little hamlets a soft misty gray before the apricot splash of the sunrise! And the thrush, bursting with its matins, as if it knew that the clop of the horses along the road meant freedom. Freedom for France once more! . . . Rousseau was right. The pine of woods, shocking blue of periwinkles in the vale, or gaudy canna at a kitchen door did chasten the soul!

There, nestling in the elbow of a wood, was a cottage so like the one in which he had spent his earliest years that he caught his breath with a sharp pain of nostalgia. No formal garden there by Le Nôtre. Only stocks and geraniums in an orgy of color. He recalled Mère Dulange, with fresh white cap and copious apron, soft billowing bosom, and red, gentle hands. How many childish tears had her hands soothed away! . . . How happy they all had been between the times when the de Michelait coach rolled in to claim him—and take him for a holiday to that strange, inhibiting place called "home"!

A blur of memories came back, bittersweet: the feel of damp snails in his hands; the warmth of summer mud between his toes; the comfort of velvet moss; the lullaby of June breeze as he lay dreaming,

dreaming, in a low branch of an apple tree. Summer had been the vastness of sky and earth; winter had been the fragrance of a hearth fire, Pierre on his lazy belly before it.

He recalled snatches of song, pungent odors of pine and herb, and bubbling milk. Sensations too. A nameless joy filling him to bursting with shouts in the meadow; infinite sorrow at the finding of a limp, silent bird; wonder and reverence at a stream sparkling with snow; delicious curiosity at the naked beauty of his tiny foster sister. Then resentment when the world had opened beyond the vale and woods and he had been dressed as a gentleman, his head and feet covered for the approbation of Paris.

The smile of the little peasant girl in Normandy—that too, had belonged to another world. Her lips gentle and curling as the tendrils of a fern . . . all of her fresh and beautiful as a newborn day. Disturbing memories! thought Pierre. Too sweet for life when one lived it among people, among realities. How good it would be to lie in the sun now, sensations drifting like a winged seed! To feel the soil, believing it to be God's, not man's. Thoughts pure, radiant, inchoate—unconfined as wind or rain.

Yes, these tender, suckling years now seemed like the heart torn out of one, leaving the shell. Pierre thought: "If one does not close his eyes to the beginning, he is blinded by the light. . . . One must forget, to live in a world of men."

The last whimpering note of an owl rose from a grove of oaks shimmering with sun. The knoll reminded Pierre of Marly, of Hyacinthe— how Hyacinthe had seemed a flower the first summer moment he had possessed her. Was he still in love with Silvie, he wondered? Silvie with the soft blond curls? He thought of her white hands without veins or knuckles; her toes, restless as the bells of Paris. Silvie was in love with him. Rather, Silvie loved him: deeply, painfully—as Catherine loved him. Silvie would have ploughed with him in the fields. He envied her. What was it like to love painfully, he wondered? Perhaps it was better never to know. . . . He had not even been able to bear the torture in Marie Antoinette's eyes when she parted with the Comte de Fersen in Bondy. . . .

Victoire too was in love with him, wasn't she? How would this incongruous marriage end? What was it that drew him so fiercely to the flecked green eyes, the quick, impulsive yielding of her large mouth, the hard union with a body which was neither beautiful, nor feminine nor inviting? The thought of his appetite for her was at variance with the mystic beauty of this summer morning. And yet, he no longer quite loathed her. She amused him with the hard sparkle of her laughter, her inexhaustible wit and imagination, her elegant effrontery. "What a dazzling knowledge has Mme de Michelait!" said one admirer after another to Pierre. Men who embroidered, men who swallowed her dashing tales as a fish, a fly, but did not read, he thought. Was her appeal to men their instinctive knowledge that no man would ever fully possess her? And what was it about Victoire that she withheld? . . . Yes, it was a curious marriage, he thought. The first of two, the Vicomtesse du Luvin had predicted. That would mean that Victoire would die before him, since they were both Catholics. But what could that old witch know about the future? He sighed. It was unfortunate that he had married so soon. Now with the glory of France returning and the security of the old régime in sight, he might have lived a bachelor a long time without money. Or he might have married any number of beautiful young women at court, as poor as himself, for Marie Antoinette had always rewarded the faithful with colossal pensions. . . .

He yawned. He could hear the voice of the little Prince now, refreshed after his sleep. He looked back and waved to Louis Charles who was hanging out of the coach window. The King would be hungry. Surely his appetite would go down in history like the gourmandizing of Henry VIII. . . . If only Louis would exercise his head as assiduously as his stomach, things would never have come to this critical pass.

Breakfast was begun, and the bodyguards rode beside the coach now. Squeaking hampers were opened and silver platters were loaded with chicken, fruits, and pastries. Louis smacked his lips cheerily over his white wine. Marie Antoinette handed Pierre a glass of orgeat, a liquor made of sweet almonds and barley.

A sense of adventure and the freshness of early dew and sweet growth had stimulated their spirits, thought Pierre. There was almost merriment within the coach. Louis, his lackey's hat at a provincial angle, was shining with chicken grease. Mme Elisabeth, dressed as a maid, her crucifix still in her hand, watched her brother with brightening eyes. Marie Antoinette, in her simple gray gown, sipped at her orgeat. The large gypsy hat and the thick purple veil thrown back rippled with the motion of the carriage. But now little Louis Charles had to urinate, and Papa King unbuttoned the royal panties and extracted the silver closestool from its cupboard. The child giggled be-

cause he was dressed as a girl, and it was hard keeping the skirts out
of the closestool and the hot yellow stream from jiggling out toward
the coach door.

Only poor Mme de Tourzel was miserable, stricken with the indig-
nity of hiccups.

Mme Royale finished her drumstick and cried: *"Tenez!* Here it
comes!" as she thrust the bone from the coach window. *"Tenez!*
Monsieur de Mich—" At a tug from her mother she finished lamely: "I
mean—Monsieur Vorsdeaux."

Louis, nibbling on a fig, settled back in the coach with maps on his
knees and began to follow the route from village to village. Pierre rode
on ahead once more; the elation of the royal family made him jubilant,
too. He remembered how as a child he had always hurried to his
mother with any little ill that worried him. "It will be all right, *mon
cher,"* Catherine had said. And her words were balm. Today Marie
Antoinette's smile was all the reassurance he needed.

It was a singing morning. Butterflies drifted in the breeze; bees raped
the hollyhocks; now and then a cloud of dust turned into an herb merchant on a mule or a wagon of cabbages. Châlons . . . after they had
once reached Châlons, thought Pierre, there could be no possible doubt
of safety.

At the next change of horses, six in the morning, no one troubled
to ask the Baroness de Korff for her papers. The ostlers were the only
ones astir.

One of them, with eyes so bulging that Pierre was sure he never slept
at all, broke into eager conversation with him.

"You're elegant as a new cheese in your yellow brocade," he said,
setting down a bucket of meal.

"Mme la Baronne de Korff is very rich."

"Oui. I can tell by the coach. It's wide as a calving cow—and well
sprung as a grasshopper." He leaned over to sniff the fresh varnish,
and his eyes lingered on the windows, but the shades were drawn.

Pierre turned away from the ostler; he would have liked to punch the
fellow in his officious nose.

The entourage moved on, quickly now, with fresh, spirited horses.
Pierre had a feeling that the ostler lingered in the thickness of dust,
watching them sprint out of sight. It had been stupid, now that he
thought of it, wearing these new flaming yellow liveries. Conspicuous.
As well as the lavish coach that could only attract attention. Pierre had
argued over the coach with the Comte de Fersen. But Fersen was a

man madly, hopelessly in love—a love for Marie Antoinette not so platonic as Pierre's. She must be comfortable as if she were at Versailles. She must have every luxury at her fingers' tips; a silver dinner service, a clothespress, a cupboard for food, a built-in wine cellar, and a wardrobe befitting a queen for her stay at Montmédy, as well as ladies-in-waiting for her toilette.

"A light post chaise with two horses would only take five minutes at a posting station," Pierre had contended in the thick of their intrigue. "A new relay for a big coach will mean half an hour's delay."

"The more splendid, the less it will seem like a flight!" insisted the Comte. And as the King and Queen had been practically penniless and Fersen had supplied the necessary funds, likely he had the right of decision, thought Pierre.

But every hour counted like a bead in a rosary. And they had not made up time. As a matter of fact the journey had been postponed from the nineteenth to the twentieth, for Marie Antoinette suspected one of her maids of betrayal. Well, perhaps Fersen was right about details. He had long ago sent the Queen's diamonds to Brussels through Léonard and the Duc de Choiseul. Also, Marie Antoinette had insisted on shipping ahead her *nécessaire* under a pretense that it was a gift to the Archduchess Christina, her sister, governess of the low countries. Pierre had approved of neither of these moves, but Fersen had and no ill had come of them. . . . But since his talk with the ostler the morning was not so beautiful somehow.

Although the day passed uneventfully Pierre felt a tightening in his breast. Failure was impossible. He would not let himself think of it! . . . He knew well enough what it would mean. Prison . . . the gallows. *Dieu,* but the day was beastly hot and the sun was ravaging as the London fire. His eyes were filled with the grit of the road; the dust choked him like diphtheria. Neither water nor wine quenched his thirst. Soon, soon they would be at Châlons, and less than half an hour's drive from there, at Pont-de-Somme-Vesle, the Duc de Choiseul would be waiting with the first squadron of cavalry.

At four o'clock in the afternoon, Pierre jumped down from Volante at the posting station. People gathered magically like fruit flies: a farmer with a hoe; women with brooms, buckets, babies; men trusting their tills to their empty shops. An undercurrent of gossip began to trickle from one to another, like honey. The couriers were accosted.

"What a deal of baggage has the Baroness de Korff!" (As if she meant never to return!). . . . "Would you carry this letter to Sainte-

Ménehould?" . . . "I should like to use my scissors. A *métre* of that courier's lace would buy my children bread for a year." . . . "They are snobs, not even passing the time of day." . . . "The first party I've seen that didn't want to stretch its legs and cool off with a glass of wine!"

"*Queue du diable!*" thought Pierre, "but I am going mad!" Yet, what was there to fear? All friendly—all of them . . . natural to ask questions, to make remarks. A *coup de soleil,* perhaps, from the infernal sun (that crack which ran tortuous down the middle of his scalp.) Or nerves . . . now that they were safely away, the strain of the weeks behind him would tell. *Dieu,* the crack of the whips at last! Half an hour and then Choiseul. The false passports could be torn up, tossed blithely to the wind. Louis could discard his sweaty wig. . . .

"If there are more than ten chickens in this next barnyard all will be well," thought Pierre, reverting childishly to a game which he had always played with himself. One, two, three—eight chickens. But how ridiculous! The game had never worked out right from the time he was little. . . . "If Jean cracks his whip before we reach the curve we are lost. . . ." Jean did not crack his whip. Pierre laughed at himself and relaxed. Mme Elisabeth was leaning out of the coach window often now, wanting to be the first to see Choiseul. At any moment the cavalry's sabers would flash in the sun. . . .

But soon a horseman appeared alone and gave the countersign to Pierre. Choiseul was gone, he whispered, and the hussars too, after a long wait. What had caused the delay of the party? Choiseul had been certain they weren't coming.

Pierre cursed and dismissed him. Night coming on—and no guard! But Sainte-Ménehould was only two hours away. "Surely, there . . . *surely!*" he whispered to the Queen as they moved on.

Marie Antoinette was hopeful, smiling.

No two hours in Pierre's life had ever seemed so long. His linen was drenched with a quick sweat; his pulse rushed like a turgid waterfall.

Sainte-Ménehould—and no guard! The cavalrymen had dawdled away a whole day there, tippling and waiting, tongues free and easy, it seemed. Another posting station here. Another crowd, bigger than the crowd before. But so like it: brooms, babies, buzzing.

"See how the commandant of the cavalry greets these strangers . . . saluting the whole time he talks!" . . . "How elegant the coach!" . . . "The fat steward looks familiar." . . . "What news of the Great Louis these days?" . . . "Baggage enough for a prince!"

Pierre saw one of the onlookers step up to Drouet the posting master and whisper in his ear. The posting master stared open-mouthed, then meeting Pierre's eye, snapped his mouth closed and smiled blandly.

Pierre felt that the devil himself pursued them. But here at Sainte-Ménehould the commanding officer promised he would gather his drunken men back from the eastern road where he had sent them, confused by Léonard's message. They would follow at top speed to Varennes, would soon catch up with the royal party.

One hour more, thought Pierre as they left Sainte-Ménehould. After all these grilling weeks certainly he could wait one hour more. He wasn't being a weakling, was he? He stiffened, tightened his proud lips, and forgot the ache in his muscles as he rode beside the chariot. Whatever happened, his Queen must be safe . . . nothing else mattered.

There was a late afternoon apathy in the cooling air. The day had burned itself out, lay exhausted, dying. Marie Antoinette was holding the drowsy little Louis Charles, singing an Austrian lullaby. Mme Royale fussed aimlessly with a red-cheeked doll. Louis's maps were sliding from his knees and his head wobbled.

Finally the Queen leaned from the window and handed Pierre a ravishing peach from Montreuil.

"How exquisite is the sunset, Monsieur Vorsdeaux!" she said, and the mellow rose light touched her face and glorified it.

"A memorable sunset, Mme Rochet," he answered, smiling.

They looked into one another's eyes to find courage.

CHAPTER XVI

IT was eleven o'clock. The night was thick. The Korff berline had halted on the hilltop at the south end of Varennes awaiting a relay of horses and hussars from Bouillé, for the little village had no post. The berline was now six hours late and Varennes had gone to bed.

Thirty long minutes passed. Pierre felt a sweep of desperation. What could they do? Certainly not force these tired horses until they dropped frothing dead. . . . Bouillé must have gone to bed in the little village. He must be found at once—and the horses and hussars.

Pierre gave the order to the postillions to start ahead. The berline and cabriolet rumbled wearily down to the gates of the town. There was no sound but the stertorous breathing and tired clop of the horses and the faint rush of the river Aire below.

Quite suddenly a nightmare sprang into being in the light of lanterns. Men, tumbrils, wheelbarrows, chairs, and ladders blocked the road, swinging into red entity and out again with the dancing beams.

The horses bolted, frightened as cries and men broke loose.

"*Halté-là!*" exclaimed a hoarse voice behind a National musket. "Your passports, *s'il vous plaît.*"

Pierre backed up to the carriage, cursing under his breath as a lantern revealed the heavily veiled face of the Queen.

"You must not detain us. We must reach Frankfort tomorrow," she said, and the steadiness of her voice gave Pierre mettle. "We are pressed for time, Monsieur."

The voice behind the musket laughed. Pierre stared as the light flashed across the man's face. But surely this was the posting master who had gaped, open-jawed at Sainte-Ménehould!

"We are advised to escort you to the shop of M. Sausse, procureur of the Commune de Varennes."

The order was echoed by a dozen voices, spirits in the dark. A drum began to beat in the village square—or was it only his sick heart, thought Pierre. Pounding, pounding a *generale*. Candles began to appear at windows, small eyes prying into the secret of all France. . . .

"*Dieu,* we must plunge through this handful of Patriots before more gather," Pierre whispered into the depths of the coach. "On through Varennes, on till the hussars reach us."

But Louis had already yielded.

They drove a short way beyond, to the shop of M. Sausse who was a grocer. The traveling party entered, ushered in by the triumphant M. Drouet, posting master of Sainte-Ménehould. He had taken a short route through the fields and woods to warn Varennes that the steward in the chariot was the image of the engraving on the Louis *assignat*.

The shop was a small place, stifling with summer heat and the odor of rancid oil, sausages, and spice. Crowded shelves of bottles and herbs closed them into a breathless prison cell. M. Sausse, fully dressed, sat at a table behind a large cheese and a placid candle. A thin little woman, in nightcap and chemise, a quilt hiding her middle, stared white-faced from a shadowed door. In a moment other faces and figures appeared, half-formed, like lepers sneaking up on one without a bell, thought Pierre.

The shop boasted one other chair beside that of M. Sausse. Louis shooed a cat from it and drew it up behind the Queen; she sat down, her back straight, her head high. And then he saw two flushed red spots appear in the face of M. Drouet, who gave M. Sausse a triumphant look. The rich Baroness de Korff had been left standing; her companion, Mme Rochet, had been seated! The hand on Pierre's sword tightened. . . . Stupid Louis! Was there a possible way of saving a king whose lovable head was filled with sawdust?

M. Sausse examined the passport minutely. "It seems in order," he said, "but send for Destez—he has often seen the King at Paris."

The royal party waited, unable to speak or look at one another. Mme de Tourzel began to hiccup, and M. Sausse offered her a glass of warm, bubbled water which stood on the table. Louis toyed with the braid on his coat. The little Prince, lolling sleepily against a treacle barrel, worked out two fancy initials, "L C," on the dusty lid.

"Louis Charles!" thought Pierre, in agony. "You are writing out your own sentence!"

In getting out of the carriage the little Prince had torn one of the ruffles of his skirt, and his blue sash was tumbling open. He made a poor girl. None of them was very adept at pretending. . . .

It seemed an infinite wait until Destez arrived, and now it was impossible to keep out the curious neighbors, men buttoning their pants, women attempting to hide a bold breast.

The stranger, still in his nightcap, threw himself at the feet of Louis at once. "Ah, Sire," he exclaimed, his voice filled with emotion.

"Yes," said Louis, "I am your King."

The early morning hours passed painfully. The royal family retired up a companion ladder to a bedroom and parlor above. The ceilings hung low and stained, threatening. The air was tainted and thick and more stifling than that below; the covers of the bed were gray and patched. Heavy-eyed, the two children fell asleep at once, with Mme de Tourzel's cloak between them and the quilt. Marie Antoinette sank into an easy chair, the heavy veil still hiding her face. Louis delved into the cheese and wine that poor M. Sausse, a Royalist at heart, had laid on the table. Louis's forehead was pink and damp although he had removed the wig, and he smelled sweaty as a stoker.

"The hussars must come soon," Pierre said to himself over and over, pacing the floor. "The hussars must come. . . ."

The door was guarded by two farmers with pitchforks. In the street below was a constantly growing throng of people, half naked, wildly brandishing lanterns and improvised weapons. The noise grew with the tireless tocsin. It began to sound like the distant ominous roar of the fifth of October. Finally, Pierre heard the clatter of many horses and a cry of "The hussars!"

The haughty Duc de Choiseul appeared, breathless . . . he had been on the wrong scent. He could spare seven horses, and the royal family could ride away at once with the hussars before the National Guard of the commune had been assembled.

"But might not the Queen or one of the children be hit by a bullet?" asked Louis, wiping the crumbs of cheese from his limp linen. "Better, I think, to wait till the dragoons quartered in the inns have been roused and united."

"Oh, Sire, I beg of you, reconsider!" cried Pierre. "Every second counts. The people are gathering like flies. And Her Majesty is an excellent horsewoman."

But Louis detested bloodshed. It was always safer to wait. . . .

The Duc left to assemble the dragoons.

"Sit down, M. de Michelait. Rest yourself," said Marie Antoinette wearily.

Pierre dropped onto a rough milking stool. He was so tired he could easily have slept standing. In the little adjoining parlor he could hear the gentle voice of Mme Elisabeth telling her beads, and Mme de Tourzel's hiccups, mockery to the cries below: "To Paris!" . . . "Long live the Republic!" . . . *"A bas l'Autrichienne!"* . . . There was the thunderous roll of an antiquated cannon over the cobblestones. . . .

His fancy ran wild again. They would all be dragged back to Paris— to prison, to the gallows. It would be the end of the world. The end of *his* world, at least. Why did one want so desperately to live? Why did the old life at Versailles seem a panacea? Hadn't he been bored there with the gilt and the women? Why hadn't he the courage, the serenity to die? Catherine would die calmly when her hour came. Was it just faith in an ideal that made the difference? But no, with faith, with accomplishment, one must want the more to keep on, to further in the world his burning purpose. . . .

Dieu, why couldn't he forget this thing of faith? It was beginning to blister him like the boils of Job. One spot healed, another festering. . . .

Louis sighed loudly as he popped open the lower buttons of his coat (the cheese had dwindled by a pound) and slipped off his shoes to air his feet. Pierre looked up, surprised to find himself in the attic room. Now and then Marie Antoinette fanned a horsefly away from the children. Otherwise her hands lay folded firmly in her lap—those hands that had so often played spiritedly on the clavecin . . . waiting.

A lot of trapped animals they were, with the hunters riding closer. But he wouldn't give up, thought Pierre; the Duc would surely return with sufficient force.

His face sank into his hands again. Nearly two days' beard . . . he could well use a razor. There'd been only a bath of dust. How he would like to rip his soiled clothes from him and leap into a cold river of oblivion! . . . Victoire. He could see her sprawling in her tepid bath *à la Dauphine,* with its sea salt, wild thyme, laurel leaves, and marjoram. Bath *à la Dauphine.* Lovely paradox, with the Queen a prisoner . . . *Dieu,* would the shouting never cease! It rent his head like a cleaver. How he would like to close his eyes and shut out the noise and the mouse dirt! But if he closed his eyes they would be glued shut at once with sleep. At any moment he might be needed to defend her. . . .

What would Paris say when they all returned captive? What would Grégoire say? They would have their Republic now, the Girondins. Pierre felt a sudden surge of hatred for Grégoire who, though he had always advocated a government with a king, tolerated Mme Roland and her ideal of an Athenian republic. They would have their aristocracy of intellect, pulling all men down to a selfish level, raising none up! The perfect leveling—only down to one's self, Pierre thought cynically. Little sympathy they had for the coarse, unlettered man—for the masses—while they condemned royalty for that very same failing!

Dominique had said one day: "Freedom, M. de Michelait, is anything we can't possess." . . . No faction would ever have all it wanted. The Bourbons gone, the Girondins wouldn't last either. There would be bedlam—the end of France.

He looked up then, for Louis was dozing, a soft, puffy sound coming from his lips. Flies were buzzing around him and the cheese. The Queen raised her veil at last. M. de Michelait had seen tragedy in her face before. She smiled at Pierre and there was a vague, far-off look in her eyes, like the bewilderment of the haunted at the Bicêtre.

"You were too young to remember . . ." she mused, softly. "The coronation at Rheims. When the crown was placed on your sire's head he exclaimed: 'It hurts me!' . . . When Henry III was crowned he said: 'It pricks me!' "

Pierre recalled the assassination of Henry III; and her insinuation gave him a feeling of nausea.

"Soon the Duc will return, Madame," he whispered, "and all will be well again."

Dawn was beginning to seep through the window, a dawn murky through the gray, limp, uneven curtain.

"If only you could sleep a little . . ." Pierre suggested softly.

"Sleep is for children," Marie Antoinette answered.

Louis had slunk in his chair like a sack of flour. Mme Royale shifted restlessly, her dark rich curls a damp tangled mass. The little Prince still clung to a grinning pirouette clown; his one plump leg dangled over the side of the bed. Both children looked feverish from the heat.

"You have been very faithful to me," said Marie Antoinette to Pierre, "from the time you were not much bigger than Louis Charles. Like him, you were a gay, sweet child, M. de Michelait—filled with spirit. . . . I should like to have rewarded you. Now I can only hope you will add to your burden the safekeeping of my son. . . ."

Pierre felt choked, unable to answer.

"I can only hope," she went on in an impassioned whisper, "that whatever happens to me, if you are free you will continue to fight for his safety and for the good of France."

"I swear it!" he answered, and his words were mumbled and husky. "I swear it by all that's holy!"

He would have liked to drop at her feet, to lay his tired, muddled head on her knee, to cry out his sorrow into her soothing white hands as he had sought out Catherine when he was a child.

She was so beautiful, Marie Antoinette, in the haze of the summer dawn . . . the light of a Madonna in her eyes as she gazed at the child on the bed; the dignity of Maria Theresa in her bearing; the thrilling warmth of mingled love in her voice; the faint scent of roses clinging about her like perfume in a tomb.

Pierre, deeply roused, stood before the window staring at the wanton masses below.

Worshipping her, adoring blindly, he felt once more that she was France incarnate. He would fight for her, for his country's soul, unto death. Here was a sublimation too sweet for any sanctimonious Abbé Blafond . . . for any Roland martyr. Here was the real Godhead—the spirit of one's country. . . .

Louis stirred, and the chair creaked with his leaden bulk.

Six o'clock, and a new furor arose outside with the coming of a Paris carriage. Romeuf and Bayon, two deputies of the National Assembly, clattered up the companion ladder with a decree that the King return to Paris, that his rights had been suspended. Paris was in a state of wild excitement. . . .

Suddenly Choiseul appeared, and M. Sausse and his wife, the thin little woman, with a patched apron instead of a quilt around her middle.

Louis read the decree; total silence within, the uproar of thousands in the streets. Romeuf and Bayon shifted from foot to foot, sheepish under their arrogance.

"There is no longer a king in France," Louis said thickly, and brushed a fly away from his nose.

The return to Paris took three days. Pierre, bound with ropes to the other two bodyguard couriers, was jostled in the blaze of the sun atop the berline.

Over and over the last hours of Varennes plagued him. Couldn't *something* have been done the last moment although the drunken hussars were cheering with bakers, butchers, farmers? But every subterfuge had been tried. Louis had begged for a few extra hours of rest before the return journey. (Bouillé's cavalry squadrons *must* come within that time, followed by infantry and artillery.) But this expedient had failed.

Louis had demanded a meal; he was hungry. The meal served, he had eaten but a few bites, Marie Antoinette refusing to join him. Yes, Louis had been resourceful—too late. Even Mme de Neuville, one of the ladies-in-waiting, had fallen in a pretended epileptic fit, but a doctor had soon been summoned to give her a sedative. All entreaties of help to M. Sausse and his wife had proved in vain. They were loyal—but if they collaborated, their lives and those of their children would be at stake.

The party moved snail-like to Paris, surrounded by sixty thousand National Guards. Barnave and Pétion, commissioners of the Assembly, crowded into the berline with the royal family, sharing the cold chicken and wine with insolence. At several points there were grave disorders. Insults were hurled at the berline; scythes and muskets and pitchforks ushered the family at night into the inns at Châlons, Dormans, Meaux. At one point Barnave saved the life of a nonjuring priest who was threatened by the outraged people. At another the Comte de Dampierre, attempting to reach the berline to avow his loyalty, was killed mercilessly in the sight of the royal family.

As the cheering, sweaty army approached Paris, entering the Porte de la Conférence to traverse the Champs-Elysées, it was greeted by a Paris of absolute stillness. Posters had announced that: "Whosoever insults Louis shall be caned; whosoever applauds him shall be hanged." Silence escorted them to the Tuileries. But St. Antoine and St. Marceau waved loaves of bread on their pikes to prove that the King's absence hadn't starved them.

Pierre and his companions, drunk with fatigue, heat, and the pain of open sores from the friction of the ropes, were tossed from the berline like baggage and bandied about the crowd.

"*A la lanterne!*" Pierre heard once more, and deep within his paralyzed emotions thought: "*Dieu*—am I then to die again?"

But the National Guards intervened. The noblemen who had helped to "kidnap" Louis were only tossed to the rats in prison.

Within the palace the lackeys, as usual, were drawn up in obsequious line. The magnificent table was set, as always, for the evening meal. Louis ate.

❊❊❊❊❊❊❊❊❊❊❊❊❊❊❊❊❊❊❊❊❊❊❊

CHAPTER XVII

Early August 1792

VICTOIRE had just bade her several dinner guests good-bye. She felt out of sorts, perhaps because her curls couldn't compete with the muggy weather. Life in Paris was becoming a bore and she decided to take her ennui out on the harpsichord. Her strong fingers pranced up and down the keys, making the Haydn a welter of chords. What difference if she struck the wrong notes so long as the effect was brilliant!

Pierre would probably be coming along soon, though he certainly

used the house on the rue St. Germain as if it were a tavern. At any
rate, since his imprisonment last year it was obvious he didn't spend as
much time with that little Mlle Marguerite. It still angered Victoire
that she had missed him those three months after the Varennes fiasco.
Bu she hadn't wasted time. The Chevalier de Tuite had finally won his
cause. Poor little snipe! She was sick of his languishing poetry to her.
And there wasn't as much virility in his whole pomaded body as in
Pierre's laugh.

Society was certainly a farce these days, with the war on and everybody important running to the border. At first, after the King had
signed the Constitution and General Lafayette had effected Pierre's
release from prison, it seemed as if things might be reverting to normal.
The acquiescence of the King had increased his popularity for a while,
though Pierre said the withdrawal of many moderates from the Revolutionary party had only left its strength to radicals. And since the
attack by the mob on the Tuileries in June, one might as well be in a
convent, like the Marquise de Bussac. What joy was there any more in
entertaining when the gold plate and jewelry had long ago been buried
and one was looking for a suitable cache for the silver? And the tables
—they looked naked without their villages of confection. How selfish
of San Domingo to have a sister insurrection and create a sugar short-
age way across the water!

Perhaps she had been a fool not to flee with her mother and father.
Émigrés had left by the thousands and it was said that Brussels and
Coblentz were very gay. Of course, it was galling to be declared suspect
by the government and have your estates confiscated. But the *émigrés,*
led by the King's brother at Coblentz, had enlisted the aid of Austria
at last, and when they invaded France the confiscated estates would be
returned, of course. The *émigrés* even threatened that when they made
their triumphal entry into Paris the nobles who had remained slothful
in France would be degraded to the bourgeoisie.

Imagine Pierre demoted to a boxkeeper at Mlle What-you-ma-call-
her's Opéra. Or a clerk at Le Jay's, the bookseller's shop! Pierre humble,
hands gritty from books! His arrogance salted down to no quarters instead of four! Would she continue to live with him, she wondered?
Who would be manuring his lands then, *s'il vous plait?*

A year and a half of marriage, she thought, and still she had not
been able to make a conquest of Pierre although she did amuse him
. . . Victoire gave her lap dog a smart kick as he played with her toe
at the pedal, and when he yelped tossed him a *gimblette* and called him

"sweet Leander." . . . It was mostly because Pierre had urged her to
escape with her family that she had been adamant about staying. Why
should she go just when she was beginning to make a little headway
and leave the field wide open to Mlle Narcisse! Moreover—and she
might as well admit it—she would miss the flashing of his black eyes,
the tightening of his proud lips as she taunted him, and the triumph
she felt as he begrudged her his kisses, angrily yielding to a force
stronger than his hatred.

Dieu, but he would have a surprise when he learned that she was
enceinte, that he would have an heir to carry the bourgeois taint of the
de Varionnet blood. Perhaps she would tell him tonight when he returned from dinner with his father. . . . How differently he would
react from the heroes of novels, in which M. X.'s heart fluttered with
paternal feeling and he kissed Mme X tenderly on the forehead, mum-
bling solicitous nothings!

Hot tears began to blur Victoire's eyes, and because she could not see
the keys she played with increasing venom.

"Sweet Leander" whined, as if stabbed by a porcupine, and ran away
from Haydn into a corner.

"Scissors, knives and, combs!"
"My fine boot laces!"
"Fresh salad!"
"Voilà le plaisir des dames, voilà le plaisir!" The spice of fresh gingerbread tantalized Pierre as he strode to Venua's, the Girondin haunt
close to the riding school. He had been asked by his father to meet him
there for dinner.

Paris wore the same garb as three years ago, thought Pierre, when
his world had been a miracle of joy in the pursuit of Mlle Hyacinthe.
The same tempting shop fronts, scurvy beggars, rag pickers, performing dogs. And the same cacophony: carriages rumbling to cafés and
promenades, jabbering stockbrokers and jobbers crowding to the
bourse, thousands of peasants clattering in with fruit and vegetables
and flowers for market. Bells and bells, shouts and shouts, cries and
cries. . . .

But the heart of Paris had a new cry: *"Ruban National!"*
Blue, white, and red—National ribbons cried everywhere. In soft
feminine satin, in varnished leather, in stiffened tape—to suit all fancies. One was hardly safe on the street without the cockade. And *"bou-*

quets à la nation," flowers of the three colors imbedded in myrtle, worn on the bosom, in the *"bonnet à la citoyenne,"* at the waist. The world was slowly turning blue, white, and red; and everywhere was the *"Drapeau Rouge"* of the National Guard.

Picking his way through the clamor, Pierre wondered if Paris would ever be light of heart again. It had the artificial gaiety of a Spanish dancer awhirl on a table top. The table was not so solid for caprices as mother earth. . . . And as for himself, he felt constantly keyed to sharp emotions. He was young and so strong, in spite of those three black months in prison, that he had no realization of his strength. The incarceration at Vincennes had given him a new challenge, a new personal motive for upsetting the table of the Revolutionists. He had come out of prison no longer blinded to the politics of the day and full well knowing the penalty of failure. Had Mme de Staël taken Victoire's remark about saving the Queen literally? Had she been responsible for the pursuit of the royal family to Varennes—for the dreadful fiasco? No doubt he would never know. But with his twenty-three years and their optimism he was confident that after many sacrifices on the part of the Royalists "everything would come out all right." Another Pangloss to another Candide.

His three months of imprisonment had given him the conviction that Paris consisted of eyes, vengeful eyes (though Grégoire assured him that his suspicion was at least half the fault of his early Jesuit training). Aristocrats were being watched maliciously. The Jacobin Clubs had covered France like a strangling fungus, promoting constant strife with the nobility. More châteaux had been burned in spite of the Constituent and Legislative Assemblies, which tried to preserve order. The Paris Jacobin Club alone bragged of six thousand members. Twelve thousand eyes, thought Pierre defiantly, wondering if at this moment he were being followed.

Life at the Tuileries had been almost worse than prison. After Varennes the royal family was under strict surveillance with doors to apartments always open. Since the attack on the palace in June the King and Queen, terrified of being poisoned, ate only plain roasted meat and substituted wine and pastry smuggled in by Mme Campan for supplies sent up by the kitchen. The Tuileries was filled with spies and Patriots and potential assassins in the guise of servants. In public, Louis wore a coat of mail beneath his clothes. Marie Antoinette scorned this precaution. And yet it was the Queen who was in greater danger, for her letters in cipher to foreign agents and to Fersen in Brussels went out of the palace hidden in boxes of chocolate or in linings of jackets. And every door and window was watched by avid Revolutionists.

Pierre himself breathed in deep relief when his duties as librarian were fulfilled and he could join Silvie in the rue d'Anjou or Victoire in the rue St. Germain and eat an adequate meal. He was loath to close his eyes in the stuffy *mansarde* room and closet that he and Dominique shared in the Tuileries. During recent weeks he had often been forced to enter or escape from the palace in disguise.

He fingered the gold ring Marie Antoinette had given him on his release from prison. It contained a lock of her hair turned white the night of her apprehension at Varennes. The inscription said merely: "Blanched by sorrow." Possession of the ring had given him a feeling of redoubled intent and adoration along with a pride that his fate was inextricably involved with that of his Queen.

Pierre came to Venua's. It was clammy with steaming roasts and with the outer atmosphere of rain-drenched sunshine. But the food here would not be poisoned. His mouth began to water in anticipation of pigeon boiled in barley.

His father had not yet arrived. Pierre chose a table in a far corner and blew out the candle. He wondered what the Marquis wanted with him. Pierre had seen little of Grégoire the last year, for his father still sat in the Assembly and was allied with the Rolands and their Girondins. M. Roland, lately dismissed from the Ministry of the Interior for his brazenness, now openly aimed at a republic.

Both Grégoire and Pierre had wanted the war that was declared in the spring, but for different reasons. Grégoire wanted war because he thought the King would lose his power through French victory; Pierre wanted war because he thought that Louis would recover his power through foreign victory. Now with the two armies about to clash in the east one of them must soon be victorious. And there was Gilbert, fighting with the French army, therefore fighting against Marie Antoinette and Louis. What an anomaly, thought Pierre—like the rest of this battle for freedom!

He ordered a bottle of Tokay and began to look around him. Men were playing earnestly at piquet and chess, some of them smoking long white pipes. Playing with Barbaroux was one of the juring priests who had taken advantage of the new law that priests might marry. Just the other day Pierre had heard Louis quote Gouverneur Morris the American ambassador: "I have lived to see a new religion arise. It is a denial

of all religions and its votaries have the superstition of not being superstitious. They have as much zeal as any other sect and are ready to lay
waste the world in order to make proselytes."

Pierre's conscience twitched. For the sake of Marie Antoinette and
Louis and their two children whom he adored, he pretended to be a
devotee of the Pope. But in truth he had no religion and was untouched
even by the fact that divorce, no longer a sin, was rampant. He felt a
sense of relief in admitting this to himself after the spiritual struggle
of the last few years. It was something like the imperturbable peace of
death. One no longer had to think. The physical aspect of living was
enough of a challenge at the moment—the race for survival of the
fittest.

And yet, Pierre's heart ached as he thought of Catherine at the convent of the Carmelites, unable to endure the secular world since Louis
had been forced to vanquish the nonjuring priests. How proud she had
been of Maurice, "Bishop of Agen" at eighteen! The solemn, near-
sighted Maurice had always been her favorite. He had been a clumsy
little body, awkward at sports. He had never understood the bawdy
jokes that Gilbert and Pierre had invented to shock him. The advances
of little girls had made him blush and cringe. Strangely enough, although Gilbert and Pierre had ignominiously taunted him and led him
by a ring in the nose through the daily routine, it was Maurice's word
that was command in a crisis.

"Thank God for Maurice," Pierre thought, "for mother would have
been bereft of hope without him! . . . Maurice was born of immaculate conception."

Maurice would be banished now along with the others. Where
would he be, Pierre wondered?

The bottle of Tokay was half empty when Grégoire hurriedly arrived. He and Pierre greeted one another with lavish affection and
then settled down to the business of ordering the meal.

Grégoire was dressed simply in a black frock coat, unjeweled, a practical man of business. The soft batiste of his jabot was spotless. His fine
ivory skin was flushed from the heat: the handsome gray eyes were
tired, the lines at their corners deepened.

Grégoire kept his voice to a whisper. He had seen Maurice a few
days before. Maurice had come to Paris to comfort his mother, had
traveled dressed as an herb merchant. He lived in a room of the stable
of the rue de Grenelle mansion, which had been closed. The Abbé
Blafond was hiding with him.

Finally Grégoire came to the point. "I beg of you to leave France while there is still time—you and Victoire," he said so softly that Pierre could scarce hear him above the clatter of the dishes. "Another few weeks, a few days perhaps, and Paris will be a prison from which no aristocrat can escape."

No pretense now that Pierre's fears were from his early Jesuit training! . . .

"I shall stay with the Queen as long as I am needed."

"She has become a fetish with you then. . . . Aren't you putting your heart before your head, *mon Pierre?*"

"No more than you and the Girondins."

"Come, Pierre, you oppose new views with the relentlessness of a Jacobin. At one time you were not so averse to Mme Roland and her idealism. You have become a second Edmund Burke."

"He was right when he said: 'Liberty, when men act in bodies, is power.' You attempt to level all France and what do you do but raise up a dictator? There's never any equalization of the people by law. It's not a matter of politics, but education. A long process—"

"When you say dictator I assume you mean Danton." Grégoire wearily straightened the ruffles at his wrist.

"I know you hate him," Pierre expostulated, "but if you don't collaborate with him whom do you have? Robespierre or the eighty-four-axed Commune? . . . What are you Girondins working for, anyway? You preach moderation but none of you have the courage to attempt to enforce it. You never lift your voices against riot or massacre until your own skin is endangered."

"We fought for the new Constitution, didn't we?" returned Grégoire sharply. "We've abolished all feudal rights, given Protestants liberty of worship, granted Jews the status of citizens with political rights."

"*Oui.* You've won liberties for the people—but how you cringe from any contact with them! Aren't you losing your hold in the Jacobin Clubs for that very reason? Poor, weak enthusiasts! How far do you think your golden tongues can carry you?"

"The kingship is still hereditary." Grégoire's gray eyes were dark with bitterness.

"So you too want to depose the King—to establish a confederacy like that of America. . . . But you Girondins want your confederacy run by intellectuals. . . . Well, it won't work. You can't win the people with snobbery. . . . Poor Louis—wrenched from the throne because he's too kind and democratic! Because he won't adopt the harsh methods of his predecessors! *Dieu*—at least we know the evils of a monarchy. Why then should we turn to the new evils of a republic?"

Grégoire laughed at last. There was no use trying to argue with this firebrand. The boy was under severe strain at the Tuileries, living with dead royalty.

"You remind me of a man having his tooth pulled," he said. "There is not so much pain, my dear Pierre, if he does not resist."

"Any day Austria and Prussia will come to our rescue," groaned Pierre. "Perhaps the tooth will not have to be pulled after all!"

"You aren't fool enough to believe Austria has any love for Louis and Marie Antoinette? . . . The foreign powers will only fight because they want royalty on the throne—any royalty—to dispel the ideas of Republicanism which are so fast taking hold throughout Europe. And don't deceive yourself that they haven't annexation in mind."

A waiter appeared with pigeons boiled in barley, and the men fell silent. Pierre found that now he was not hungry.

"Come, eat," urged Grégoire. "You're growing lank as a barber pole. . . . You're still confused, aren't you?"

"On the contrary, I never have been more determined."

"In your sense of values, I mean. I think of you often, Pierre. In the middle of a long harangue at the Assembly, in the middle of a game of chess, in the middle of the night. I know something of the struggle that has been going on within you. You are neither Jesuit nor Jansenist. Neither atheist nor deist . . . a little of all. But the fact remains that you were raised a Jesuit. That is why you cling to your mania of monarchy, raised hand in hand with it. Although by instinct you have always striven for liberty and initiative, you have been trained by the Abbé Blafond to obedience and direction. . . . Once a Jesuit, always a Jesuit!"

Pierre was angry. "You were the one who sent me to court."

"It seemed the lesser of two evils."

"You think me a lost soul, don't you?" Pierre went back to the Tokay, only toying with the pigeon.

"Sometimes I think that in your bewilderment you are only living through the church history of all France. The Edict of Nantes—massacres, dragonnades—the revocation of the Edict of Nantes. . . . The religion of France has evolved snail-like, just as the building of the Madeleine: a natural thing for a country—and a natural thing for a thinking man. . . ."

"Did you ask me here to upbraid me like a child?"

"No, no, no. I asked you here to warn you that if you do not leave France now it will make little difference what you think. Pierre. . . ." And Grégoire's kindly gray eyes were warm and pleading. "I have always loved you more than anyone in the world!"

The soft words penetrated the clank of dishes and wine glasses, the laughter of restless men, the sound of thirsty rain on the window panes, the cries of the street.

While his father went on feverishly about the coming dangers Pierre thought of Maurice and Gilbert. Gilbert and his father had only hunted and cleaned guns together. Maurice and his mother had only prayed together. But Pierre and Grégoire had shared many things, material and spiritual, in the few rare hours of their companionship: the beauty of a rainbow over the Seine, the bandaging of a limp dog, the love of a midnight candle over a book, a passion for pigeon cooked in barley. In their hearts they had often wept and rejoiced together; their eyes had met in understanding when words failed them.

Pierre believed that Grégoire was telling him the truth, that Grégoire loved him more than anyone in the world—more than Gilbert, or Maurice, or the son of Mme de Chenault, who so resembled him and was now in the east of France in a Protestant college.

Pierre was swept again with nostalgia for the early days. He knew that he and his father had lost one another, each thinking the other a weakling—just as he and his mother had lost one another after his marriage by Talleyrand. Today in spite of the love of his parents he was orphaned and alone. No one wholly shared with him his hopes or bafflement. No man, no woman, no child. . . .

He finished the Tokay, which tasted bitter, and mumbled something to his father about an appointment. Grégoire embraced him tenderly.

It was the last time they saw one another.

When Pierre returned to the house in the rue St. Germain, Victoire was still at the harpsichord. The delicate mahogany instrument with its inset of Wedgwood medallions jingled like a pocketful of coins. Dressed in elaborate yellow, a huge bowl of tea roses behind her, Victoire was part of the room's golden elegance.

But the room was stuffy, the shutters closed against the damp heat of August. (Moreover, Victoire's complexion was at much better advantage in taper light.) It seemed to Pierre that Victoire and the old

régime were already in hiding behind the closed eyes of the windows.
Or had his father's warning made him unduly melancholy?

Pierre greeted her indifferently and picked up the *Gazette of Leydon,*
a digest of all current opinions.

Victoire's answer was swallowed up by the ruthless sweep of her
fingers.

After a few moments Pierre laid the paper beside Victoire's smug
wedding bouquet, *sous cloche.*

"Victoire," he shouted above the jangling, "I would like to talk with
you."

Victoire ended abruptly on a discord and turned to him, curious at
the note of urgency in his voice.

"I have just dined with my father. He feels that you must get out of
France at once. There is to be further insurrection—more serious than
before."

"*Dieu merci!* I'll enjoy a good brawl. Life has become very dull."

"You mean—you prefer danger to safety?"

"*Pourquoi non?* . . . A powdered head on a pike gives one a delicious zest for living . . . and I am told the line at the Hôtel de Ville
waiting for passports is a mile long."

"My father can arrange for a passport if I fail. He has—influence,"
said Pierre with a certain bitterness. "And as for the head on the pike,
ma chère—if it happens to be *your* head the zest for living goes
with it!"

How altruistic of him, she thought, wanting to get rid of her! Wanting her "safe," far enough away that he would be under no obligation
to her. . . . Mlle Muguet must be a charmer indeed that Pierre would
prefer her alone, poor, to sharing her with Victoire and her fortune.

"I have no desire to relinquish my dowry to the state, my dear *ci-
devant*," she said acridly. "I shall stay here on the battleground and
fight for it."

Pierre shrugged. "Very well," he said. "*Vous êtes bien le maître.*"

And he went back to his reading.

She was unbalanced by the quick impetus of her success. So—he
didn't really care more than this if her head should be paraded up and
down the boulevards on a pike. One feeble argument and he was willing to have her murdered before his very eyes. . . . Perhaps now was
the time to enlighten him. . . .

She went over to the table beside him and leafed brusquely through
the *Journal des Dames.*

"Pierre," she said, with an attempt at softness, "I have something to tell you. . . ."

"*Oui, Mme Moqueuse?*" He continued his reading.

"*Je suis enceinte.*"

It took a few seconds for the truth to penetrate his muddled emotions. Somehow he had never dreamed that the giddy passion they shared with one another could beget a child. He leaped to his feet, staring at Victoire. What a boor he had been all these frenzied months! How interminably he had hurt her! Small wonder that she had been caustic and flippant. Natural for a woman with any sensitivity at all. And she *did* love him, poor thing, didn't she? He had guessed that long ago, and forgotten. . . . A son, a human being in his own likeness! A small Pierre de Michelait with all his father's virtues and none of his foibles! Already Pierre felt less alone. His hope began to swell within him like the seed within Victoire.

"I am very happy, Victoire," he said simply. His lips swept her forehead as his fingers drifted over her fichu.

Victoire was somebody new—a magnified part of himself. For the first time she felt soft in his arms, pliant as a reed, beckoning his heart as well as his flesh. He wanted to taste the newness of her, wanted to touch the tautening muscles of her belly. Her eyes too—they had lost their challenge—were almost frightened. . . .

Victoire was baffled, at once triumphant and defeated. An unborn child could evoke a fire in his eyes that she had never been able to stir, could rouse a tenderness in his touch that made her go limp. Fingers brushing her softly, so inviting that the memory of M. de Tuite's fumbling enraged her. Lips that no longer crushed a mocking smile from her own but trembled, lightly burning. The M. de Michelait of Mlle Violette. M. de Michelait, the lover. . . .

Chagrined, bewildered, her eyes became tawny. A dark flush of red covered the patches of scarlet on her cheeks, the thick coating of powder on her face and neck. She jerked away from him and began to run from the room with a whish of silk. In a few strides he snatched at her wrist.

"Victoire—you don't believe me?" he asked.

"*Oui, oui, oui,* but I want to be alone!"

"Now I insist that you go to Coblentz, *mignonne.* If you stay in Paris you might not even get a *surgeon-accoucheur* for the birth."

"And you might lose your precious son!" she exclaimed, her voice choking with angry tears. She wrenched her hand away from him.

Pierre's heavy brows contracted as she ran from the room. The moment of tenderness had been short-lived, he thought cynically, had evanesced like laughter in a dream . . . too new a sensation for them both, perhaps. But it would come again as she recovered her poise. A woman *enceinte* was emotional. . . . She was his wife, bearing him a child. Strange. . . .

❀❀❀❀❀❀❀❀❀❀❀❀❀❀❀❀❀❀❀❀❀❀❀❀

CHAPTER XVIII

Late August 1792

PIERRE and Dominique shared an attic room in an alley off the rue de Richelieu. It was a voluntary prison, the third hole Pierre had crawled into since the insurrection of August tenth at the Tuileries.

Pierre fingered a book on his knee as he sat in a lumpy armchair. Mice had long ago appropriated most of its curly stuffing. As his eyes read the words of Diogenes his mind wandered. For Jean de Batz had learned of his hide-out from Dominique, whom he met on the street, and the little Gascon was coming at any moment to see him. Baron de Batz would want to enlist his help for the royal family, he was almost certain.

The attic room was long and narrow with a slanting roof toward the street and two *mansarde* windows that would not shut. In several places bare laths with stringy balls of plaster gaped from the haggard walls. Someone had once made an attempt to cover them with prints of duchesses and hunting scenes and pink-beribboned cats. The pictures were helter-skelter over the room, some even at knee level; but in the end the laths had persevered. Four mouse-colored strings, cut from a grimy bed curtain, hung at the windows, which were murky with months of summer dust and rain. There was one bed; it slanted away from the wall so that Pierre found his feet pushing against the foot-

board when he awoke. Dominique slept on a trundle bed that boasted
its share of bedbugs. The rest of the furniture hinted of grandeur.
(The landlord had a secondhand shop on the ground floor.) A Louis
XIII wardrobe of cherry wood had been painted blue, white, and red;
as the brass handles were gone and the doors usually swollen from the
dampness, Dominique had to pry the latter open with his knife. Beside
the bed was a marble-topped table, minus a pie-shaped niche of marble.
The washbasin of gay, flowered china was glued together; Pierre had
to splash in a matter of forty seconds to race with the water as it
trickled to the floor. The room was strewn with books and pamphlets,
a few odd bits of clothing, a gallon bottle of wine, and a half-eaten
cheese. In the very center of the floor was a pot; it was not only handy
there but prevented Pierre from unwittingly twisting his ankle in the
gully beneath it. In a far corner was a tangle of junk to be repaired
before its swank appearance in the secondhand shop: brass firedogs, a
Wedgwood soup tureen (filled with spiders), a marten muff, a lyre, a
saddle, a pile of yellowed music, a doctor's kit. The assortment was
covered scantily with cheesecloth, and at night in the moonlight it took
on the form of a hunchbacked ghost with two heads and numerous
legs.

Several times Pierre heard quick footsteps that he thought must be
those of the Baron de Batz, but they dwindled away on the floor below.
It was painful trying to concentrate on printed words these days. Pierre
wondered for the thousandth time if Victoire had reached her parents
safely. She had fled to Coblentz the very day before the six hundred
reds arrived from Marseilles, singing that brave new marching song,
the *Marseillaise* which had so inflamed Paris. Once again, on the tenth
of August, the people had attacked the Tuileries; once too often Louis
had compromised with bloodshed and his Swiss Guards had been
brutally slaughtered. (A young lieutenant, Napoleon Bonaparte, jostled
by the crowd, had remarked scornfully that a quick sally by the Guards,
a handful of gunshot among the canaille would have scattered them
like hailstones.) The royal family had been escorted to the Assembly
and later had been taken prisoners to the Tower of the Temple where
the Commune allowed them to live at first in a grandiose manner.
The Tuileries was at once deserted and sacked, an empty beehive,
nobility hiding in the crevices of the city. Somehow it angered Pierre
immeasurably that his father had been able to warn him of the insurrection.

The tenth of August had seemed the end of everything. Seals had been put on Pierre's effects in the rue St. Germain and the rue d'Anjou, and a warrant was out for his arrest. Silvie had fled with Javotte to a room in the Palais-Royal. He had only dared to visit her once—in the early morning. She was thin, pale as porcelain. No, of course she was not working too hard, she said. But could she help being worried about her lover? And one no longer could dance with her heart in her toes. . . . The Opéra, the theaters, were filled with strange people who roared out patriotic songs. Women, *"tricoteuses,"* came with their knitting; tattered men, mud-bespattered, bloodstained, carried large knotted sticks and started brawls. One scarcely knew whether to keep on dancing or run to hiding.

Pierre watched the little motes of dust that floated through the hot August sunshine—like people floating through the ages. Straight ones, crooked ones, small ones, large ones. Slow ones, and fast. All drifting along in one direction. Some aimless, others with a purpose. Where did they come from? Where were they going? And what did it matter? *Guingette* or gallows—what does it really matter, he questioned? Relentless, the whole system, from the stars down to the dust. The stars, swept along in their course; the dust, swept along in its beam. And the little people, swept along in their social strata. Only now and then a shooting star. . . .

> *Men at some time are masters of their fates:*
> *The fault, dear Brutus, is not in our stars,*
> *But in ourselves, that we are underlings.*

What conclusion was it that he was coming to? That a priest can fight as well as a butcher, given a pike? Or must he come to some conclusion? He had never had any desire to be "master of his fate." Life for him had been a comfortable thing with little intervention—pleasant enough to return to after the allies reached Paris. . . .

Louis on the throne again. The gaiety of Versailles little tarnished by its recess. The whole episode of the Revolution an insignificant nightmare, like a heavy loss at *trente et un.* . . .

But somehow as he sat there trying to revive Versailles it refused to breathe. It lay heavy on his mind like some half-masticated banquet lying heavy in one's stomach. No thought of promiscuous shimmering white breasts or saucy red heels excited him. When one is nauseated no display of cream puffs can be tempting.

The truth of the matter was he had no desire to go back to Versailles. He wanted Versailles again only for Marie Antoinette and the royal family. The idea struck him like a boomerang. What he wanted for himself now with a curious fervor was threefold. Three things he had looked upon casually a few weeks before: the chance to look upon the face of his own son, the comfort of holding Silvie Hyacinthe in his arms, and a warm bath.

The Baron de Batz appeared suddenly without the noisy footsteps Pierre had been listening for. He entered with a swift knock, attempted to bolt the door behind him, and laughed silently with a shrug when he found the bolt was broken. He was dressed in the uniform of the National Guard. A Gascon, he was small and swarthy as a Spaniard.

"It's good to see a familiar face without a mustache!" Pierre greeted him and offered de Batz the privilege of the lumps.

Jean de Batz waved aside the offer and squatted down on a pile of books, panting from the many stairs and the heat.

"You make a charming sans-culotte," he whispered to Pierre, who was pouring bad wine for the two of them.

They grinned at one another. Jean de Batz's fingers were already gnawing at a pamphlet he had picked up.

"You know why I have come?" (The noblesse had learned one thing from the Revolution—that "time is of the essence.")

"I can guess."

"I've been trying to find you since August tenth. You have a reputation, you know, for wanting to die for Marie Antoinette."

Pierre made no answer. He had thought a good deal of death in the last few weeks. The idea was distasteful.

"No doubt you've had wind of the various attempts to get the royal family out of the Temple . . . Talon, in England, definitely has the sympathy of the British ministry. Louis de Noailles, in England too, is planning to get to France and rescue the Dauphin . . . M. de Versigny was actually in the Tower enclosure with a patrol of fifty bribed National Guards (they're easy to bribe as a child with candy), but there was too strong an opposing guard on hand. I wonder if you remember Lady Atkyns, that clever little ex-actress? She's been in to see the Queen (smart little thing, disguised as a sailor), but Marie Antoinette refuses to leave without Louis. So Lady Atkyns will concentrate on the Dauphin . . . and I—well I have bribed police spies all over the city. I have Republican officials and magistrates eating out of my hand . . . eating money, of course! Do you know Commissioner Michonis the lemonade man? He's one of the hungriest."

Jean de Batz paused to chuckle softly.

"You think nothing of your neck!" Pierre said.

De Batz looked up quickly. "Did you, *mon ami,* when you went to Varennes? Or when you saved the Queen at Versailles? . . . Besides, I've learned to dodge the Assembly like a trained flea. I've a dozen names and disguises—little attic holes like this all over Paris—as well as a hide-out in the country. . . . Money has never brought me more excitement. . . ."

"How is the Queen?"

"Her legs are badly swollen—the damp."

"*Dieu!* I can't bear to think of her suffering . . . You've seen her?" Pierre fingered in his pocket the ring that Marie Antoinette had given him. He could not think why he should be nervous facing the little Gascon, though the latter reminded him somehow of a busy scissors.

"I saw the Queen only a week ago while I was on guard duty at the Temple . . . she inquired for you; her faith in you seems unlimited."

"What can I do for her?" asked Pierre, staring at the rotten boards of the floor while his words rang metallic in his ears.

"That's what I've come to talk to you about. . . ." Jean de Batz whipped a fly away from his sweaty face and leaned so close to Pierre that their knees touched. "There seems little chance for the family's escape. And—there are rumors that the King will be brought to trial."

"How can a king be tried by citizens?" asked Pierre sharply

Jean de Batz laughed. "In a revolution anything can happen. Robespierre and the extremists know that a trail of the King would stir up the mob. There's been too much indifference to the Revolution lately—in spite of the excitement of inflation and the stagnation of industry. Then too, what better way is there for Robespierre and the Montagnards to get rid of the Girondins and their 'moderation'? Wouldn't a trial undermine the Girondins? If they don't vote the death sentence they'll be accused of lacking Republican zeal. If they do vote the death sentence they'll be accused of plotting for power for themselves, of being hypocrites about their ideal 'legal order.' Robespierre would have them caught nicely between two fires. And the field would be open to the demagogues."

"*Dieu!* Would a trial of Louis really mean death?"

"Death."

There was a creak in the hall and the two men jumped up, hands on their guns. Jean de Batz jerked open the door as if he expected an eavesdropper to fall in upon him. The hall was empty except for a cat.

The men laughed and slumped back to their seats, but they leaned closer together.

"If the King dies," whispered de Batz, and his small, thin fingers toyed with his sword, "the Queen will go next, *sans doute* . . . then—"

"The Allies will be here soon. They've got to come!"

"But if they don't! . . . We can't wait to see. We've got to plan *now* for the worst. . . . There's no safe place in Europe for the Queen. America is the only place that's safe."

"What do you have in mind?" asked Pierre, and he stirred uneasily.

"If the King's brought to trial will you go to America to plan an asylum for Marie Antoinette and the children? . . . Louis de Noailles has connections there, made when he was in Rochambeau's army. He's the one who suggested it—if his plans to get the Dauphin to England fail. A little colony in the wilderness—Pennsylvania perhaps—where the Queen and the children could be hidden till the Revolution is over. . . ."

"*America!* It's the end of the world!"

"But you'll do it?"

Pierre stared at him, waiting for the fanatic sense of loyalty to Marie Antoinette that had obsessed him all these years. He thought of the Queen in the Temple, her legs puffed and veined. He remembered his vow to her in the cottage of M. Sausse. He told himself that until the last few weeks no one but the Queen had mattered really. But he felt only a coldness within and without, an apathy humiliating, real. He could think zealously of nothing but the chance to see his son, to hold Silvie Hyacinthe in his arms again, to have a warm bath. Shame filled him as water fills the drowning.

Would it be such an outrage to leave Marie Antoinette and the children to their fates, to be master of his own fate for the first time in his life? To find his way to Coblentz and Victoire and be with her at the time of her confinement? Would it be cowardice to spirit Silvie away from this France that terrified her? How pale she had been, how passionate and pathetic that early morning he had roused her from her dreams! It was the first time he had accepted her love with gratitude. It was the first time that he and any woman had had a spiritual need of one another. Silvie was frightened. He couldn't leave her now. There were hundreds of able men who were eager to help Marie Antoinette; there was no one but himself who cared what became of Silvie. . . . If he went to America he would never see Silvie again. He would never see his child. And of what avail would his sacrifice be?

He groped painfully for the old obsession, shocked at its loss. But it was as if he tried to call back a loved one from the dead.

"What would come of it all?" he asked Jean de Batz, and his mouth was dry and his sticky clothing seemed to strangle him. The two eyes of jet were boring into him as if he were a traitor. "What would be the end?"

"The old régime again—Marie Antoinette on the throne. Or Louis Charles on the throne. . . . We can do it! I know we can do it!"

"And Versailles again?"

"*Mais oui.* With a ministry for you, and châteaux lined with francs!"

"I don't want a ministry! I don't want all the old rot for my son," exclaimed Pierre, aghast as if he were making confession of a murder. "Did you know I am going to have a son? I want to see him. I want—"

"I know, I know!" And Jean de Batz ran his fingers through his black hair spiked by perspiration. "You want to live on in him. . . . That's fear of death. Everyone's got it, hiding like this in a garret— waiting for a stab in the back. It gets the nerves worse than any battle. . . . You want peace. But how can you get it if you aren't willing to meet struggle and danger first? What's come over you, *mon ami?* You were the bravest man at Versailles on the fifth of October! Has your liver turned so pale?"

"I don't know," faltered Pierre with a lack of resentment that amazed and baffled him. If he were any kind of a man he would strike de Batz on his impudent mouth! "I've always vowed I'd give my life for Marie Antoinette. But America—it's the end of the world!"

"Obviously Marie Antoinette has misplaced her trust," said the little Baron cruelly.

Pierre flushed, jumping up, and stalked to the window. "Oh God, I'm not the coward you think!" he exclaimed. "You look at me as if I were a yellow rat! . . . I can't say what's come over me. I'm half dead inside!"

"I know what's come over you. You're human like the rest of us, my young hero. . . . You miss the down of your bed in the rue d'Anjou, and your crêpes suzettes, and your bath! Well, if you want these things again you've got to fight for them. Come, Monsieur, say you will go to the States and you'll find the words give you as much courage as a Versailles meal."

"There are others who can go to the States."

"Other men have sons!"

Jean de Batz jumped up too, challenging Pierre like a tiger.

"M. de Michelait, would you desert France and your Queen?"

They glared at one another. For a long moment neither of them moved . . . then Pierre downed the glassful of wine at a gulp.

"I'll let you know," he said grimly. "I'll let you know through Dominique—in a few days."

"*Bien*," said Jean de Batz, and the frigidness that was more cutting than the small, black eyes thawed out a little. "Tell him to ask for M. Forget. That is my name in the National Guards . . . But I know your answer. It could be nothing else but yes. Marie Antoinette gets into one's blood. . . ."

He raised his wineglass, whispered huskily: "To our Queen!", swallowed the bad wine with a grimace, and smashed the glass on the bed post.

Then he left as abruptly as he had come.

CHAPTER XIX

September 2, 1792

"I KEEP THINKING that any minute I'll hear it!" murmured Dominique as he stooped over a torn gray shirt he was mending. "I keep hearing the tocsin ring—but it's only in my ears."

Pierre lay sprawled on his bed as if he were racked on a wheel. He stared at the broken tiles of the roof beyond and tried to turn his mind from the cries and bells in the street and the horror of the tocsin. But he could bear still less to think of himself. He loathed himself, loathed the coward that Jean de Batz had seemed to make of him. And the vow he'd made Marie Antoinette at Varennes to give his life to her service: "I swear it—I swear it by all that's holy!" . . . But that was before he knew he would have a son. . . . *Dieu,* what was wrong with his thinking? He hadn't been eating enough lately, that was the trouble. Although there were *assignats* stuffed behind all the laths of the leprous wall, he and Dominique had been afraid to market. And how could one think clearly hidden from light like a rat in the sewer, waiting breathless now for the new massacres at the prisons?

Three hundred assassins, recruited from released convicts and tradesmen and the newly arrived Marseillaise, had been employed by Danton. At a given signal they would break open the prisons and fall upon the aristocrats. The bourgeoisie had been removed from their cells.

Several nights before, domiciliary visits had been made by communal officers to detect weapons hidden by suspected persons. The city's barriers were now closed and guarded so no one could escape. Three thousand more of the nobility had been thrown into prison. Pierre knew his own name must be among the first on the police list.

"This will be the worst slaughter of all," Dominique said dry-lipped, his fingers trembling as they picked up the needle again.

"Because the masses believe what Danton tells them," Pierre exclaimed. "That the *émigrés* and Austrians are already at the gates of the city to destroy them."

"Today the baker said to me—you know, the one with the wart— 'Shall we march to the frontier and leave our wives and children to the mercy of aristocrats who may break prison and kill them? *Non, non, non*—not if we can break into the prisons and get at them first!' "

"Then the people believe that infernal propaganda of Danton— that Louis plots with the nobility to fall upon the common people within Paris while the Allies push on them from without. . . . *Dieu!* It's just a dictator's lie to get what he wants. Danton and the Commune have ordered this attack on the prisons in cold blood simply to terrorize the aristocrats and so thwart the advance of the enemy."

Dominique shook his head and his eyes began to water. "They say all's fair in love and war," he mumbled. "*Dieu,* M. Pierre, you are fighting for a lost cause."

Pierre felt the angry thud of his heart. Dominique himself had brought to Pierre the news that Verdun must fall to the Allies—the very news that precipitated the massacres. Of course, nothing could prevent the massacres now. But the cause was not a lost cause, thought Pierre. Another week, another two weeks, perhaps, and there would be victory for the Queen. No need for a refuge in America—no need for him to make a decision! The trick, of course, was to keep one's noble neck in hiding until the Prussians and Austrians reached the gates of Paris and released the royal family.

A new church bell began to clang loudly and Dominique jumped to his feet. But the bell was only striking the hour. He sank onto his stool again, his olive face turned scarlet and his hands trembling and mottled. The heavy beard that he wore now was gristled with gray like the hair that hung to his shoulders.

"This time I was sure it was the tocsin." He laughed, unsteadily and went on with a high nervous pitch to his voice: "*Oui*, M. Pierre, you are fighting for a lost cause. You must know by now that the people will be free. You wish to be free yourself. You have proven that in your unorthodox marriage."

"Who knows what freedom is?" Pierre retaliated bitterly. "For you it is one thing; for me it is another!" And falling back on his bed again, he closed his eyes so that Dominique would stop this chatter.

It seemed to Pierre that of late Dominique was like a sputtering candle. It was quite different being served by him in a palace and living with him in a tenement. Dominique snored; he languidly picked his toes; one could see his tongue swish in his mouth like a cow's when he ate; and at every new sound he lurched like a coil spring set in motion. A dozen times a day Pierre reminded himself of Dominique's long, faithful service to the family only to be irritated by the valet's squint again.

Dominique had a mole under one shoulder blade too. Nothing about the mole. It didn't bother Pierre. Why should it? Just that Pierre noticed the mole every time Dominique removed his shirt. It was curious to think the mole had always been there. For years, when Dominique had been serving him at Versailles and at Paris, the mole had been hiding under his shoulder blade. Pierre had never supposed that there was anything about Dominique that he didn't know. It had never occurred to him that Dominique might have a crooked toenail, or that Dominique would have to use the china pot over the gully in the floor boards. Now it seemed as if Dominique were a hypocrite.

In the one moment that Pierre forgot the tocsin it began to sound. It began with one agitated bell and then in a flash there were a thousand echoes clanging. Through the jumbled notes of the scale came the booming of cannon, the incessant roll of drums. Paris was in arms! In the street below were shouts and people tumbling from the shops. Pierre and Dominique, each at a window, watched the holocaust.

Pierre's heart thumped like the tocsin. *Dieu,* but it was agony to have to watch the fight from his cage, to remain in hiding! He sank down on the edge of the bed again, covered his face with his hands.

Dominique's face had grown lavender, and his words sputtered like fat in a spider. He would follow the throng, would be back in an hour to report the news.

Pierre was left alone. M. Valdeux the landlord and his daughter Angélique would wonder why he hadn't joined the mob with a pike. A good sans-culotte like himself. . . . He laughed and rose to look at himself in the mirror, a golden sunburst with half the mirror missing. . . . His beard was of three days' growth, and his hair hung in greasy black curls about his neck. The coarse cotton pantaloons were red-and-white striped. (He had cut a hole in one knee so that Dominique could patch it.) A tricolored carmagnole covered the blouse he wore, which was gray and smudged and short-sleeved. At first the sabot had made blisters on his feet. (How soft were these aristocrats, Dominique had bantered!) The earring, thought Pierre, gave him a good gypsy mien . . . how Silvie would scream at his disguise if she could see him!

But Angélique would never scream, he thought. *Nom de Ciel!* How long would the tocsin go on ringing? Already his head was split with a thousand clanging axes. . . . Not that he had ever touched Angélique. On the contrary, he always avoided looking at her as he went out of the house and passed the shop. He had never stooped to an eight-franc *fille!* At least it could be said that a de Michelait had more pride than a d'Orléans.

What agony it was to wait, wait, wait! . . . By now, he supposed, the prisons would be assaulted. At this moment perhaps someone he knew was being hacked to pieces. Why had Maurice come to this fomenting Paris? But Maurice, of course, was safe in hiding.

He drank freely of the wine as if it were water. There were times when a man couldn't forget . . . he must drink until he could lie quietly on the bed, to defy the waiting and the confusion of his mind.

Finally he slept. He wakened with a lurch.

A strange tomcat, which had entered by the window, meowed on his chest and sent his pulse flying. He whisked it angrily to the floor. But at least the cat had brought him to his senses. The sun was going down. The roof tops were red, very red—too red, he thought, for September. If he closed his eyes the roof tops shimmered red beneath his eyelids like a sea of blood. He would have to move, to swim, or the sea would engulf him. He would have to get out of the room if he didn't want to go mad. Dominique tried to keep him here like a chained monkey. . . .

And how could the wine jug be empty? *Sapristi,* the cat must have drained it! . . . Well, he would risk a trip to the cabaret to fill it.

He remembered that he had washed his hands at noon, so he went over to the pile of junk and ran his arms and hands across a filthy ottoman. Then he dug his finger tips in a flower pot with a dead geranium on the sill. He could feel the earth jamming uncomfortably under his nails. His linen seemed to suck at his skin. *Dieu,* but he wanted a bath—a warm bath!

He seized the empty wine jug and billowed down three flights of rotten stairs, cracking his head once or twice against the wall. One floor reeked of tobacco, another of boiling leek, and a third of cheap cologne. At the attic the odors combined in a stinking miasma.

Pierre passed the dozing concierge and paused at the door that gave onto the street. The façade of the ancient house was of crumbling plaster and rotting wood peppered with rusty nails. It slanted ominously toward a cabaret next door. From a yawning crack in the wall hung a sign with three gilded balls.

The folded shutters of the shop, open by day, exposed a few pieces of jewelry on a slab, *"bijoux à la constitution."* There were plaques of china enameled in blue, white, and red; earrings of white glass with *"la patrie"* on them; and souvenirs of the Bastille, pieces of crushed stone in rings and brooches combined with flashing gems. In the window also were other decoys: an ivory needle case, not too yellow; an ermine scarf minus a few tails; a pair of eyeglasses (with just a small crack in one lens) mounted in gold and enamel.

Pierre did not look into the shop as he passed for he knew that Angélique would be there in the shadows.

Angélique was plump, with the pink satin skin of a redhead. She never moved but stood like a tinted wax statue in the doorway or at the shop window. The wavy titian locks escaped languorously from her limp cap; her full bosom blossomed from under a sleazy shawl. Pierre had noticed the first time he saw her that her eyes seemed to follow him like the eyes of a portrait. Small brown slits, they were, with lashes absurdly long clinging to her baby cheeks. Her wide mouth rippled, hinting vaguely at a smile. The girl irritated him beyond reason—everything about her, from the overflowing hips to the scanty petticoat.

Pierre had no idea how long he stayed in the cabaret. Bits of news drifted in with each newcomer. Nobody paid attention to one more sweaty sans-culotte lolling in his dirty corner guzzling wine.

"*Ventre St. Gris!*" cried a clogmaker, flinging his arm about an *ébéniste* beside him. "How they ran! . . . Like the three blind mice from the carving knife!"

"*Comment?*"

"The nonjuring fathers. At the seminary of St. Firmin. One was thrown from the top story and met his death squashed like a piece of raspberry tart! . . . He, he, he."

The little *ébéniste* trembled. He was a good Catholic at heart. "But the priests were to have safe escort from Paris to a place of deportation!" he exclaimed. "And three livres a day for the journey."

"Priests! Fooh, our enemies! Accomplices of those who gave up Verdun. Waiting to murder my wife and children. The nonjuring aren't safe while my saber can cut butter, *ébéniste!*"

"They were dragged to the Abbey," added a burly goldsmith. "And the assassins were waiting. Zip, twenty-one heads! . . . And at the Convent of the Carmelites, zip-zip—a whole garden full of priests! The roses'll bloom large there, come the summer. The Archbishop of Arles, the Bishop of—"

"He was a stubborn one, the Archbishop," cried the clogmaker, "the way he fought. Those that raise their arms peaceful are wise, get it more direct—don't make the sword curl into their throat or heart and suffer longer. The *bêtes!*"

Pierre's glass relaxed in his moist fingers and he was forced to set it on the table so that he would not drop it. *Nom de Dieu,* could his mother have witnessed this carnage? And Maurice—why hadn't Maurice stayed in Agen instead of coming to Paris? But it was like Maurice—nearsighted. There was the time when Maurice had walked into the bonfire and his blouse had burst into flames. . . .

Why did the tocsin begin again, as if it were frightened, running? . . . *Mais oui,* to remind all good citizens that the Commune ordered an Assembly at the Champ-de-Mars tonight. By the morrow fifty thousand more soldiers must leave Paris to meet the enemy.

"Come, little *ébéniste,* you will make a brave soldier!" mocked the clogmaker, half tossing him into the air. "Let the army buy your bread at six sous the pound! . . . Don't starve, little *ébéniste,* join the army!"

"And get shot by the Austrians?" cried the thin little cabinetmaker. "Then my good wife won't even have my sixteen sous wages a day!

Non, non, non," and he struggled to free himself like an incommoded bug.

"While you're gone let her live two days a week on potatoes as Santerre orders! Or let her hang the dog! He'll fry juicy. And if the Austrians get you, *ébéniste,* she can throw away her bread ticket from the mayor and marry the baker!"

The goldsmith started singing the *Ça-Ira,* and soon the whole cabaret had joined him.

There was a great guffaw of laughter, for the little *ébéniste* shrank from the horseplay. Pierre kept his eyes glued on the wine glass before him. He felt sorry for the little cabinetmaker—but one could not afford to feel sorry for anyone out of his own class. Give the *ébéniste* a pike, brooded Pierre, and he would dash out the heart of Marie Antoinette as soon as the clogmaker. Marie Antoinette . . . Would Jean de Batz ever tell her about Pierre de Michelait the coward?

Tossing down a remnant of biscuit, he picked up his wine jug and went out onto the street where the red of the sunset had been swallowed by evening. The street lamps were unlighted, for there was a full moon. For a moment he stood in the vast shadow of the stone tablet that bore the name of the street, and leaned against the iron pole; the cries of the city had dwindled but there was a new tension in the nightfall. A sudden slamming of a door, a shrill cry of a parrot, a quick step running down the cobblestones, a child's whine. Groups of men were talking heatedly and now and then there was the figure of a woman in a doorway, fanning herself with her apron. Lights twinkled in the windows, mostly in the upper stories for below there were shops.

Pierre passed the window of the secondhand shop. The shutters were not quite closed. But he did not look in. Angélique would be standing there. Angélique who, like his conscience, never slept! Or she would be standing at the peephole that her father used, to look down on the street from his living quarters on the floor above.

Angélique . . . her skin would be like a pudding to the touch, he thought, revolted. Soft and cool and the color of maraschino beaten into egg white. Paris was filled with men, he thought; what did the girl want of anyone sullen as himself?

He stopped inside the closed door of his attic and listened. Was it the scream of dying priests and nobility that rose like a siren? Strange, the minute he halted the sound stopped and there was only the creak of the aged stairway.

Then he knew suddenly that he was not alone. Fear ran through his body like wind over water.

"*Soyez le bienvenu!*" he exclaimed, tautly on guard, his hand at his pistol.

A laugh greeted him. It rolled over lazily like a porpoise in the sun. Then he saw the outline of Angélique's figure in the moonlit frame of the window.

He was angry, both because she had frightened him and because she presumed to come here.

"*Qu'est-ce que c'est que vous voulez?*" he demanded. Couldn't she tell he had no need of a sloven with billowing hips and soiled linen? The anodyne of a bourgeois!

She slipped noiselessly over to him and he felt her hands on his shoulders. Her fingers had a curious warmth through his shirt, and it flashed through his mind that it was their plumpness and pinkness that gave him the burning sensation.

"So—you can move!" he exclaimed. "You can laugh and breathe!"

She laughed again. And now he could feel the warmth of her breath on his face. He tossed her hands from his shoulders roughly.

"Ah, so you beat your women, Monsieur!"

"*Mais oui*—if they like it!" he said gallantly.

And now he felt her hands on his shoulders again, fingers slipping into the strands of his long hair.

His pulse suddenly went headlong, like one released from the top of a toboggan slide. And he pulled her to him, his lips against the rippling mouth with its vague moist smile. The roundness of her cheek and the large bosom yielding to the hard pressure of his body reminded him of a feather bed. Yes, she was the kind of woman a bourgeois would want to beat. . . .

She was the anodyne of a bourgeois. He pushed her from him and brushed the moisture of her kiss from his lips with the back of his hand.

"Get out!" he commanded quickly.

He had no proof of her leaving, no motion, no sound. But she was gone. He listened for a step on the stair. And then he laughed aloud. Could it be he was foggy with wine? And that he had fancied? . . . He knew for certain that the girl never moved—that she was a wax figure whose eyes only seemed to follow him onto the street, whose breasts only looked like a pudding, soft, the color of maraschino beaten into egg white. . . .

He flung himself down on the bed and was immediately asleep.

During the night Pierre wakened.

Dominique had returned and was on his knees before an improvised *prie-dieu.* The candle guttered on the seat of the armchair. Propped against the back of the *bergère* was a faded print of the Mother Mary partly torn from frequent folding. Dominique's rosary lay on the lumpy cushion and he fingered it nervously.

Pierre stared at him, fascinated. Dominique's hands were red-streaked, shaking. Once Dominique held out his hands before him, palms down, then palms upward. The fingers trembled as if with palsy. The back of his shaggy head stood out in sharp relief against the gold of candlelight. There was something sinister about the bent head, the cringing shoulders. Pierre felt a sickening in the pit of his stomach and said sharply: "Dominique!"

The servant stumbled to his feet with a startled cry and for a moment stood gazing down at Pierre a little crazily.

"What is it?" demanded Pierre, sitting upright.

Dominique raised his fluttering fingers to his mouth, then quickly tore them from his lips, staring at them incredulously. His face was blotched with purple; the small, piercing eyes were blurred.

"Maurice . . ." he whispered.

Pierre jumped to his feet and clutched the shivering Dominique with two strong hands.

"They've murdered Maurice!" Pierre cried sharply.

Dominique nodded. "At the convent of the Carmelites," he whispered. "But when it was dark I . . . I. . . ."

He stared at Pierre, his body swaying. Pierre was unable to speak. For a long time they stood taut, gazing at one another. Finally Pierre shook him roughly. A torrent of words broke loose like a hemorrhage.

"I found his body in the mound of corpses in the convent garden. I dragged it to the rue de Grenelle. The Abbé Blafond blessed it. . . ."

Pierre dropped the streaked wrist and looked at his own fingers in anguish. He expected them to be scarlet.

"We buried him," whispered Dominique, "in the garden—under the window of the bedchamber of Mme la Marquise, your mother."

❁❁❁❁❁❁❁❁❁❁❁❁❁❁❁❁❁❁❁❁❁❁❁❁❁

CHAPTER XX

PIERRE jammed on the red nightcap of the sans-culotte and slipped on a leather jerkin. He wanted to see the fresh grave in the rue de Grenelle. Dominique clung to Pierre, pleading with him not to go. But Pierre was determined. He had never loved Maurice before. He had only taunted Maurice, who could not run fast enough. But now that Maurice was gone he loved him. *Dieu,* he would give a hundred lives for one more glimpse of the warm Maurice with his bishop's miter!

The early dawn was mouse gray and roofs were ectoplasm against the sky. Even in this hour of rage and sorrow he could not escape Angélique. As he stalked down the street he was obsessed with the thought that she stood within the shop, watching, watching. Not only her half-closed eyes now, but her wayward, drooping mouth with its rough pink tongue. He would never have kissed the slut if he hadn't been drinking. . . .

He walked past the Palais-Royal, longing to rouse Silvie and pour out a flood of emotion in her arms. She would be sleeping with her hand across her face, like a lily hiding under a sheath before its unfolding. Silvie loved him.

Creeping over the Pont-Royal, he clung to the shadows, avoiding the market wagons returning home and the shivering clerks hurrying to their business. A few stragglers and milkmaids and beggars were abroad. Now and then he saw the deserted carriage of an aristocrat. The traces had been cut and the horses seized to go to battle with fifty thousand men recruited at the Champ-de-Mars.

The boats of the Seine stirred and stretched for the work of the day. On the Left Bank washerwomen and anglers grew out of a roll of fog. Watermen's barbers and dog shearers were setting up trade, and dockmen and sand carters and tollmen came to life and whistled. Another day had begun as usual as if Paris had not just ripped open her own belly!

It was no longer the Paris of friendly cries and familiar odors and mad haranguing, thought Pierre. It was a monster that had thrown the gauntlet—a maniac who had killed Maurice, an aristocrat. Until now, the word "Révolution" was a matter of five round syllables rolled from fanatic tongues; a matter of hide-and-seek till the Allies should come marching with laurels.

The sky became saffron with dawn as Pierre reached the Hôtel Michelait and slipped into the garden from the rue du Bac.

The garden, bordered by the coach house on the north and the mansion on the south, was overgrown with weeds. High walls hid the marble benches and bird baths from the street. It seemed impossible that in so short a time the fountains looked parched. Two gravel walks, flanked by parterres, met at a small shrine under a row of linden trees. The flowers were tangled and gave out a strong funereal scent. Gilbert and Pierre had sometimes played hide-and-seek in the garden, and the shrine of the Mother Mary was "base." Some little Protestant urchin had once climbed over the wall and put a mustache on the Mother Mary.

Under this lazy sod with its tangled flowers—a few feet away— Maurice lay then dead with rusty wounds? There where the ground sagged a little and the broken roots and bruised petals hid the secret of murder? Yes, here was the spot, clots of brown earth overflowing onto the gravel. The grave of an aristocrat who had escaped the ignominious common grave of quicklime. Pierre wrung the loathsome red nightcap of the sans-culotte in trembling hands.

He felt cold and weak, assailed with misgiving. Had Maurice been draped in a winding sheet or had Dominique slung clods of earth over his face in the frenzied fear of discovery? Had Maurice a cross in his hand? What words had the little Abbé stammered with his tears and blessing? . . . There was the small, neat footstep of the Abbé pressed firmly into the soil—firmly, even as he had pressed into the heart of Maurice his Jesuitism. Here also was buried a part of himself, Pierre knew, a part of Catherine, Grégoire, Gilbert, a part of his caste.

For a moment Pierre had a strange conviction that it was he, Pierre, who lay in the ground dead; that it was Maurice who stood staring down at the earth, sobbing.

"You see," Maurice said distinctly, "I am not dead. I have faith. The kind of faith does not matter. Jansenism, Jesuitism, Buddhism . . . what matters is that one has faith, a virile faith to carry him safely over into the Beyond."

Pierre hid his burning eyes in his hands. He was not sure whether Maurice had spoken or not. And he wanted to seize the word "faith"

in his fists—the cursed word that had plagued him for years—seize it
and tear it into a thousand filaments.

It was faith that had struck Maurice into the ground—faith that had
sent him tumbling into a bed of worms. Faith—he would scream like
a madman if he ever heard the word again! Ah, how his head careened,
like a carrousel! . . . And there was something about Angélique he
did not understand—if he had really kissed the soft, pulpy lips or
dreamed it. . . . *Dieu,* the sweetness of petunia was more than one
could bear before the sun came up! . . . and the thought of Maurice,
stiff and cold; the thought of his eyes, glazed with death, clotted with
dirt from the spade. . . .

He would like to rush out to the cold nirvana of the river, rush out
with the river to meet the sea. Or he would like to fill his body with
some ineffable joy.

"Sorrow and joy," he thought, shuddering, lucid for a moment, "sorrow and joy are two depths of emotion, two opposite poles. But they
both flame within one. Joy bursts its bounds so that finally the elation
and the body seem to rise into the blue like two butterflies, floating,
soaring, mating. . . . But sorrow is caught, confined within the shell,
straining, storming to be released until every fiber of the body pains
unbearably with the imprisonment. A world, an eternity of tragedy
caught within the small human bounds of one heart. Joy and sorrow,
both of them flaming. . . ."

"Joy and sorrow," began the twittering of the birds in the linden
trees. "Joy and sorrow."

Pierre fell on his knees and began to pray glibly, a gushing of empty
Aves out of his spiritual vacuum. But it was what Maurice would
want, to help him out of purgatory. . . .

Maurice, his fat fingers toying with the silver flute; Maurice, clinging
wildly to a branch of the apple tree; Maurice, his nearsighted eyes
adoring Catherine; Maurice, humming out of tune; Maurice, getting
only one cherry if there were five to divide. Maurice, who always lost
a game. Never able to run fast enough, stumbling, always overcome—
as in a dream. Maurice, Maurice, Maurice! . . .

At a sound from the carriage house Pierre leaped up and rushed
through a web of ivy and honeysuckle to the street beyond. Leaning
against the wall, breathless, he waited. If the grave were discovered
Maurice would not even be able to lie dead in peace. . . . Perhaps it
had only been the Abbé Blafond creeping down from his hiding place

in the stable. But Pierre never wished to see the Abbé Blafond again.

He listened to the furious clamoring of his heart. "Maurice, Maurice, Maurice!" it said. "Or was it "Silvie, Silvie, Silvie!"? He wanted nothing at this moment but the sweetness of revenge for the blow the Revolution had struck him, for the part of himself that lay strangled below the earth. There was only one way to meet murder, and that was with murder!

And then he heard the voice of Maurice again, soft, blending with the chirp of the birds: *"Merci, mon Pierre,* for the tears. They water the soul and make it bloom in eternity . . . but do not fret that I could not run fast enough from death. One does not even have to run, if one has *faith."*

Seven o'clock in the morning found Pierre at La Force prison, swept along with the tide of the hungry underworld. The massacre had started there shortly after midnight. Now as he was jostled in the courtyard under the black boulders of the building, the sun flashed brightly over the carnage, over the hundreds of shouting people. At regular intervals, an aristocrat was tossed from the mouth of the jail like a fish to a seal, and met with eager, jabbing pikes. A few screams, perhaps, before the blood, spurting fresh from another corpse, gurgled over the cobblestones of the yard and into the sewer.

Pierre scarcely knew how he had come here. He only knew that his being here had vaguely to do with revenge, that the desire to kill surged faster through his veins than the blood of the murdered over the paving stones. He must wet his feverish lips over and over; he must stare and stare at the victims who were thrust out on the doorstep fresh from the tribunal that convicted them; he must cry out with madness when each one fell. No one knew that his cry was not one of triumph. No one knew that he was waiting, trembling, for the moment to attack. . . .

The tocsin had begun again, and now it was not a sound of bells but a jingling of addled brains in his own head. A few feet away a score of men and women were doing a wild, ancient dance; their drunken voices screaming to the beat of their wooden shoes on the stones:

"Dansons la Carmagnole, vive le son! Vive le son! Dansons la Carmagnole, vive le son du canon!"

It was a savage orgy, with a flinging of arms and legs so abandoned

that they seemed detached from their bodies. Now a yellow arm leaped
skyward; now a gleaming saber. A bloody shoe hit Pierre on the shoulder, leaving a smudge of red on his blouse.

Under the wall a group of *égorgeurs* devoured soup brought by their
wives; when the assassins began to flag they were spurred on by brandy
mixed with gunpowder. The assassins were drenched in blood. It
was clotted in their hair, dried in their ears; their clothes were stiff
and reeking.

One of them, cross-eyed, reeling, slobbered soup from his wooden
bowl down the bosom of a fishwoman he was embracing. She screamed
lustily.

"*Dieu!* Such noise!" he howled at her. "I'm weary as a hodman
that's been beating plaster all day. *Scélérat!*"

And as he brandished his ax she vanished.

But now there was new refreshment. An old woman, her skirts
caught up in the basket of hot rolls she was carrying, halted coquettishly
before the *égorgeurs*. They attacked the bread like vultures with new
cries and cheers. But the soup was gone! . . . What, must they eat the
rolls dry? Never! Not when there was the blood of an aristocrat!

The cross-eyed man with the bludgeon wheeled about to the pile
of corpses awaiting the dead wagon. Slung across the edge of a stone
block was a young man, his eyes staring upward, his body convulsed
with the last death gasp. From a wound in his thigh, the blood bubbled
over the rich yellow brocade of his suit. The man with the bludgeon
dipped his hot roll into the gash, swished the roll about a few times
so that it might absorb the blood better, and sank his teeth into the
tasty red sponge. With shouts of envy other assassins crowded over to
the mass of dying, shoving the corpses about like apples, to find one
that was sufficiently bleeding.

Pierre felt that the time had come to strike. It mattered little to him
that if he sank his knife into the man with the bludgeon a thousand
pikes would sink at once into his own flesh. He tried to lunge through
the mass of onlookers, crushing those near him with a new strength
that was brutal and superhuman.

But now above the din of the Carmagnole was a scream so piercing
that a comparative hush descended on the hundreds within the courtyard. The Princess de Lamballe, confidante of the Queen, beautiful
and childlike, was facing her doom.

Pierre forgot the man with the bludgeon. He tried to call to the
Princess de Lamballe, to shout that he would save her or die with

her. But nobody heard him, for like a sea closing in on an island, the mass swayed and pushed toward her. A moment later and she had dropped from sight. Shouts arose. Pierre could see the pikes lunging crazily, like hail.

"Let me through—let me get to her!" he cried, trying to force his way with the point of his knife, and the human flesh began to open for him like the Red Sea. What an avid young sans-culotte that he could not even await his turn, laughed a crony with two fangs for teeth.

Princess de Lamballe, limp on the pavement, was already dead.

An eager ghoul had torn her clothes from her, tossing them like confetti on a heap of burning rags. The heart that had held so much love for her Queen was torn out and hoisted, dripping red and pulpy, on a rusty harpoon. Her belly lay ripped open like a fresh-caught fish, her bowels oozing slimy gray serpentine from a froth of blood.

Pierre gazed at her, retching. The horror in her staring eyes clutched at him, held him hypnotized. He did not know whether the cold tremor that he felt went through his body or hers, for her lips were still twitching, and he thought that she breathed. . . . Oh, God, she couldn't be breathing! God strike her dead at once, now, before another excruciating second!

Amid the shouts of *Ça-Ira* the intestines were snipped in small bits and passed about for souvenirs; the old woman with the fangs lost her footing on the slippery mass and shrieked out a joke about jelly.

A giant of a man sliced the soft white breasts of the Princess de Lamballe from her bosom, deftly as a tailor slashing through a length of white silk. He held one aloft in his ham of a hand and sucked noisily at the nipple of the other.

"*Ah, c'est frais et tendre comme beurre!*" he bragged.

A shout of envy and adulation rose from the crowd.

"How the Queen would be jealous!"

"Pass it about like a loving cup!"

The second tidbit was tossed into the air and a dozen hands scrambled for it.

"*Dansons la Carmagnole, vive le son!* . . ."

"*A bas les aristocrats!*"

"*Allons, enfants de la patrie!*"

"*Donnez-moi un gôut!*"

And now a thin little man, with lips like a blowfish and a birthmark that might have been dried blood, knelt beside the body. With his penknife he cut off the golden-brown hair of the pudendum. As he held it up to his lips for a mustache the applause was maximum, and a virago gave his rakish mouth a kiss.

For a moment Pierre felt no more than a mote of dust, and prison and people swam in a great black shadow. But if he fainted he could not strike back. . . . He came alive again with a stupendous effort. He would not kill the man with the bludgeon. He would kill the man with the mustache, with the birthmark. He began to force himself again through the gallery.

By now the comedy of the mustache was forgotten; the head of the Princess de Lamballe was being hacked from her body.

"To the Temple!" cried the man with the birthmark. "Let the Lamballe call on the Queen at the Temple!"

And now the head of the Princess teetered on another pike, the eyes jutting, the golden hair clotted, the neck in vermilion shreds.

Pierre tried to think. He must get to the little man with the birthmark. . . . Somewhere before, he had seen the little man with the birthmark, had hated him then too. *Dieu,* it was hard to push his way through to the little man! It would be sweet to sink his knife into his filthy vitals, to see the ugly blood spurt out. . . . Strange to be a murderer, like these others. Strange and sweet. . . .

"To the Queen . . . to the Queen! Give the Queen her lover again, her blushing little Princess. . . ."

With cheers a procession had already started for the Temple, Princess de Lamballe's head leading the way on its pike. Pierre, only a few feet now from the man with the mustache, was swept along with the current. His hand dropped, inert. They would have to live a while longer; the thin man and himself.

The thin man, attracted by Pierre's savage eyes, stared at him curiously and a flicker of recognition passed over his face. But his attention was drawn to a new victim.

An aged aristocrat, his body transfixed with lances, his face singed with torches, was being compelled to walk on his knees while the blood poured from his side. His groans penetrated the laughter like distant thunder. Behead him? . . . Not yet, *bêtes!* Not so long as he made funny contortions like a drunken octopus! Here, let him drink a glass of his daughter's blood. That would strengthen him!

Neatly begging the old man's pardon for walking before him, a sergeant with a sack of dead aristocrats' jewelry for the town hall picked his way among the cheering.

The triumphant horde that possessed the head and torso of the

Princess left the courtyard, the men outdoing each other with obscene songs and joking. Pierre among them avoided the carts that jogged out to the street. They were filled with naked corpses, a grotesque medley of staring eyes, faces cleft in two, and fingers stiff as the twigs of winter trees. The throng flooded into the rue des Ballets, and while they stopped at a hairdresser to have the lovely ringlets of the Princess washed and powdered, the women, always energetic, began the Carmagnole. It was a wonderful show for the streets of Paris, a vast diversion from the sweeping of stairs, the cooking of soup. It gave the September morning a piquancy, like sherry in a sauce. People began to accrue to the parade in hundreds. And watches and earrings changed hands like April sun and shower.

At last the head was washed and curled and back on its pike. But the face was too chalky blue, cried a chorus. Ah, now someone was rouging the cheeks with a blob of house paint.

It was a gray-haired man, not an old man but a man who looked old. The back of his shoulders had a familiar stoop. When he turned about, his hawk eyes glowed like a lantern in the night. It was Dominique.

Pierre was horrified. He felt as if he, like the aged man in the prison yard, were walking on his knees to the Temple. A hundredweight of iron seemed to press on his head along with the new agony in his heart. He tried to retreat but the tide swept him on to the Temple.

Finally they reached the tower of the Temple, squeezing through the double doors of the palace courtyard. The cries rose in a common roar: "The Queen . . . The Queen!" Below the windows of the imprisoned royal family the frizzed head of Princess de Lamballe pivoted on its pike. The glazed eyes of the faithful Princess bulged heavenward.

But the mob was not satisfied that the Queen shrink from the sight at her window. Why not force its way up the dank stone stairways; why not wave the head at her very feet? . . . Let her kiss once more the cold precious lips of her confidante! Hadn't the little Princess been Marie Antoinette's lover?

There was a cry of suffocation as a dozen tried at once to crowd into the doorway of the Temple past the guards.

If they reached Marie Antoinette she too would be murdered, Pierre knew. She suddenly became alive for him again, returned from the dead. There was no longer any thought of Silvie or his son or a warm bath. There was only the harrowing need of saving Marie Antoinette from murder. . . . Once before he had saved her from the mob. What had he said—what had he done that day at Versailles? . . . Was it possible that one man alone could save her now?

He leaped up on a stone block and began to rant, waving his tricolored sash. At first his voice was drowned in the uproar. He kept on shouting, "*Allons!* . . . through the city of Paris. . . . Let all Paris see the head of the Princess de Lamballe! Let all Paris taste her blood! . . . To the Duc d'Orléans, her enemy. . . . Let the Duc gloat! . . . *Allons!*" His voice was shrill as a hawker's and the veins stood out on his forehead. The rabble began to listen to the young sans-culotte with the bloody shirt and the rakish beard, a fine specimen of a citizen. The pulpy body of the Princess de Lamballe was at his feet, slashed open now from the chest to the pudendum. It was like a rack of lamb hanging on a butcher's hook. Cheering beside him, a coal heaver swirled a dripping rag that had been the Princess's chemise. The fresh powdered head on its pike swayed so close to him that he felt waves of insanity mingling with his logic. He called the murderers "heroes"; he cried out their "glory"; his arguments carried the fire of a Brutus.

The crowd in the doorway turned. He was right, thought the fleshmongers. Why not make a day of it? When would they have such a prize again as the head of the Princess de Lamballe? Why not make the carnival last? Why not incite all Paris against the Prussian enemy that was pushing on to the gates of the city? . . . Give the jaunty head a great showing before it was dumped with the corpses at the place du Châtelet—before its brains were finally bashed out in the common dump heap. The Queen had seen the head from her window; now let the people of Paris celebrate!

The mob cheered and began to rush to the street. They had the frenzied strength to parade to Jericho!

Pierre, dropping from the stone block, found himself face to face with a National Guard, the Baron de Batz, who was wrestling with the crowd.

Their eyes met like two streaks of lightning.

"My answer is yes, M. Forget!" cried Pierre.

Late that afternoon Pierre returned to his lodging. Hours of brandy drinking had benumbed him, tempering the madness of the day. As he came to the shop window of M. Valdeux he was forced by some cursed instinct to stop and gaze at the display. There were only a few new articles; a bust of Voltaire with a chipped nose; a *badine* with enamel knob; and an exquisite miniature of the Princess de Lamballe.

He tried to focus his eyes on the frame jeweled with sapphires. It was certainly the very same that had stood on the console of the Queen's closet in the Tuileries! He felt the blood rushing through his body like a torrent, felt that any moment he would go headlong.

But he must own the miniature. He must keep the image of the Princess intact before him or he would go insane. There was money enough for the picture hidden in his mattress. He tried to move on without looking up because he knew Angélique was there, and her figure in the shadows hypnotized him.

Angélique's hair caught a gleam of light from the sunset. Her hair was the color of the copper pots in Mère Dulange's kitchen. Her drowsy eyes were fastened on him as if they would nail him to the shutter. The memory of her soft, naked kiss kept his eyes for a moment on her lips. Had he kissed her really or had she come to him in a drunken reverie? . . . But no, he remembered now the feel of the pink, swollen bosom against his blouse, the soft, pink-pudding breasts, like maraschino beaten into egg white.

Bitterly angry with himself for this moment of weakness, he strode into the dark hallway. His back burned from the two brown slits of her eyes, and now the burning traveled into every nerve of his body.

In his room he could not remember what he had come up for, but he knew that he must look for something. Slinging his red cap of liberty on the floor, he burrowed into the huddle of secondhand goods, upsetting firedogs, scattering books and music. But whatever he hunted was not here. He would search for the thing among his pamphlets and papers. *Dieu,* but his head was reeling! He might better throw himself down on his mattress. Mattress, that was it! He found the mousehole and extracted the money.

As he staggered across the room to the hall door he came headlong on the blur in the mirror. He was as filthy now as he looked—his face streaked with blood, his body wet with the sweat of terror. The fast-growing beard added a dozen years to his age, he thought vaguely, the mirror swimming with brandy. How he had always prided himself on his clean, sleek look! His nostrils contracted with scorn at the enforced role. But he would have revenge! If he did end by cutting his own throat, first he would have revenge.

And now he would go down and buy the miniature of the Princess de Lamballe, for he had plenty of *assignats* in his pocket.

He flung open his door to the impact of odors, and Angélique stood before him. She was like a cat, soundless. And she had the same wide mouth of a cat, with the faint suggestion of smile like a Cheshire. *Dieu!* Why did she bother to cover her great pudding breasts at all?

"What do you want?" he demanded, the same as he had the day before. As if he did not know!

"I have a customer for the marten muff," she purred softly, and again he had the impression of bubbling oil.

She glided across the room. Even as he watched her Pierre was convinced that it was not Angélique that moved, but a figment of his fancy.

"How much is the miniature of the Princess de Lamballe?" he asked thickly.

"Too much, Citizen. . . . So you know the Princess de Lamballe?"

"After today all of Paris knows her!"

Angélique slipped the muff from the mutilated ghost and rubbed it softly, sensuously across her cheek.

"Why do you want the miniature of the Princess de Lamballe?" she murmured.

"I want to grind my heel into it," he said warily.

"An expensive whim for a poor sans-culotte!" As she glided toward the door again she paused close to him, and he could smell the oil of her hair and her strong body odor and the dust of the shop in her clothes. "Then you do beat your women! . . ."

"*Chienne!*" he exclaimed under his breath, swaying now more with desire than brandy.

He thought he had never loathed anyone as he loathed this pink chunk before him, her cheeks flushed a dark red, her shawl trailing the floor, her eyes, watching. . . . Suddenly she filled his arms; her red curls tumbled from the soiled cap as he forced her lips apart with a boorish satisfaction.

The great pudding. The great pink pudding, he thought. Why shouldn't he taste of her? Why shouldn't he consume her?

Her weight lolled heavily in his arms, sharpening his lust. And he had a sense of lust he had never had before. With hands blackened from the grime of prison courtyards he began to strip away the flimsy skirt and blouse. There was no more resistance than if he had been stripping a dummy, and when she was naked she melted into his violent embrace as casually as water finds its level. Her pink-pudding body was moist and soft and clung to him like a leech through the deepening twilight.

But for a while he forgot the blood as the room darkened and became more stifling with Angélique's soft panting. Even with Angélique a part of the shadows now she filled him with stark, crude sensations. His lips tasted the salty sweat of her skin; his muscles quivered with the billowing fat of her body; the sly smile that crept into his consciousness weeks ago lingered in his core like a taint, a black fungus, spreading, spreading. . . .

Finally, lying drugged on the hard mattress of his bed, Pierre watched the girl fumble about for her chemise. He loathed her, for he had not meant to weaken; an hour before he had been of a gentleman's world in spite of the blood and grime on his clothing. He loathed her even as he had the man with the birthmark he had meant to murder.

His eyes drifted shut for a moment and the brandy pulled him away from himself as a strong rein pulls horses. *Dieu,* but he could sleep, with the pain of the morning diffused by brandy and the tingling of his flesh . . . tingling! . . .

Pierre bolted to his feet, caught his breath sharply. The Princess de Lamballe was before him. She stood there with her stump of a neck, and the blood trickled down from the red mash and dyed her white gown crimson. The room was not so dark that he could not see the white of her gown as white as snow on the pines of Satory, the red of her blood as red as Marie Antoinette's rubies. An endless quiver seemed to sustain the body with its wild gesticulating arms pleading, pleading for the head that lay at its feet. He lurched for the head with palsied hands, and his fingers met the cold of the china pot.

Dieu, was he going mad? It was not the Princess de Lamballe hovering over him, but Angélique.

"M'sieu?" she whispered, and the long foolish lashes swept her cheeks.

Pierre fumbled in his pocket for the *assignats* and thrust at her a fluttering handful.

Angélique's hands were on his hard bare chest, drifting down his nudeness lightly as an insect. He thrust her away from him. *Nom de Dieu,* some women were insatiable! . . . She laughed her lazy porpoise laugh and it maddened him to sadism. He reached out and seized the straggling red curls, tossing her like a sack of meal onto the bed. It was not too dark to see the brown slits of her eyes, glazed a little with the orgy, watching, watching. She was the world that had attacked his world, that had murdered himself and Maurice and the Princess.

He began to beat her, and she gave him a lashing blow across the face that almost blinded him. The strength of this soft-pudding mass amazed him. He could feel the thin sharp nails in his beard like steel; and her hot-garlic spit stinging his eyes like grapeshot. . . . Here was no lacy Mme de Frivouac, no evanescent Silvie, no volatile Victoire. Here was a woman who wanted to be beaten. And he would deal her a thousand blows for every one her kind had inflicted on the poor tender body of the Princess de Lamballe.

Here in this grimy attic hell, thought Pierre fiercely, they would fight out the fate of their two worlds between them. She was the thing that had haunted him for weeks, that had lain in waiting to destroy him and all that belonged to him. She was the thing incarnate. She was the Revolution.

It was sweet to feel a raging fire within one's hands, to feel that nothing mattered now—neither life nor death. To let insanity flow untrammeled.

The girl's small rodent teeth clung avidly to his arm, and he loosened her jaw with the grip of his free hand on her throat. He would choke that damnable smile from her lips, that watchfulness from her eyes: he would leave her blue and dull-eyed as the Princess de Lamballe.

Together they heaved about the room, crashing into the bergère, upsetting the pot of urine.

Angélique fought like a panther, silent. The cries born in her throat seemed to die there gurgling, stifled as the voice of dawn in Paris.

Pierre swam crazily about the room, like an octopus blinded by ink of his own making. Drunk, of course; he knew he was raging drunk. If he were not drunk he would be able to pummel the life out of this steaming pink pudding. . . .

Dieu, what was he thinking? He must get rid of her or he really would kill her. . . . With one desperate hand he forced the door and they bolted into the tiny square of a hall together. It was black as the sod under which Maurice lay suffocated. Pierre heard his laughter cutting the quick, pasty dark as he gathered violence to thrust Angélique's hot clinging body free of him.

There was a strange concatenation of sounds: a rip or a squeak, as of kindling splitting; the heavy thud of a bag of flour bounced on the floor of a mill; a muffled choking, like water damming; and then the noise of the streets again, loud against the silence within.

He was free of her. For a few seconds he stood there floundering, breathless. In his head was the hammering of a hundred hammers.

It came to him that he had thrown Angélique down the stairs—that without a doubt he had killed her. He felt a rush of triumph, an appalling freedom. The exultation lifted him to the skies and dropped him.

And now all he wanted was to sleep—to forget. He prayed to St. Geneviève that his legs would carry him as far as his mattress.

An hour later Pierre had three visitors with a lantern.

One of them, thin as a reed, had a birthmark on his face and a mouth like that of a blowfish. He said gruffly: "Citizen Michelait, we arrest you in the name of the law."

Later, in the prison of the Abbaye, Pierre remembered that as he was dragged past the window of M. Valdeux's shop, he saw the puffed face of Angélique, one eye closed, one lip like a jellyfish—watching.

❀❀❀❀❀❀❀❀❀❀❀❀❀❀❀❀❀❀❀❀❀❀❀❀

CHAPTER XXI

January 20, 1793

PIERRE shoved aside the remains of the prison dinner that had been brought in to him from a fashionable restaurateur. The Baron von Drinsbach, who had an insatiable appetite, had finished his Strasbourg sauerkraut and was pacing up and down the cell to keep warm, patting his fat, round belly. (The Baron was married to a French lady-in-waiting and had been imprisoned because he wore striped silk stockings, which made him suspect, and because, although he had done nothing against liberty, he had done nothing for it.)

Pierre and the Baron, being wealthy, were "pistoliers," and had the advantage of sharing a bed together in a separate cell. The nation generously supplied them with straw but they had to pay the porter twenty sous a day for the bed and furniture. Candles and coal for the brazier were extra.

Pierre huddled into his greatcoat. They had allowed him a suit of his own clothes, praise God, when he came here. Money had bought him the privilege of course. He smiled at the hungry little Baron chafing his stomach. He and the Baron were men of prestige; they also fed a dozen poor prisoners, *"the pailleux,"* who lay huddled in dens or lairs on piles of straw.

But being privileged was little comfort, thought Pierre. His *côtelette de mouton* was no less like tallow when he came to eat it than the stew of potatoes, rice, and kidney beans the *"pailleux"* subsisted on. Feast days were no different from fast days.

And if the food ever arrived with a semblance of heat Pierre himself was too cold to eat it. He thought he had never known before what it meant to be cold. Winter had always been an *apéritif*. In the rich furs of a sleigh he had breathed in the December frost, his ears and nostrils tingling; but his body had been warm with the lynx robe and the warmth of a courtesan beside him.

Now the blood in his veins seemed to have stopped flowing. His veins were tiny springs, frozen, stiffening. His mind, too, often refused to move, like a hapless plant, immotile in any icy brook.

Pierre took a pinch of snuff with fingers that were numb. His thoughts clung to Louis, who was to be guillotined on the morrow. The prediction of Jean de Batz had come true. Sieur Gamain the locksmith had played directly into the hands of the Montagnards by revealing incriminating papers in Louis's iron cupboard. Could anyone now doubt the court's intrigue to restore the old régime? Who could be indifferent about the Revolution now? . . . Well, Louis had been tried and condemned.

Pierre thought bitterly of the Girondins. They were cowards, weaklings, all of them! Grégoire, his own father, was a coward. They had fallen into the neatly set trap, voting for execution when the time came though they had always been opposed to it. A minority in the Convention, they had not dared to lose their standing. Yet without their vote of "Death" the Jacobins wouldn't have triumphed.

Pierre had read avidly of the harrowing days of trial in newspapers bribed from a turnkey. Then too in spite of the *"moutons"* or spies who infested the prison, he had been in constant communication with a traitorous porter through a cipher and a deaf-and-dumb language. For instance, scratching of the right ear meant that Michonis (erstwhile lemonade vendor and now Inspector of Prisons) would appear that day on his rounds. But Pierre had made no attempt to reach his father. He was glad now that he had concealed from Grégoire the fact that he was in prison; he would rather die on the guillotine than accept help from a coward!

"Life seems to be a matter of waiting," Pierre said aloud grimly. "Once I waited impatient for the hour when I could toss books aside and play ball. Soon I was waiting for my next rendezvous with the Comtesse de Frivouac. I waited frantic to find Mlle Hyacinthe. . . . Then I waited for the escape to Varennes—for the Duke of Brunswick's capture of Verdun."

The Baron paused long enough to look down at Pierre's cold mutton with longing. He said: "After his defeat at Verdun who would dream that Dumouriez could force back the Prussians at Valmy? Or that the Austrians would be beaten at Jemmapes? Who would have dreamed the Allies could be forced to retreat?"

The Baron sighed and bit his thick lips. He hadn't meant to mention Valmy, where M. de Michelait's brother Gilbert had been killed in action. He would change the subject.

"Waiting can be the thing most pleasant in the world," the Baron observed sagely. "It whets the appetite."

"Oui, oui, oui," said Pierre sharply. "But not five months of waiting in the Abbaye. Sometimes I think I am losing my mind . . . and now I am waiting for tomorrow!" His voice dropped to a whisper. "Oh God! Do you think Louis can escape on the way to the guillotine, M. le Baron? The plans are all set. Jean de Batz, you know . . . *mon Dieu,* if Louis is not saved what then?"

The Baron halted. His fingers toyed with the edge of Pierre's greasy plate.

"What does one wait for then, do you mean, my friend? . . . What does anyone really wait for the world over?" he asked, his blue popeyes caught by Pierre's black gaze. "Both the Kaiser and the little man who lives by his clock—they wait for the end, *nicht?*"

"The *end?*" Pierre's teeth were chattering with cold and emotion.

"Yah." And at last the Baron picked up the chop bone from the plate and nibbled at it with relish. His lips were like two soft caterpillars, thought Pierre, sickened.

"I don't wait for the end!" Pierre burst out savagely. "I'll escape somehow!"

The turnkey came and escorted Pierre and the Baron von Drinsbach to one of the guard halls used as a common room after dinner. Although the walls were defaced with pornography and the reeking heat stung one's chilblains, a château elegance prevailed.

Pierre watched the usual groups assembling to play cards (appointments were kept punctiliously) but he avoided an invitation to whist. He could not forget Louis.

"Come, join us in charades," coaxed a flimsy looking girl.

"*Non, non, non,*" interfered a massive matron, well powdered and feathered. "He's going to dance with us. M. de Lechitreux has his violin."

"*Je vous demande pardon?*" said Pierre slyly as one of the guards drifted by.

"The *Citizen* Lechitreux has his violin," corrected the matron.

The room was filled with commotion. Pierre dropped down on the straw-matted chair he had brought with him and watched a group of men playing with a "toton," the new English gambling top. Would Louis escape, he wondered? And would Marie Antoinette be brought to trial before Jean de Batz completed the plans for her flight to America? Now that Grégoire had betrayed the King, Pierre felt a fiercer obligation than ever to help the Queen.

Jean de Batz had sent messages frequently to Pierre by Cortey the National Guard Captain. Cortey was one of the thousands of Royalists holding Communal trusts, ostensibly turned Republican. Victoire's M. de Tuite himself in order to insure his safety was a clerk in the *Bureau des Pièces Accusatives,* an office in which the lists of all prisoners were registered. Like many of Pierre's *ci-devant* friends now in public office, the Chevalier lived in security and comfort.

Jean de Batz assured Pierre that the well-bribed M. de Tuite could keep Pierre's name off the daily lists of the doomed—provided there was no slip, of course! . . . And certainly in a matter of a few weeks now some escape from prison could be effected. It was vital that Pierre get to America at once.

It was vital, thought Pierre. Yes, it was vital! But here he was—waiting! Trying to forget how long it was since he had had a glimpse of Silvie; trying to keep the courage of his decision the day the Princess de Lamballe's head had been dragged in the dust before him; trying to forget that he would never see the son that would be born so soon in Coblentz!

He thought often of Victoire in her bath *à la Dauphine;* envied her with a passionate, childish envy as he scraped the vermin from his body. He still had no assurance that she had reached Coblentz. It was even possible that she had obtained a divorce *a vinculo matrimonii.*

Divorce was so simple now and such a protection to the *émigrée!* . . .
But Victoire would not divorce him. There was that formidable tie
between them. Oh, my God, how one's thoughts went round and
round in a circle—if one were warm enough, of course, to think of
anything but the cold!

Beyond the group a pretty little milliner with pricked fingers was
arranging the hair of her sister. At present the little milliner was
scratching her lice. Up and down before them in time to M. de
Lechitreux's fiddle—alone and up and down stalked an old Chevalier.
He was a member of the Académie française and he wore his palm-
embroidered coat and mother-of-pearl sword. The coat was smudged
with old gravy. Every night the Chevalier stalked up and down desperately trying to recall his panegyric on the Cardinal de Richelieu,
founder of the Academy, which he had been required to give when
he was admitted. For the Chevalier meant some night to regale the
company with a rendering of it.

Oh, there was plenty of éclat here better seen with myopic tolerance,
thought Pierre bitterly. His eyes drifted over the throng. Brocaded
men tête-à-tête with their brocaded wives. Not enough benches and
chairs, of course, and a precedence given to a Marquis over a Comte
by common consent. But who is able to stand with more grace than
a Frenchman? . . . And hundreds of yards of lace, delicately frayed;
hundreds of sparkling gems, slightly dulled. Sweat more pungent than
cologne. For who merited enough water for a bath when it must be
dragged to him from the river Seine?

Certainly not the old Vicomtesse du Luvin, who had once told
Pierre's fortune. There was a buzz around the smelly old hag now
as she sat there in her corner fingering a greasy pack of cards. A
protégé had sent her a box of bonbons. There were crumbs of sugar
mixed with snuff bobbing on her mustache. Near her skulked the
African with whom she had held séances in the bowels of her *hôtel*.
No longer naked, the African—but whimpering at his lot and the
occasional slaps the Vicomtesse gave him. . . . It was said that her
hôtel had been taken over by Fouquier-Tinville. Many prisoners' and
emigrants' houses had been bought from the state by members of the
Convention or others in power. Robespierre had acquired Monceaux;
Couthon had moved into the Comte d'Artois's Bagatelle. Little clerks
who were unable to purchase got themselves lodged in the most magnificent of national buildings. All of them enjoying the luxury they
had so condemned in the nobility of the old régime. Would the Revo-

lution only serve to make the little emulate the vices of the great, Pierre
wondered?

The great . . . were these the great, huddled together like cattle
awaiting a storm? The young scholar, wearing the broad black ribbon
of St. Michel, making love every night to the English governess; the
Marquis de Brieffe, flaunting his broad red ribbons of St. Louis to
show he was a prince of the blood. The Comte who was always wanting to deliver a lecture on the stars. Close to the Comte, his valet. Pierre
thought of Dominique with a sharp stab. He had last seen Dominique
rouging the cold blue cheeks of the Princess de Lamballe. It gave him
less pain to think of Maurice and Gilbert who had died the deaths of
heroes than to think of Dominique.

A scurrying of dogs over Pierre's feet suddenly roused him. How
well he understood them and their antics to get away from one another's fleas! Now they were climbing over the two nuns. But the nuns
paid no attention. They stood with their backs to the grilled window
praying, their lips moving like water with an evening ripple. Here in
prison they were free to say the prayers that free nuns were forbidden.
Were they praying for Louis? Somewhere, was Catherine on her knees
praying for Louis? How cool her fingers had been on his forehead!
. . . cool as the earth that pressed Maurice's eyelids; cool as the steel
that had ripped the lungs of Gilbert.

Pierre shuddered and felt hollow. It must be good to feel the soft,
round words of prayer in your mouth as the nuns did. He himself
had so long been hollow. Although he remembered the fullness of
prayer one could not pray without the love of God in him. He thought:
"I no longer have the love of God in me . . . I am become another
Helvetius, an *esprit fort* living for myself. But it's true, there's nothing
but physical sensation. . . ." He was saying these things like a cate-
chism.

"*Pardieu, Citoyen Michelait,* how can you nap in this bedlam? Three
times I've offered you Mlle Mansoine's ringlet; she wouldn't be very
flattered."

Pierre jumped to his feet and stared at the coquettish porteress. She
was dressed flagrantly in blue, white, and red, and wore a small wooden
guillotine on a ribbon about her neck.

"*Pardon!*" he exclaimed, trying to conceal the fact that his groin
itched abominably. "Mlle Mansoine?"

"*Oui.* The blond little barmaid who was overheard praying for
Marie Antoinette. Don't you recall, today she 'sneezed into the sack'?

I lent her some rouge. She refused to look pale in the basket. This morning she cut off this lock with a piece of broken bottle. She said she would like the Citoyen Michelait to have it."

Pierre reached out for the crescent of hair and felt a twist of pain in his stomach. He had once touched Mlle Mansoine's curls and said they were pretty. He thought now of her trembling lips and wished that he had kissed her. He thought of the lock of white hair in the Queen's ring, hair "blanched by sorrow." The ring had disappeared with Angélique. The next day, no doubt, it had lain on a velvet pillow in the shop window.

He turned his back on the chatty porteress and began to walk up and down, stumbling over romping dogs and children. Every now and then Angélique came back to him. It was hard to remember exactly what had happened that night in September. It was as if he had lived in another world for a few days, as if his spirit had departed from his body like the spirits of the two thousand who had been murdered on the thresholds of the prisons.

He had no sense of shame when he thought of Angélique. He knew what the Abbé Blafond would say in confession—that it was the filthiest act of a life tainted with sacrilege and adultery. No doubt the Abbé would be right. But Pierre had no desire to analyze that drunken emotion. He simply accepted it like the riddance of foul excrement. To Pierre, Angélique was still the victorious soul of the Revolution skulking in the shadows. At first, in the fury of being imprisoned he had been sorry that he had not killed her. Just as he had been chagrined that Romain, Silvie's flutist, had escaped him. In the long days of brooding that followed he always associated one with the other.

Dieu, he must learn to be gay in prison like these others—to live fully the life of the moment! It was just tonight when he wished to God he had it in him to pray for Louis. . . .

There was a piercing scream at his feet and Pierre seemed to collide with it.

"*Eh bien,* Monsieur, now see what you've done!" cried a lad of fourteen in a tangle of benches and chairs. "Yolande was just about 'to look through the little window.' And you've spoiled it."

Pierre apologized. He had interrupted another guillotine rehearsal. The lad, with all the austerity of Sanson the executioner, had tied the hands of the rosy-cheeked Yolande behind her back, had prostrated her on a bench, pretended to cut her hair, and was about to let down on her neck the small lap escritoire which served as the knife.

"Shush!" cried Yolande's mother from the card table. "How can I remember what is trump!"

But a moment later the guard room was still enough for Yolande's mother. The Commissioner had appeared.

The time had come again—the inexorable time of night.

In the quiet one could hear the stertorous breathing of Mme de Stenjac. Two days before she had tried to commit suicide with a mixture of pins and copper coins soaked in vinegar. She had been revived with milk. But the pains gone, she still breathed as if she were running.

The Commissioner coughed and paused.

"To appear on the morning of January 21, 1793, before a Tribunal of Five Judges, a Public Prosecutioner, and a Jury, the following, in the name of the Republic, and in the name of Liberty, Equality, and Fraternity: . . ."

Faltering, he read a list of a dozen names. The silence continued, but now there was a racking scream as the name of M. le Baron de Stenjac was called. The Baron drew his wife to his breast.

"Vive le Roi!" she cried with a pitiful wheeze. And her name was added to the list of the condemned with her husband's, as she knew it would be.

Pierre did not hear the names of others on the list. One only knew if his own name had been called, if his own name were missing. It was a matter of a minute; it was a matter of eternity.

Pierre's name was missing. He felt his body take form again and his heart begin to beat. The blood began to flow through its arteries. The nerves came alive in sharp twinges. He moved his hand because he was not certain that it would move. He had no fear of death. It was just that for one minute—at the Time of Night—he was paralyzed. Always after he found that he could move his hand again, there came to him the putrid smell of the fish oil in the lamps and a momentary illusion that he heard the roar of the ocean.

The company began to stir like a willow swayed with the wind. The group beside him returned to its *toton*. The fiddle of M. de Lechitreux struck up. The little milliner scratched her lice and giggled.

But Sister Gabrielle Marie was on her knees singing *"Veni Creator,"* the hymn to the Holy Ghost, in a thin, piercing voice. Although the mother of Yolande had left her card table forever she had already been replaced. The old Chevalier stood still in the center of the room. He would not need the panegyric. He struggled now to compose a poetical adieu.

As the Commissioner led his chosen away Pierre stood close to the iron-barred door. He stared with amazement at the Baron von Drinsbach, who had paid thirty thousand francs in gold to the jailer to effect his escape. The Baron's caterpillar lips were trembling. He raised his finger in the sign of death as he passed Pierre. In a moment the doomed were gone. The room was a clutter of noise again. There was another eternity until tomorrow, till the next Time of Night.

Soon it was time to go back to one's cell. Three tipsy turnkeys came to call the roll. At their heels were as many savage hounds. The lap dogs squealed, and there was a snarling and nipping of legs. The turnkeys couldn't read well and passed the list from one to another. Often they read out the wrong names and swore when there was no answer. The company marched in and out several times before the turnkeys were satisfied that all were present. It was like a game of musical chairs with a certain condescension.

Then came the tour through the dark passages, following the flares. The corridors, blockaded with foul plates and bones, stank of onions and cabbage, rotting apples and cheese, and food *réchauffé*. Now and then Pierre tripped over a dog, a slop jar.

It seemed very strange to be in his cell alone. He was more conscious of the little Baron von Drinsbach now than when he lay shivering beside him in bed. Pierre drew on his greatcoat and crawled under the blankets. They were no more than gauze in the dampness, and his teeth began to chatter again. First he listened to the chatter, then to the disputes of the riffraff that slept on the staircase at night. One man was accusing another of spitting on his head.

He could not imagine the Baron von Brinsbach without a head— without a mouth—soft caterpillar lips lying still. Strange, he was sorry for Louis and the Baron because they would never eat again.

In the blackness of his cell Pierre lived through the coming hours of Louis's execution. Tomorrow. Eight o'clock of a day filled with gloom and rain. Trumpets sounding. Drums beating. The entire military force of Paris abroad under arms. Shops closed; shutters drawn.

He pictured the place de la Révolution, once the place de Louis XV. And there was the scaffold set high, facing David's stone and plaster statue of Liberty. Paris waited there, wet and freezing on wooden stools and straw chairs, on handcarts—six to twelve sous for the best places! Lucky the housewife who could rent out her windows! What if one did have to wait throughout the night in order to see the royal performance? There was always the heat of a bonfire, a brazier. There was always the vender crying pies and hotcakes and coffee. There was always singing and drinking. . . . Of course guillotining was not so thrilling to one who had watched a criminal die on the wheel in the good old days.

Pierre tried desperately to sleep. The scene only returned to him doubly intensified. He imagined the city bells striking ten o'clock. There came the coach at last. Louis rode beside his confessor, the Abbé Edgeworth de Firmont, a nonjuring priest. Louis had been reading his prayers. His fat figure descended from the coach steps awkwardly. There was not the loud yelling and jeering one expected. Although every time a head fell into the basket someone in France was being born, this beheading was different. The end of a king was finite.

Louis's coat was removed by an executioner, also the handkerchief about his neck. Sanson, the long-haired Sanson, whisked out a scissors and cut Louis's hair. Quietly mounting the scaffold with the Abbé, Louis cried out to the hypnotized throng:

"People, I die innocent. I pardon—" But at the order of Santerre the drums smothered his voice.

(Where was Jean de Batz? What had gone wrong? Oh, *mon Dieu* —was Louis really to die?)

Louis lay his head on the block. He still tried to talk:

"Sirs, I am innocent of all of which I am accused; I wish that my blood may cement the happiness of France."

Sanson had never before been in such great haste to release the spring of the ax. Louis's neck was not even properly placed. *Nom de Ciel,* but he was mangled! . . .

The severed head was raised to the crowd. "Long live the Nation!" they cried.

There was a wild scramble for the scaffold to tear apart the brocade coat, to escape with bits of Louis's hair and ribbon that were being sold, to dip a finger into the royal blood!

"Café! Café!"

"Gâteaux! Gâteaux!"

Off to the dancing on the Pont de la Révolution! What if one slithered about in the rain? Wasn't the body of Louis Capet already bouncing along in its cart to the cemetery of the Madeleine, to the thirsty bed of quicklime? Off to the Pont de la Révolution, and tonight to the theater! For wasn't France free? . . .

Pierre was no longer chattering. His clothes were drenched with sweat from the nightmare. In his chest was a pain so great that it seemed like the bursting of cannon. Holy Mother, if only he could relieve the pain by praying for Louis's escape! But he could not pray. . . .

Thank God, for the rush of tears then!

It was in June that Pierre was moved to the Luxembourg Prison. Transference was common—though not transference for the better. No reason was given for the change, but Michonis the Prison Inspector winked broadly at Pierre, inferring that Jean de Batz had used "influence."

The former palace of the Comte de Provence was, above all, the prison of the aristocrats. Its wide windows had been fortified with bars. The ballroom, picture galleries, salons, and bedchambers had been honeycombed by small partitions of rough lath and timber to accommodate the hundreds of nobility who suddenly arrived. Here were chairs enough for everyone in the salons of an evening, however, and the parade on the grand staircase was impressive and deceiving. Here, the brocade was not so tarnished.

Prisoners were free to come and go within the walls of the palace. Letters were sent and received; friends called. A confectioner supplied the tables. Benôit, the gentle and genial old concierge, was lenient and respectful.

Pierre's hopes rose magically. The months of patient planning would soon bear fruit, Baron de Batz informed him through friends. Pierre would be removed in a tumbrel from the prison, allegedly to be transferred to the Conciergerie—the last stopping-off place before the guillotine. On the Pont-Neuf a horde of wild dogs would be released, causing total confusion. The guards of the tumbrel would be well bribed— and Pierre would suddenly be swallowed by Paris.

He would hide for a few days in the near-by house of a druggist-grocer. Awaiting him would be the clothes and medicine kit of a doctor, and through M. Lepitre—whom the Commune had unwisely made President of the Passport Commission—a passport for said doctor to leave Paris. Also Pierre would be equipped with a medal commemorating his Republican deeds of bravery at the Bastille. Concealed on his person he would carry small opium pills wrapped in pieces of glove, undiscoverable unless he was searched with the utmost indecency.

Within the month Royalists would try to smuggle Marie Antoinette and the children from the Temple, sneaking them to Bordeaux—and surely this latest plan was foolproof. Pierre would be at Bordeaux before them, would arrange there for their passage to America. Louis de Noailles was already in America founding an asylum on the bank of the Susquehanna.

It was simple enough for Pierre to keep abreast of the intrigue within the Temple, that had baffled the Commune all during the year. Marie Antoinette had refused to be abducted without Louis while he was living; once in widow's weeds, she had bent all her energies toward escape and especially toward the rescue of her son. Workmen signaled from adjacent housetops; Royalists communicated messages with a violin played at midnight; bribed news venders shouted the day's news near the Temple each evening. Notes came in with clean linen or appeared in the stoppers of carafes. The Commune had become so desperate that it probed into loaves of bread for hidden missives, shook out the napkins of the royal family at meals, and finally removed everything sharp and made a thorough search for writing materials.

But the leak continued, for Jean de Batz had offered a million francs for success, and the Commune was forced to take volunteers very often in place of the National Guards who dreaded duty at the Temple. Lady Atkyns was still conspiring; General Dumouriez contemplated a raid on the prison with his cavalry corps; Toulon and Lepitre, volunteers, had planned an escape that hinged on the lamplighter who came every afternoon with his two children. The scheme had so nearly worked.

The Commune, exhausted at last from its vigilance, had separated the Dauphin from his mother, putting him under the care of M. Simon. What did it matter that the Dauphin had been ill with worms, a pain in his side, convulsions, a recurring fever, and an injury due to riding on a stick? He would recover on a diet of veal soup, frogs' legs, and plant juices. Ah, poor little Charlot, playing with the officers in the guard room, learning lascivious jokes, drinking brandy to make him gayer, laughing at the name "stupid aristocrat," studying nude pictures, and having pretty ladies caress him when he was naked. Poor little Charlot, who had been born such a showman, and thought this was fun because everybody seemed to love him!

When the Queen, grossly accused of incest with her son, was removed to the Conciergerie in August, Pierre resolved that he would challenge a thousand deaths to help her.

He found that the time went faster now that he could keep himself busy. Having no valet, he fetched water, swept out his quarters, and even took a turn at the spit in one of the huge fireplaces.

Moreover, Silvie came every day to see him. One morning in September she arrived with a basket of fruit, which prison guards had inspected carefully.

Her smile was so reassuring that Pierre knew she was trying to hide some new heartache.

They sat on a love seat, overlooking the many acres of park where they had so often loitered. He cursed the lack of privacy of his quarters, for he lived in a small alcove at the top of a stairway; and there was no corner of the palace that was not teeming with people.

"Silvie, what's wrong, chérie? . . . Something has happened!" he whispered, and he held her to him with a desire that had become desperate.

A child bolted into the alcove for a ball that had gone astray, and stood staring at them raptly.

For a while Silvie chatted of shops and boulevards but at last she burst into tears and laid her head on his shoulder. The story came out. When *Pamela* had been given the night before at the Théâtre Français, a troublemaker in the balcony cried out that the actors were giving a counterrevolutionary piece. Fleury had shouted from the stage that the play was being given as approved by the Committee of Public Safety. But the drunkard had gone to the Jacobin Club, denouncing the theater as a den of aristocrats. The theater had been surrounded by the military and there had been dreadful brawls, and finally an order had been issued for the actors' arrest by the Commune of Paris. The men had been sent to the Magdelonnettes and the Picpus, and the women to Sainte-Pélagie and the Anglaises.

"You're afraid the Opéra will be next!" Pierre said, unnerved by her trembling.

"*Oh oui, mon Pierre* . . . I am so terribly frightened."

With a joke Pierre snatched the ball from the child and tossed it down the stairway. The child bounced after it.

"When I escape I won't go to Bordeaux," he whispered. "We'll go to the border together!"

"Oh if we could, *mon Pierre!* . . . If only we could be together! . . . But it will never happen. You'd hate yourself for a coward and then I would come to hate you!"

"Damn America!" he said violently. "Damn the Revolution!"

She smiled a little in spite of her tears.

"You do love me at last. . . ."

"Yes, little Silvie . . . if you knew how tempted I am to forget the States you'd know how much I love you!"

He kissed her with such longing as he had never known.

"You'll come back to me, won't you?" she pleaded.

"And you'll wait for me, won't you, darling? . . . Oh, Silvie—how did we ever feel so free? . . . How did we look at the flowers as if we would always see them growing? And talk and laugh as if joy would go on forever?"

A group of young men squatted at the top of the stairs and began to shoot dice.

"Do you remember one day at Meudon," she said softly, . . . "you snapped off one of the flowers of the woodbine I'd picked, and I wouldn't let you dissect it. . . . You looked at me so queerly and said: 'Silvie, you have a soul. . . .' "

"Yes, I remember."

"Don't be afraid for me while you're away, *mon Pierre*. . . . It will be such a little while . . . and now that I've cried I feel so much better."

The bell that warned visitors to leave began to clang like that of a scissors sharpener.

Although he knew that one of the young men gaped at them, Pierre touched the cheek that seemed white as the gauze fichu above her black gown; kissed the gold ringlets moist at her neck; kissed the lashes still damp from tears.

"I must go," she said softly. "What if they shouldn't let me come again? What if you wanted pears and I couldn't bring them? . . . This is the juiciest pear . . ." and she touched the smallest one wrapped in white paper. "The greengrocer says this is the pear that you'll enjoy most. . . . *Comprendez-vous?*"

"*Oui, oui, oui*—I understand."

She turned to go.

"Silvie. . . ."

"Why do you say Silvie like that, *mon cher?*" Her voice was tense.

He faltered for words. He had such a dreadful premonition that he would never see her again.

"I was thinking how much I would like to see you dance."

"Ah, Monsieur, dancing is for the young."

"And for the brave!"

They smiled at one another and Silvie drifted down the stairway. The young men watched her too as the black folds of her gown slipped slowly from stair to stair.

That evening when he was alone Pierre held the paper of the special pear to candlelight. The invisible ink revealed one word in the hand-writing of Jean de Batz—"Tomorrow."

⁂⁂⁂⁂⁂⁂⁂⁂⁂⁂⁂⁂⁂⁂⁂⁂⁂⁂⁂⁂⁂⁂⁂

CHAPTER XXII

September 1793

To PIERRE, riding through the countryside on horseback, the earth had never been so beautiful. The air was sweet with the first hint of frost. Today in spite of his melancholy he had a sense of roundness; the many months of prison had been a long desert plain, flat. He had not thought of an earthworm for years. An earthworm was a good thing. An earthworm was reality; terror, the stink of cabbage, and the Commune were the maggot.

At each village Pierre was forced to show his passport to a National Guard, to collect a new visa. Every stop was a test of his courage but he answered boldly. He, Citizen Dreux, was en route to a village near Tours. He hoped to give the nation's blessing to his old mother before she died. Fate willing, he hoped by some miracle to save her. *Oui, oui, oui,* but of course he was *"bon patriote"!* In a cabinet at home he had a scrap of Louis's guillotined stocking.

There were few travelers abroad. Now and then he met a diligence or some *dames des halles* going to market. The women were barefoot, their shoes slung on a stick. Why not be comfortable till they reached the town's outpost! All of them wore vast aprons in which they stored juicy weeds to take home to their cows.

Occasional droves of cattle cluttered the road—and thin, ugly hogs hardly fit for the spit. The precious convoys of wheat or flour on their way to Paris were escorted by troops, for since France had declared war on England and Spain in the winter the scarcity of food and the torpor of industry had caused insurrection throughout the whole of the country.

People were not merely hungry, they were starving, brooded Pierre, as he passed raped fields of peas and turnips and beets. And although the maximum price fixed on corn and wheat had encouraged black-market selling, how many were there who could afford black-market buying?

It was on the third night of his journey that Pierre met his first challenge.

As he was undressing in the drab room of an inn he was sharply tempted to retreat his steps, to go back to Paris, and hide there until he found Silvie. During his few days in the house of the druggist-grocer he had made every attempt to find her. She had left the Opéra, his messengers said, and this time the ballerinas thought she would not return —Silvie had known the message in the basket of fruit!

Pierre felt defeated. There was nothing to do but go on to Bordeaux and to America as he had promised.

The three days of journey had smothered all joy he had felt at first being in the open. This was no longer France, this strange countryside where "Trees of Liberty" and guillotines crowded the village squares. And why not be honest? . . . he was as frightened as Silvie.

His pose as a doctor was dangerous and made him constantly uneasy. Once more he began to rehearse the remedies for a fluxion on the jaw, gout of the stomach, a trembling in the limbs. He thought of the ugly clinging leeches in the jar, of the black dose with its mummy powder, a physic to cure all evils.

There was a knock on the door. In a spurt of fear Pierre blew out the candle. For a moment he waited, then answered, annoyed at the folly of his delay.

At the door were the innkeeper and a scrawny priest.

"You are a doctor, *n'est-ce pas?*" inquired the priest.

"Mais oui."

"Bon! Come at once with me, *s'il vous plait.* A poor girl down the road is in labor. And the village doctor has gone to Blois. Her husband doesn't trust the midwife."

Pierre felt himself shrinking to an iron weight. There was nothing to do but go. *Mon Dieu,* this would be the end of him!

The priest guided him up a cobbled road with a lantern. Pierre's legs took him one way, his volition another.

The priest was obnoxiously chatty. What were conditions in Paris?

The same as in the country, where the rich with their special war tax were fearing seizure of their property? Merchants distrusted *assignats,* which had fallen forty per cent below par, as *M. le Docteur* knew. Small retailers were pillaged for not selling cheaper than they bought. The poor murmured at the price of bread and the numerous levies for the army. Even here in the village the lower class squandered their wages and drank and gambled; prices had increased fifty per cent, but why save valueless money? *"Par ce que ce n'est que du papier!"* was the cry of all of them.

Pierre was not listening, absorbed with his own immediate predicament. There must have been some pretext he could have used to escape this dilemma. Suppose the child should be a forceps baby like that of Mme de Frivouac? Which of those deadly steel instruments in his case was the forceps? (Why hadn't he paid more attention to the druggist-groceur's instruction?) Or, *mon Dieu,* a Cæsarean birth! . . . In that event he would have to sham an attack of gallstones. And infants were sometimes born freaks—with two heads! He recalled suddenly the fairs he had been to. . . .

The priest held the lantern considerately before Pierre's tottering footsteps.

Of course, he said, he was a juring priest but at any moment he might be thrust into jail, regardless. No wonder, when informers against persons or families were paid from fifty to one hundred livres for an accusation! It was an easy way to make a living. Perhaps it was all the fault of the Girondins, who never should have made an attack on Marat. After all, the Girondins had represented the bourgeoisie, and when they lost their battle against the Jacobins the power was handed to the populace on a silver platter. Did *M. le Docteur* know any of the twenty-nine Girondins who had been arrested by the Convention in June? Did *M. le Docteur* think that those of the deputies who had escaped into the countryside would ever be apprehended?

Pierre shuddered. Grégoire, he knew, was among those still under surveillance.

The scrawny little priest lowered his voice to a whisper. One did not know what to think since Robespierre the Incorruptible had begun to climb. One thing was certain: the assassination of Marat by Charlotte Corday had made place for him. Some people called this the Reign of Terror and said fear was the only weapon to forward the Revolution.

It was necessary to show this jabbering hypocrite that he could talk, thought Pierre, and answered:

"Others say that the Republic, which began with idealism and hope of liberty for everyone, has become a government of selfish interests—a government interested only in war and expansion."

The priest coughed equivocally.

"*Et vous, M. l'Abbé,*" Pierre asked, his words sounding hollow as pebbles dropped in water, "*vous êtes bon patriote?*"

"*Ah, mon Dieu, oui!*" answered the priest in a hasty whisper. "*Il faut bien l'être à present.*"

They turned in at a clipped thorn hedge. The moon shone on a thatched cottage and spectral peach trees in a garden beyond.

The abbé knocked and entered, Pierre following him. A woman's cry began with a low moan and rose to a bellow. Pierre felt that he must turn around and run. But a tremendous old midwife in a large white apron was talking to him.

"She is in the second stage, *M. le Docteur,*" she said.

The room was dark with grimy walls. A few rudely carved chests and cupboards of pearwood glowered from the corners; a bed loomed from the rushlights, a great bedstead with curtains of green serge set high above the damp ground floor. Near the bed was a table with remnants of bread porridge, cold kidney beans, salt herring, and cider. It was within close nibbling distance of the billowing *sage-femme* as she stood at the bed.

"Open a shutter," Pierre demanded, stifled with fear and a crackling heat from the hearth.

"There is no glass at the windows, *M. le—*"

"Open a shutter or the child will suffocate!" A shutter was opened.

The *sage-femme* relieved him of his coat and led him to the bed. The young girl's blond hair was matted and straggling over the pillow. Her eyes were fastened on him with the glaze of death. She wore only a linen shift crumpled with sweat, which barely covered her pendulous, blue-veined breasts. A long wash pole was suspended with ropes from the top of the bed, and hung crosswise, close to her taut, mammoth belly. Her fists clung to the pole fiercely. The balls of her feet dug into the footboard of the bed, her knees raised, her great thighs trembling with pain.

Pierre felt a quick surge of bitterness. Another sans-culotte was being born into the world. He, Pierre, was to deliver a child who would some day set a castle on fire, who might some day murder the son Pierre had conceived. If there was a just God the child would be born dead.

"Do you think it will be brief?" asked the *sage-femme* with professional etiquette. She knew to the moment the time of birth.

Pierre's bitterness gave him courage.

"*Dieu!*" he said. "*Otia dant vitia.*" He knew the Latin would be impressive.

The *sage-femme's* rheumy eyes widened. "Is that serious then, *M. le Docteur?*"

"*Oui, oui, oui, Madame.*"

Several people grew out of the shadows, the scrawny priest among them.

" 'Leisure makes vice'—*serious?*" the priest questioned.

Pierre's heart contracted.

"Merely a joke, *M. l'Abbé.* I was only philosophizing . . . less leisure, fewer infants."

"Scarcely a vice, an infant, *M. le Docteur!* Annette was properly married in my own chapel."

Pierre's eyes lowered then to the long quivering gully of blood from which the child would come. He felt sickened. He heard himself sharply ordering everybody to leave the room—to go to the barn, the closestool, anywhere else. He turned to the table where he had laid his satchel, opened it, and began to fumble with essences, oils, tinctures.

"You will give her a narcotic?" asked the *sage-femme.* "She has only had brandy."

The old woman picked up a flake of salt herring. As she had no teeth she sucked it loudly. She watched Pierre's confusion.

"I believe in Hippocrates's method: few remedies—let nature take its course."

The *sage-femme* shrugged and returned to the bedside, rinsing her herring hands in the basin of bath water for the baby.

"Come, Annette," she said as the pain began again and the girl writhed and cried out. "Bear down. It won't be long now and here is a *surgeon-accoucheur* all the way from Paris."

She pressed her hands on the girl's belly. The girl gave a swelling grunt. At the top of the crimson gully a dark veined, red, rotating ball grew larger and larger. It was like a firm mass of sweetbreads.

"*Bien—très bien!*" encouraged the *sage-femme.*

Pierre stared. It was as he thought. The thing was deformed.

For of course it was the head that came first. He knew that much. He felt a sweet sense of retribution. The dark, bloody ball was larger now, then smaller as the piercing cry of the girl abated. *Dieu,* how one struggled to enter a world of travail and sin!

"It's almost over!" cried the old woman, and she poured down Annette's throat a splash of brandy.

The pains were coming closer. The cry began again. The girl's fists were white with tension. The rushlight, flickering with the draught from the window flung fickle shadows on the green serge bed curtains. Now Annette's livid face sank into gloom; now it leaped into a glassy mask. The footboard of the bed creaked from the force of her feet. It was as if thunder had shaken the cottage to its roots in the ground and now lightning would strike again in the piercing scream. The restless red ball began its burrowing. Blood oozed down the gully to widen the pool in the sheet.

"Help her, for God's sake!" cried the *sage-femme.* . . . "*Nom de Dieu,* you do not even have your hands oiled!"

Pierre turned to the table and groped for a bottle of oil. The cork rolled off toward the hearth, the bottle upset. He held his hands under the stream that drooled from the board. He could feel his nostrils tightening, quivering. His heart was a knot of string. Mère Dulange's barn —that's where he had first heard this frightening cry—when the cow calved. He had hid then in his feather bed, stuffing his ears, weeping softly with the cow's pain. But he must not let the pain of this peasant soften him . . . he was no longer a little boy. He was a man, persecuted by Annette and her kindred.

The smell of salt herring was stronger and stronger, the heat of the room engulfing. He snatched up a lancet and let it slip just a fraction. . . . He dropped the lancet as the shriek reached its climax . . . *Nom de Dieu,* the girl was dying without a doubt! They would say he could have saved her. He must remember his own sacred mission—must pretend to help. . . .

He collided with the *sage-femme* who rushed to the foot of the bed; the bloody ball burst its bounds and the child's face shot into view like a lavender gargoyle. The dark veins became glued strands of wet black hair.

Pierre was utterly shocked. The infant's eyes were closed. He knew it was dead, and felt triumphant. But he would be blamed. He had no intention of sacrificing his life because of this dead idiot. Annette's great sighs had paused with the silence—the most penetrating silence he had ever known. He could not move his eyes from the gargoyle. He could only seem to see the detached head of the Princess de Lamballe, with the same faint blue of mountain twilight, the same trickling stream of blood for a neck.

But the *sage-femme* seemed pleased. She gazed at the head through strands of ratty gray hair that escaped her cap. She took a quick draught of cider.

"Ah, a boy, I'll wager! . . . *Allons, M. le Docteur,* aren't you going to give him a helping hand at last?"

Pierre tried to think. His hands trembled so that he put them behind him, out of sight. He could feel the sweat trickling down his cheeks, down the middle of his back. His linen was soaked. He must say something, something. . . .

"In Paris, Madame, the *surgeon-accoucheur* only directs. It is the *sage-femme* who works."

The old woman grumbled. *"Par Dieu!* It is the same the world over. It is the woman who works. The man who orders and collects the fat fee. *Soit!"*

She heaved him aside, and her strong, withered hands grasped the baby's head, turning it deftly to the right. It was as simple as uncorking a bottle. She pulled and screwed, and in a moment the blue body of the child slipped from its bloody pocket. She gave it a brisk spank on the buttocks, holding it casually in one hand like a kettle of soup. Annette moaned and lay still at last, her eyes closed.

Pierre gripped the footboard of the bed.

"Come," cried the *sage femme* with excitement, "blow into his mouth. Blow hard! I haven't the strength and he needs breath. *Dieu de Dieu, hurry!"*

The child could live then, thought Pierre. He could give it breath. He could give it life to burn castles and murder its betters. Perhaps even to murder the Dauphin for whom he risked everything. But to rescue the Dauphin now, to escape from this plight and get to Bordeaux, first he must save the infant. He was caught in the senseless whirlpool reasoning of the dark ages: if the accused man drowned he was innocent; if he swam he was guilty and met the death sentence!

"Monsieur!" ejaculated the midwife.

He stared at Annette, the poor cow—Annette. The poor, bellowing cow. . . . Why did he think of the little girl years ago at the county fair? The child with the sky-blue sash who had dropped the apple? He had given the apple back to her and she had smiled at him.

Mechanically Pierre took the slimy child in his hands, fitted his mouth to its own, and blew with the strength of a bellows. The *sage-*

femme continued to spank its buttocks. In a moment the child gave a gasp and was scrambling like a spider. It was neither dead nor an idiot.

Pierre loathed himself for the brief sense of triumph. He had been a traitor to his class—to Maurice and Gilbert.

But there was something wrong. Something he had not noticed before. A filmy gray cord, the width of his little finger, dangled from the child's navel to its mother's vagina.

"A boy!" cried the *sage-femme*. "As pretty a boy as I've ever seen, *chérie!*" And she planted the baby on the girl's belly. "Cut the cord, M. *le Docteur, je vous implore!*"

"Cut the cord." The words fitted into his memory somewhere, or into a book he had read. The cord! Everyone born into the world trailing a cord. A cord and a conscience! Both to be dispensed with! . . . But who would know this was a cord? . . . He had a wild desire to stand there and laugh and laugh—to guffaw like a peasant, holding his sides.

The *sage-femme* was tying a bit of string close to the child's stomach. She handed Pierre a scissors. *Mon Dieu,* where should he cut? Somewhere near the fat thumb and finger which seemed to be patiently waiting? How the infant writhed and cried its angry cry! And how almost impossible it was not to guffaw like a peasant! And yet, one false snip and he would feel the scissors of the guillotine! . . . Now it was the cord or the guillotine. He held the scissors for a moment between the twine and her thumb. She made no objection. This must be right. He clamped the scissors together and a spurt of blood shot from the cord into her face.

"*Sacrebleu!*" she howled. "I've brought a thousand infants into the world and never have I seen such a *bête* as you!"

She wiped her face on her sleeve, and Pierre had to laugh aloud at last.

There was no way he could possibly stop the laughter. It bubbled up in him like a geyser. If she had not had the child in her hands he knew she would have struck him. As it was, she dug her heel sharply into his toe. And rightly! What made him laugh when he knew she had seen how his hand was shaking? She must know him now to be a charlatan. In a moment, when she had wrapped the child in its blanket and tucked it into the cradle, she would surely denounce him to the mayor. . . . *Dieu,* he *must* stop this laughing! He thought of the opium. Yes, he would cheat the mayor and the guillotine with the opium! . . . But what was she saying between her curses? . . . The *afterbirth?*

"And I suppose, *M. le Cochon,* that in Paris the midwife also removes the afterbirth while the surgeon stands by and laughs?"

"Oui, Madame, but only when a midwife is so skilled as you!" Words seemed to be released now with the hysteria. "On my word of honor, I have never seen a midwife perform with such art, such genius! For your invaluable aid, Madame, I make you a present of one hundred francs!"

("And of the afterbirth, whatever that is!") he thought rashly as he thrust a note into the hand stinking with blood and herring.

He shoved the bottles into the satchel and slung his coat over his shoulder, giving a last look at Annette. A month from now, dancing the Picardy jig at a vintage dance with her arms akimbo, she would be charming.

The *sage-femme* stood staring, her face blank with amazement.

"Alas, I must go on!" he exclaimed, and kissed her parchment cheek. "I must bleed a man at the inn. *Mais vous êtes un bijou!"*

Pierre had only gone a few paces from the cottage when Annette's husband caught up with him.

"M. le Docteur!" he whispered, "a word with you."

Pierre halted, terrified.

"I have not paid you your fee." He reached for Pierre's hand and pushed a few coins into it. *"M. le Docteur, je saute de joie!* The boy is beautiful, Monsieur. I am overcome with gratitude. . . . But a word of warning, Monsieur—the midwife is a jealous old bitch. She says but for her the child would be dead. That you are a quack or you would not have given her all that money! Tomorrow morning she will denounce you to Citizen the attorney. *Chien de mon âme!* These women! . . . I am eternally grateful to you, *M. le Docteur,* and wish you God-speed."

Pierre fumbled his way to the inn, his face aching with laughter. But his thoughts were racing. A hundred francs to a midwife was a fortune! He had been stark crazy.

The inn was settled for the night. He stole to his room and flung himself on the bed. It seemed he would never stop laughing, consumed with terror. . . . But he must go at once. The stables would be locked and he could not get his horse without arousing suspicion. Where could he go by foot to be in hiding? He was only a few leagues from Blois. With luck he might get on the ferry and cross the Loire before dawn. If he left at once . . . *if he could only stop this infernal laughing!*

CHAPTER XXIII

PIERRE was fortunate in gaining the confidence of a fisherman starting down the river from Blois at dawn. He had changed his story a trifle: his sick old mother now lived in a village near Chinon. He had made up his mind to head for Grenauld, the feudal castle of his father between Usse and Azay-le-Rideau on the Indre. He had no assurance that Grenauld would be standing; but here was a Gothic fortress it would be hard to destroy. (And if Grenauld were standing he felt certain his father's bailiff would not have deserted.)

As the day broke and they began to pass little hamlets, Pierre pleaded vertigo and lay in the scaly bottom of the punt. Few boats were afloat. Here, although the Loire had hips as wide as those of *Madame la sage-femme,* the water straggled through the shallows like the wisps of hair on her bald pate. It was a great tranquil stream with only enough current to carry along a twig. Yellow diamonds glistened in the distant river, growing larger and duller only to pass—dreary patches of sand.

Castles drifted by, tinted mother-of-pearl by the sunrise, half-screened by the wooded banks of the flat shore line. The pompous Chambord; the elegant Chaumont, guillotined by the side of the trawl. Now and then Pierre sat up to drink in the beauty of their staked vineyards luxuriant with ripening fruit.

He could scarce keep his mind off the droll tragedy of the night before. He began to think of the mothers he knew. Mme de Frivouac— *Dieu,* if he had first seen her in childbirth he would never have deigned to touch her! . . . Then his own mother. He could not endure the thought of how she must have suffered. It was no wonder she prayed for his soul. He had been poor comfort to her. Why couldn't he have been killed instead of Maurice and Gilbert who had brought her pride and glory? How she would mourn his impiety more than the loss of Maurice who had died in faith and its consecration! He tried to pray for her sorrow now as he watched the clouds tangling. As in the prison his hopes were inchoate. No prayer would come from his heart, only from his lips. He was angry—proof that there was no God if God refused meditation! Through God he wanted to explain so many things to Catherine, things to which he did not know the answer.

And then for the first time he thought of Victoire in actual childbirth. Victoire with the same glazed eyes, the same sweating pallor, the same straggling hair as Annette in the cottage. Nature was partial neither in birth nor in death. Victoire, like a peasant, had been reduced to primitive suffering. Strange to think that it was his own seed she had nurtured to fruition. He thought that if he had been with Victoire at the time of her travail, that if the weird little gargoyle had been his own, a new bond might have been created beyond the bond of their passion.

He wondered why he cared for a further tie between them when Silvie was all that he wanted. He remembered the challenging cry of Mme de Stenjac at the Abbaye. *"Vive le Roi!"* No doubt Mme de Stenjac had had her lovers. But she wished to die with her husband. What did the filth of prison, the shadow of the guillotine do to one that in his extremity he thought only of the family unit? What was this bond of mother, father, son, sister, so weak in prosperity, so strong in crisis? In the New World, no longer *"un homme sans aveu,"* there might come to him the solution.

He longed desperately for news of his son. Six months old, the child would be. Could the boy walk? Could he laugh? Did he look like Victoire or like his father? If only there were some way to get word through to Victoire. . . .

Thoughts had a way these days of colliding, shifting, evanescing, like the amorphous clouds he watched as he lay cramped in the boat. No beginning, no end. *Dieu,* it was only when one had to lie still that he knew how sick was his mind, how sore, how despairing!

The fisherman dropped him off at a little village across the river from Langeais, casually as if he dropped a fish back into the water.

He would stay at the inn, he thought, for the night. It was a tiny place, with only stable, kitchen, and common sleeping-room. He did not like the eyes of the innkeeper's wife upon him as he ate his couple of eggs and plate of peas.

In the common sleeping-room there were several others. The air was bad and the bed-bugs vicious, and Pierre wakened early. He had had a night of excruciating dreams. He had handed the Princess de Lamballe her head; he had seen Silvie plunging from the Tower; he had delivered Annette of a pig. . . . After his breakfast he was confronted by a gendarme. Madame the innkeeper's wife had fetched him. Would Pierre show his passport please?

Pierre watched the man with anxiety as he tried to scan his thumb-marked list of nationally proscribed people. The name of Pierre de Michelait, accomplice in the flight to Metz, recent fugitive from the Abbaye prison, would be on that list—would be on the list of every hamlet in every province. But the *sage-femme's* denunciation of M. Dreux, *surgeon-accoucheur* of Paris, could surely not have arrived before him.

"Where is the horse described on *M. le Docteur's* passport?"

"Ah, that is a tragic story," said Pierre. "A favorite mare—too timid. She bolted at a stampede of cattle near St. Amand, and backed into a ditch. Her leg dangled like an earring. We had to shoot her. And I rushing to my dying mother near Nantes!"

The gendarme continued to stare at Pierre's passport in his dirty hand. Pierre suggested a drink to the nation. Between them they soon consumed a bottle of fine sauterne. The innkeeper's wife, glowering, disappeared and returned with the municipal. The municipal examined the passport. Pierre was in the middle of a hilarious story, a joke he had heard on old Louis Capet. Pierre ordered another bottle of wine. It made a disastrous breakfast. He had no notion, however, of losing this tilt with the innkeeper's wife. He drank only enough to keep his tongue glib, his memory for ribald stories flowing.

Madame the innkeeper's wife went off to fetch one of the committee of superintendence. Pierre ordered another bottle of sauterne and began to sing *"Oh, Homme, mon frère."* Soon there was close harmony. Pierre began to feel desperate. There was no end to the woman's prosecution. One could not be highly amusing forever. The Commissioner came and examined the passport.

"My son has a fluxion on the jaw, *M. le Doc—"*

"Ah, a creeping plaster's the very thing. Remind me before I go." Pierre hastily drew out his medal of July fourteenth and began to brag about the assault on the Bastille and his bravery.

At last he decided he must take the initiative. He talked of his old mother near Nantes, how he must get to her quickly.

"Dieu, if I should be too late because I have drunk to the nation with my citizen brothers! . . . Your visa on my passport, *s'il vous plait, M. le Commissaire."*

The Commissioner's handwriting staggered with wine.

The innkeeper's wife sullenly overcharged Pierre for the sauterne. As he took his departure, leaving a plaster and some black dose with the Commissioner, the men began to rile her. What an ass she was to mistake such a jolly good patriot for an aristocrat!

Pierre heard them singing as he went down the road. He had an almost uncontrollable desire to run, to look behind him. His carpetbag and satchel seemed filled with bricks, and the countryside swam dizzily with sunshine. From now to Bordeaux, thought Pierre, he must avoid the villages; he must sleep only in a thicket or deserted barn.

It was only four leagues to Grenauld. Once at the castle, he could shed the ill-fated doctor's guise for that of a sans-culotte. For an hour he cooled his head and his tongue, lying in a copse from which he could watch the road. He was not sure that someone would not follow him for he had taken the opposite road from the one to Nantes.

At last he approached Azay-le-Rideau, filled with wine presses and coopers' shops. It was dusk. There was the comfortable smell of fermented grapes in the breeze; this was a countryside enchanted, drowsy, intoxicated with its own perfume. He and Gilbert had loved to come here with the bailiff when they were little. He longed to wander in the familiar, picturesque streets, to find lodging for his cumbersome body. He cursed the shoes that grew smaller with every step and the blisters that grew larger. Walking had never been a gentleman's forte.

But he dared not stop, for here a de Michelait might be recognized. Circling the village, he groped his way through a tangle of vineyards and limped among the hemplands of the Indre valley.

The towers of Grenauld had long since emerged from the evening sky, *Dieu merci!* It was many years since the family had gathered here for Catherine's name day, since he had seen the stream with its beloved sycamores and silken willows. He was suddenly filled with nostalgia. He had been happy then without knowing it. It shocked him to realize he had never really been happy since his childhood.

There were lights in a little nest of houses at the base of Grenauld's hill. Beyond was the turreted wall that enclosed seven hundred acres of park and woodland. In many places the stones of the wall were crumbling. The park was a drab wilderness in the deepening twilight, the castle a menacing ogre. Hundreds of years ago the ground he trod had first been pockmarked with every kind of hidden snare and pitfall. He remembered he had once broken his ankle in a trap of stones. Now the undergrowth swirled like a jungle. The early moon lighted the grim skyline of pinnacles, chimneys, and dormers. He had never seen Grenauld so black. Where were the thousand tapers? He shuddered, almost loath to go on. But now he could distinguish the various wings: the *Salles de Preuses* added at the time of Francis I; the Henry IV *donjon;* the Louis XIII chapel.

He came to the moat, supplied by a dam head of the Indre. Now it was dry—like shining glue in the moonlight. He thought of the great iron rings let into the walls, where visiting barques had once been fastened. He and Gilbert had had a game. They had nicked coins and dropped them into the moat in the springtime; they had tried to find them again in the drought. Mad, senseless days! . . . The ache to see Gilbert at this very moment was unbearable.

The portcullis was down and he slowly crossed it. He saw a light now through the curtained slit of its guardian turret. The wall would be covered with green and gold mold, half hiding scars of cannon balls and bullets. Old Duchâtel the concierge had told him many a fantastic story of the fortress. . . . His initials, too, were scratched on the pointed stone arch. Suddenly he wanted to cry. He stood for a long time, his throat aching.

But he would get no farther than this if he did not knock. There was an inner moat, a dry *fosse,* twenty feet deep. *Nom de Dieu,* but he was hungry and tired dragging his carpetbag and his doctor's satchel! He must knock, of course. He must take his chance. . . . There were always his two strong fists and his sword cane. He drew a deep breath, banged at the door, and stepped back into the shadow. His heart gave a leap of joy when he saw the old concierge.

For days Pierre lived in the castle. Mme Duchâtel, a hunchback, brought him his meals. She seemed to him like a shrunken gourd but she was still nimble. Duchâtel was also forbidding, with eyes crossed, but the more shrewdly observing. If Pierre was shocked anew at their ugliness they were equally shocked at his gauntness.

Duchâtel spent hours with Pierre relating the outrages of the peasants. The bailiff had been recently guillotined. Pierre had to talk to Duchâtel about Paris although he wanted to forget Paris. His mind seemed porous. Events and images slipped from him as if they had been spirited away. Now and then he began a story and stared at Duchâtel in the middle of a sentence. He had forgotten what he was saying. It was Silvie's fault . . . she was crossing the *Salle de Preuses,* her white train drifting down the great paneled room with its painted ceiling. Pierre watched her as she paused beside the huge chimney.

Here was a row of marble life-sized females representing the ladies of the chief knights of chivalry. Silvie floated among them, then was still as the motto carved in Gothic. *Dieu,* he knew now it had been an hallucination but a moment ago she was real as Duchâtel! Pierre felt a hot wave of embarrassment.

"Pardon! What was I saying?" he asked the concierge, who gazèd at him strangely.

"You were saying, M. Pierre, that you thought the garb of a sansculotte would be very satisfactory. . . ."

"*Oui, oui, oui!* . . . and your Royalist friend at Azay-le-Rideau. He is surely to be trusted?"

"*Mais oui!* He has been a professional letter writer for forty years. He is a very skillful penman. He will forge you a passport to fool the cleverest official."

"*Bien!* But the seal of the districts I have passed through on my way from Paris?"

"They will be wanting. Unfortunately M. Flons is only an artist at visas." Duchâtel pulled on his pipe, gazed keenly at Pierre, and added as he departed: "Try to eat more, M. Pierre, and try to have patience."

But Pierre felt more confined here than he had at the Abbaye. There was the dullness of dust over everything, like the pall of black hangings after a funeral. There were small, dead moths from the woods, and mammoth gray webs. The portraits of his ancestors were dim and wraithlike. Although the great halls had the chill of a mausoleum he was afraid to light the logs; smoke against the sky or a red slit of casement would be invitation to a curious peasant. Escape was possible, of course, through the sliding panels, hidden doorways, or the secret cabinets that had so delighted him as a child. But he might implicate Duchâtel, who had been so kind to him. Even now he endangered both himself and the concierge by warming his marrow at night at the hearth in the *conciergerie.*

Duchâtel supposed that Pierre lived alone in the castle. But he was never alone. At night he dreamed of Silvie. They wandered together in the woods of Meudon, filled with rapture until the flowers grew thick and huge and finally strangled them. Sometimes Pierre saw his son, a big boy now, tossing a ball to him. Marie Antoinette often sat on one of the carved Gothic seats of the Great Hall, embroidering. But she was always behind him. When he turned with a quickening hope she was gone. He knew by the rose scent she had always used that she had been there and for a long time it quivered in his nostrils. Sometimes he heard the Princess de Lamballe playing the lute. That was more tuneful than the little bell that tinkled persistently in his ears like that of a leper.

One day he asked Duchâtel: "Why does the bell in Azay-le-Rideau keep tolling?"

"There is no bell, M. Pierre."

"But I hear it distinctly . . . my ears are very sharp!"

"Perhaps it is the bell of the convent," answered Duchâtel, his brow puckered. *"Dites-moi, M. Pierre,* you have everything you want here? . . . Have you been sleeping?"

"How can I sleep when I am consumed with eagerness to be gone? *Dieu,* will your M. Flons never be finished with his embroidery?"

Pierre tried to read, but his head was leaden, split now and then with a pain that cleft his skull in two. The magnificent library with its two thousand volumes and old manuscripts from the abbeys of Fontrevault and St. Florent seemed to shrink, to close in on him. Silver fish scrambled from the pages he touched. He hated them; he swore at them. Grenauld was gradually eating itself away with silver fish, and dust, and darkness. And he no sooner began a paragraph than Gilbert intervened. Gilbert was always fond of playing practical jokes. Now he caused the armorial shields above the wainscot to change color . . . or was it the diluted sunshine? . . . *Dieu,* how could one's mind wander so?

The echo of his footsteps throughout the rooms was regular as the fall rain on the windows. He could not be still. Once, passing a mirror, he stopped to stare at himself. This was no one he recognized. It was a bearded man with a lean, hungry look. But he must raise a fine pair of mustachios if he were to be a convincing carmagnole. Of course, this was his own reflection. And yet, he had a distressing belief that he was two people, that he was literally beside himself.

He roamed from Catherine's chapel with its pale rose window to the towers. Then down again, down the interminable steps to the *donjons.* In the moldy cells he imagined the smell of leek and cabbage and human excrement. It was like the smell of the corridors in the Abbaye. In this black belly of the earth there was a death chill. He and Gilbert had sometimes come here to try to decipher the inscriptions and sketches traced on the walls by despairing captives. One even stumbled over bones. Gilbert had always shrieked melodramatically. Maurice had never been frightened. He said that even in *donjons* God was with one. . . . But oh, the joy, the relief it had been to get back to the great halls with their rich fringed tapestries, the warmth of red velvet, familiar suits of armor, and the sweet pungent perfume of spiced wine!

When the castle became so oppressive that he was not sure but he had screamed, Pierre trod the quadrangle of the interior court, onto which gave the doors and windows of the apartments. Here no one could see him but the bronze equestrian figure of his ancestor. In the waning moonlight he stalked the outer parapet that served as a communication from one wing of the castle to the other. The walls were battlemented and machicolated, with loopholes between the embrasures of the battlements. Now and then his toe slipped into a machicoulis, a hole in the stone floor between the brackets supporting its projection. Through the cavities boiling water or hot lead had been poured upon the enemy; or stones upon the head of an adventurer. Gilbert had had a game . . . but Maurice crossed himself and said it was very wicked.

How the frost ate into one's flesh here on the parapet! But here the air was alive, sprinkled with stars. It drove from his mind fragments of crocketed gables and finials, traceried balustrades, leering heraldic animals.

Nom de Dieu! was he losing his mind? . . . What made him so confused? What made him see patches of blood on the stone floors— blood that vanished like a mirage when he touched it? What made him shiver and sweat by turns so that he could no longer drag his legs behind him or swallow food? What made him feel that he, Pierre, was outside of his body? What gave him the sickening urge to leap from the *guette* to the cliff below? So strong an urge that he fought with his will, his nails cutting his palms, until he was overcome with chills and fever and faint with exhaustion! . . .

And then one night Duchâtel came to tell him that Marie Antoinette had been guillotined. And Pierre was grateful for the blackness of the sea that engulfed him.

CHAPTER XXIV

FOR A WEEK Pierre lay very ill and it was the beginning of November before he was strong enough to set out on his journey. He wore a complete carmagnole with an enormous saber dangling at his side and a brace of pistols in his belt.

The passport M. Flons had made was a masterpiece, convincingly soiled and limp. It carried the visas of mayors, lawyers, and municipals who claimed they had seen pass Citizen Jacques Mourat, an honest sans-culotte going to Bordeaux on secret business of the Republic.

For several days Pierre made good progress although his legs were not so strong as his will. But he must keep moving. That was the one way he could keep his sanity. His world had become hollow without Marie Antoinette, like a cup one lifts to parched lips only to find it empty. His thoughts dwelled on her with a morbid sweetness—the ivory of her hands, the grace of her carriage, the rose perfume, the alluring curve of her lips. Yes, even the rhythm of her fan! The Abbé Blafond was right. She had been his religion—a woman one died for, even as Silvie was a woman one lived for—and now Marie Antoinette was gone.

But there was the Dauphin, he told himself sharply. And there was the Queen before him in the little attic room at Varennes, her voice impassioned: "I can only hope that whatever happens to me, you will continue to fight for his safety, and for the good of France. . . ." He looked back on his lapse of loyalty, on his selfish desire only for Silvie and his son with a painful chagrin. From this moment on he would let nothing interfere with his sacred purpose.

At night Pierre slept in a deserted monastery or hen house, avoiding settlements as much as possible. Sometimes he longed to be dead rather than to measure each word and each step, to stifle a sneeze in a haymow, to sing the *Ça-Ira* at a village guillotine. Only now and then he dared to take a diligence between two large towns when he was exhausted.

Brooks, marshes, fields, groves, and hillocks . . . he waded and climbed, blinded with fatigue and hunger. Squirrels and rabbits scurried close and he heard the impudent squawk of the pheasant. He longed to shoot one, to flay and roast it. He thought of the Hôtel d'Aligre in the rue St. Honoré. Baked hams, cooked tongues from Vierson, wood hen from the Pyrenees . . . and the little delicacies that he loved: pickled cucumber, princess almonds, Chinese lemons in confection. His saliva was sharp and piercing as vinegar.

When hunger overpowered him he took the risk of buying bread or sausage or cheese in a village. Once he ate at an inn; but hadn't he learned at the inn across from Langeais that that was dangerous? He could demand food at a farmhouse, of course, but a fierce-looking sans-culotte might not be welcome. In the meantime he munched on some chicken corn stolen from a bin, or extracted a few walnuts from his pocket and cracked them on his gun. What if the meats were still a little green and bitter?

One morning he was overtaken by a "strolling deputy" who traveled alone in a post chaise. He urged Pierre to join him. The deputy made it a point to pick up a brave sans-culotte whenever he could, he said. Weren't they the very backbone of France since Robespierre was President of the Convention? Why should the sans-culottes walk? Let the *ci-devants* walk!

Pierre was grateful. The night before in leaping a brook he had wrenched a tendon. His leg was so swollen and rigid he could hardly drag it. And the company of a strolling deputy would be more protection than a troop of volunteers, he decided.

The deputy was a tall, wiry man with the éclat of a swirling pennant. He wore a dusty frock coat with high, turn-down collar and lapels, tight breeches with ribbon below the knee, a large felt hat with the brim pinned back by a cockade, and soiled linen. His long tapering fingers might almost look like a gentleman's, thought Pierre, if they were not so dirty.

The deputy was garrulous. The revolts in the provinces had been nearly unmanageable, he told Pierre. It was not so much that people loved their King and religion as that they feared conscription. *Oui,* the rebels kept him busy as a fly at honey. Sometimes he even had to make laws on the spot to bring the fools to reason. Now and then he assisted at a guillotine. Had Pierre ever helped with an execution? It reminded one of pressing grapes at the vintage. . . . Now, the noyades in La Vendée (an idea Carrier had borrowed form Nero) were much more efficient. So simple to pack the victims on a boat and dump them through a trap door into the Loire. The people preferred it, so a fellow deputy had told him. One young girl, falling into a drowning heap of corpses, had even cried out: "Help me! I have not enough water," and an official had obligingly pushed her to a deeper spot of the river. There were only two defects in the noyade method: the waters were so corrupt they were beginning to spread pestilence; and drenched skin did not make as good wash leather for the tannery at Meudon. Amazing that a man's skin was superior in toughness and quality to chamois!

Pierre laughed and clenched his nails into his palms.

They jabbered to one another of liberty, of Pitt and the coalesced tyrants, of *l'amour de la patrie*. Pierre showed him his Bastille medal, embellished his story.

What did Citizen Mourat think of the new Republican calendar, asked the deputy? Strange to think that this was no longer the month of November, but Brumaire, the Year Two. And that the Christian Sabbath would now shift for itself while the Decadi, every tenth day, would be the day of rest. What place was there in a new, a virile France for a moldering religion?

Their passports were examined casually. Here was a pair of patriots dirty enough that no one could doubt their loyalty. Pierre dreaded a stop at an inn. But they drove on through the villages. At high noon the deputy shared with Pierre bread, fruit, and chestnuts that he had stuffed in his pockets.

"What do you think, Citizen Mourat, of the *Autrichienne* sneezing into the basket?" the deputy said blithely, his mouth bulging.

Pierre made some indistinct sound.

"They say she trod on Sanson's toe when he tied her hands, and begged his pardon!" The deputy gave a loud guffaw. "Once a Queen, always a Queen!"

Pierre's voice failed him.

The deputy turned to him and their eyes met with the swift, keen glance of the hunter. The deputy whipped his horse and they flew along at a gallop, silent for a moment. Then the deputy said: "I'd like to get my fingers on the Girondins. Not the mess who were just executed in Paris," and he laughed coarsely, "but those who escaped in June and wandered through Normandy and Brittany to the Gironde. . . . It is only a rumor, of course, that they are being hidden by Mme Bouquey in a cave at Saint-Émilion. Yet she left Fontainebleau at once by diligence when she heard that her brother-in-law was being pursued."

"Mme Bouquey . . ." repeated Pierre in anguish, because he dared not ask which Girondins had been guillotined.

"*Oui,* Mme Bouquey. And Tallien is doing a wretched job as proconsul in Bordeaux. Very lax—letting many a chouan get away with his head. It's all the influence of his tender-hearted mistress, la Marquise de Fontenay. If I were in the Gironde I'd ferret out the rats."

At nightfall the deputy suggested that they stop at a cottage for supper and the night. Why should a deputy pay for his meals, he laughed? At one dwelling after another there was no answer although the deputy pounded on the door and called through the cat holes with great bluster.

At last they surprised a peasant entering his cottage with an armful of wood. He wore twisted straw about his bare legs to keep him warm, and his ragged shoulders were thatched against the November rain. The cottage was a filthy, dilapidated place, overflowing with rabbits and cabbage leaves. The hutch, brought in for the winter, was but a step from the decrepit bed, a few feet from the spit on which the poor creatures roasted.

The peasant and his wife stood transfixed in the center of the hovel. Young, they looked old, with a skin dried and sallow from their limited diet.

"I understand you have done nothing of late for the Republic," shouted the deputy, picking his nose. "*Viens,* we will talk over your bad manners at supper."

Pierre's stomach turned over. The air was fetid. He would never be able to swallow a morsel.

The man pushed two stools forward and the woman sullenly went to a cupboard, producing half a roasted rabbit and some black pudding. Pierre wondered if the trap door going to the cellar did not conceal plenty of cheese and butter and wine. How could these people be sure *M. le Député* was not a tax collector? It was an advantage to appear poor in order not to pay taxes. For if the poor peasant could not meet the demands someone richer had to meet his deficit.

Just then a pig emerged grunting from the corner.

"*Bien!* We'll have sausages for breakfast," announced the deputy with relish. "I am not overfond of hare. . . . Slaughter the pig at once and get the grinder to work."

"If I slaughter the pig, Monsieur, we'll starve before the end of the winter!" pleaded the man in a patois hardly intelligible.

The woman was muttering angrily now as she tossed some nicked earthenware on a table.

"The guillotine is sharper than the grinder," the deputy reminded him. And he winked at Pierre.

Pierre rose. His stomach was churning. The fresh news of the Girondins had completely unnerved him. If only he dared ask about his father. . . . He must keep moving, must get to Bordeaux. Thank God, he was not so very many leagues now from Bordeaux!

"But I must go on," he heard himself saying. "My business with Tallien is very urgent."

The deputy was disconsolate. He had never had so charming a traveling companion. He was *désolé* that Pierre would no longer accompany him. And he made a bow with a grace that was surprising for one who picked his nose.

Pierre spent the night in an outhouse.

The next day on a byroad he approached several women who were gathering horse dung in baskets. When they saw him their laughter ended abruptly. Pierre stopped to chat with them a moment to reassure them, and learned that the strolling deputy had been apprehended, that he was an impostor, a nobleman from Normandy. That he had blown his brains out in the cottage of a peasant. But, *hélas,* his companion, whom the police hunted, had escaped. Another nobleman, they thought, posing as a sans-culotte. For a moment the women had wondered. . . .

Pierre laughed. "Like as not he has already been found, the *chien!*" he said. He gave the women a flattering smile, wished them good findings, and sauntered off, whistling the *Marseillaise* very much off-key.

He must find a hide-out as soon as possible, and remain under cover until the flurry over the deputy abated. Saint-Émilion . . . it was not so far. Of Gallo-Roman origin, the little village was honeycombed beneath with enormous, winding grottoes. Pierre had often heard Grégoire speak of his childhood visits to them. The ancient quarries extended in a vast network, and almost every house had access to the grottoes, parts of which, walled off, served as cellars. The Girondins hidden by Mme Bouquey would be confreres of his father. For Grégoire's sake they might shelter him. And Saint-Émilion, on the right bank of the Dordogne, couldn't be more than ten leagues from Bordeaux.

Pierre hid by day and limped along by night. Curse the deputy, the brazen *ci-devant* who had so delayed his mission!

In the early morning a week later while it was still dark eight men emerged from the house of Mme Bouquey, Pierre among them. One at a time they left the kitchen to creep to the square well in the garden.

Situated on the slope of a hill, Saint-Émilion was hemmed in by doddering ramparts of the twelfth and thirteenth centuries. Ditches, hewn in the rocks, encircled the medieval buildings. A fine belfry commanding the town was built on a terrace beneath which were gouged from the rock the oratory and hermitage of Saint-Émilion. Mme Bouquey's house lay in the shadow of an ancient monolithic church that adjoined them. The buildings were now part of the starless sky, undistinguishable.

Pierre climbed over the parapet of the well. The same thought always came to him: one false step and he would splash in the water a hundred feet below like a bucket. Better that way, perhaps, and he would not have to think! . . .

But each morning his hands gripped the stones firmly. In the masonry, holes had been cut on opposite sides at different levels. By now he knew how far down to feel for the slimy niche. Then twenty feet below ground and there would be an opening into the cave.

A second grotto thirty feet underground opened from the "salon," as Louvet gaily called it. The deeper gallery was reached by slipping through a hole closed by a board. It was here that they sat all day, not daring to speak above a whisper, for the caverns caught their voices and screamed their words to unknown grottoes beyond. In case of emergency there was a spade, a jar of mortar, and a pickax so they might block up the entrance of the "salon" and entomb themselves in the little closet.

Pierre and Gaudet dropped onto one of the two mattresses Mme Bouquey had let down the well with the long iron rod and its hook. Marinette was an angel and Gaudet might well be proud to claim her as his sister-in-law. Here was a young woman who had the courage of a Marie Antoinette. A charming young woman who cheered them by her fire at night and struggled to find food for them by day, risking her life because she was filled with the milk of human kindness.

The other men settled down too with quiet resignation. These men, eloquent and impractical, who had fought for Mme Roland's ideal republic. Barbaroux, once *"beau comme un marbre grec,"* now fat and puffy and afflicted with rheumatism; Buzot, the ardent lover of Mme Roland, wearing her miniature at his breast; the brave Valady, who could not sit still for more than a minute; Louvet, the author of scandalous tales, living a tale more dangerous than any he had ever fabricated; Salle, the solemn country doctor; and Pétion, who had once been chosen unanimously mayor of Paris. It was Pétion who had brought back the royal family from Varennes, riding jauntily in the royal coach. But even Pétion had asked no questions of Pierre and had accepted him simply as a man fighting for life. It was scarcely the time for Pierre to evince his hatred of Pétion.

The grotto was not without some comforts. Mme Bouquey had let down two chairs, a small table, and some blankets in which they wrapped themselves like mummies. As the iciness of the catacombs penetrated like needles and it was impossible to light a fire, they passed a hot-water bottle from one to another. Mme Bouquey had thought of spoons and forks, books, ink and paper. From the first, of course, there had been a lantern, its light flickering wanly in the strong air currents.

Salle's pen began to scratch. He was working on a tragedy of Charlotte Corday. Buzot, Barbaroux, Pétion, and Louvet were writing their memoirs.

Now and then there was a whispered snatch of conversation.

"Some of your speeches are of inordinate length," said Pétion, leafing through Salle's *Charlotte Corday*.

"I recommend you to imitate M. Shakespeare," remarked Barbaroux, trying to rub the pain out of his swollen fingers.

"The love element does not belong in Corday's story." This was the wiry Louvet whispering now. And Louvet had published.

An argument began. "Come," said Pierre finally, "where there is France there is love—even in the story of a Jeanne d'Arc or a Charlotte Corday."

Only Buzot was silent. With his miniature of Mme Roland on his breast, he paced up and down, up and down, his hands behind him. He had no thought but for her in the *Conciergerie* at Paris.

Gaudet exclaimed irrelevantly: *"Dieu,* what I would not give for a generous pinch of snuff and a generous sneeze!" and he toyed with his snuff box.

There was quiet again except for the scratching pen of Salle going on with *Charlotte Corday*.

Pierre settled onto one elbow. He had been framing in his mind a letter to Victoire. He hoped that he could send it by ship from Bordeaux to Coblentz. He would tell her that he must go to Asylum, the colony in Pennsylvania, and that if she could safely make the trip he would expect her to join him there with the child.

When he thought of his son he trembled with an inward weeping. Every day it seemed less probable that Pierre would ever see him. Sometimes he thought it would be better if the child didn't live. What future was there for him in the chaos within chaos, as the scrawny village priest had called it? Even if Grégoire were dead and Pierre in the eyes of royalist France were now the Marquis de Bussac, Comte de Grenauld, Baron de Brithon—the inheritance of these estates would be swallowed by the government because Grégoire had been guillotined.

Moreover, Danton, who had at least made an honest attempt to unite all partisans of the Revolution in defense of the country, had begun to lose his power along with the Girondins. The Committee of Public Safety ruled France, and the Jacobin Club ruled the Committee of Public Safety. It was Robespierre who now planned the ideal state, and not Mme Roland.

"No, there is nothing for the boy to live for," thought Pierre, over and over. "I am only a scarecrow grateful for warm water to wash my feet. For bread of fern meal, or snails and eels for my stomach. Why should I wish my son to inherit my misery?"

And the little Louis Charles—would he ever really gain the throne out of this chaos? At Louis's death the Comte de Provence had proclaimed the Dauphin King of France and Navarre under the name of Louis XVII. Provence had declared himself regent, and his brother Artois Lieutenant-General of the kingdom. But weren't these blustering declarations beyond the border, in defiance of a demand for the execution of all the Bourbons?

What hope really was there for the child in Coblentz or the child in the Temple?

Dieu, if only he could twist the necks of the little noises that seemed so thunderous! The incessant whisper of dripping water; the scratching of Valady's stone as he etched a guillotine on a stalagmite in the ancient manner; the soft paddling of Buzot's feet on the plastic clay floor; the gnawing of Salle's pen on the paper; the crackling of Barbaroux's knuckles as he kneaded them.

A clanking noise above him caused Pierre to jump to his feet with the seven other men. It was the same each day when the clank came although they expected it. Mme Bouquey was lowering vegetable soup to the cave in spite of the "banditti" of Saint-Émilion who threatened to burn alive in his house anyone who concealed proscribed persons.

Valady reached out and clutched the steaming kettle of soup, which slopped a little over the slippery floor. Gaudet produced the bowls, and except for Buzot who continued his pacing, they ate silently, lustily. How could Mme Bouquey furnish the daily soup? How could she manage the milk and eggs, the bit of poultry she gave them at supper? She lived alone and was entitled to but a pound of bread a day and a small ration of meat. When they questioned her she only laughed. But Marinette grew thinner.

After an eternity of hours the men crawled up the well again, creeping back through the dark November frost to the heat of the house.

It was a night that remained vivid in Pierre's memory.

A fire roared in the kitchen fireplace. The room was cheery and heartening with its high-backed chairs under the great over-hanging chimney piece. But Pierre felt depressed with the sudden heat, as if he had taken an opiate.

Buzot and Barbaroux sank onto stools before the fire, chafing their hands. The curious Pétion peered into an omelet pan, exclaimed "Mmmm," and began to draw some chairs up to the table. Anne Bérard, the wisp of a maid, was sniffling as she brought over the blue plates from the olive-wood cupboard. But where was Mme Bouquey who usually fluttered about the kitchen, joking with them as gaily as the bunch of keys that jingled at her apron?

At last she joined them, but her great black eyes were dull and her laughter forced. They had no sooner started eating than she burst into tears.

The whole town of Saint-Émilion was filled with a terrible suspicion and malevolence, she sobbed. Only two nights ago the house had been searched for a refractory priest . . . and the baker had said there was rumor of the Girondins—that a pack of hounds was to be let loose in the vicinity. . . .

She did not tell them that for days she had resisted the pleas, the demands of her husband and relatives to force her to give up the men in hiding—that M. Bouquey was adamant—that she had been just as adamant.

At news of the hounds there was a cutting silence. Then Anne Bérard began to sob with her mistress and the men groped for words of gratitude and consolation. They would leave at once, of course.

"We will be gone by midnight," exclaimed Louvet. "Rather all eight of us be caught in the streets than one hair of your head be injured!"

It was a noble speech but it could not conceal his weariness and desperation.

"*Non, non, non,* never!" insisted Mme Bouquey. "I forbid you to leave me."

"Ah, but if they should arrest you some day and we are still in the cave, what would become of us?" Pierre bantered.

"My poor children, I have thought of that so often! There is a little den at the shop of the wigmaker, M. Troquart," Mme Bouquey wept. "He has promised to help you!"

There was a bustle of preparation. Valady went down the well to fetch memoirs and souvenirs, which were entrusted to the little maid. If the authorities came she would throw papers, pictures, and strong boxes down the privies.

The men lounged before the fire then while Mme Bouquey knitted. It was a long evening of brooding filled with nervous chatter.

But one thought lay behind every word that was spoken.

They could not remain with Mme Bouquey; yet neither could they leave her.

CHAPTER XXV

AT TEN O'CLOCK there were five muffled sounds on the shutter. Though this was the customary rap of Anne Bérard's lover the men warily disappeared into the rooms beyond the kitchen. A moment later Mme Bouquey followed them, white-faced. There was not a second to lose. The authorities were coming and the men must go to their hide-out. When it was safe to return to the house again she would give them the signal.

The men snatched their coats and went out into the blackness. Mme Bouquey stood at the door; her eyes were still red from weeping, but the fire in them was heartening.

With a quick premonition Pierre, who was last to leave, leaned over the tiny woman and kissed her.

"Good-bye, little mother," he whispered. "God keep you!"

The men disappeared down the well into the underground like a flight of jackdaws.

"Tonight we must block up the entrance," whispered Gaudet as they crawled through the hole to their closet.

It was a job quickly done.

Alive, they were sealed in their mausoleum.

Salle as a matter of habit seated himself at the table and strummed on the board where a few hours before his manuscript of *Charlotte Corday* had lain before him. Pierre and Gaudet, who had sealed the closet, huddled in blankets for their sweat was turning to ice now. Pétion was openly chattering. Pierre handed him the hot-water bag, but it was colder than the wet moss in the well niches. Barbaroux puffed from his exertion; his breath came in short pants for so long a time that Pierre knew he was wildly frightened. Even Valady's obvious joking did not distract them.

Brave Valady, thought Pierre gratefully, how would they ever bear up without him? If only Buzot would stop his pacing . . . *Mon Dieu,* pacing would not get Mme Roland out of the *Conciergerie!*

But the entombment would only last a few hours at most. A cursory search of the house and the authorities would be satisfied. Then Mme Bouquey would signal. . . .

But Mme Bouquey did not signal with the clank of the anchor. Two hours went by—and three hours. Barbaroux's watch lay before him on the table when he did not play with it or wind it. Salle was dozing with the fatalism of a doctor.

Now and then Buzot stopped short in his pacing and said: "There, I hear it!" and they would jump to their feet. But there was no sound but the distant dripping in a cavern, so loud if one listened carefully that it was like the ring of an anvil.

Morning came—by Barbaroux's watch. All but Buzot had slept fitfully. They took turns slapping a little circulation into each other's thighs.

Gaudet pulled from his pockets some bread and cheese he had thought to take from a cupboard. He dealt it out sparingly. The fact that he used only half depressed them all but they knew this was necessary. Buzot refused his share.

"I'll eat it," cried the puffy Barbaroux eagerly.

Pierre thought of Louis at Varennes and the Baron von Drinsbach in prison.

Gaudet himself did not eat.

"I am worried," he confessed to Pierre as he poured wine for him. "Something has happened to Marinette. I feel it."

"Perhaps the house is still guarded and she doesn't dare leave it."

"If that were all I would be thankful. I can't help but fear the authorities have taken her—"

Pierre laid his hand over Gaudet's mouth and he felt the lips tremble. It was a bold show they were putting on for one another, he mused, when their hopes were crumbling, their fears rampant. Valady and Pétion playing dominoes; Louvet revealing the plots of books he would some day be writing.

The only opening now from the little cell was the size of a manhole. Through it one could see into the dim caverns beyond—gaunt shadows, threads of light, a distant bead blazing like a blue zircon. Buzot, listless now, lay on his belly staring through the opening. When at last he began to sneeze, and each sneeze roared through the caverns with a thousand echoes, Salle covered the opening with a blanket to bar the draught. He gave Buzot a pill from his wallet; it would allay a cold, he said. And Buzot slept.

The air was becoming putrid and heavy. Sometimes caves gave out poisonous gases, thought Pierre, and shivered. But no, this was only guano. He had seen the bats himself in the adjoining grotto one day when he had gone wandering. And there was the smell of clay and wet rock and rotting animals fallen down pits onto the bedrock.

As the day went on, relentless, Pierre's mind began to wander. Now and then he dozed in spite of the pain in his leg. Dreams and memories mingled. He remembered the Wieliczka salt mines in Austrian Poland. There was a chapel below with salt crystals glittering like diamonds. The underground was thrilling, not frightening. It had given to man iron, silver, gold, diamonds. Was he in a diamond mine now? His eyes were glued shut with diamond dust and he wanted to reach out and touch the blazing Kohinoor. . . . Yet now it had turned to coral. He was not in the diamond mine after all but in a coral cave of the South Sea Islands. . . .

He stirred and opened his eyes. He should not have drunk so much wine; his wits must be keen to save him. Any moment Marinette might clank the anchor. But wine warmed the ribs and mellowed the faltering of time. His thirst was as much a vulture as the appetites of Louis and Barbaroux.

He laughed to himself at the memory of a visit to a wine cellar in the Jews' quarter of Warsaw. There was the sort of underground a man relished. The wine cellar had stretched two or three miles under the rumbling of carriages in the street above—a modern wine cellar, only a few hundred years in existence. The casks had been covered with dust and cobwebs, some bottles on the shelves undisturbed through the reigns of many kings. The proprietor had broken a bottle covered with mold, barely distinguishable. It was not the only wine they had tasted. They had gone from one to another like bees in a flower garden. Pierre had sat on the bottom step of the cellar and refused to leave with his party. It was a joke for weeks that the Comte de Frivouac had had to cuff him to bring him to his senses.

But here was no wine cellar like that of Warsaw. Here when the jug of wine gave out would be a dugout far worse than those of the ragpickers in Paris. Another night, another day in this tomb and they would have zest for the chiffoniers' common kettle of soup made of dead dogs and the garbage of restaurants. No chance of a *"bonne bouche"* here, with the *"hasard de la fourchette"*!

Pierre finished his wine and sank back, drowsing again.

"The grave is dark; but the paths that lead from it are, to the right-eous, strewn with eternal flowers. . . ." "Be not proud or boastful, O Mortal; for this is the end of the loftiest ambition and the highest glory. . . ." What were these words that stood as high as a mountain before eyes tightly glued with diamond dust? . . . Ah, he knew now, as the words dwindled to dim inscriptions in the catacombs of Paris. The dump of Saints, poets, princes, *grisettes,* and pickpockets. He was reaching for Maurice's hand as he stumbled down the circular steps to the catacombs, and the wax taper in his hand was shaking. *Dieu,* one did not have to end smothering underground like the persecuted Christians under Nero!

He raised himself with a cry of protest and wakened to find Salle leaning over him, upbraiding him. Silence! There must be the utmost silence! He knew it, of course. One's voice might carry tenfold in volume to a guard at the top of the well pit. He was ashamed, profuse with apology. He would stay awake from now on, would no longer indulge in nightmares. Shivering, he settled back in his blanket.

But his waking mind was still filled with the agony of the catacombs. The Abbé Blafond had taken the boys to visit the Church of the Cata-combs in Rome. Gilbert had laughed hysterically at the monks' bones arranged in patterns, the neat designs of metatarsals, the ceiling bold with skull bones. Maurice had kept crossing himself, and Pierre, choked with human dust and terror, had clung to the Abbé's garments.

The sunshine later had been like nectar. They had drunk it in, laughing and crying at once, feeling volatile. The sunshine! It seemed years now since Pierre had seen it. The sun was the core of life, the pivot of happiness and freedom. America would have abundant sunshine. If he would ever reach it! Ah, the thirst he felt suddenly for America and freedom!

He looked at the men about him. Living so close to these men, they had become a part of him. He was a drop of an ocean, the shred of a tree split into splinters. Humanity was one man; men were only facets of the Godhead. One knew this instinctively under the ground where the silence and mold had already begun to claim them. Marie Antoinette too was a part of him; she shared his agony of mind just as surely at this moment as he shared her decomposition. One man, one God . . . but there was no God, for Pierre had reasoned him non-existent. When one could not pray to God, surely God was hypothetical. . . .

Pierre's eyes drifted to Gaudet, who was telling the beads of his rosary. There was a God for Gaudet. But either a God existed or he didn't. And who was to judge? Pierre's soul and body filled with the pressure of bursting as if he were drowning, and he buried his head in the mattress. It was more than one mortal mind could endure, this uncertainty of the Godhead. Could it be like this struggling for salvation in a hereafter?

By the time the next evening came the men had become silent, impassive as statues. It was Gaudet who roused them at last.

"I can no longer endure this," he whispered grimly. "Now I know something has happened to Marinette."

Twenty-four hours had passed and there had been no word from her. Should they take the risk of going up the well again and face the authorities if need be? Death in the open would be a boon compared to subsistence in the dungeon; they agreed on that unanimously. Without food or water they would be able to hide down here another day or two at most. But would that other day or two insure their safety? Would the suspicious authorities get tired of waiting and watching and wondering?

All but Gaudet and Barbaroux voted to remain. Another day below ground might spare the lives of all of them including Mme Bouquey.

Their minds were suddenly changed by a pitiful incident. It was discovered that Buzot was missing. During the night he had slipped through the opening to the outer cavern. Pierre volunteered at once to search for him for he knew the crevices and pitfalls from his adventuring.

He tied one end of a rope to the table and the other end about his waist and slid through the opening on his belly. Valady passed the one lamp to him, leaving the men in darkness.

It was a gruesome errand. Looking back, Pierre could see the feverish eyes of the men at the opening like the eyes of cave rats hypnotized by a light. He crept down the long narrow corridor that Barbaroux could not have squeezed through. It seemed to shrink as he advanced, pressing in on him. His feet slipped as he shoved along in his own little aura of light. Hearing a loud pounding, he stopped once only to find it was his heart beat.

At last he had to turn left and slide through another opening on his stomach, pushing the lantern inch by inch before him. He was alone now; the feverish eyes could no longer see him.

The cave he entered was vast and deceiving. The floor and ceiling, the limits of the cave, grew opaque out of the shadows of the lantern. Pillars of stalagmites and stalactites grown together reminded him of banyan trees in the forest. Hundreds of interstices led to smaller caves on various levels.

"Buzot! Where are you?" Pierre whispered. The words became a hiss like a wild wind whistling and the syllables returned to him jumbled and babbling.

Not even the ravenous cold was so frightening as noise in the cavern. When his own whisper died down with a lingering sigh he heard the sweet note of a flute repeated at regular intervals. He knew that the sound was produced by water dripping into a tube it had hollowed. He had located the tube one day, had fathomed its mystery. Or had he, he wondered confusedly? Were these the voices of fate which the Cumæan Sibyl consulted, and lived with?

Unthinking, he laughed aloud—and his laugh was a hundred hyenas.

Beyond the singing flute was a small bowl of water that looked to Pierre like a lake. Buzot might have drowned in it—Buzot and his miniature of Mme Roland. There was no way of telling the depth of the water. The placid ink with its lightning streaks from the lantern might be a mile deep; again, it might be a shallow fish pond. He turned away with a growing sense of frustration.

The rope was not long enough to allow him to explore beyond a

few of the crevices. As he groped his way in and out, the conviction
that he was strangling became more persistent. And now the iciness of
the cavern was close to unbearable after the lesser cold of the small cave
he had been inhabiting. Pierre had no idea how much longer he could
move his frigid legs and his hands with their icicle fingers.

Once as he shoved his way between two pillars he stopped horrified
when his lantern struck a stalagmite and a deep, sonorous note filled
the cave, beautiful as the note of a carillon; the life of the note seemed
eternal, the call of doomsday, vibrating not only in his ears but in the
very core of his being.

At last in a very small cavern, strong with the stench of guano, he
found Buzot. The deputy was a giant in the glow of the lamplight.
His eyes were bright and piercing though a tremor of his lips gave him
a pathetic, childish expression.

"I can't find her," Buzot whispered.

Pierre took a step toward him and Buzot backed away as if he had
been threatened.

"Stop!" warned Pierre quickly.

He had been in this cavern before. On the wall behind Buzot hung
a pack of bats huddled together against the chill and darkness. Clinging by their feet, their heads down, their bodies were shrouded by
their long, folded wings. They looked like the brown, dried pods of
milkweed.

Pierre knew that they were not easily roused from their hibernation,
that fire or water might not stir them until they were ready for their
midwinter mating. Only the other day he had picked one, cold and
shriveled, from its brethren, and it had shown no signs of life beyond
a shiver of the wings and a feeble whimper.

When Pierre had told the men about it later Buzot had shuddered
and said that the bats in these caves were blood-drinking vampires.
He must not allow Buzot to be frightened.

"Stop!" Pierre said again.

But Buzot, unheeding, lurched into the wall, which slowly became
alive and trembling. There was a quivering of wings, a few plaintive
cries. Buzot threw up his arms, striking the furry mass in a frenzy. The
bats began to take flight, blindly careening, their small atrophied eyes
agleam like fireflies.

The cavern had turned into an inferno of sound. Buzot's scream and
the flight of the bats produced a rumble deep and terrifying, a thunder
that would have split the eardrums of Vulcan.

Buzot fought clumsily with his fists, fought like a demon, only rousing more of the creatures to madness. Pierre seized him by the shoulder, and it took every ounce of his energy to force him out into the larger cavern. He pinned Buzot's arms to his sides, and Buzot, exhausted and weak from no food, crumpled together like a scarecrow.

Pierre stared into the bewildered eyes as if he would hypnotize them.

"Come," he said gently, "let us look for Mme Roland—the two of us."

Buzot took his hand and followed him.

When the men heard Pierre's story they decided they must leave their hiding place, must get Buzot up into the open. The closet was unsealed with difficulty. It was midnight by the time they climbed the well.

The Bouquey house was dark, the kitchen door standing open to the winter wind. Neither Mme Bouquey nor Anne Bérard was there.

Gaudet, Salle, and Louvet sneaked away to one of the quarries in the hillside where the poor had made their homes for generations. Valady went off by the Périgeux road, where he hoped to find another asylum. The rest of the men crept one by one through the deserted streets to the shop of M. Troquart the wigmaker, who hid them.

Pierre decided that he must take the first diligence to Bordeaux. He was expected there by a fanmaker in the rue de Gorgons who would have word from de Batz; and the captain of an American vessel awaited him. He must take the chance that the search for him had slackened. He had no idea what he would do without the passport of Citizen Mourat, whom the police were hunting, for the passport must be destroyed. But he must keep moving. . . .

Pierre left for Bordeaux the next afternoon. The diligence in which M. Troquart procured a seat for him was an enormous wooden vehicle. The top was so laden with baggage that eight gasping horses were needed to drag this beetle over the waffled roads.

As there was no glass in the windows one of the leather curtains was drawn back for light, and the children sneezed and the women guarded their wayward locks with muffs. The ten or twelve passengers with their bundles and colliding knees were like a school of minnows, thought Pierre. And the air was that of a manger, tempered with leather and snuff and cheap scent. But it was no longer the air of a tomb!

His own seat was placed against one of the doors. Beside him was a fashionable young lady wearing a fur-lined cape with a hood. She was saucily pretty. On her fichu she wore a miniature Bastille and earrings cut of the Bastille sandstone. Often Pierre felt that she was staring sidelong at him, but when he turned, her mouth was set in a mysterious *moue* and she was glancing out the window.

The journey begun, Pierre had started at once to confide in a jaundiced old courier beside him. He talked boisterously with a coarse language to suit his outfit. He had a plan that must work if he were to get to Bordeaux safely. And he wanted everybody to hear him. For eight years, he said, he had loved the daughter of a stonemason. He himself was a bleacher and scourer. Finally they had scraped together enough money to marry. He was conscripted at the very moment when she lay in childbirth. On his way to Tours, whither he had been ordered, he was overtaken with the news that she was dying. His one hope was to reach Bordeaux in time to see her alive. . . .

If the story of his addled brain was not too feasible no one seemed to discount it. The women clucked, the men sighed, and the little bride of the National Guard wept aloud. When the driver announced that they were soon to reach a village and that they must have their passports ready, Pierre fumbled through his pockets and broke out with a harrowing cry:

"*Diable!* My passport! I've lost it!"

He hunted with seeming desperation. Everyone in the diligence hunted. To a man they wanted Pierre to get back to the dying wife. All but the young woman beside him perhaps. He knew that her brown eyes were mocking.

As they neared the outpost Pierre wailed: "If I'm held for a passport I'll be too late. . . . *Nom de Dieu,* can't you hide me?"

Of course they could hide him. He scrambled under the straw on the floor and they smothered him with hatboxes and petticoats. The children were warned to keep the secret. The ankle of his pretty young neighbor nestled close to his chin. Soon they bolted to a stop. Pierre heard a guard swing onto the steps of the diligence. He looked over the passports with perfunctory routine. They were off again. There was a good deal of laughter in the coach when Pierre emerged with straw in his hair. As he took his place again the young lady's calf pressed gently against his leg. He began to be annoyed with the impudent hussy.

In the early evening they came to the city gates of Bordeaux. The game was to be played once more. The travelers loved it. The trip had not been nearly so dull as they anticipated.

"Everyone out!" ordered the gendarme.

There was every sort of remonstrance from the travelers who had stifled Pierre again with straw and baggage. One had a sleeping child on her knee; another took cold in the evening damp; the National Guard's bride was allergic to the night smell of fish near the seacoast. But the young lady of the brooch and earrings distinctly giggled and Pierre felt her heel give him a saucy dig as she rose.

The guard was insistent. "You will do as you're told!" he thundered, waving his lantern irately. "How can I be sure there's no one in hiding?"

The little bride began to sniffle, the courier began to cough. The guard, brandishing his lantern, chased them all out in the darkness.

Pierre in his coffin of straw lay taut and suffering.

The guard tossed aside cloaks and hampers; he struck angry blows on the leather of the seats; one of his military toes dug into Pierre's sore thigh as bundles and muffs and carpetbags were bandied about. The guard was in a fury of resentment, a dog unrewarded at a cat hole. At last when the coach had been stirred up like a batter, the guard swore lustily and departed.

The passengers settled themselves noisily for the ride through the city. Pierre disentangled himself again from the baggage and straw. The soubrette beside him leaned close to his ear.

"A sou for your thoughts, M. de Michelait," she challenged.

Her words were a stab through the heart.

"Who are you?" he demanded in a whisper.

"The kiss, my dear M. de Michelait, was stolen behind a door from the maid of Mme Campan."

"I have no recollection," he said coldly, lying.

"*Non?* . . . From the fire of it I should think you might. . . . Your memory has become uncommon short—now that you are M. le Marquis de Bussac!"

A week later, Pierre's business in Bordeaux was transacted. He was rolled aboard the *Sally* in an empty wine cask, soon to set sail on a sea infested with English cruisers.

America!

What was it Rabelais had said as he lay dying? *"Je vais chercher un cher un grand Peut-être!"*

PART *Two*

CHAPTER XXVI

Asylum, Spring 1794

PIERRE, who had been hacking at a chestnut tree all day, dropped his ax and straightened up slowly like an old man rising from a chair. *Ma foi,* but he was soft! And he'd supposed he had muscles of iron. A week had made of him a semi-invalid. Would he continue to ache like this throughout his long, indefinite stay here at Asylum?

He wiped the energetic sweat from his face with his sleeve, and paused for breath. If one had time to look about he found this Pennsylvania country very beautiful. Mountains hemmed in the luxuriant plateau in the bend of the river. The river itself was a sparkling freshet. Wild geese and clouds of pigeons were beginning to fly northward, following the valley, their whish mingling oddly with the blows of ax and hammer. Willows were sprouting a golden lace and between the stumps there were lush beds of violets.

Behind him, running into the high woodland, lay the larger farm plots—though these at present were only squares drawn with ink upon a map. The road on which he stood meandered up into the woods, going south toward the Loyalsock Creek.

Before him, toward the ruddy east, lay the village. The streets were laid out evenly like the warp and woof of a loom. Fifty feet in width of mud—this had meant a lot of chopping, he realized with agony. Luzerne, Chestnut, Oak, Elm, Pine, Walnut, Cherry, Plum, Vine— going east and west; Washington, Lafayette, Hamilton, Sullivan, Mouchy—crossing north and south. (Would these great men be flattered, he wondered?) Victoire would have called these new roads snake trails!

He sank down for a moment on a tree stump, though he had already learned of the wood lice—little improvement on prison vermin.

A week ago he had arrived by horseback. In Philadelphia, Louis de Noailles had told him of Asylum in detail—except for the wood lice. . . . Coming to America, Noailles and Talon (Advocate-General at the Châtelet when the Revolution broke out) had appealed to Robert Morris, founder of the Bank of North America. Mr. Morris, who had recently acquired tremendous acreage in northern Pennsylvania, approved the plan for a French colony there and was willing to back it along with John Nicholson.

Two scouts had been sent up at once to select a site. The plan contemplated a stock consisting of a million uncultivated acres. Agents of Morris had procured Pennsylvania patents for the land; Hollenback, a Wilkes-Barre judge, secured titles from the Connecticut squatters so that here in the new colony of Azilum (as the charter called it) there could be no disputes such as had started the Pennamite Wars. Agents were selected to sell the land abroad.

Bué Boulogne, one of the two scouts, had attacked his project with a frenzy in the fall of 1793, importing artisans and craftsmen in large numbers. Two-story houses were begun, hewn of logs, roofed with shingles, and dug with ample cellars. A wharf for the ferryboat had been constructed. The small clearing had soon taken on the semblance of a village. And because the nearest post office was at Wilkes-Barre a weekly pony express to Philadelphia was started. There were still no stores, of course, the nearest being Hollenback's trading post at Tioga Point thirty miles away.

But progress had been slow, for the ice in the river delayed boats coming up with supplies, and building operations had been suspended over the winter. To Pierre the village seemed little more than a hunter's camp though the mansion begun for Marie Antoinette and the children was almost finished. Talon, as resident manager, occupied la Grande Maison.

Émigrés were beginning now to drift in by way of Wilkes-Barre, Catawissa, and Bethlehem, some of them by boat. Here was a medley of people, thought Pierre, but at least a medley with a single purpose. Secular clergy, soldiers, merchants, nobility; a baker, a weaver, a shoemaker, a wheelwright—even a gingerbread vender. Few of the laborers were French; they were men who had been imported from Philadelphia or Wilkes-Barre, or those who had early settled here in Schufeldt's Flats—the Johnsons, the Hermans, and the Vanderpoels.

This was hardly what Pierre had expected and yet he could not say exactly what he had expected. He was smitten with the first case of homesickness he had ever known. The six months since he had escaped from prison had been filled with excitement and danger, feeding him with a superficial kind of hope and energy.

Suddenly there was no outlook but the wilderness, a half-broken back, and blistered hands. The probability of the Dauphin's coming here seemed doubly remote now that an ocean separated them, though Talon with whom Pierre had privately conferred was most optimistic.

And why had he been idiot enough to believe the letter he had sent to Victoire would ever reach her, and that if it did she would leave a luxurious refuge to join him? Well, it was fortunate she had never received the letter. Asylum for Victoire would be nothing more than a slow suicide.

The atrocities he had lived through seemed accentuated by this quiet grandeur. Grégoire, dead, took on the dimensions of a martyr. It was torture not to know what had become of Catherine—of the Girondins with whom he had been entombed. And little Silvie, whose courage had so outshone his own—he was not able to think of her at all. His concern for her and the memory of their happiness would hardly keep a man adamant in his purpose. . . .

Pierre's thoughts mellowed a little as he saw Aristide du Petit-Thouars coming up Luzerne Avenue on horseback. Pierre had felt an immediate warmth of friendship toward the man although du Petit-Thouars was ten years his senior.

Born of an old family of Touraine, he had early left the estates and châteaux along the Loire to go to the Military School of Paris, becoming a captain in the French army. Intrigued by the fate of the missing geographer La Pérouse with whom he had served in the American Revolution for five years as a captain, du Petit-Thouars had outfitted an expedition to find him. The venture, made with great personal expense and sacrifice, had not been successful. A malady had carried off one third of his men; the Portuguese had seized his vessel and, arresting du Petit-Thouars, had sent him prisoner to Lisbon. On his release he had come to America, his patrimony spent, and Noailles had urged him to come to Asylum. At first he had been a guest of Talon's, then had wanted to help build up the embryo colony, overseeing construction in the village and paying off the workmen. In the dense, unbroken wilderness twenty miles west on a four-hundred-acre tract, he had built his own cabin as an ultimate refuge for the two little sisters, Félicité and Perpétue, still in France. By day he slaved for them; by night he wrote his memoirs, carved model ships, or arranged his butterfly collection.

As du Petit-Thouars approached, Pierre returned to his chopping with a sense of guilt, like a little boy who has been dawdling at the piano and gets down to scales with the whish of his mother's skirt. Somehow one couldn't seem lazy in the eyes of this dynamo.

And there was the bark-and-puncheon house Pierre had determined to build himself on the five-acre plot that had suddenly made of him a potential farmer. At present there was little sign of a cabin. A few logs eighteen feet high had been set into the square trench two feet deep. It would be weeks before he could finish. He shouldn't have been so stubborn about refusing the help of the workmen. . . .

Aristide du Petit-Thouars tied his horse to the signpost that said crudely "Washington Street and Luzerne Avenue," and Pierre paused gratefully to chat with him.

Small, dark-haired, with frank brown eyes and a humorous smile, Aristide was mild and simple of manner. He had lost his left hand in a fight with pirates, but his right hand did the work of two men. The sea-leg sway of his walk, his love of adventure, and his tawny skin had earned for him the soubriquet of the "Little Admiral," though he dressed in the buckskins of a backwoodsman.

"Are you going to be really rustic and hang your door on withe hinges?" he teased.

"Why not?" replied Pierre with a laugh. "This won't be a Versailles, you know. Only a Petit Trianon."

"M. Talon says he'll be sorry to lose you as a guest," said Aristide. "Your adventures have been so extraordinary."

They began to discuss then the building of the colony houses and Pierre's cabin in particular. The chinks could be filled in with moss and mud and in the autumn banked up outside with earth for warmth.

Suddenly Pierre, facing the downward slope of the hill, saw a look of alarm cross du Petit-Thouars's face. At the same moment the toy sounds of hammer and ax in the distance were drowned by a great heaving and creaking like that of a ship being split by a storm. The Little Admiral made a lunge at Pierre with the quick cunning of a panther, his impact so great that the two men fell together in the trench in a whirl of arms and legs.

Pierre, struggling with mud and insensate anger, saw the chestnut tree crash across the very spot where they both had been standing; it shivered and showered him with twigs, then lay morosely silent.

The Little Admiral burst into laughter as he disentangled himself from Pierre.

"God protects children and fools and the French nobility!" he exclaimed.

"*Comment?*" asked Pierre, sulkily wiping mud from his eyes—too startled yet to be grateful that du Petit-Thouars had saved his life.

"One doesn't chop at a tree on all sides and wait to see where it falls," warned Aristide, still grinning. "There's a certain technique—come, I will show you."

"*Mon Dieu!*" muttered Pierre, returned to his senses at last. "I might have been no more than wood pulp without you. . . . I'm ashamed, Monsieur—and very grateful."

"*Pas du tout!*" cried Aristide with enjoyment. "This is the very reason Asylum is never dull."

"I'll get the better of the wilderness!" vowed Pierre as they scrambled out of the trench on all fours.

"I doubt it."

"Why do you say that?"

"The wilderness is so close to God!"

Pierre shrugged good-naturedly.

"But in the meantime, *mon ami,*" said the Little Admiral, "I'd better show you how to fell a tree!"

Victoire, dressing in her Philadelphia pension for a party the following August, looked back at her image with the shrewd eye of a hawk. There was one virtue she had, she thought. She had never had any illusions about beauty. No man in his right mind would tell her that the jaded skin was rose petal or that the long, stiff curls were silken. Fortunate that her teeth weren't poor, with this clown's mouth! *Dieu,* but the American women had bad teeth and thin hair and shiny noses! Pretty at fifteen when they married, but wilted at twenty-five, haggard at thirty-five, and ready for the rag bag at forty.

How Mrs. Morris and Mrs. Willing and Mrs. Bingham and all the other select envied her exotic wardrobe. Having Nicolas Claude had only improved her figure. There was more of a bosom now under the low-cut, squarish bodice; and the new puffed sleeves and high waist and satin sandals lopped off a little height. (All men were not so conveniently tall as her husband.)

Victoire's heart gave a twist at recall of Pierre's angry embraces. Months ago he had written to Coblentz for her to come. It was the child, of course, that he wanted. . . . How the four weeks had flown since she landed in America! She had meant to write to Pierre each day. Everybody thought she had written, of course, and condoled with her because she had had no answer. But M. Talleyrand had introduced her to society at once and there had been so many distractions: dinners and teas; Rickett's Circus; the plays of the New Theater; Lady Duer's reception for the artist Gilbert Stuart; strolls with Nicolas Claude on those lovely innovations called sidewalks. Nicki dawdled so, wanting to pick up every bug and stone with the curiosity of his year and a half. And Victoire must needs dawdle too, and that all led to sociability.

The French colony was exceedingly gay and cosmopolitan, almost as much so as Coblentz. Coblentz! There was liveliness for you, with Louis's brothers holding court, and gambling and dancing and intrigue enough to make Versailles green with envy! She doubted if she would ever have left if her mother had not died of apoplexy *"de peur de la guillotine,"* as any natural death was facetiously labeled, and life had become dull with mourning. Of course America meant adventure, and no lover had ever set her aflame as had her own arrogant husband. Yes, tomorrow she would write to Pierre; and he would come to her. She would buy her proud Marquis a jolly little house in Philadelphia with some of her mother's emeralds, and they would be very gay here until the Revolution was over.

"Hurry!" she exclaimed to her *femme de chambre*. "After a certain lateness one is not noticed, eh?"

Frau Gresch, her eyes dim with homesick tears, handed Victoire her fan and reticule and gave a last tweak to the flowing blue satin sash and the draped gauze turban with its blue ostrich plume. Then she stood back to allow the peacock an unalloyed view.

Frau Gresch was a jewel more valuable than the Regent. A middle-aged widow with no children, she had become nurse to Nicolas Claude when he was born. The shapeless avoirdupois of Frau Gresch and the myriad warts on her face and neck, which he picked at as he rocked, were both security to Nicki. Half the time her broad, fat face was moist with tears; half the time it was moist and *gemütlich* with smiles. When she was *gemütlich* Frau Gresch hummed little tuneless notes that seemed to drift through her mind like feckless seeds in a whiffet.

It had taken no bribery to get Frau Gresch to America. Although the fact that Nicki called her "Frogra" or some such mumbo jumbo would have made her follow him to Borneo, it was her dream of an eagle that had been the deciding factor. The dream book interpreted an eagle as freedom.

Even Victoire confessed a dream to Frau Gresch now and then and challenged her to predict its meaning. Not the more personal dreams, of course, that had no business even in a dream book!

Ah, how the jewel could do the work of ten! On the ship she had washed and mended, read to Victoire who lay quivering and green, and cooked tempting meals for Nicki over the spirit lamp—potted hash or soup, or an omelet of the greased eggs they had carried with them. No hard ship's biscuit and dried fish for the son of a Marquise!

Victoire left the French pension at Race and Second Streets and took the waiting sulky for the Binghams' party. The city had been a glorious surprise after the tedious trip on the ocean. Philadelphia was Gallic *à la mode*. There were exquisite shops. There were French masters in schools of dancing, fencing, and language; and these schools were admittedly the best in the country. One read the *Courrier de l'Amérique* with one's morning chocolate and *grillés*. Inns and taverns had become hotels; bakers and pastry cooks were restaurateurs; French dishes, customs, books, names, and music were the rage. The *Marseillaise* was sung everywhere, along with America's *Hail Liberty, Supreme Delight*.

And too, Philadelphia was so cozily full of bachelors, a real asset in a smug land where men married their wives for love and forthwith became insuperable prigs. . . . Well, perhaps she might have been faithful to Pierre too if he had loved her. But she had been so freakishly jealous of that little Mlle Marguerite or Lis or Hyacinthe, or whatever her name was—rotting now in the Madeleine, no doubt, with so many of the theater people.

What airs these Americans sported without even a title! she thought, as the sulky pulled into the Binghams' driveway. The whole mansion no more than one of the servants' wings in the Comte de Varionnet's château at Passy. . . .

By eleven Victoire had a circle of men about her in the mirrored ballroom. Supper was about to be served. Although the Binghams, as well as the Morrises and others, had French chefs, Marinot had been called in to cater. Marzipan represented the façade of the Tuileries; there was blancmange in the form of men and women of the court; elaborate ices and sorbets accompanied cakes wreathed in rose garlands. Victoire approved.

Mrs. Bingham, who was a celebrated beauty and hostess, was obviously annoyed with the Marquise. What did this hussy talk about that Mr. Madison deserted his Dolly? And random members of the Senate and House of Representatives clung to her words as if she were Alexander Hamilton! Well, here was a bolt out of the blue—the handsome young husband of the Marquise, M. de Michelait! So—at last he had come for her and the child! Strange they hadn't come to the party together! Mrs. Bingham watched M. de Michelait shake hands with Senator Bingham. As a great friend of the Vicomte de Noailles, Senator Bingham's partner in the merchandising business, Pierre had a standing invitation to the mansion.

The Senator greeted Pierre cordially.

"What a surprise, M. de Michelait. And a very pleasant one indeed! When did you arrive in the city?"

"Two hours ago—on business for M. Talon." News of the Dauphin was expected on almost any ship, and Pierre would remain in Philadelphia until he heard from an agent of Jean de Batz.

"Two hours ago! But does Madame—"

"The Vicomte de Noailles's landlady was shocked when I told her I was tired and had better stay home. She swore no one in his right mind would miss a party at the Binghams'."

The Senator beamed.

"But why didn't Mme la Marquise tell us you had come at last?" he exclaimed.

His words were drowned out by the chatter of the room and the penetrating voice of Mme la Marquise herself.

"—and because he was so mad for beauty, no one ever considered the Duc de Menneville a lecher. The intendant of his pleasures traveled all over Europe, you know, with portraits of old famous beauties, until he found young women who looked just like them. Imagine! And when they were properly bribed and brought to Paris, they were dressed in the costume of the ancient one. *Dieu!* Think how picturesque—finding Mary Queen of Scots, Cleopatra, Nell Gwynn, and Ninon de L'Enclos all at the supper table together! The Duc de Menneville was notoriously impartial; I believe he'd been educated in Turkey or—"

For a second Pierre stood electrified.

Then he said without volition: "Pardon, Madame, but are you not speaking of the Comte de Friche and not the pious Duc de Menneville?"

The men of the group made grudging room for the newcomer.

Pierre's eyes met those of Victoire's. The little mouse released from the mousetrap of the convent in the rue de Bellechasse! His face turned a dull, bronze red. He felt a humiliation unequaled by the sans-culotte filth of his attic room in Paris, the bites of rats in prison.

Victoire gave a little shriek and rushed to him.

"Ah, mon Pierre!" she exclaimed. "At last! I thought you would never come for me, never answer. I have been *désolée*. But chagrined! What kind of *poste* do they have in America?"

He wanted to bite the full red lips that closed over his in a demand for silence. But there was one's pride. . . .

The company responded at once to the romantic reunion. There were questions and congratulations, curses on the postman who abandoned letters on inn tables, and a long and anguishing toast by the entire party to the separated lovers.

"But he is beautiful!" thought Victoire, in triumph. "More beautiful than I ever remembered. More lean, yes, and brown as an Indian—more of the man." There was a hard, almost brittle expression in his black eyes, like the snapping of twigs. Before, she had never noticed the lines about his eyes and mouth when he smiled; they gave him an air of concentration, a tightening of personality. He was taller too; but surely he could not be taller. Just the simple cut of his black clothes, and the tight, immaculate fit of his breeches, perhaps. *Dieu,* how could she ever have wasted these months of boredom, she wondered, away from the exciting challenge of his indifference? Ah, poor little Mlle Violette, so very dead! . . .

"Two years . . . an eternity." This from a young man newly in love.

"The piracy of mails on the water is a crime!"

"M. de Michelait—a Marquis?"

"What a charming couple!"

"And he has not even seen his son!" It was the quivering voice of the motherly Mrs. Morris.

So it was a son then, thought Pierre. His fingers tightened their grip on the arm of the Marquise de Bussac.

"If you will be so good as to excuse us. . . ." He bowed low before Mrs. Bingham.

The women warbled sympathetic nothings. Of course he would want to see his child at once! The gentlemen knew better. The fancy of the young man newly in love wallowed in ecstatic love scenes.

Pierre assisted Victoire into the carriage of the Vicomte de Noailles, which had been ordered to see them to her pension. The night was delicious with flowers, bursting with moonlight.

"You little bitch!" Pierre exclaimed as Victoire's blue-gloved hand closed over his.

"Pierre, *mon cher!* But you are cruel! . . . After I have dreamed of tonight for two years—through all those desolate days in Coblentz." Strangely enough Victoire was convinced by the faltering of her own voice. Coblentz suddenly narrowed down to a fatuous German town of stifling dimensions. "You don't believe that I've written either from Coblentz or Philadelphia!"

No, he did not believe she had written, although British men-of-war patrolled the seas and the Barbary corsairs and French privateers veered to and fro, and some said that only letters that were charmed arrived at their destination. (Yet—there was the note of the little Hyacinthe that she had assuredly written and that had never reached him.)

"I would like to believe you," he said, "after the hell I've lived through."

"Tell me of the hell, *mon cher*. Tell me everything. Tell me why you are here, why I am here . . ." and she proceeded to prattle on of the insufferable Coblentz; how she had almost lost her life at the birth of the child; the death of her mother.

They came to the French colony and entered one of the frame houses with its imposing marble front. She lighted one candle from another at the foot of the stairway. Pierre followed her into a large room, heavy with mingled shadows and walnut furniture, its plain gray walls bare of hangings. His heart thumped as crazily as it had the day he found Silvie Hyacinthe at the fair. . . . But what was to assure him that the boy was his, he thought bitterly.

Victoire held the candle low, close to the child in the trundle bed. Pierre fell down on his knees beside the tangle of covers. The child was so like him that he felt a swift pain. Damp, curly black locks escaped the nightcap and clung to his forehead; beneath the flush of heat his round baby cheeks were the tint of fresh cream; the hands, thrust above his head, seemed boneless, made of dimples. Even so his brows were dark, well defined, with a patrician look old for the jolly, formless little nose and red lips.

Pierre leaned over swiftly and kissed him, but the boy did not stir. Nor did Victoire, holding the candle.

The beginning of life for himself and the child, thought Pierre. A new life, a sweet life, untainted by madness. In the fresh beauty of Asylum the boy would grow tall and strong. The child would be happy there, free as he himself had once been in the Dulange barnyard.

The child . . . "What is his name?" Pierre asked at last, rising.

"Nicolas Claude Adrien Louis Pierre de Michelait."

"I am glad he's been christened Louis. . . ."

"*Hélas!* He's never been christened . . . I was so ill; and then *Maman* died."

Pierre was shocked. Immediately he wondered why he should be shocked.

Victoire put the candle in a sconce on the wall. Frau Gresch in the next room gave a great snort and sigh, and the snoring continued in a new minor key.

Pierre thought suddenly of Catherine, the night in his father's library when she had pleaded so pitifully for his soul. What had she said? . . . "A loveless marriage, without the sanction of God . . . it will be a curse to you—a curse on the children your wife bears you. . . ."

He looked at Victoire, her green eyes hungry, impatient. Her old challenge was tempered somewhat with a new, impalpable fear. And he began to laugh. She joined him recklessly.

"Good night," he said. "I'll be back in the morning."

"But you're not going!" she exclaimed in the tone she used for Frau Gresch.

"*Oui.*" He picked up his hat.

"So—you have turned ascetic!" she cried with a deep scorn. "Pure, in the virgin woods!"

"Only honest, perhaps."

"You have a mistress in Philadelphia."

"*Non, non, non* . . . in Terrytown, six miles down the river from Asylum. Very discreet. One can skate there easily in the winter. . . . In Philadelphia I am impartial, like the Duc de Menneville. . . ."

The expression of her green eyes was that of a panther in a tree branch ready to spring. . . . He had grappled with one but a month ago. And he had won.

Here was the old Victoire beating the tom-tom. The muslin and soft blue sash were a paradox, garb for a wisp of a flower like a Silvie Hyacinthe.

Curious to know what he would feel, he took her in his arms, loathing the sensuous clinging of her lips. They had not been together long enough for the old impetus of loathing . . . and the boy had stirred in him a different kind of fever.

"Good night," he said again, "Mme la Marquise de Bussac."

CHAPTER XXVII

PIERRE WALKED briskly toward Race Street the following morning. He was more eager to see Nicolas Claude awake, to have the eyes of the child on his, than he had ever been for a rendezvous with a mistress. He had scarcely been able to concentrate on the reports of the Vicomte who managed the Philadelphia affairs of Asylum.

He thought again how crude he had been the night before and wondered if that was how the wilderness affected one. He and Victoire must live together, and the life at Asylum was not easy for a woman. He wondered how he had ever presumed that she would meet its challenge, but when he had written from Bordeaux he had not thought beyond the fact that he wanted possession of his son—and she belonged with him.

Victoire was having her chocolate when he arrived, not in the slandering sunshine of the window but in a more lenient corner of her boudoir. She had already made her toilette and wore the green peignoir that made her look so maternal. Her curls hung as faultlessly over her shoulders as the curls of her grandmother in the mantel portrait at Passy. Victoire had lain awake campaigning into the small hours of the morning. From what Pierre had told his friends at the Binghams' it was plain he expected her to return to Asylum with him. Here in a decorous America Pierre unfortunately had the advantage over her. If she refused to accompany him to that dugout up in the sticks Mrs. Bingham and Mrs. Morris and their social brigade would ostracize her. And although Robespierre had just been guillotined in the wake of Danton and Desmoulins, Paris was still a stewpot and would never countenance a returning *émigrée*. Moreover, her feeling for Pierre, which had gone on holiday in Coblentz, was again attacking her with renewed vigor. Very definitely they belonged together, she thought. Life had twice the zest when their minds were grappling; and the marriage bed had all the delicious lust of the lewdest venery. Besides she adored Nicki and would never part with him—nor would Pierre. On then, to the adventure of Asylum!

"*Bon jour*," she said with that surprising energy in her voice which had first astonished Pierre at Passy. "*Ah, mon cher,* I see your eyes are all for Nicki. Frau Gresch has taken him for a stroll. He'll be back any moment. He is a beautiful child, *n'est-ce pas?* And no sooner did he learn to say mama than I showed him your miniature and taught him to say papa."

Pierre sat down on the horsehair chair and smiled. One accepted Victoire's gauntlet to pleasantry even as one accepted her gauntlet to battle.

"I want to hear about Nicki," Pierre said simply when she paused for a moment from her satire on American customs.

"But of course, *mon cher.* How incredibly stupid of me!"

She began to talk about Nicki, how he had been the idol of the French colony in Coblentz. (She failed to specify that the orbit had been overwhelmingly male.) He had walked when he was but eleven months; he had already had the measles; although babies never put words together until they were two, Nicki at a year and a half said "mama pretty," and "papa gone"; he adored flowers—had a passion for pulling them to pieces. Mr. Bartram, the botanist friend of the Binghams, predicted Nicki would be a great scientist. Were there flowers in the colony of Asylum?

"But of course," said Pierre, "flowers and even a little finery."

Victoire brightened. "Tell me about Asylum, Monsieur. If a woman thrusts her head into a kettle she has a right to know if the water boils."

"What do you want to know . . . how the colony started?"

"*Certainement.* Where the water was fetched from."

He smiled again and accepted the cup of chocolate she poured. He began to remember that Victoire had never been dull.

As he talked Victoire thought: "But his eyes are black and bottomless! No pupils—only black pits that deepen and finally swallow one. . . ."

"She is actually interested," thought Pierre gratefully, and he went on, with reckless ardor.

"*Mon Dieu!*" exclaimed Victoire at last, completely aghast at the barbarism he lived in. "I shall have to learn to scalp the *Peaux-Rouges!*"

Pierre laughed. "But we seldom see an Indian now. After their Teedyuscung was burned to death thirty years ago the Delawares began to migrate north. Oh, now and then a few come up the river in search of game or hemp—or drift down the river with a sweet-grass basket to sell."

Victoire gave him a wide, hypocritical smile. It was obvious that Pierre intended to remain in Asylum—that he reveled in being a farmer. *Incroyable!* She instinctively glanced at his hands. They looked coarse, already weather-beaten, not so skillfully tender as the hands that had caressed little Mlle Muguet. The entire project seemed an outrage. Who in his right senses would leave the sophistication of the capital?

"And why, *mon cher,* do you invite these hardships?"

He would have to lie to her, of course, he thought, or tomorrow all Philadelphia would know he awaited news of the Dauphin.

"The answer to the age, I suppose—desire to be an Émile, to live simply in a sublime little world of my own . . . desire for 'Le Contrat Social.'"

Bilge and fish water! thought Victoire—and she sipped a last mouthful of thick, cold chocolate. . . . Well, a few more bear raids and glaciers at Asylum and he would be ready for the house of emeralds in Philadelphia! But if she would have to make this suicide lunge she would put it off as long as possible.

There was a scrambling and chatter in the adjoining room as Frau Gresch and Nicolas Claude returned from their amble.

Pierre jumped to his feet. He knew he had only been talking swiftly to pass the time. He felt greater stage fright than the night he had played Othello to the Queen's Desdemona at the Petit Trianon.

Nicki waddled into the room, still conscious of his legs. He looked like a little girl in a long white dress exquisitely lace trimmed. But the dress belied him. He was all swagger and manhood. The pink sash was askew and the lace had been tweaked by a neighbor's parrot. His black hair escaped from his bonnet in rakish curls. He stopped short when he saw Pierre and stared at him with large shy eyes.

The eyes were green. They were Victoire's eyes, Pierre saw with a shock. Somehow he had forgotten the child was Victoire's and he felt a flash of resentment. The son he had thought of so peculiarly as his own had slept in Victoire's womb for nine months, and now the child clung to her as his large green eyes stared at his father—and in Victoire's protecting arm there was something of condescension.

What had he expected? He had seen babies before who were even shy of the fathers who lived with them—the child of Mme de Frivouac, for instance, who screamed at the Comte's approach to the nursery although he had always greeted Pierre with a joyous onrush.

"Non, non, non!" warned Victoire, as Pierre stooped and began to reach impetuously for the boy's hand. "To Nicki you are still a stranger. . . . *Nicki, c'est votre papa!* Papa is no longer gone. *Papa est donc ici."*

Nicki's lip trembled and he took to sucking a dirty thumb for consolation.

"Your watch," suggested Victoire, gratified by Nicki's diffidence. How the hurt pride filled Pierre's face, making him a mere schoolboy in a flogging and drawing the three of them irrevocably together! "See, Nicki, the pretty bibelot . . . it says tick, tock, tick, tock."

Pierre held the watch to the bonneted ear. Nicki reached for it, dropped it, of course, picked it up, and held it again to his ear.

Then he said: "Ti-ta," and smiled, still keeping a safe distance.

"You see?" said Victoire. "The watch tells him it is high time he learns to know his father."

Pierre moved into the pension at Race and Second Streets. In a few days he and Nicki became friends. Now it was Pierre who took Nicki for his morning stroll—another Æneas and Anchises.

The August days slipped away. Then one morning a French sailor sought out Pierre through the Vicomte de Noailles.

He was small and angular and red and reminded Pierre of a boiled crab. From one ear dangled an Oriental earring. (Having his ears pierced had evidently not kept his eyes from being sore and rheumy.) As they swung toward the Pennypot Inn he talked casually of the storms around the Horn.

They ordered grog, and the sailor promptly delivered a purse of money from Jean de Batz. Spreading his rough red hands out on the table, he leaned toward Pierre and began to talk in an intimate whisper.

Le Petit was still imprisoned in the Temple. For a year he had been separated from his aunt and sister. As conditions became worse in France there had been an even greater fear that the Dauphin might escape, that an aristocratic party might rally round him. And conditions *were* worse! *Mon Dieu,* thousands were starving and hordes of wild dogs infested the city of Paris! The Convention had had to set maximum prices on food, one third above those of 1791. There were severe penalties for infringement, whispered the sailor, gulping his grog. But the law had done no good. Farmers brought neither butter nor eggs to market, butchers refused to slaughter, and nothing could be purchased openly. Country people were sneaking provisions to private houses, where they got munificent prices. Things had come to such a pass that farmers were being released from prison—even those who had been accused of hoarding—in order to harvest. *Sapristi!* M. de Michelait did not know the advantage of living in a country where one had no gripes in the belly! . . . The sailor's brother-in-law had committed suicide—a poor shopkeeper who had purchased foreign goods at double the price he had been allowed to sell for. With a new law that he must not shut up shop in less than a year, he had been ruined. The guard had found him hiding his goods the night before the law went into effect—and Christophe had taken poison. . . .

Ah, France was *très malade!* In May, of course, the saintly Princess Elisabeth had been guillotined. Nearly every nobleman's house had been pilfered by servants or agents of the government, some of the mansions requisitioned for blacksmiths' forges or a crew of tailors making clothes for the army. One never knew what the new day would bring; Hébert and Chaumette, heads of the Commune in Paris, who had forced the new calendar and the new religion of Reason on the people, had become too powerful. Whisk!—their heads in March. Danton's too in April because the bloody old man had actually sickened of bloodshed. Then came Robespierre's dictatorship and the Great Terror. Heads, heads, heads in the basket!—till at last the green face of Robespierre tumbled in with the others. . . . But M. de Michelait had heard all these things, perhaps by former ships? . . . Ah, it was hoped now there would be a moderate Republican convention. There were signs of a monarchial party, demanding restitution of the Bourbons though not of the old régime.

"And le Petit?" pleaded Pierre, his glass of grog untouched.

"Sans-culottes will never be lenient toward a Bourbon until they gain their rights of soap and bread!"

"But how do they treat the Dauphin?"

"Ah, Mother of Mary, what can one expect of a people who worship a Goddess of Reason, a prostitute on a throne on the altar?" The little sailor reached for Pierre's untouched grog and began work on it. (Another Baron von Drinsbach, thought Pierre. Greed was the one bond of humanity.) M. de Michelait did not know half the atrocities. Blacksmiths' hammers had hacked down chapel rails; stonemasons had chiseled out all titles of nobility in sculptured epitaphs; monuments and tombs were attacked by ghouls; saints were torn from their time-honored niches; even scaffoldings had been erected to destroy the beautiful painted ceilings. What happened to chasubles, crucifixes, church plate, and altar cloths? If these were not cried out for sale on the streets by carpenters and locksmiths, they were burned in public places along with confessionals and books condemned by the Jacobins. The chapels were only dives for dancing and feasts and debauching. The new religion, with its lavish pagan show, was far more gross an appeal to the senses than the Catholic processions which the Convention repudiated. *Sang de St. Denis,* but one was afraid of being a Christian! Even the Archbishop of Paris openly confessed himself an impostor, a charlatan.

"It is le Petit I want to hear about," insisted Pierre, "I've learned these other things from the *émigrés.*"

Ah, to be sure, le Petit . . . the very reason the sailor was sitting drinking grog here in America. From the first of the year le Petit had been cared for by a succession of Commissioners, no longer by the shoemaker Simon. There were rumors that Louis Charles had been smuggled out by the Simons before they left, that they had supposedly given him a gift of a hobbyhorse in which a substitute dumb child afflicted with rickets was brought in to fill his place. Alas, the rumor was not true! Louis Charles, suffering from constant dysentery, his face and hands puffed, his body covered with sores and vermin, was now on the third floor of the Temple. There was no one to wash the child. His bed was a tangle of foul sheets and fleas and bedbugs. The room stank so of human excreta that the jailers could scarce approach to shove bits of food through the grating. He was left to himself in the dark and quiet to stare at the walls, forbidden to see his sister. He was never mentioned at the Commune, so confused with its own struggle for existence. That was the one hope: that he was gradually being forgotten by the Commune—easier then to abduct him.

"Oh God!" exclaimed Pierre.

Le Petit! The little Prince who had been "born gay"! The child whose toys had been of the essence of fairyland: kites of golden silk, tops of enamel, bowls of boxwood, a collection of singing shells from the sea, cages of birds from the tropics. A child of bridling spirit and tantrums, but sensitive, sweet, and lovable. . . . Frightened easily— alone now in the dark. Simon, at least, had been fond of him—had let him play in the garden with the dog, had seen that he had baths and clean linen. Simon too, simpleton though he was, had given the boy birds because he loved them—not birds of exotic plumage from the tropics but roosts filled with pigeons in the lonely turret.

Vermin . . . blank walls . . . excreta . . . the guillotine had been kind to the child's mother.

"Thank you, my friend," stammered Pierre, rising; and he lurched against the table as if he had drunk all the grog of the sailor. "Tell Jean de Batz . . . tell him I'll be here when he needs me."

❦❦❦❦❦❦❦❦❦❦❦❦❦❦❦❦❦❦❦❦

CHAPTER XXVIII

PIERRE WAS READY to leave at once for Asylum. He was well supplied with secondhand books in English and French and German. He had found maps too for Talon; a syringe for Mme Homet; drugs for Dr. Buzard; cologne for M. Carles (lately the canon of Guernsey). And out of his own money it had been impossible to resist a ship's model of the *Santa Maria* for du Petit-Thouars.

But if Pierre was ready for the journey, not so Victoire. The fall goods were beginning to arrive from London at Clifford's Wharf, and the shops would soon flame with new muslins, calicoes, and chintzes. Also Nicki had not yet been to see the tame alligator; and the Société Française de Bienfaisance de Philadelphie was giving a charity ball for the refugees.

Pierre was lenient at first. After all, soon the wolves would howl and the snow pile high at Asylum. Let the Marquise de Bussac have her memories and her conquests! He spent hours in the Library Company on Fifth Street and browsed among the five thousand volumes, many of which had been bought from Benjamin Franklin's personal library. Even to handle books for which he had been so starved gave him a renewed strength and ambition.

David Rittenhouse, a self-taught mathematician, invited him to the American Philosophical Society to hear his paper on the isosceles triangle. There were lectures by the president of William and Mary College or the editor of *Le Courrier politique de l'univers*. Stephen Girard the merchant took Pierre to see his first boxing match.

Dinners were legion. Everybody wanted to celebrate the romantic reunion of the Marquis and Marquise de Bussac.

But the days, a Versailles orgy of pleasure and activity, began to drag. The endless vivacity of Victoire's mind wearied rather than amused Pierre, especially in the confines of a pension room. The scent she used drenched the very drapes, seeped into his clothing. Every toilette had the intensity of that of a courtesan preparing for a royal presentation: Victoire never sang (little Silvie had often chirped like her birds) but she talked to herself wittily with the same flash she used for a circle of gentlemen. She wore pearls and rubies strung like a child's chain of gaudy berries. *Mon Dieu,* but the woman had jewels! And how Victoire loved color! She would wear orange and green with a flair unequaled in polite society. The effect was almost like that of sound, thought Pierre, the cacophony of a waterfall.

Nicki adored her and often waddled over with a catapult snatch at her knees. She would seize him, laughing, showering him with pet names, and then spank him playfully and send him back to the jealous Frau Gresch.

Nicki, it seemed, was not too young a moth to scorch himself at the candle. . . . All male blood accelerated with her quick, almost gauche, impulsive manner.

A few weeks ago, for instance, he, Pierre, could have sworn he never again would want the touch of her small, naked breasts on his body, her full, mocking kiss on his lips. Desire for her sometimes stung like a poisoned arrow—always when he hated her most.

Pierre felt melancholy and restless. His hands were used to work. And he realized that his mind was still very sick, far from free of images of blood and horror. The news of the Dauphin haunted him from one hour to another. And his vow to Marie Antoinette burned in him like a brush fire. He dreamed of her often at night, of the pathetic faith that she had placed in him.

At last one Monday he made arrangements to leave for Asylum the following week end.

But Victoire couldn't possibly leave the following Saturday. She had been invited to take the air with Mme Washington in the very coach presented by Louis. It was a miracle of glass-covered flowers and cupids, with green Venetian blinds and servants in white-and-scarlet livery.

"You have ridden in a hundred finer carriages," exclaimed Pierre angrily.

"But not with six horses *and* Mrs. Washington!" (How obtuse men were.)

"The yellow fever is spreading again through the city."

"*Oui?* But being sick is so dull and unbecoming. I have never been sick, *chéri.*"

He tried to tell her that Bronze John was no respecter of temperament. Of course this was no epidemic like that of 1793 when thousands had died like sandflies, but there was Nicki to consider. Perhaps the child did not know that sickness was dull.

Was it really so fatal, asked Victoire? And what were the symptoms?

Strangely enough the day before they were about to leave, Victoire was attacked by a severe headache, chills, and acute thirst. The vomit, which had been black, she had hastily disposed of in her shame, she said. She was so weak she could scarcely move.

Pierre called in Dr. Benjamin Rush at once and moved Nicki and Frau Gresch to another pension, he himself taking the room they had vacated.

"All the symptoms of the yellow fever," Dr. Rush whispered to Pierre in the gloomy corridor, "except, oddly enough, the fever."

In a day or two Victoire felt quite well enough for company, she announced. Flowers and books arrived from the Mmes Willing and Bingham and various distressed gentlemen, but nobody called—not even one of the eligible bachelors. It was tedious.

Although Victoire was suddenly fit as a fiddle Dr. Rush advised that no trip be attempted until she had overcome her weakness.

The dinner parties began again (Victoire was quite strong enough to go out to dinner!), and Pierre resigned himself to the delay.

When Victoire was able to go horseback riding with M. Talleyrand, Pierre decided she could certainly make the trip to Asylum, and once again he made definite plans to leave.

He returned to the pension one afternoon to find Nicki in bed. Victoire was dressing for a dinner at the home of Lady Kitty Duer.

"Do hurry, *mon cher,* or we shall be late," she said. "And this evening *j'ai un peu de fièvre. Mais vraiment.* No, not yellow. A fever of curiosity. . . . Do you know that a Mr. Thomas Twining has just arrived from India? And he has brought with him a small Bengal cow and a great sheep he calls a Doombah? Mrs. Jay says Mr. Bingham has offered Doombah his fine lawn on Fourth Street for grazing!"

Pierre's black eyes narrowed to slits. "What is the matter with Nicki?"

"Oh, he's all right. It's really nothing! I have been so worried about the smallpox since he was born that today I called in Dr. Caspar Wistar and had him inoculated."

"Que le diable vous emporte!" he thundered, dropping on his knee beside Nicki. The little boy breathed heavily. The tiny face was scarlet, the lips dry and open. The green eyes too, puffed and glazed like marbles, stared at Pierre with indifference.

Pierre took one of the hot hands in his own and he felt tears of fear and anger welling within him.

"You might have asked me!"

Victoire shrugged. "I have had his responsibility so long alone. It never occurred to me."

Would the unique Mr. Twining prefer the corsage here among her curls or in her bosom?

"You've sacrificed Nicki for the sake of a few parties! You aren't even human!"

"Fooh!" she exclaimed. "Don't rant like a madman! A few more days and Nicki will be playing around as usual. You were at Versailles when the Dauphin was inoculated. You know it's nothing. One would think I had had him bit by a viper."

Pierre sent his regrets with Victoire to Lady Kitty Duer, dismissed Frau Gresch, for the evening and nursed Nicki himself.

The day the child's temperature was normal he announced to Victoire: "We are leaving for Asylum tomorrow!"

Her fingers paused on their needlework.

"It would be dangerous for Nicki."

"I have spoken to Dr. Wistar."

"Eh bien. But the ball of the *Société Fran—"*

"We're leaving for Asylum tomorrow!"

Damnation! So the time had come at last. . . . "Mr. Albrecht says my piano—"

"It can come later."

"Why are you in such a hurry? Is it the little mistress in Terry—"

"I think it's time we understand one another," he said, turning from the window. His heavy eyebrows met in one glowering line. "I have work to do in Asylum."

Dieu, but he was beautiful when he was angry!

Her green eyes met the engulfing black ones with mutual malice, her high brows arched like the back of a cat on guard.

"So—you are commanding me!"

"I am commanding you!"

"And if I refuse to go?"

"I shall leave tomorrow and take Nicki."

She considered, bending over her needlepoint industriously. She knew he was entirely capable of carrying out his threat. She meant to go of course. She had decided it was the only thing to do the night they had met at the Binghams'. She loved and hated him so madly, with his ink-black eyes and his damned blue blood of Henry IV! She recalled the night of the pastoral fete at Passy—how she had humbled him with tears. She let her anger overflow now, though the tears were skimpy.

"Dieu!" he said curtly. "You act as if Asylum were a prison. We are very gay at Asylum. We have parties and picnics and even a theater. It's just that we're not always gay. We all have our work. And then the play is like water on a desert. . . . *Dieu,* work is medicine! I do not think the same since I am working with my hands. One does not think with his hands. And yet somehow one thinks differently when he works with his hands. . . ."

There, he was now in control of his fury.

"A nice little point of discussion for Plato!" she taunted, breaking the wool with a flip. "But you were never meant for a pedant. You're far more charming as a lover—or even as a husband."

"That has nothing to do with the question. You had better begin packing."

"I would loathe Asylum."

"You won't have time to loathe it. You will be making soap, baking *gâteaux,* making violet dye from the iris."

"Impossible!"

"I think we could even be happy, with Nicki to share."

"You and I could never be happy together, even in Valhalla!"

"Et pourquoi non?"

"Because you think you're the sun and I'm only a constellation!"

"Come, Victoire, why not be reasonable?" (What in hell was there about a woman's tears! . . .) "I want a home, and a wife, and my child. I want to believe in something. And I could be faithful to you if you were only half human. You have brains and wit and a *joie de vivre* which is very bracing!"

She wiped the tears with the wraith of a handkerchief. She had humbled him once more. Really, it was quite simple . . . but she must learn to humble him without self-abasement.

"I'll go to Asylum, but only for a visit," she compromised, tossing the work frame away from her. "I shall come back to Philadelphia for the New Year."

He smiled charitably. The New Year would find ice floes in the Susquehanna.

⊛⊛⊛⊛⊛⊛⊛⊛⊛⊛⊛⊛⊛⊛⊛⊛⊛⊛⊛⊛

CHAPTER XXIX

THE TWO-HUNDRED-MILE TRIP to Asylum was palling to any traveler.

To Victoire it was appalling. A dozen times, attacked by sore muscles and ennui, she threatened to turn back. Pierre listened to her bombast mildly.

"But of course," he agreed, "go back if you like. And I'll promise to take excellent care of Nicki."

West to Harrisburg by wagon they went, joggling over rocks of Gibraltar. Victoire said the advantage of riding from the *Conciergerie* to the guillotine in a tumbrel was that the ride was shorter! And suppers at the inns! Warmed-up potatoes, salt pork, and ginger cakes! Garbage!

Then the trip by horseback from Harrisburg to Catawissa, dodging tree stumps and mud holes like acrobats. Nicki rode with Pierre; Frau Gresch flounced around in her saddle like a pancake on a skillet. She was always dropping things in the puddles. And once Nicki made a lunge for a firefly that entranced him, and splashed like a ball into the mire, coming out a mulatto. Pierre laughed and wrapped him in his greatcoat. Only Pierre had the stoicism of the pack horses that plodded behind them.

Wasn't the scenery magnificent? What could equal the grandeur of the broad, meandering river, the crimson of the sumac and woodbine on the mountains? Victoire heard him talking to Nicki, whose eyes grew heavy with the joggling. Those were the kildees, with their plaintive calls, gathering for the fall migration. The screech owl wouldn't hurt one, nor the bat, which was only frightened and trying dolefully to avoid collision. Night in the woods was the same as day. God had just blown out the candle.

At Catawissa they took the Durham boat to Wilkes-Barre. This was a miracle of modern convenience, and the reason it could travel as fast as twelve or fifteen miles a day upstream was that it was made of the lightest wood available. Two polemen on either side propelled the boat, which was twelve by sixty feet, pointed at both ends like a Turkish slipper, and gave the appearance of a huge canoe. Small decks at the bow and stern were for the passengers, and the freight was placed in the middle. Sails could be hoisted on the small mast, if needed.

The party, including two men from Reading who were going to Judge Hollenback's trading post at Tioga Point, set out on a hazy pink morning. The Captain, who was ruggedly handsome and young and Victoire's nemesis for several days, stood at the stern, his hairy hands guiding the rudder. Each of the four polemen dug his pole into the muddy river bottom and, heaving a shoulder against the other end, walked slowly the downstream length of the boat, pushing it upstream. Much of the time they were silent, but as they ate their sandwiches of cornbread and salt fish they broke into song, *Yankee Doodle* or something more rakish, and the songs were followed by bawdy joking.

Frau Gresch, all in one piece, devoted herself to a debauch of dreams and dozes. She had dreamed of molasses! . . . That meant failure in one's enterprise. Could the trip to Asylum end in failure? Victoire, who chatted with the Captain or worked on her needlepoint, nodded in triumph. Pierre paid little attention to her, talking most of the time with the traders or reading. Nicki, ubiquitous, at last had to be tied to one of the cowhide trunks, for Frau Gresch had dreamed of sliding down a banister and that meant drowning!

The party stayed at the Old Red Tavern Inn at Wilkes-Barre for a night while food supplies and freight were taken on for the rest of the journey. (Wilkes-Barre was a metropolis of two hundred and fifty inhabitants.) At night the passengers slept in narrow bunks built into the side of the cabin under the deck. Now and then a glum September rain kept them huddled below, and the baggage was covered with a tarpaulin.

The river coiled gracefully like a snake among the mountains, and the polemen guided the boat with cunning among the rocks and their foaming water. Maples and oaks burned scarlet in the sunshine. The air was sweet, almost perfumed. Now and then they saw a rattling buckboard on Sullivan's trail, and the passengers called and waved to them. Or a lone rider on horseback in the buckskins of a woodsman. Travel on the river was more frequent; lumber rafts going from the upper counties to Philadelphia; arks carrying several hundred bushels of grain or potatoes; floating bridges and ferries with peddlers, crossing the river.

Pierre was so excited at being in the Asylum country again that he deserted his books and talked to anybody who would listen: back in the hills were flourishing trout streams; there on the west bank was Forty Fort—the Battle of Wyoming had taken place there, fought by the Connecticut settlers—only a stockade now of logs. . . .

"Look, that's an old Indian trail," and he pointed it out to Victoire. "I must teach you how to tell sweet cicely from the poisonous musquash. Does the squawk of the pheasant remind you of anything? I always think of a shrew with a cold in her larynx."

Victoire laughed, settling down in the hot noon sun, a sunshade balanced on her shoulder. Although she was painfully bored pouting was dull.

The night before they reached Asylum, Pierre and Victoire stood on the deck together while "Frogra" tucked Nicki into his bunk. The air was cool and fresh, with a sweetness rising from the damp of the foliage. Grasses and rocks slithered past them, and the heavens were bewildering with starlight.

Pierre stood with his head thrown back, his hands locked behind him. It was as if he drank from some invisible chalice.

Victoire was amused.

"You remind me of a small boy going to the Isle de St. Marguerite on an excursion," she said.

"I wish I were. . . . Those were days of real beauty. I believed in everything—in sugarplums, my father, and the immortality of the Bourbons. I even believed in God."

"You do not believe in God now?"

"Do you?" he asked suddenly.

Victoire laughed. "But of course, *mon cher;* God is very convenient."

There was a moment's silence.

"There is much beauty in Asylum," he said, his voice no louder than the lapping of the water. "It will mean a great deal to me if you like Asylum."

Victoire stifled a yawn and drew her pelisse about her. She did not bother to answer. She was wondering if Omer Antoine Talon had a mistress. It surprised her when Pierre took her suddenly in his arms and kissed her. He had not so much as touched her hand since they left Philadelphia.

Her lips met his with a quick ardor. Asylum, Siberia . . . any place with Pierre never could be intolerable.

But the moment was cold, unfruitful. Their lips had never met before in the spirit of beauty.

The following evening in the dusk they approached Asylum. There had been no sunset and the air was damp and piercing.

It seemed to Victoire that they were being insidiously smothered by mountains. To the south and the west they rose grimly—gray peaks lost in melancholy restless clouds. From a distance Pierre had proudly pointed out Rummerfield Mountain across the river, noble, precipitous, stark with dark-green firs and naked boulders. Now even Rummerfield was a mingling of clouds and mist, its autumnal beauty hidden in glumness.

The small boat plodded on in the rising fog of the river. The Captain blew a gusty warning on the conch shell, and the note lingered, like the eerie call of a wolf to his mate on the hillside. Someone lighted a lantern. Frau Gresch coughed from the fog. Nicki, who was hungry, wailed on her shoulder and picked at her warts. Pierre was assembling the baggage; a bat, disturbed by the conch shell, flew dizzily over the boat, lunged into the mast, and fell, limp and fluttering. Pierre paused, picked up the animal, felt the blackness of the cave at St.-Émilion, and dropped it, shuddering.

Victoire stood beside the Captain, her hands gripping her red velvet jewel box. So, the great plateau in the horseshoe bend of the river was Asylum! This smattering of muggy lights in the opening hacked from the forest! Her eyes strained to see the cross on the chapel, the stockade that the Captain said surrounded the village—because of the wolves. The wolves that came down in winter—hungry! From low on the left bank out of gray nothing came the strumming of a gourd guitar, thumbed by some homesick Negro slave. It was here that she would bake *gâteaux,* make candles, squeeze the dye from the iris. . . .

There were calls now from the dock as men came running down to meet them, their lanterns like facetious, winking eyes in a vacuum. Night had come suddenly, a dim, moist night, enveloping them. The polemen were blindly but skillfully working the long boat into the slip of the dock from which the ferry ran to the Sullivan Road opposite. There was a final lurch and a bump. Victoire clung to her jewel case angrily.

Pierre's hand was guiding her off the boat now onto the phantom dock and then to the bank—a mesh of browning wood fern and skunk cabbage. Her heart was raging against her bosom like the clattering of a wind-blown shutter. What was this groveling slavery to sex that made one cross the river Styx with a man into a black inferno—to a woods where the wolves howled, hungry, in winter? She would no longer abide him—no longer suffer the torment of his mastery, not for a thousand ink-black eyes that consumed her! Once and for all, in this godforsaken spot she would get the better of him, and then she would leave him!

And then Victoire laughed. Her laughter screeched out in the quiet like the crazy laughter of a hyena. Frau Gresch, who still held the sleeping Nicki on her shoulder, turned to stare at her. The Captain, who stood alone, raised the lantern in his hand, and shafts of milky light jerked over her, striking fire on the red of her jewel case.

Pierre stared too. Her head, tossed back, framed by the fur hood and collar of her pelisse, seemed detached from her body. He saw only slits of sharp green eyes—only stark white teeth and a shivering tongue within a blood-red circle.

He felt himself begin to tremble. It was the trembling of a crater when lava begins to bubble within it. He had no thought, no emotion, only a subconscious need to stop the laughter.

With all his strength he struck her across the mouth, and he felt the marks of her teeth in the palm of his hand, stinging.

The laughter stopped. He and Victoire were glaring at one another. He felt emotion now, a sense of burning triumph and degradation. Of course she would strike him back with an equal fury. But she did not strike him back. . . . She would prefer some more subtle revenge of a Borgia.

"So! . . . You beat your women! That is your secret."

He felt that the words came from the two slits of eyes, not from the smeared, rouged lips. He was not even certain he heard them. She had drawn herself up to her full height, and he had the impression that she looked down at him like an Amazon.

He had lived this before . . . somewhere in the wallowing hours of the Revolution. But then the laughter that had enraged him had been lazy, like the rolling over of a porpoise, the voice fawning, like oil upon water. Pink-pudding breasts . . . *Nom de Dieu,* he remembered now! One beat women because they wanted to be beaten. . . . A beating to a woman was victory, part of an overwhelming surge that she had created—a confession sweeter than caress.

He wanted to crush her to him now, to feel the soft, wide lips closing in on his with a maddening satisfaction. His eyes, blazing, showed what he wanted. And he knew it. Victoire's eyes and lips answered with invitation, slightly scornful.

The night had stopped in its course. The noises of the wood, the confusion of unpacking, the greeting of friends—all of them halted. Even the very stars, somewhere there behind the fog, would have delayed their twinkling. Everything, it seemed, waited upon his decision. And he could not tell why it seemed so momentous. Surely as a gentleman he owed this woman an apology. As a husband he owed his wife contrition. And yet he stood trembling, struggling within an unknown voice while the universe, tongue in cheek, awaited the outcome.

While he was waiting too his legs began to move, carrying him to the rutted road that led away from the river.

And the Captain, smiling, lowered his lantern.

CHAPTER XXX

Pierre on his horse gripped Nicki stoutly by the waist. The young man squirmed like the eels so abundant on the river's edge, but he clung tightly to a chestnut burr the early frost had opened. Pierre was wearing again his buckskin shirt, skintight breeches, and high-top boots. His hair hung loose about his neck, free of the queue or black bag of the city.

They were coming from the new shop of Bec-de-Lièvre near the landing, where they had bought a mirror for Maman. They had been at Asylum for two nights, the first of which they had slept in luxury at la Grande Maison. M. Talon, as manager of the colony, always extended his hospitality to newcomers.

The day was a masterpiece of autumn, thought Pierre, with the sky a timid blue, gently clouded. A faint, magic haze softened the boldness of crimson and ocher, and yet the sassafras hedgerows of Rummerfield

Mountain blazed like bonfires. Through the fringe of trees along the river the water sparkled saucily as it flowed southward. Smoke curved lazy and snailwise from the chimneys; a few thin cows munched languidly at the browning grass. There was the squawk of pheasants, the rumbling of a buckboard, the faint ring of M. Aubrey's anvil. And the perfume of wood fire was sweeter than attar.

Now as Pierre reached the hitching-post before his five-acre plot and looked down upon the snug colony in the flats, his eyes had in them a depth of satisfaction, almost a covetousness he had once reserved for ballet ankles.

Far down to the left, close to the river, rose la Grande Maison, the largest log cabin in America. To the south of the ferry on the fringe of marshland, lived the Negroes brought by the San Domingans. And close to them—though the slaves did not like it—the little cemetery of three white crosses. One suicide, a homesick Frenchman who had hung himself in the forest with a silk handkerchief; a stillborn infant; an octogenarian of one of the Yankee families who farmed for the French.

In the middle of the village, bordering the market place of two acres, were now the theater, the inn of M. le Fevre, and the chapel. The whitewashed cross of the chapel caught the sun and blazed silver, stirring in Pierre a small nameless emotion that hurt him. Yes, he thought, Asylum had been a panacea for the moment—no blood, no hiding, no *visés*—protecting one with an extravagance of mountains and heaven— A kind of Olympus where there might be pain and heartache and struggle but none of the ugly strategy of the gods.

If only Victoire could be fettered! She had continued to laugh, although not like a madman. Asylum was a naked woman, she said, with warts and patches of hair and shriveled veins on her body. M. Talon's mansion, no bigger than one of her father's hunting shacks, was the only civilized place in it. And Pierre's house—it was no more than a shelter for cattle! She and Nicki would take the next Durham boat which went southward.

And she sat before the fire that first day and read or embroidered, receiving the women who came laden with offerings of food or candles. It was Frau Gresch who went to work at once, scrubbing and sanding the pine floors and preparing soup in the fireplace. The one day Victoire had lived in the house Pierre had built seemed eternal . . . not even a mirror! If they were to dine with M. Talon again tonight she must have a mirror.

Until Victoire came he had not realized how much he loved the small cabin for which he had hewn the logs, and the sprinkling of thirty-odd houses that lay within the stockade surrounding the house and town plots. For he had watched them rise, log by log, shingle by shingle. Nothing to be ashamed of: two stories high, with cellars, fine chimneys, and sturdy staircases. And no oiled paper for the French but real glass windows! Each house on its own naked clearing, raw stumps strewn about like the shining mushrooms that sprang up so legion after the first rain of September. Yes, these little houses were palaces to their owners—set among a few stalwart spruce firs or wandlike birches, hovering close to the great groves of primeval oaks.

His own house had seemed manorial to him when he lived here alone, he thought as he followed Nicki over the twisting path that led to the doorway. Now he could see that it was tiny; the few great chestnut trees towering above the chimney dwarfed it. Three rooms it had: the kitchen below with its fireplace in the rear center, the few stairs on the right leading to the two sleeping cubicles of the loft.

It was not a house for a woman, with its stiff ladder-back chairs and stools, its crude, homemade table, bunks built into the walls instead of beds with brocade hangings. It was a house for a lone man who read Shakespeare or tussled with his lack of faith by rushlight—a man who used the fowling piece over the mantel, who thought the fan of birds' tails an adequate ornament.

He opened the door with a sense of depression. Four chairs were strung in a row the length of the room, covered with the red couch cover Mme d'Autremont had gratefully given him in return for his Philadelphia mission. They formed a sort of screen so that he could not see the hickory flames that were soaring.

Shadows and firelight capered on the long poles above the mantel and across the low ceiling on which hung strings of peppers, pumpkin rings, herbs, and dried apples. A warm, pungent, spicy smell filled his nostrils, a breath of thyme, a waft of laurel leaves, the fragrance of marjoram. And there was a little lapping of water, like a whisper.

Nicki tossed his chestnut aside, joyfully cried *"Maman,"* and scooted around the barricade of chairs. Pierre brazenly looked over them.

Victoire was in the tub he had used in the summer to clean the trout from the brooks. She was taking a bath *à la Dauphine.*

La Grande Maison lay just outside the village stockade, but there was a fenced-in path to the mansion.

Victoire approached it that evening with anticipation. Here in Asylum women were deliberately losing their figures, deserting embroidery for the dough tray, heedlessly staining their hands. The whole venture was absurd in view of the fact that Marie Antoinette was headless, and the Dauphin a caged idiot. It was nothing less than a desecration of her sex. In defiance she had never prepared her toilette more carefully, had made it an all-day ritual, beginning with the bath *à la Dauphine* in the morning.

The house had the charm of a little music box, she thought. It was a mere toy, only eighty feet long, with candles shining behind the small glass panes of the square windows.

Wallois, Talon's Negro butler, admitted them. The long hall was cheerful with tapers burning in niches; Louis XVI chairs, burnished floors, and great urns of fall foliage gave it at once a note of elegance. Huge staircases of walnut at either end of the hall held the shadows, which at last merged into one great shadow consumed by the upper story.

As Victoire entered the salon to the left her fingers relaxed on Pierre's arm and she gave him a dazzling smile that was meant for the assembled company. He was so like a little boy, she thought, who brings a mutt home from an alley. He wanted so much that they should like her—that she should fit into their prescribed manner of living.

Now if Pierre had brought her to la Grande Maison to live, a winter here might be conceivable. The "French ladies' drawing-room," as the salon had been styled, had sophistication, though here were walls and ceiling of polished walnut, not cupid-guarded moldings. On the river side toward the terrace was a double door, its upper half twinkling with colored panes like jewels. Lush crimson hangings of satin were drawn across the French windows, which reached from floor to ceiling. Twin fireplaces, one at either end of the room, had high carved and colonnaded mantelpieces and branching bronze candelabra. Here were the things one was used to, thought Victoire: a petit-point fire screen, backgammon table, porcelain clock, a portrait of Maria Theresa. How Marie Antoinette would have been touched by that and the *clavecin!* And mirrors! . . . Asylum for the Queen—picture frame now for a marquise!

M. Talon kissed her hand graciously. Mme la Marquise would be a genuine asset to the colony, he was certain. Backs might be stiff at night, minds might be weary; but whenever two or three Frenchmen were gathered together there would always be conversation and levity. Madame's reputation for wit had arrived before her.

Victoire took a quick census of the male guests, cataloguing them as Good, Bad, and Indifferent, as was her custom.

M. Talon, polished but undistinguished, not too young and not too old. Eyes, a nose, a mouth, and two ears, as usual. No calluses here, but the soft hand of a gentleman—more than amenable, no doubt, with his wife across the water—generous, too. Hadn't he kept open house for his distressed countrymen in Philadelphia? *Dieu,* it was good to know someone here lived like a human being—an undisputed czar of the colony! What else then but *Good!*

M. Carles, rector of the log chapel, and a farmer, dressed now in trim wine velvet. The girth of a lollypop, the stockiness of a miller. Bad skin like herself but no feminine wile to conceal it. Lively, but with the dyspepsia and bad breath of a gourmand. *Bad to Indifferent!*

Charles Homet, former steward of Louis—young, not much older than Pierre. Ah, this was more like it! Almost handsome and certainly vital; how could she ever have overlooked him in the lottery of Versailles? What was the story about him? He had fled to the Bay of Biscay to escape on a ship that already had his effects on it. And when he had found the ship was five miles out to sea he had swum to it. Admirable figure and muscles of a Neptune . . . but of course, he was the one Pierre said had married Maria Theresa Schillinger of Strasbourg, one of the Queen's waiting-women, after they had crossed on the ship together. There was Mme Homet admiring the painting by Chardin. Victoire remembered her—even remembered the olive-green brocade with its nasturtiums. Shabby elegance! Mme Homet was annoyingly beautiful, it was true, with her skin of rose-tinted ivory—but rumored ten years older than her devoted husband. Charles Homet, looking at least like a prince of the blood. By any reckoning, *Good!*

And then Dr. Lawrence Buzard, a planter from San Domingo. Here was an enigma: dark, almost greasy-complexioned, obese, and yet with an eye and a manner of persuasion. Certainly no rival of M. Homet or Adonis. (Now that she thought of it, the former steward did remind her of blooming raw cauliflowers and sturdy capons.) But there was a leashed look about Dr. Buzard that was intriguing, and Victoire enjoyed playing Pandora. Dr. Buzard, then, certainly *Good!*

She gravitated toward him and was presented. He and M. Carles were talking of du Petit-Thouars the little Admiral.

"Ah, the Castor to Pierre's Pythias!" she exclaimed.

"Could Mme la Marquise mean Pollux!" inquired Dr. Buzard, looking at her from the black eyes of which the whites were a tired yellow.

"Things equal to the same thing are equal to each other, *n'est-ce pas?*" laughed Victoire with a hot flush.

The men laughed. She was indeed witty, thought M. Carles, quickly scoring her blunder into a triumph; likely she had intentionally trapped them.

"As I was saying," said Dr. Buzard, "du Petit-Thouars thinks we should get more yield of maple sugar from a tree. Perhaps two and a half to three pounds a year. The soil on the Loyalsock is certainly excellent."

"That's a concern of spring," replied M. Carles, stifling a hungry belch. "My present concern is my cattle with winter coming and a lack of decent fodder."

"*Oui.* What little milk they give is poor . . . and my children rebel at cider."

"Thank God, I don't have to eat that mash of turnips and gourds and Indian corn," M. Carles ejaculated.

"But you must make Herculean efforts," warned Victoire, "you and the cows. We women must have our milk baths."

The eyes of Dr. Buzard and M. Carles focused on her. Neither of them answered.

She flicked the seed-pearl fan as if she were shooing flies, and drifted away from them. Bores! She would leave them to their cattle. As she passed Pierre and Mme Buzard she heard the voluptuous Sultana say: "But our chains and tools are poor. The iron breaks like butter. M. Aubrey—"

There was the welcome announcement of dinner. Victoire went into the adjoining dining-room on the arm of M. Homet and sat between him and M. Talon. She would begin with the story of the lecherous Duc de Menneville and his impartiality. . . .

The beautiful table was reassuring. Sèvres china, silver goblets, a compote of fruit and nuts, a cloth of exquisite lace and linen monogrammed "M. A." The row of wine glasses in steps like peasants' children indicated that the cellar of la Grande Maison was stocked to overflowing.

And then the dinner itself: broiled trout dressed with chives and parsley, grilled quail with mushrooms, venison, an inimitable salad, a crêpe suzette burning with maple sugar and almonds.

M. Talon adroitly led the conversation, assisted by the sweet little widow d'Autremont on his left. Congress had estimated the adult support of a refugee at thirty pounds a year; French brandy was $1.30 per gallon; the last census claimed there were some five thousand people here in Luzerne county; Bishop Carroll was reputedly annoyed because the abbés of Asylum had never asked his sanction to exercise their ministry in America and had become farmers.

For an hour Victoire felt like a river-bank weed, stirred by conflicting eddies of water. The Duc de Menneville and his impartiality were dangling. Such a gauche lot of society had never been inflicted upon her before. Her heart pounded proudly under the high, blue-muslin bosom. What had happened to these Frenchmen, who were dressed tonight like courtiers, kissed her hand with a charming obligation, and forgot her? There certainly wasn't a woman here who could compete with her. Their dress clothes even smelled of camphor. Every time that she glanced at Pierre she knew that his eyes had just shifted from her, and his surveillance was highly irritating. But the evening was young. If she could not manage Talon she could certainly manage the young cauliflower Homet.

Victoire turned to him once more but he was intent on Pierre's news that a hundred new books were ready for circulation. Through the chatter and gesticulation she learned that Mme Homet was helping Charles to weave a shad seine of willows. Dr. Buzard thought a serum for yellow fever could be made of the juniper; M. Homet had bought new grapevine shoots from Priestley's vineyards at Northumberland.

Victoire tried to interpose a few words on the new fashion of sandals but her words were muffled and carried downstream. Mme d'Autremont—if you please!—interrupted to say her sons had decided to make tar and pot-and-pearl ash from the forest refuse.

There was a wild applause.

Victoire made up her mind that she would hold the floor if she must raise her voice to the pitch of a fishwoman's. There—someone had just mentioned a thief. This would be the apt moment to tell them the story of the Comte de Teaufaché and how he had fallen in love with a beautiful courtesan in England, not knowing she was the Mme de Lamotte of the Queen's necklace scandal until he had discovered "V" for *voleuse* branded on her shoulders.

"The Comte de Teaufaché is said to brand his lovers," she began boldly, engaging Homet with the vulgar tap of her fan against all convent approbation. In a moment he was all absorption. Now M. Talon and Mme d'Autremont were listening. Victoire's voice rang clear over the clank of dishes with a certain practiced note of secretiveness that had always proved inviting. The Sultana, it seemed, was continuing her gesticulations and the story that went with them. M. Carles was giving her and his ill-controlled belching his undivided attention. Well, Victoire would have to be content with half the audience; at least it was a beginning.

She had only arrived at the fabrication of the Comte's forcing the lock to Mme de Lamotte's boudoir when M. Carles clapped his hands loudly. Pierre's eyes, which had been fixed sharply on her, turned to his San Domingan partner. Dr. Buzard, who had just exclaimed: "Ah, the scamp!" to Victoire, said *"Qu'est-ce que c'est?"* to the former canon.

"Magnifique!" cried M. Carles loudly, reaching for a bunch of grapes. *"Attention, mes amis!"*

"Mme de Lamotte shrieked and—" Victoire was loudly insistent.

"Une proclamation!" cried the canon.

"—mais avec un soupçon de poivre—" came the last triumphant words of Mme Buzard.

Another clap of M. Carles's hands and his voice boomed over Victoire's like a bolt of thunder.

"Miracle of miracles! Mme Buzard has found a new way to use our large supply of pumpkin! But *délicieux*—and not too much San Domingan pepper!"

The white Creole teeth of the Sultana gleamed. Mme de Lamotte was consumed with the tidal wave of praise, forgotten.

M. Talon rose. "A toast to Mme Buzard in the American way! . . . A toast to all the ingenious women of our colony!"

Pierre, his voice singing praise with the others, glanced again at Victoire. His words were excluding, as the black glance shot between them.

She was a derelict, he thought, and she belonged to him. He was chagrined as he toasted the valiant women of the colony. In spite of their gala clothes, in spite of their homesick longing, their hearts beat warm with courage and determination. If Victoire's heart might be bared one would find on it only the imprint of the arms of a Marquise. Yes, he had hated her from the beginning, and if his son grew like her he would kill him! He tossed the wineglass onto the hearth, seeing only the slits of Victoire's eyes, which were black as his own as she sat in ramrod defiance. She could take the next Durham boat out of his life, and be damned to her!

The dinner over, the group went to the salon for coffee. Victoire disappeared, slipped above to one of the numerous bedchambers. It was dimly lighted with tapers, smug with chintz and rosewood and delicate French paper.

She sat at the dressing-table, stared into the ornate mirror. She was so angry that she was frightened. Her breath came hard and irregular as if she had been running; two invisible iron hands seemed to choke her. She was nothing. She, the Marquise de Bussac, lost in a tangle of wood stumps and cabins and cattle! She who should have been the toast of the evening . . . nothing, nothing, nothing! *Dieu,* she was even ugly, skin mottled, eyes witchlike, mouth drooping! She hated life, she hated herself, she hated Pierre. And he despised her—even as he had always despised her. Because she had money that he lived on. Because he had blood of the Charlemagnes. And now, because she was nothing. Well, she would have the showdown at last—would leave him his pride without money—would take Nicki and break Pierre's heart with the theft of him—even as he had threatened to do if she did not come to Asylum. . . . Pierre might scorn her but the rest of the world was filled with esteem for a marquise. She would flaunt his name over Europe and have a thousand lovers. She would crowd her hours with dancing and jewels and embraces. And she would soon forget him.

Nom de Dieu—but would she forget him? He would hibernate here in Asylum, would be sated with silly fox sparrows trilling in the laurel bushes. He would forget her and she would live with the cancerous envy of his contentment—gnawing at her always—eating away her conquests.

It was folly to lie with no one here but herself and the harpy in the mirror. Nothing, nothing, nothing! She refused to accept this humiliation and yet she could not leave him. Rough hands, consuming eyes, lean strength, struggle—it was still what she wanted, more than the thousand lovers of Europe!

She told herself again that in a few months she would wheedle him into going to Philadelphia. But three months of exile! Her years at the Convent de Panthemont, chained by the irksome minutiae of religion, were not a long enough apprenticeship to patience—to three months of the dominion of the fatuous Sultana. . . . Dominion. But why should there be any dominion but her own? Wasn't she shrewder than any woman in the colony? Why not make a deliberate campaign against them and their potash and their peppered pumpkin? If that was what the men wanted, the fools, she could give them their candle-grease soup and confiture of mushrooms! In a week she could have them eating out of the palm of her hand. Why should Mme Homet act the part of Juliet in the coming play for the holidays? She, Victoire, would be Juliet; she, Victoire, would organize the fete for the Noël, the dancing class, the New Year's ox roast on the river. She would lead Asylum a breathless pace that eventually would be the death of it—and Pierre, of course, would adore her. The ordeal should not be longer than three months, and the game would be well worth the playing!

She began to feel exhilarated. Her eyes gleamed hard as crystal and the corners of her mouth widened and lifted as she smiled at the Victoire of the mirror. A little powder now, and some lip rouge. . . . Ah, the poor Sultana! . . .

She returned to the salon, her curls flouncing with a new resolution; no one saw her as she stood in the doorway.

It was a moment that impressed her, a moment that she felt afterwards fate had prepared for her. For instead of the usual after-dinner jocularity and laughter, here were six people listening raptly to M. Talon, who stood with a brandy glass in hand, his back to the fireplace.

"Ah, if only we had bolting cloth!" he was saying as he lifted a fleck of cork from the brandy with a delicate little finger.

It seemed there was a new grist mill driven by horse power. Strong millstones of Lackawanna flint had come from Wilkes-Barre. It was a little gem of a mill, forty by thirty-four feet, double-geared, with a good pair of stones and a fireplace in the corner. Part of the lower story already stabled the horses as well as some cattle. In the upper story was fodder for the entire winter. Everything was in readiness to produce flour—except for the bolting cloth.

"M. Hollenback says it may be months before the cloth arrives from Philadelphia," Pierre said. "I just saw him in Wilkes-Barre."

The Sultana sighed darkly into her coffee.

"What a treat it would be to have our own bolted flour!" said Mme Homet wistfully. "Not to have to wait for ground corn meal from a dinky little mill in the next county!"

"What is bolting cloth made from?" asked the Sultana, her great dark eyes lugubrious.

"We could use any fine new cloth. If such a thing were only to be had in Asylum!" M. Talon drew the bell cord for the playing cards.

Yes, this was her moment, thought Victoire in the doorway, unnoticed. She walked grandly into the center of the circle.

"I shall give my new white silk gown from Coblentz," she exclaimed, and looked directly at the Sultana, "for the bolting cloth."

The seven despondents broke into a babel. Victoire was accolated. M. Homet kissed her fingers with a flourish. Mme d'Autremont clapped her little hands in ecstacy. M. Talon turned to her with astonished joy. The expression in Pierre's dark eyes was one of puzzlement.

M. Carles, swaying slightly, raised his brandy glass and cried out: "To Mme la Marquise—heroine of Asylum!"

CHAPTER XXXI

February 1795

VICTOIRE HAD BEEN like a shot of adrenalin to the pulse of the colony. Her rendering of Juliet to M. Homet's Romeo had been almost poignant. Half of the women in the audience had come to Victoire for advice on the remodeling of a fraying satin. Once a week she held dancing classes in la Grande Maison (Aristide du Petit-Thouars had taught her the hornpipe). She worked with the Sultana's indolent little daughter on the *clavecin* and instigated concerts, boldly interpreting Mozart, Gluck, Scarlatti. If Mme d'Autremont played with more sweetness, Victoire played with more mettle. Her own piano had not yet come, but M. Talon was generous.

The men revolved about her once more, for there was no woman in Asylum more interested in a good bargain and she had a way of transposing business into pleasure. M. Heraud discussed with her his new inn for which he had just been given a license. Where could he get a housekeeper for the inn?

At Victoire's suggestion M. Homet opened a bakery. He lived eight miles south of Asylum in a further retreat that had been begun for Marie Antoinette and whose buildings he had been in charge of erecting, but he often came down to the village for supplies.

Yes, Asylum was growing. The novel bolting cloth had proved most successful at the mill, although the mesh of the silk was too fine to take out any but the whitest and finest of flour. The brewery, built before Christmas, was steadily producing. A road was being surveyed toward the Loyalsock so that the colony might be connected with the immense forest tracts on the Muncy, the Lycoming, and the Loyalsock to which the Asylum Company held title.

During the winter Victoire and Frau Gresch worked over two large kettles at the kitchen fire, making candles of deer suet and moose fat. Victoire was impatient at first and dipped so fast that the candles grew brittle and cracked. But if Mme d'Autremont was proud of her output of one hundred and eighty candles one night, the next day Victoire must keep her kitchen cooler and work more slowly so that she could boast of an even two hundred.

Although Victoire was shocked and furious that she could not leave Asylum till spring, no one knew it. Least of all would she have given Pierre the satisfaction of thinking he had tricked her. She was both annoyed and amused that she wasn't actually miserable here. The days passed swiftly; her opinions and help were so sought after that she felt more important than in the most select court circles. There was a keen pleasure in being more resourceful than these other women in making a synthetic blancmange or in fashioning a ravishing muff of a bobcat.

Pierre was proud of her. She had borne the winter so stoically that sometimes, Pierre thought superstitiously, it must be the calm before the storm.

"You are a hundred times superior to these other women," he exclaimed. "You even manage through some black magic to keep your hands white as a courtesan's."

Yes, thought Victoire, here in the woods Pierre forgot there was a nobility of the sword and a nobility of the robe; she was humbling him although it was taking all of her time and ingenuity. She even felt that in an abstract fashion he had come to love her. By spring the leveling of the sword and the robe would be complete and the three de Michelaits would go to the emerald mansion in Philadelphia.

Pierre was in and out all day, smelling of sweat, dragging slush about the fresh sanded floor. He pruned the pathetic little fruit trees, chopped wood, mended tools, cleaned game, set traps, helped break through the snowdrifts. Nicki's fat legs toddled after him, and Nicki's pet crow with the split tongue and nipped wings flapped after Nicki.

The worse the news that came from France, the harder Pierre worked. The fate of the Girondins with whom he had shared the cave had reached him: Buzot and Pétion, having killed themselves in a wheat field, were found at harvest time, faces half eaten. In death, Buzot still clung to his miniature of Mme Roland. Salle and Gaudet had been executed in Bordeaux. Barbaroux, having shot himself at Castillion, was guillotined when half dead. Of the group only Louvet escaped, and it was rumored that he had defiantly set off to Paris to find his Lodoïska. Four hundred men with bloodhounds had attacked Mme Bouquey's house, and she with her old father had been apprehended and guillotined. Where in the world were enough snows to be ploughed, enough trees to be pruned, to make one forgetful?

One afternoon as the dusk became palling, Aristide came to see them. Pierre greeted Aristide joyously, for the Little Admiral had been snowbound for two months in his cabin. In the early winter he and Pierre had hunted bears together, had blazed new trails, defanged rattlesnakes, trained a fox cub. Many a night, whittling before a fire, they talked of the Touraine they knew and loved, of Aristide's botanist brother in Africa, of a projected trip to Niagara Falls by canoe and foot. Words and ideas tumbled from one to the other like those of lovers in their first budding harmony as they discussed forest fires, the habits of a beaver, ships, the manufacture of potash, the works of Calvin, the eternal war between the Connecticut and Pennsylvania settlers. And always, always there was talk of France and the endless Revolution.

"Ah, Mme la Marquise," said du Petit-Thouars as he came forward to the fire, "but you look charming this evening! I always expect to hear the bells of Paris when I see you."

Victoire extended her free hand to be kissed. She was sprinkling herbs in the venison ragout. (It was Frau Gresch who peeled the potatoes.)

Nicki gave a cry of delight and deserted the wooden blocks that Aristide had made for him.

"Present for Nicki! Present for Nicki!" he clamored, pulling at the fringe of Aristide's leather pouch.

"But of course," laughed Aristide, "if you can find it!"

Nicki's small hands scrambled through the miscellany of the pouch until he came upon a ring made of an acorn. Pierre laughed as Aristide pushed it on the stubby little finger, and said: "Now we're married and our fates are interlocked forever."

Nicki laughed because the others laughed (all but "Frogra" who was not *gemütlich* today).

Pierre went back to his boot polishing, and Nicki clambered on Aristide's knee, content for a full moment to be close to this wonderful gift giver.

The conversation always began the same way.

"Gone!" wailed Nicki, touching the stumped wrist that was half hidden by Aristide's cuff. "Gone!"

"*Oui,* still gone," answered Aristide, stroking the black curls with his right hand.

"Because M. du Petit-Thouars is brave," said Pierre.

"Brave," repeated Nicki, slithering off Aristide's knee and away to his blocks again.

A few minutes later the peace was interrupted by a terrified squeal from the hogpen. Pierre, Aristide, and the dog Neige dove from the cabin in time to see a bear spring on one of the hogs, grasping him in his forelegs. The bear, lean and hungry from his recent hibernation, waddled off quickly on his hind legs with his load.

"Don't shoot!" cried Pierre to Aristide. "We'll make it man to man. I was going to butcher a hog tomorrow anyway."

The squeals of the smothered hog were like those of a strangled baby. Brandishing a club he had snatched from the lean-to, Pierre pursued the bear, which ran through the snow fast as a rabbit. The Little Admiral flew along beside Pierre with his knife unsheathed.

The bear paused at the fence, hugging his writhing armful, and glowering down at the two men, let out pants of breath that smoked in the chill of the early night.

Pierre began to pound at the great black animal with his club, suddenly too angry to think of danger. The wretched hog, the fattest in the litter, was a sow and the very one Pierre had no intention of slaughtering. Her gasps became weaker and weaker like the faint wheeze of an accordion as the iron arms locked around her. Soon only small sighs escaped her as the bear's paws dug into her belly.

The bear was frankly puzzled. Dodging, swaying, snorting, loath to give up his prize, yet he had no legs with which to combat Pierre's onslaught. Moreover, there was the problem of an icy fence to hurdle. At last in desperation he dropped his victim and made a drunken lunge at Pierre, who evaded him, landing a blow on his rump.

"Stay back!" cried Pierre to Aristide, who was attempting to run his knife through the thick, black fur. "He's mine!"

But Aristide had already made the thrust. The impact of his knife, jabbing into the hard wood of the fence instead of the soft belly of the bear, threw him.

Pierre pommeled the bear as he might beat a rug, and the animal, insane with pain, parried with him. At last, unable to cope with the ruthless bludgeoning, he reeled toward the fence, swung over it dizzily, and staggered off into the grove of oaks. Aristide shot quickly, on his feet again, but the bear escaped.

Pierre and Aristide turned to one another and laughed hilariously, not even hearing the shrieks of Frau Gresch and Victoire at the door.

"We've scared him off," cried Pierre, almost breathless. "We've gotten the better of the wilds once more."

"Have we?" countered Aristide, pointing to the hog that lay like a sack of meal between them, a dirty smudge in the snow.

Aristide's brown locks swung over his forehead like an idiot's and his lips twisted into a grimace. He was a small, unleashed fury, no bigger than Pierre's shadow at midday.

The sow had nearly breathed its last. The two men dragged it by the legs to the hogpen, trying to dodge tree stumps hidden by the snow and the quickening dark. Pierre alternately cursed and whistled a funeral dirge.

On second thought he decided to lay the hog in a heavy steel trap concealed on the edge of his property. It would be an invitation for Bruno to return. Victoire wanted another bear rug.

"You mark my word," exclaimed Victoire angrily as the men trudged into the house calling for a hot toddy, "one of these days your son will be chewed alive!"

"One of these days," returned Pierre, swinging the wide-eyed Nicki to his shoulder, "my son will be old enough to handle a gun better than M. du Petit-Thouars!"

The following day when Pierre told his story at M. Heraud's inn, the men decided to have a ring hunt. There had already been two drives or large hunts during the winter, but these had been rather for the purpose of taking a few deer and turkeys. Wolves had been avaricious lately and a bear or two had been seen, for after a severe winter there was an early warm spell and little food.

The ring hunt was planned for the following day. It was an ideal time since the snow had dwindled to a smattering and pursuit through the woods would not be difficult.

Louis Paul d'Autremont rode to Terrytown and Wyalusing to round up all available men from that community both old and young enough to handle a gun. The Hermans and the Johnsons and the Vanderpoels were all recruited; language was no barrier when it came to the chase, and the critical feeling between the French and the English seemed to dissolve in whetted anticipation. A little bourgeois tailor volunteered to ride the eight miles to Homet's inn and order the bear barbecue that was to follow the hunt. Even the very dogs of the village yapped excitedly at the prospect. There was a great sharpening of knives and cleaning of guns. The women began to freshen the gowns they would wear when they joined the hunters in the afternoon for the feast.

The men of the village gathered before the last star had melted into sunrise. The Little Admiral, who had stayed at Heraud's inn for the night, came for Pierre so early that even Frogra was in curl papers and redundant nightgown.

They ate enormous breakfasts and began to gather their equipment: a quarter pound of powder, a pound of buckshot, flint, a pint of rum, cheese and dried fish to gnaw on.

Where were they going, and why? demanded Nicki, at large in his night shift. What did they have in their pouches, and why? Neige could go with papa, and Nicki couldn't. Why?

"What shall I bring you?" Pierre asked Victoire. "Our yesterday's visitor—for a bear rug?"

"Why not the phantom white stag of the mountain?" she challenged.

The plot of land that had been selected for the focal point of the kill was a couple of miles from Homet's inn and was a broad plateau surrounded by woodland in all directions. Major Hoops, who stood six feet three and had a fire-red beard, made an impressive captain. He and his four subordinates were mounted. There were Captain Beaulieu who had served in the Pulaski Regiment in the Revolution, James de Montullé, an ex-cavalryman who was now superintendent of clearing of Asylum, and the de la Roué brothers, both soldiers.

The meadow, five miles away, was approached by concentric lines of men who kept equally distant from one another and always within sight or hearing of the hunter to the right and left. Radii of blazed trees guided the men toward the field, as well as the horns of the mounted leaders. Those who were attacking the meadow from its far sides had left the night before, taking with them the buckboards on which the game would be loaded.

It was a feverish moment when Captain Beaulieu, who led Pierre's section, blew the signal on his trumpet. The Little Admiral, stationed at a cut in the woods near Picnic Rock, gave Pierre a salute and cried "Ahoy!" M. Carles, far off to the south, waved a red bandanna. The dogs began to scamper wildly, vying with the echo of trumpet and horn to waken the sleeping animals of the hillside. The men too as they advanced cried and shouted like Tartars, for no animal was to be left in his winter den.

The beginning of the hunt was slow until the first ring of blazed trees was reached, and Major Hoops and his staff made a circuit to see that the men were evenly distributed and all of the gaps closed. Pierre knew how the dogs felt as he waited for the trumpet signal to start on; his voice was already hoarse from his challenging cries, and his impatience knew no bounds.

It was almost at once that Pierre saw the tracks of his enemy Bruno. They began in the woodland beyond Pierre's acres. He knew they were Bruno's for the imprint of the two forepaws was clear and there were also the marks of the iron-clamped hind paws, with an occasional lacy design of a chain. Splashes of dark red blood tinged the thinning snow of the forest floor. Pierre's terrier, scrambling ahead of him, sniffed and whined with excitement, rushing back to Pierre at intervals to leap up on him and warn him of his prey.

The excitement of the wilderness was in Pierre's blood again, and it flashed through his mind that he had felt like this outside of the Abbaye prison rubbing elbows with the sans-culottes.

For a couple of hours Pierre followed the tracks, now losing them in a trout stream, now finding them in a hemlock thicket. It was wonderful to be alive in the frost of the morning! It was wonderful to be in pursuit! Turkeys began to squawk from the brush, and the first herd of deer leaped startled between him and Aristide as the wary shots of the men drove them inward. Coming to a rocky ledge, where he paused for a moment for breath, he almost stepped into a knot of rattlesnakes that had gathered on the rocks for the warmth of the morning sunlight. He escaped them with a laugh. How the women would cringe tonight when he told them! . . .

By the middle of the morning the nip of the air had gone. The woods were denser and alive as a jungle, and although Pierre knew he was closer to Aristide and M. Carles they were often lost from sight. Bobcats mewed fiercely; simple little birds like the juncos and bluejays fluttered about in terror; a fox skulked now and then behind a tree and if he refused to be driven inward, was shot as he bolted to hiding. There was no time to measure his tail or skin him, although there was an excellent bounty on his jacket. The day flew on, filled with small victories and defeats. Often, great clumps of fern swallowed the tracks of Bruno, and a hundred times Pierre despaired of ever finding him. . . . Here was the carcass of a sheep—one of M. de La Roué's, no doubt. He was the only one in the colony who dared raise sheep in defiance of the wolves. And here were enough beechnuts under rotting leaves to keep an army of squirrels gorging throughout a winter.

As Pierre rested now and then in a clearing he sampled his cheese and fish and biscuit, gazed at a bewildered chipmunk or some lost spotted fawn, which he pitied.

Shortly after noon he was beginning to feel a little despondent. For a mile or more he had lost the bear tracks. If Bruno fell into the hands of M. Carles or Aristide he would never forgive them! Then suddenly he came upon the tracks again, looking fresh and more enticing than ever.

"Hey!" he cried to Aristide, who was not more than fifty yards away now. "Our old love, Bruno!"

Aristide was too busy to heed. He had met his match in a full-grown panther, the size of a hundred-and-fifty-pound man, the size of Aristide himself. Pierre gave a cry as he saw the brownish red ball of an animal leap at Aristide with a sly cunning from the branch of an oak. For a few deadly moments there was a tussle fast as the spin of a pin wheel. Pierre tore between trees, through a soft bog of brook and rotting leaves, falling, scrambling forward, crying, unable to shoot—for neither Aristide nor the panther held one spot for more than the flash of a second. Once he all but collided with a wounded buck that flew snorting past him. His shouts were lost in the holocaust of gunfire and horns and cries, for the men were drawing in close to the meadow.

Pierre had just determined to take a low aim at the panther (for now he was only ten yards from the fight) when the animal fell back under the knife of the Little Admiral, and after writhing gave a lurch and was still.

Pierre leaned against a tree, the sweap dripping from his chin.

"Mon Dieu!" he panted. "I thought he had you!"

"With my nine lives?" gasped Aristide. "Never!"

The Little Admiral was still staggering and his face was streaked red like that of an Indian. But his soft brown eyes shone happily through smeared locks of hair.

They took a draft of rum, exchanging excited notes on what they had seen and done, and Pierre retraced his steps to the halfway point between M. Carles and Aristide. But he was to have his innings too. For the first time since dawn he had entirely forgotten the bear, thinking only of Aristide's escape and of the short time before the men would meet in the open to surround their bounty. As Pierre reached his trail he tripped over the gnarled root of a tree and fell headlong. Neige, rising on his hind legs with a sudden cry, gave him brief alarm. The bear, crazy with pain, was so close to Pierre that as he stumbled to his feet its breath was warm on his face. Before Pierre knew it the great forepaws had closed about his chest, crushing him like a boa constrictor.

He had no breath to cry out, and the knife he carried in his hand was pinned to his side and trembled in the weakness of his fingers. The bear seemed to be grinning at him, his long pointed teeth like the stalactites of the caves at St.-Émilion.

The terrier flew at the bear viciously, his bark one long continuous howl as he made at the maimed, clamped claws.

Pierre, unable to gasp for breath, felt his lungs fill with pain as if he were drowning. The forest seemed to be coming down on him; and now it had turned into a hot oven—or was he slipping into hell? Something roared past his ear and there was an explosion. He had no idea if it was sound or the stab of a thousand teeth in his shoulder. . . .

When he became conscious again he was lying flat on his back on one of the buckboards. Aristide's hunting jacket lay over him, and the warmth of the mid-afternoon sun poured down on him. For a few moments he was content to soak it in, vaguely listening to the great uproar of shouts and shooting. His left arm burned as if someone had set a flare to it, and he pulled himself up on his right elbow and yanked the jacket away. His arm was bound by strips of gray wool through which the blood soaked. He was humiliated and utterly angry with himself.

Other buckboards ranged about the meadow were being filled with bloody carcasses. A flock of deer, desperate, under constant fire, stumbling with exhaustion, mad with wounds, nevertheless leaped over the heads of a line of men who had guns, clubs, and pitchforks raised to vanquish them. Hunters and dogs were scouring the fringe of woods surrounding the meadow to retrieve dead or wounded animals. There was no end to the fracas of the dogs; they leaped and frisked, sniffed and whined, tore at fallen animals, snapped at one another.

Major Hoops was trying to gather the men together with a blast of his horn and a wave of the arm, his red beard flashing in the sun like a beacon.

As Pierre pulled himself together and teetered dizzily to the ground, he saw a familiar black lumbering giant dash crazily from the woods, dragging the chain of a trap. The bear was perhaps fifty feet away and mad with fright and pain, blindly fighting for freedom.

Others had seen him too. He cavorted through a shower of bullets, refusing to die.

Pierre pulled his flintlock grimly from the buckboard where it had lain beside him, and leaned against the wagon to steady himself. To raise his left arm took the courage of a dozen Jobs; his left hand refused to flex enough to grip the barrel of the gun, but he hadn't a moment to lose and he rested the barrel on his wrist. With his right hand he cocked the gun and pulled the trigger with trembling fingers.

The shot was wild for his head and his eyes were swimming.

But the bear threw up its forepaws to heaven and sprawled forward in the slush of the field. A shout of acclaim went up from the men who had been chasing him.

"Bravo!" exclaimed the Little Admiral, who was suddenly beside Pierre, bolstering him up.

"What in the devil happened to me?" Pierre demanded dizzily.

"Not a thing, *mon ami*," laughed Aristide. "You just got the better of the wilderness once more!"

CHAPTER XXXII

THE HUNTERS straggled to Homet's inn in twos and threes, guided by the road that was still a rutted trail and the fragrance of smoke belching from numerous chimneys.

A cluster of Lombardy poplars marked the site of the house that had barely been begun in the back woods for Marie Antoinette when news of her death reached Asylum. M. Homet, in charge of erection of the buildings, had finished the house on a small scale for himself, turning it into an inn for an occasional transient and the workmen who were building the Loyalsock road. A long, low bunkhouse had been added to the inn on the other side of the taproom fireplace, and as need for further beds arose log houses were erected. It was an impressive little colony, with three acres cleared and to the east a large bakehouse with storerooms and workrooms.

Hot grog awaited the men in the long bunkroom, which had been set with trestle tables and decorated by little Mme Homet with boughs of rhododendron and pine. A contingent of women from Asylum had come early to assist her, and bustled about with aprons over their finery, heating gallons of rum and carrying in from the kitchen trenchers of food. The bear, sputtering brown in the huge fireplace, sent out so inviting an aroma that it seemed he could not wait to be eaten.

The food, shouted the men; hurry with the food for the starving!

Everyone was in everyone's way. Mme d'Autremont, who always looked helpless as a doll and was efficient as a drum major, was sugaring the pumpkins that had been baked in the ashes of the bakery hearth; Mme de Blaçons, the ex-canoness of Bon-Bourg, poured buttermilk into dozens of birch-bark cups; Mme Seybert, the rich widow of a San Domingan planter, elegantly cut the Juneberry tarts; Mme Homet toasted waffles with a long fork over the coals of the open kitchen fire. Pervading all was the smell of sizzling fat and the fresh, long crusty loaves of bread. Mme Buzard, the Sultana, dripping with jewelry, hovered about with a ladle in one languid hand, her eyes drowsy from the heat and the exertion. Tied with a napkin into his high chair, Master Homet, not quite a year, pounded a silver spoon with the insistence of a gavel.

Dr. Buzard conducted a clinic. There was a sprained ankle, a shot through the shoulder; Aristide's gashes wept continuous tears of blood; the flesh of Pierre's arm was a raw pulp and needed heavier bandaging.

Victoire played nurse, cutting lengths of bandage for Dr. Buzard, her own sleeve flounces pinned back. The snipping was interspersed with lively epigrams. The women who really liked to mess around with food could handle the meal. She preferred working with something animate.

M. Homet staggered in under the weight of a punch bowl (he had returned in time to toss together brandy, sugar, tepid water, roasted crabapples, and a little muscat). The men drank it like water alternately with the grog. Everyone sang. Everyone wanted the rostrum. Let the bear revolving on the spit take his time now!

"Two bears single-handed!" boasted one of the Johnsons, cockily wearing a moth cocoon over one ear.

"I've got the thickest wolf skin you've ever seen. What a rug for Julie!" cried one of the de la Roué's.

"Did you say a total of seventy wolves?"

"To His Excellency George Washington!" shouted M. Carles, patting his lollipop girth.

"To His Majesty Louis Charles!" returned Pierre stolidly.

George and Louis received equal applause. In this melee of guns, lost leather jerkins, discarded boots, pouches, remnants of stale lunch, no incentive to drink was needed. Hot wool smelled as strong as roasted bear. Muscles relaxed and the Johnsons, Hermans, and Vanderpoels sprawled with the titled.

And such diversion! Mme Renaud had been spattered with hot fat—apply the lard! Master Homet was screaming with fright as the red-bearded Major Hoops swooped him to the ceiling and back. A waffle turned to fire was gobbled black and hot by one of the dogs. M. Heraud's sleight-of-hand trick was gone wrong and Mme Blaçon's best handkerchief cut in two. The little storekeeper Bec-de-Lièvre, too drunk too soon, rushed for the privies.

The meal was ready? But who had time for food?

Pierre, with a pain in his arm so great that no amount of punch or ribaldry could make him forget it, lounged on a stool at the corner of the hearth. His stomach gave a rebellious twist as M. Homet and two of the men began to carve great chunks of bear meat and pile the trenchers high, and he drifted out to the taproom. A late group of women was just arriving from Asylum. The runners of the bobsled had been glued to a pool of mud and snow. But what had happened to M. de Michelait that he had his arm in a sling? *Dieu,* were any of the other husbands injured? M. de Michelait, Pierre informed them drily, had been out conquering nature again. The other husbands were not so presumptuous.

He dropped down at one of the deserted taproom tables, mulling over Aristide's remark for the dozenth time. It was a foolish fear that beset him: he, Pierre Louis Bertrand Marie de Michelait, Marquis de Bussac, would never get the better of the wilderness! The wilderness was insatiable as Angélique.

And then as the newcomers dispersed he saw the girl. She stood at the taproom fireplace warming her hands.

He could not exactly guess her age, but she was young, and although not tall held her shoulders so straight that they gave her a look of height. Her hood was tossed back, revealing a curious mop of short brown curls, suggesting that her hair might recently have been cut after a fever.

Pierre noted the small frown between her gray eyes, and her lips were puckered as if half in mischief and half in defiance. It was almost the naughty little face of a child who doesn't want to go to bed, he thought. The face of a little boy rather than a little girl, for the freckles sprinkled about the slightly retroussé nose were vaguely reminiscent of summer and the old fishing creek.

Yes, definitely, thought Pierre, one would not be surprised to see her romping in a garden with kittens or with a flock of children gamboling about her—a nice little wife in a large white apron, flushed with the excitement of baking a pie. He yawned and braced his reeling head with his hands.

They were alone in the taproom. The two men with whom she had come in had wandered into the bunkroom to explore the gaiety and no doubt to find the proprietor. For a brief second Pierre felt disposed to extend a greeting to the lady and offer his assistance. But either the fact that she was escorted or that he was still lethargic from pain and punch detained him. She had not seemed to notice his presence, moreover, although she glanced quickly about the room with its deserted tables and iron-grilled bar.

Strange he had thought her eyes were gray. They were brown now with the casting shadows of the fire and the guttering candles. Well, what did it matter? . . . she certainly looked disheveled and muddy, as if she'd worn the same clothing for days—elegant clothing too, come to think of it. She would not be good at baking pies after all and, not being beautiful, would not even be good at simply being a woman. The green velvet pelisse with its hood tossed back, the muff of sable and ermine and flecked snow had cost some man a pretty penny. How Victoire would envy her the simple gown of dull gold with its low bodice and the sole ornament of a miniature on the bosom! Perhaps she was pretty after all. *Dieu,* what a low state he had sunk to when he saw a strange woman for the first time in months and couldn't make up his mind about her! Perhaps food was what he needed after all. . . .

As he rose the young woman left the fireplace and walked into the bunkroom ahead of him.

There was a clatter of benches now being drawn to the long table, and many of the guests were already seated. The young woman took the place between her two companions, who looked like teamsters and who already were diving into the food. At their end of the table was a rabble of Hermans and Johnsons and Vanderpoels, obviously sitting below the salt and so obstreperously drunk that they were throwing pellets of bread at the ladies. Pierre found a place at the opposite end between M. Carles and Mme Buzard. The priest, his plate loaded with victuals that oozed into one another, gripped a loaf of the French bread and was "cutting a wheel on the thumb," peasant fashion. Mme Buzard was smothering her food with pepper.

The feast seemed to go on interminably. Pierre wanted to lie flat where it was quiet and cool, but he refused to admit defeat.

As the supper came to an end M. Homet, hurrying in from the kitchen with a platter of cheese, paused before the strange young woman who was standing before his hysterical baby trying to quiet him with an apple.

"*Ah, merci, Madame!*" he said gratefully. "What an evening is this! He is teething, you know, and Mme Homet is distracted with so much company. . . . You will pardon me for being such a slack host? First M. Heraud wants cards for a trick, then Captain Beaulieu wants cider to make a champagne toast. . . .

The young woman smiled and sank down on the chair before the *clavecin* that M. Homet had moved from his wife's boudoir for the company's amusement. As the girl twiddled the red apple before the baby M. Homet was not certain whether the smile was meant for him or the child. It was a provocative smile.

"*Dieu,* I'd forgotten the music!" he exclaimed. "It's music we need to quiet the bullfighters! No more cheese! . . . You will be kind enough to play something, Mme—?"

"Mlle de Louvenne."

"But of course, Mlle de Louvenne, I apologize for not recognizing you. And now I beg of you, help me out."

"I play very badly."

"Not if Madame's smile is any criterion." His handsome face was so filled with pleading that Mlle de Louvenne turned about and struck a minor chord or two in an aimless fashion.

"You must name the piece," she said.

"But of course—'*O Richard, O Mon Roi.*'"

She hesitated a moment and began to play. At once everybody was singing. A few gentlemen, waving their glasses, huddled together behind her and began to harmonize.

An hour or more of music frittered away the time that the women spent in clearing the board and stacking the dishes.

M. Homet, the host once more instead of the servant, came to the *clavecin* to request an old Irish song in honor of John Keating, one of the company owners who had arrived from Wilkes-Barre the day before.

Pierre, quietly drinking brandy on his hearth stool, watched the Little Admiral with amusement. Aristide, whose forte was whistling, was trying to sing. He had not been more than a foot from the *clavecin* the entire evening.

Someone exclaimed about the time and wondered if the hot bricks were ready for the bobsleds, and the ladies began to put on their wraps.

Mlle de Louvenne stopped playing and rose.

"But this was enchanting!" cried Aristide. "A pity it can't continue into the morning!"

The young woman smiled at him.

"We are indeed indebted to you, Mlle de Louvenne," said M. Homet, and he went off to fetch her wrap.

A few of the Asylum group gathered about her, all thanking her at one time for the charming entertainment. M. Homet returned and held her wrap behind her.

"This is Madame's pelisse?"

The little frown came between the girl's eyes, and she glanced about her with hesitation.

"You're not starting off on your journey at this hour of night!" exclaimed Mme d'Autremont with horror.

"*Non, non, non,* I am staying here if M. Homet has room for me. My friends of the trading post will guide me to Tioga Point tomorrow."

"Then Mlle de Louvenne did not come with you from Asylum?" M. Homet asked the company in astonishment, and he dropped the pelisse over the back of a chair.

There was an awkward silence. The girl's face was flushed and there was a certain defiance in her eyes.

"May I inquire what is your destination, Madame?" asked the Little Admiral tensely.

"I am going to the French colony of Gallipolis."

"Ah, but that's a malarial hole! And there are hostile Indians on the Ohio River."

"I am looking for someone," she said, stoutly.

"You have relatives in the French colony there?" inquired Dr. Buzard. He halted as he draped the Sultana's shawl over her shoulders.

"I do not know."

The women looked at one another, incredulous, pausing in their flurry. The girl must be crazy, making a trip through the mire and stony woods to Gallipolis when she was not even sure! . . . Why, it was only the wreck of a colony that had suffered murder and robbery and even the perfidy of its own land agents!

"You—you do not know!" repeated Victoire with a scarcely suppressed scorn.

"No, Madame. I only know that I have come from Philadelphia and that I must go on till I find them."

"Mlle de Louvenne is lost then?" persisted Victoire, with a hint of amusement in her voice.

"*Oui, Madame,* I would like to find my family. I would like to find my husband if I have one . . . I do not know. I cannot remember. At the pension in Philadelphia a woman told me that a M. de Louvenne had left for Gallipolis."

The girl's lips quivered. The women edged away from her almost inperceptibly.

Dr. Buzard stepped forward and took Mlle de Louvenne's arm suavely.

"You are an *émigrée,* Madame? . . . Where do you come from?"

"I don't know, Monsieur. I only know that I am alone and that I am looking for those who belong to me." There were tears now in her eyes.

"You've lost your memory? You don't know if you come from France or San Domingo?"

"No, Monsieur."

There was a murmur of concern.

"A victim of amnesia," pronounced the doctor in an undertone, turning to his friends. "Very rare. Very pathetic. Most likely a victim of Le Cap. A case of memory lost from shock."

"You know how to treat this—amnesia?" asked Aristide anxiously.

"In all my practice I've had but one case—a Negro frightened out of his wits by the whip. But I've read of many a case." Then in a whisper: "Tragic and very difficult to cure."

Pierre had drifted into the group, drawn by the startling conversation.

"How can the girl have lost her memory? She has been playing the piano," he whispered to Dr. Buzard.

"Organic memory. Very simple. Like sewing or—"

"Ah, Mademoiselle," deplored M. Homet. "You may stay here as long as you like as our guest. Mme Homet and I shall be only too glad to help you un—"

"Wouldn't it be better if we took her to Asylum with us?" interrupted Mme d'Autremont excitedly. "Dr. Buzard will know best how to help her if—"

"*Oui*—" exclaimed Aristide. "We can write to Gallipolis and inquire of M. de Louvenne."

"In the meantime," exclaimed Mme de Blaçons, "she can stay with Lucretius and me. We have an extra bed."

Little groups of twos and threes began to twitter among themselves. Here was really the excitement one longed for in the long, tedious expanse of winter.

Pierre's eyes met those of the girl in a second of mutual scrutiny. They were gray after all, a cold twilight gray without expression.

"Come, *ma chère*," said Mme d'Autremont, turning from Victoire's latest bon mot, "we'll help you in no time. Dr. Buzard is an excellent doctor and he's had experience with—with lost memories. . . ."

"Someone in the Asylum may recognize you," suggested Aristide.

"And we'll send letters off by the next post to the consuls of all the big cities," urged M. Homet, his brown eyes shining with sympathy.

"How do you know your name?" asked Victoire suddenly.

"I am not sure . . ." murmured Mlle de Louvenne as she turned over the miniature on her bosom. The gold was engraved with the name "Claude Christophe Jean Nicole de Louvenne."

"A beautiful child!" exclaimed Mme de Blaçons. "And very like you. *Ah, c'est triste!*"

The girl smiled gratefully, and there was an odd little curve of her lips that reminded Pierre of the peasant child long ago who had dropped an apple on the green.

For some reason it made him feel sullen, and he walked away to find his jacket and his gun.

As the group drifted toward the taproom, Mlle de Louvenne turned back to get her deserted pelisse.

"Allow me!" cried Dr. Buzard, hurrying over to assist her.

The doctor cast a shrewd glance at the departing company—so absorbed in talk of Mlle de Louvenne that they had forgotten her—and as she drew the cloak over her shoulders he whispered nimbly: "Bravo, Mlle Félicie Roucault!"

❦❦❦❦❦❦❦❦❦❦❦❦❦❦❦❦❦❦❦❦❦❦❦❦

CHAPTER XXXIII

A MONTH LATER Pierre left Bec-de-Lièvre's shop late one afternoon and snowshoed over the billowing white waves that had been Luzerne Avenue. His arms and his knapsack were filled with groceries but he decided to look in on Aristide at Heraud's Inn before he returned home. In January Aristide had been snowbound in his cabin on the mountain; now for a week, on the verge of spring he had been snowbound in Asylum.

Pierre felt in the best of spirits. A black day before the great storm had given ample warning to the village. The animals had been well bedded, bins of fodder replenished, and boats dragged from the river to cover. Every house bulged with a pile of kindling and logs, and shelves had been filled with supplies from the stores. Out of the northwest the wind had blown with a violence, at last carrying the white raging flakes before it. The snow came thickly and grimly for two days. Victoire called it "God's tantrum." When at last it had stopped, weakly, exhausted, the village was smothered except for its indomitable chimneys and brave little church spire.

Four feet of snow and leviathan drifts almost covered the memory of one's most heinous sins, thought Pierre. It was a rebirth, a new God-given chance . . . if there was a God.

He kicked off his snowshoes at the door of M. Heraud's inn and exchanged a few words with the proprietor, whose head bobbed up occasionally from the lane he was trying to shovel to the road.

The warmth of the inn was good. The wind had swept a fine, stinging powder over his face, and insatiable, had raced through his nostrils cutting a pain between his eyes.

M. Heraud's inn was small—some half-dozen rooms—and the cubicle of a taproom with one whole wall consumed by its fireplace would have been called merely a closet at Versailles. It was steaming now with the fragrance of warm spirits and imprisoned food odors, crackling pinewood and toasted wool. Candles burned extravagantly on the few tables and in the bar cage, for drifts shut out the daylight and threatened to crush in the precious panes.

Pierre, half blind from the sparkle of sun on snow, could barely distinguish Dr. Buzard, John Herman, M. Carles, and Major Hoops— the only ones who had braved the weather. Aristide, in the absence of M. Heraud, stirred a hot toddy behind the bar.

The men sat close to the fire, old Wilkes-Barre newspapers and tankards strewn on the table before them. Pierre joined them, fumbling for his handkerchief with stiffened fingers.

They were discussing the weather. M. de la Roué's cow had frozen to death when the storm bashed in the same side of the barn that lightning had struck last summer. It was charming to see Mme d'Autremont mothering the birds at her bedchamber sill; they came there for crumbs, avid as pigeons after buckwheat. Had everyone heard about the pane breaking in one of the double doors of the French ladies' drawing-room, and how the *clavecin* had looked like a frosted cake before Talon discovered the damage? Snowdrifts had blocked up the second-floor windows of Mme Seybert's house, and she had slept through a whole night and day. It was rather funny about one of her slave families; they had been lazy about storing up food and had had to live on Indian corn cakes for two days. . . . Yes, Dr. Buzard had taken half a day to fight his way to the bedside of the shoemaker's wife and thought he wouldn't be able to save her after a miscarriage. . . . Mme de Michelait had talked of having a sleigh ride when the snow was packed. It would be good to have some merriment again. Was Mme de Michelait a woman of her word?

Pierre, with an absent laugh, assured them that she was. Nicole de Louvenne was not here. Likely she was straightening the adjoining room. Or perhaps she was mending sheets or overseeing the preparation of dinner. As M. Heraud's housekeeper she had not much time to stand about and chat with the men who came in for a drink.

"I'm surprised to see you out in this weather, M. Carles," Pierre taunted. "The way you prize your comfort!"

"He couldn't buy any cheese. He knew M. Heraud would have cheese," Major Hoops supplied with relish. Although English, the Major spoke eloquent French.

M. Carles colored, for Major Hoops had hit upon the truth.

"How many in France are eating cheese, I wonder!" sighed Pierre, thinking of Catherine. "Have you heard the price of a pound of sugar? Fourteen hundred livres! And two thousand livres for a pair of shoes!"

"That's what the Convention gets for throwing everybody into prison!" exclaimed M. Carles. "Even the farmers! . . . They say that in La Vendée six millions of acres lie fallow and half a million oxen have been turned astray—with no shelter or owner. . . . I knew a farmer who was guillotined because a few blades of corn were found growing at the edge of his pond and he was accused of throwing in his whole crop to cause scarcity."

"Yet why should he turn in his crop for a pile of worthless *assignats?*" asked Major Hoops, stroking his red-silk beard.

"M. Talon says his letters from France are pathetic since the maximum was repealed. The rich who go out to dine take their bread with them; when they bake no one's admitted to the house till every bite of bread is hidden. And the poor have come to exchange their best clothes for a small loaf of bread or a bit of flour made of peas and rye. . . . The National Guard even come with cannon to search the villages for corn."

"The armies are getting the bread," Dr. Buzard ejaculated. "A fine time for France to overrun Holland and fight England and Spain and Austria! Sometimes I think France is a maniac!"

"You're right!" agreed Pierre fervently. "When the Convention has to send representatives to the army to threaten the generals with success or the guillotine—then France is a maniac!"

"Ah, but there's hope for the maniac!" sighed M. Carles, patting his round belly. "Since a few in the Convention have started to plead for religious freedom again. . . . With Carrier executed and with the national seals put upon the effects of the Jacobin Clubs last fall, I begin to think rumors are true—that the monarchical party is really gaining strength—that the sacrifice of La Vendée of a hundred thousand men won't be in vain."

"Exactement!" cried Pierre. "Every letter or bit of news indicates that sans-culottism is dying. The suspects are being turned out of prison as fast as they were being turned in a year ago. One has to have a writ of persecution now to be tossed into the Abbaye. . . . But the best news is that the Convention demands leaders be renewed from time to time . . . and that the Girondin supporters have been released, and are back in the Convention. No more Robespierres, *Dieu Merci!"*

"No more kings either!" Major Hoops predicted. "The more strength the Royalist party gains the more countermeasures your Convention passes to strengthen the Republic."

John Herman was twiddling his dirty thumbs, obviously bored, for politics were beyond his interest and his French was not up to this whirlwind discourse. His eyes were moody and restless.

"I don't agree with you, Hoops," said Dr. Buzard. "I feel certain that the Dauphin will rule some day. And I think everyone in the colony believes it—and hopes it. . . . Just get two or three of us together and what do we talk about? The escape of the Dauphin! . . . Isn't it understood la Grande Maison was built for Marie Antoinette and the children?"

"That was before her death," said Pierre quickly. "One couldn't bring a sick child to a place like this!"

The doctor shrugged. "I don't see why not—it's very healthful. What would be a better hiding-place?"

"Switzerland . . ." said Pierre conclusively for he didn't want Dr. Buzard putting ideas into the heads of people like John Herman who might go any length for money. Moreover the asylum for Louis Charles was the business of only two people in this colony—himself and M. Talon.

Dr. Buzard shrugged and yawned.

"We of San Domingo are Royalist to the core," he rejoined lazily, "even if we do not come from France."

"You . . . come not . . . from France?" faltered John Herman in amazement. Although he could understand most of what the men said his lately acquired French was so halting that his lips lagged behind his thoughts.

The men laughed. John Herman took the prize for an addlepate.

"I come from San Domingo," said the doctor patiently.

"But you come why . . . from San Domingo?" asked John Herman. "The trouble—it is in France."

Dr. Buzard slowly explained his predicament as he would have explained it to a child. When the Revolution in France broke out there were some forty thousand whites controlling half a million colored on the island. Did John Herman know that most of San Domingo belonged to France? . . . Well, it did. The wealthy colonists were dissatisfied. They were ruled by French officials; their taxes were great; they were allowed to trade only with France, and France could use only one fourth of the island's exports. Although the colonists believed in a king they also believed in the rights of man—for the whites— wanting representation in their own government. There had been a revolt of the Negroes when citizenship rights were granted to them by the French Assembly and the whites refused them any power. Galbaud had been sent from France to keep order. But the revolt continued. There had been a dreadful insurrection at Le Cap—and that's why the doctor and ten thousand refugees had fled from San Domingo to the States. Did John Herman understand?

The foggy look on John Herman's face had not cleared, but he felt important. He still couldn't see why *M. le Docteur* wanted a king back if the planters of San Domingo had been no better off with a king than with a Revolution. However he was afraid to ask for fear the men would laugh at him. He nodded and Dr. Buzard gave him a congratulatory tap on the shoulder as if he were promoting him to the head of the class. The men laughed anyway and John Herman sulked.

As Aristide gave a last twirl to the toddy stick Nicole appeared. She wore a simple blue wool dress with a white apron, and her eyes looked blue.

She smiled at Aristide and reached for the tray of hot toddies. *"Non, non, non,* I'll finish my job," he said, carrying them to the table.

"I shall be thoroughly spoiled by the time the snow melts, Monsieur."

"Fooh! I'd explode without a little action! And you're like a clock ticking night and day. I won't even know how to sew on a button when I go back home."

John Herman's eyes clung to Nicole and he wet his lips. Major Hoops sat up straight, stroking his curly red beard. The ladies adored his red beard and the fine pink skin like a baby's.

"Mlle de Louvenne is already indispensable to all of Asylum," said Dr. Buzard, toying with an ad he had torn from the paper.

The men laughed and Nicole blushed and left them to their conviviality.

Pierre realized that he had been staring at her, but no one had noticed. It was just that her eyes had a disturbing habit of changing color—green in the pinewoods, dove gray in the winter twilight, blue with the blue of a gown.

Major Hoops relaxed again, stretching his long legs forward to the firedog.

"I've always said you're depriving some woman of a good husband, Aristide," he teased.

"I'm sorry for her," said Aristide simply. "When the bad news came from Gallipolis the other day she burst into tears. And she gets so tired sometimes—even dizzy. Once or twice I've seen her sit down, looking confused as if she didn't know what she was doing."

"Exactly," said Dr. Buzard, his dog-yellow eyes focused on the flames. "Don't the spells come directly after I've cross-examined her? It fatigues her to try to remember. Of course the amnesia victim really doesn't want to remember. That's why he's an amnesia victim. He wants to escape some painful reality—too sensitive to accept tragedy. . . ."

"How often do you question her?" asked Pierre.

The subject of Nicole had been exhausted at every gathering over the last few weeks, but it was still the most popular topic of conversation and one never knew when there might be a new facet.

"Oh, I've talked with her some half-dozen times. I've talked of everything on the island of San Domingo—sugar cane, voodoo dances, General Galbaud, Toussaint, the very fountains of Le Cap. I've described in detail my own escape from the burning city—with the battle raging and refugees packing the quay like cattle. I've talked of the *Polly* and the *Sally,* thinking she might have escaped on one of the boats. . . . There were so many drownings. It's highly possible she's seen her family drowned or killed. But—" he shrugged.

John Herman, his face dirty, his hands dirty, his heart dirty, leaned forward eagerly.

"And none of these things brings back even a spark of memory?" asked Major Hoops, although he knew the answer from Asylum gossip.

"None. And yet once when I described the punishment of one of my slaves she put her hands up to her head. And she seemed to be looking way beyond me . . . groping—struggling. . . . It's strange to be with her. I want to reach out and help her, to pull away the curtain between her and the past. It's so hard to see the poor child suffering."

"What happened to the slave?" asked Major Hoops. The grog sent a pleasant fireball down his esophagus.

"His genitals were set aflame and he was tied into a bag and drowned."

The eyes of John Herman started from his head.

"No wonder there was rebellion," said Pierre shortly.

"He deserved it," said the doctor mildly.

"What makes you so sure Mlle de Louvenne comes from San Domingo?" asked Aristide. "Why not from France?"

"Ah, that is merely instinct," replied the doctor, rubbing the oily whiskers of his dark skin thoughtfully. "Do you know, from the moment I laid eyes on her at Homet's I felt that our paths have crossed before? That I've met her at a military ball, perhaps, or seen her on a saint's day in a church at Le Cap?"

"Perhaps she's not even Catholic," mused Pierre.

"Mais oui," said M. Carles. "She told me she feels instinctively at home in the chapel. And she had a rosary in her muff, you know."

"How long can this sort of thing go on?" asked Aristide, his grog pushed away from him, untouched.

Dr. Buzard shrugged again. "Months—years perhaps. Every case is different. (This is mighty good grog you make, du Petit-Thouars.) *Dieu,* and the worst of it is some snatch of the past may come back to her and at the same time she may forget she ever traveled here from Philadelphia. It's like a shuffling of cards. Perhaps she'll never be cured. Depending, I suppose, on the cause of her amnesia. A case I read about caused by a brain tumor—"

"A brain tumor!" exclaimed Aristide, gripping his glass.

"Mais oui, it could be that instead of a shock. But I think that she's a victim of Le Cap.

"She still remembers nothing at all before she left the pension in Philadelphia?" asked Major Hoops.

"No. And to find the pension she came from is like finding a needle in a haystack. There must be a hundred of them in the city."

There was a long pause. John Herman, downing the last of his grog, shoved his tankard aside with a dirty hand, and making the supreme effort again, said in twisted French, "Is Mademoiselle married . . . or is she a virgin?"

"My examinations have been purely oral!" said Dr. Buzard curtly.

"She has the look of a virgin," said Pierre, almost as if he were meditating to himself, for he spoke to the fire rather than to the men. "The white look. The serene look. The look of a fawn surprised."

Major Hoops let out a laugh in keeping with his six feet three inches. M. Montullé, who had just entered, exuding cold air, leaned on the table, at once intrigued by the conversation.

"I have yet to see the woman who couldn't give her eyes the look of a fawn or a bitch as she willed," Hoops said. "Eh, Montullé?"

"In the ballroom," cried Montullé astutely, blowing his nose with a blast. "Not when she is surprised in the woods alone."

Aristide's lips were twitching as he met the eyes of Pierre, who stirred uneasily.

"What's this bit of gossip I've missed?" asked Montullé, sniffling.

"No news, only conjecture!" laughed the Major. "Or does any of you tongueless know?"

"Ah, if there is anyone who knows, then the lady in question is *not* a virgin!" cried Montullé, slapping his thigh.

There was a generous laugh, even Dr. Buzard enjoying the witticism.

John Herman's pale eyes sparkled. Encouraged by the laughter, he said, half in English, half in French: "She has little hard, ripe breasts; I bet they're sweet, like maple sugar."

His words dropped hard as hail.

Aristide bolted up to his full height, swinging his hand sharply across John Herman's mouth, so that the impact sent him sprawling with his overturned chair to the floor.

"Pigs, all of you!" cried Aristide.

John Herman was too much of a coward to return the blow of the one-handed Aristide. He fumbled to his feet, kicking the chair in revenge and brushing the dripping grog from his pants. Then, letting out a torrent of good American swear words, he swaggered out of the inn, leaving the door wide open to a swirl of snow. Aristide gave the door a powerful slam and stalked away from the men into the inn kitchen, leaving a clumsy silence.

Pierre too was outraged. He had often outclamored the others in similar bouts at this very table. But he, as well as Aristide, did not want the name of Nicole de Louvenne sullied by any man's lips.

He tossed on his jacket and cap and said a curt good-bye, glad to be out in the clean air again.

Little hard, ripe breasts! . . . This was what he had been thinking, too, all the while he supposed it was only of the gray or the blue of her eyes. It had taken the little pig of a John Herman to release the truth, to bring it from nights of restless dreaming of Silvie and budding chestnuts and dripping caverns to the open light. *Mon Dieu,* but the months here had been long and sedative, like the dark winters of the land of the midnight sun! Like the snow itself, pressing emotion down to an imprisoned flame, challenging it to escape! . . . Sweet, like maple sugar! . . . The hungry tongue of John Herman's filthy mouth should be cut from his head—the lascivious tongue between the mossy teeth. Aristide had let him off easy. Aristide, the only gentleman in the lot!

Pierre felt ill as he pushed blindly through the drifting snow; it seemed as if the fever of his twenty-six years had been unchained by the four small words. He began to remember little things he'd forgotten—the old Comte de Frivouac bucking into a whirl of lace and bare, pink flesh in a Versailles garden; the delirious warmth of Silvie's kiss; hours spent with will-o'-the-wisp loves in the moonlight, on the river, in a shoddy room in an attic of Paris. Some of the memories had names, some, faces. He wanted none of them now, and yet they filled him to overflowing—filled him with burning desire for a woman who seemed no more than a shadow.

He thought of Victoire, who would be waiting, and the thought depressed him. He had never really wanted her. Now even their smoldering hatred of one another was gone, leaving only a bourgeois, mutual need.

He had never had all he wanted of a woman, he thought. He did not know what he wanted; he simply knew there was emptiness when passion was over. Did any man ever have what he wanted from a woman? Wasn't it the curse of being human that one must feel this loneness, this frustration, because no man and woman were alike or thought alike? And because it was not a sense of complement that one wanted, but a sense of wholeness, as a priest with the Trinity?

Dieu, why had the filthy John Herman said what he did, just when one had begun to know a feeling of freedom from the past and its futile passions? . . . But he would forget what John Herman had said. If it was simply lust that he craved there was Victoire.

He would grip with drowning hands the peace he had earned even if it was a deceptive peace. Yes, Pierre told himself angrily, he could forget John Herman's four little words with work. There was no room in the wilderness for passion. The wilderness took strength and courage, with its blighting snows and howling panthers and its torrid summers when one dragged a plough and sweat fell like rain onto calloused hands.

He came to his house, half buried in dunes of snow; smoke tumbled from the chimney. The smoke of his own chimney smelled sweeter than that of the others. That was because Nicki would be on his belly before the fire building blocks. Nicki would rush to him with the soft, blubbering kiss of a baby.

In the wilderness there was no room for little, hard ripe breasts. No room—no time.

CHAPTER XXXIV

March 1795

FOR SEVERAL DAYS Pierre had been working with Aristide in his sugar camp. It was the second spring they had formed a partnership, Pierre assisting with the labor and sugaring-off and sharing the profits.

Camp had been set up in a sunny glade in the midst of du Petit-Thouars's four hundred acres. Helpers had dragged the butternut troughs and spouts and provisions to the glade on hand sleds; Pierre himself on snowshoes had carried for two miles a five-pail iron kettle, two sap buckets, an ax and trappings, a knapsack, and a gun and ammunition.

Aristide had selected the fifty acres and had driven the wooden spouts while the troughs were placed. Four of Mme Seybert's black slaves cleared the snow from a level of twenty feet. Although snow was not to their liking the project was reminiscent of San Domingo and sugar cane.

As there was a good run of sap the men spent several nights in camp. Pierre was happy here. There were singing and laughter as the slaves fed fresh wood to the dozen fires with their huge iron kettles and the sap bubbled and boiled with provocative fragrance. Aristide said they would soon have as guests every bear on the mountain, for the clouds of steam bore the delicious aroma up to the treetops and permeated the freshness of molding leaves and spring damp.

As the slaves collected the golden sap in bark buckets hung on a sap yoke across their necks and replenished the kettles, Pierre and Aristide superintended the final sugaring-off. Aristide stirred furiously the sap that thickened over the low fire, and Pierre poured a spoonful at a time on a snow-covered slab, frequently tasting it.

Wallois, Talon's butler, prepared meals in a near-by shack where the men slept at night. (Talon had gone to Wilkes-Barre on company business.) Although the men ate on logs and stumps about the fire with wooden plates and metal cups the food was worthy of Paris. Wallois, who was always a little tipsy with wine, was an altruist, and there was not only wine sauce on the broiled chicken and grilled venison, but wine in the dandelion greens and coffee.

At night Pierre thought he had never felt such great peace. The voodoo hum of the Negroes lolling about the fires ebbed away as the moon came up; the blazing brush crackled softly, and between the hootings of a frightened owl he could hear the steady dropping of the sap. He lay still with muscles sore and drugged, not so much by the labor as by the first sweet laziness of spring. Asylum seemed as far away as Paris.

On the third day, the work completed, Pierre and Aristide trudged back to the latter's cabin. Robinson Crusoe, who had been Aristide's boyhood hero, had inspired him to build his house of bark.

The one-room hut was neat, for Aristide was still a sailor. On the walls were hung prints of the sea, guns and knives, bows and arrows. In the center the smoothed stump of an oak formed a table on which lay a mass of manuscript, quill pen and sand-shaker, tinder box, and the well-thumbed volume of *Robinson Crusoe*. Aristide slept in a sailor's hammock, but there were several bunks along the walls under birch-bark shelves of books.

To rid his cabin of flies and insects du Petit-Thouars had suspended a hornet's nest from a beam in the ceiling. The hornets hung lazily from their house, drugged from the heat of the fire; only now and then an adventurer tacked into a draft and back again or crawled over Aristide's moccasin.

At the fireplace was a miscellany of spoons and pans, a sweet-grass basket of pine cones, the sycamore branch Aristide used as a riding whip, a fire bucket, an Indian birch broom. Water bubbled in the kettle. Pine knots burned on flat stones in a corner of the hearth, and the pitchy drooling sent up its fragrant tar smoke into the chimney.

Lying in one of the bunks, Pierre felt aimlessly content. Tonight for a change there seemed nothing better in life than watching Aristide, who sat on a sea chest, shadows playing on the mussed brown hair and over the full, sensitive lips. In Aristide there was a warmth, an understanding, a world away from the avid wolf and the crowding winter. In Aristide there was balm for the passions.

"Do you mind if I purr?" Pierre asked lazily.

"I'm glad to see you in a mood for purring," said Aristide. "Of late you've growled more than a den full of lions. Something has made you unhappy."

"Who is really unhappy here?" Pierre evaded.

"For a long time I felt that you were really happy."

"We're only waiting—all of us. No one daring to mention the future. No one even daring to think aloud about the past . . . France—there is nothing else but France."

"*Dieu,* you're fickle as a grasshopper! One moment you swear you have never been so happy as in Asylum. The next you talk of returning to France under the Dauphin. What is it that you really want, Pierre?"

Pierre avoided Aristide's eyes. They had never discussed Nicole. There was so little to discuss about her except the small quaint nose, the urchin smile, the brown tangled curls, the little hard, ripe breasts. . . .

"Like everyone else," Pierre said, "I'm made up of different selves. When I try to be selfless I want security for Nicki."

"Security—is there such a thing? One man feels secure when he has a sovereign who demands a tax. The next man feels secure when he is of the democracy making the laws. And then there are perfectionists like you and Rousseau who still expect to work out a *Contrat Social,* a little utopia where all men are all things unto one another."

Pierre laughed, feeling guilty and unhappy that he must conceal his real motive from Aristide. Aristide knew nothing of the plans for the Dauphin, Pierre was certain. Of the colony he and Talon alone waited for Louis Charles, though everyone talked of the child's escape. One month rolled into another and the news filtering through from Paris was always the same. The Dauphin, well guarded, was slowly becoming a helpless little animal in the Temple. Jean de Batz still worked for his rescue. It was all baffling, intolerable. And sometimes it seemed futile to hope any longer. If one had not vowed to Marie Antoinette

to help the child, if one had not said: "I swear it—I swear it by all
that's holy!"—there would be the temptation to break with the past,
to think only of one's own future—and the security of Nicki. But this
was not only treason against the state but treason against the heart.

"You've not found Asylum as perfect as you'd hoped, I'll wager,"
said Aristide, tidying the hearth with his Indian broom.

"No, to be frank I think I prefer laws in a community; they add zest
even if murder and robbery must go with them. And Talon is neither
king nor manager."

"He's too interested in his own Ohio investments. Keating told me
that Talon plans to sell out his interests to John Nicholson and resign
as agent. That would make Nicholson sole owner, wouldn't it, after
buying Noailles's share six months ago?"

Pierre felt his pulse quicken. Then Talon too had given up hope for
the Dauphin!

"What an odd little colony we are!" Aristide went on. "Like an
orphan buffeted from one relative to another—poor, unloved, struggling."

"Victoire wants to leave Asylum this spring," said Pierre.

"She has seemed very content here."

"No—only triumphant. And she talks of security for Nicki too. The
son of a marquis must be raised like the son of a marquis, she thinks
—prepared for the luxury he will inherit some day."

"It will never be the same again in France."

"*Dieu,* try to convince a woman of that!"

Aristide looked up. "You will leave, then?"

"No. Living in a city would strangle me."

"Needless to say Victoire will not leave either. She's very much in
love with you."

"I've often wondered. Our life together has been stormy in many
ways."

They were silent for several moments. Then Aristide asked a question which seemed totally irrelevant to Pierre. "Before you left to come
up here to camp had Guy returned with the post?"

"*Oui.*"

"There was no further news for Mlle de Louvenne?"

"There was an answer from Dr. Romaine who has the hospice for
San Domingans on Vesey Street in New York. Talon wrote to him
some weeks ago. He had no record of a M. de Louvenne."

"It's not a common name of course."

"No. Dr. Romaine wondered if we'd written to the State Department, though he said they're so pestered with inquiries about wandering wives and trunks and jewelry that they've lost their patience."

"I feel that Nicole has a husband somewhere hunting desperately for her." Aristide held up a perfect hawk moth before him. He was toying with his collection now. "The little boy in the miniature looks so much like her too."

"The child's eyes are brown," said Pierre stubbornly, and he thought suddenly that the cabin had become oppressively hot.

"She wears the miniature every day—under her gown sometimes. I've seen her holding it in her hand; I've seen her hand tremble."

"You're a tender soul, Aristide." There was almost a note of indictment in the words.

Aristide did not answer.

"Did she talk with you sometimes while you were snowbound at the inn?"

"*Mais oui.* Often we sat and talked about America. The thousands of refugees scattered all over the country. . . . She wants to leave Asylum. Feels that she must keep hunting and hunting. Think of the tragedy—to keep hunting and not know what you hunt for!"

"It would be absurd for her to leave!" Pierre exclaimed. "We can do better searching by post than she can by foot!"

"Of course, but I can understand how she feels. When one is so agitated it's easier to keep moving than waiting. . . . But perhaps someone else can convince her it's foolish to leave."

"She'll never talk to me for more than a moment alone," Pierre said. "In fact, I think she avoids me."

"I've noticed that."

"Why, do you suppose?"

"I don't know," said Aristide slowly.

"And yet every time I glance her way I feel she's been looking at me."

"I've noticed that too."

"You don't miss much," laughed Pierre shortly. "But I never quite find her looking at me. I always hope I shall. It makes sort of a game between us. . . . Funny little nose she has, like a schoolboy, and shoulders like a master with a ruler. And her smile reminds me of someone. Marie Antoinette, perhaps, except that the Queen had no dimple. It's a different kind of smile. I keep wondering why. . . ."

"She's a different kind of woman."

"It's something specific I mean. It's not—quite even. Have you ever noticed that slightly irregular teeth can be very intriguing?"

"I like the smile without dissecting it."

"You have no humor of late, Aristide."

The Little Admiral propped the hawk moth against his stump of a hand and seemed finished with the subject of Nicole. Pierre watched him enviously. If he could, Pierre would have exchanged places at once with du Petit-Thouars, who had learned to spend his passion on ships and pirates and moths instead of women. But Aristide was thirty-six. He must have been in love at some time or other—must have known the sweet torture of sleeping and waking with a woman's image pressed into his mind.

He wondered if Aristide guessed the tumult in his blood that John Herman's words had released. He was at once ashamed and complacent, like a miser who hides a valuable gem in the earth, hugging his secret with desire and sacrifice. He did not mean to have an affair with Nicole. It was not only because he knew instinctively that she did not mean to have an affair with him or any other man; it was because she did not have all the weapons of her womanhood. No gentleman would take advantage of a child with faith in her eyes. No sportsman would shoot down a nursing fawn with its first soft coat of down. Regardless of the jibing of other nations even a Frenchman had his code of honor when it came to love, he thought.

But he was alive again as he had been alive in his desire for Silvie. And his moods and his sense of sight and smell and his thinking were sharpened with the faster running of his blood. And sometimes he was so painfully alive that he wondered if he had not only dreamed the year of vegetative peace at Asylum.

He had an uncomfortable feeling that Aristide was reading his thoughts, and he reached casually for a sample of the fresh, waxen maple sugar.

"How Nicki will gobble the sugar balls I bring home!" he said.

"Nicki is your whole world, isn't he?"

"You know you can't resist that naughty little face any more than I can."

They laughed then. The crisis was passed.

CHAPTER XXXV

On Mme d'Autremont's fete day in April a party was given for her at la Grande Maison. M. Talon had arranged for music after the buffet supper.

For an hour Pierre watched Nicole dancing with other men. She seemed gay tonight, scarcely like a woman without memories. He wanted to dance with her. He wondered what the touch of her hand might be like. He knew how her hands looked. Often she had set a tankard of ale on the tavern table before him. He wondered why her fingers did not bring back memories to her when she looked at them —memories of words she had written to a lover, of flowers she had pinned at her bosom, of keys of a *clavecin* she had played in a place called home. Her hands were expressive, small but strong. They were not like Silvie's hands, soft and knuckleless. They were not the hands of a parasite, of a Mme de Frivouac, ringed and slightly veined. They seemed very sure of themselves, pliant, simple, a trifle work-worn.

And too he wanted to dance with her because for a moment he might feel the little hard, ripe breasts pressed to him through the apple-green taffeta of her gown and the black brocade of his coat.

Because he wanted these things too much he had not asked her to dance, nor had he asked anyone else. He knew there was nothing else in his eyes but these things he continued to think about, and it seemed certain that if he asked Victoire or Mme d'Autremont to dance they would read his eyes with a shock.

It was just after young Louis d'Autremont recited his poem of felicitation to his mother that Pierre walked over to Nicole. She was sitting near the fireplace beside Mme Seybert. Dr. Buzard, who had recently been dancing with the latter, was gallantly fanning away the effects of her exertion. The fiddles began to strike up a polka.

"Will you dance with me, Mademoiselle?" inquired Pierre a trifle brusquely.

Damn her eyes! They were definitely green tonight. If only they wouldn't change like a chameleon he wouldn't have to think of them so much—wouldn't have to think of them at all.

Nicole smiled at him.

"*Merci,* M. de Michelait, but I am a little tired. I have been dancing so much. You do not mind?"

"Of course I mind," he said not too suavely, his dark brows drawn together with a boyish vexation. Then he laughed with effort and turned to Mme Seybert and Dr. Buzard. "Mlle de Louvenne has avoided me ever since she came to Asylum. I find my vanity wounded."

"Ah there's certainly vanity in thinking she would take the trouble to avoid you," laughed Dr. Buzard shortly, but as he turned to Nicole there was a tang in his voice. "Come, Mlle de Louvenne, you are defeating your purpose. . . . Our Pierre was one of the finest dancers of the court, only second to the Vicomte de Noailles. And if you refuse him now he may never ask you again."

Nicole rose, almost like an obedient child, and smiled without looking at Pierre. When he took her hand it was cold. He felt a silly sweep of anger, as if she had willed her hand to be cold, without response to the agitation he felt at touching it. She was not an excellent dancer— little better than ordinary perhaps. But she danced with the abandon of a young child who romps in a field. Once she lost her balance on a patch of sticky wax and he caught her to him quickly. In that second he felt the warmth of her, felt her quick breathing and knew somehow that she had a sharp awareness of him.

He drew her arm through his when the dance was over and led her into the small salon adjoining where Wallois was drinking as much punch as he served. The room was deserted, for Victoire was demonstrating the "pigeon wing" to the guests. Pierre brought two glasses of punch to the sofa and beckoned Nicole with a smile. She hesitated, then joined him.

"And now, why do you hate me so, Mlle de Louvenne?" he asked, trying to keep the pique out of his voice.

"But I don't hate you, Monsieur."

"I've never been able to exchange more than a few words with you. I think I'm talking with you and you've escaped like quicksilver."

"Why should you wish to talk with me? I have nothing to say. I am ashamed."

"I'm not interested in your lost memories but in your ideas. . . . I don't want to hear you prattle of your conquests or your children."

"You are very kind, M. de Michelait," she said, and he saw the suggestion of a smile on her lips.

"*Pas du tout.* Now at this moment you are more your real self than any of the rest of us—like a bird just flown from the nest, past and present severed. It's only the present that counts, you know."

"Oh, Monsieur! If only you knew how I fight to remember—what the emptiness is like—"

"Shall I tell you of your past then? You grew up in Normandy. You wore a starched white dress and your sash was blue. That made your eyes blue too. You wore bright cherry ribbons on your cap. And sometimes at night you cried because you had freckles. But you always knew how to smile, from the very day you dropped the apple on the green."

Nicole sipped her punch and made no answer. Pierre was aware that he was being obtuse, that he should rather be talking of crops, of the ice jam at Wyalusing Falls, of the malt-liquor brewery to be begun. But he had a sense of immediacy. He had no idea when he might be able to talk with her again, when he might sit so close to her that the taffeta folds of her gown billowed over his knee. Tomorrow and the next day she would be remote. And now, tonight, he could watch the miniature of the child moving slightly with her breathing, could touch her fingers as he handed her a glass, could shift his eyes from the puzzling eyes that looked up at him to her softly provoking smile. Her face was shaped like a heart; he had never noticed that till now. And her skin was clear and warm as a summer noon.

"Eh bien, Monsieur! And what then?" Her shoulders lifted a trifle.

"You were a bad little girl," he went on recklessly. "You teased your brothers and sisters. You played tricks on the nuns at the convent. You hated to grow up; it was more fun sporting with your dogs. Nice young men wanted you to grow up and offered you their hearts and châteaux. You went into tantrums when your parents wanted you to marry. You'd been reading Prévost and you were waiting for passion. Your father was indulgent—because of the way you smiled at him—and never forced you to marry. Then the Revolution came along, and because M. de Louvenne was the son of a comte your château was burned and you escaped to England. You crossed the water then: only the three of you, for your brothers and sisters were married. In New York you were smitten with the yellow fever: you and your mother and father. When your parents died you couldn't endure the shock, so you forgot. And then you began to look for them."

Nicole gave him a warm, wistful smile. "But you are most kind to give me a past."

"Don't you have any stir of memory when I tell you these things? Isn't there something that comes alive like—arbutus in the spring?"

"Yes, yes, there is," she said passionately. "The whole past is so close, so very close. I seem to remember the convent you speak of and my home—but when I try to call it back it escapes like a dream, leaving only impressions: a bell in a tower, the pattern of chintz on a chair, a gallery of paintings. . . . It's like groping for the name of a place or a person that you say is on the tip of your tongue . . . you're sure that it begins with a 'B.' And you don't know why. And that and the miniature are the reasons I feel you haven't finished my story, M. de Michelait—why I feel there's a husband I love, and a child."

"They are seldom out of your mind then, these wraiths?"

"No. Because the only way to bring back the word beginning with the 'B' is to think and think how it must look, how it must sound. And sometimes I feel I can't endure any longer the pain it brings to my head. . . . Sometimes it is all so close I hear the rushing of water, and I grow dizzy and want to plunge into the water and fill my emptiness. . . ."

Pierre felt a strange sense of guilt, as if he had been trespassing.

"And that's why I must leave Asylum, M. de Michelait. These things and these people are somewhere and I shall find them."

"Nom de Dieu!—you wouldn't really be so foolish, Madame! You must wait for answers to the letters we've written; there'll be good news some day. I am certain there will be good news."

The thought of her going left him destitute. He would not let her go! He had a mad conviction that if he reached out and touched the brown curls there would be a tie between them that would force her to stay. He had often wanted to touch the brown curls. They might not be so soft in his fingers as they looked; or they might be softer, like the surprise of milkweed. His fingers burned to touch her hair, and he remembered a game they had played at the Petit Trianon, a game of mental telepathy. One who had left the room came back blindfolded and was drawn to some object instinctively by the thought transference of the others. When he came near the rose or the fan he was to touch, his fingers tingled and burned.

Pierre was about to reach out and touch the curls when a noisy group drifted in to the punch bowl.

"And do you know what the old scamp told the priest who confessed him on his death bed?" Victoire ejaculated. " 'You say Saint Peter holds the roué in *mauvaise odeur.* . . . Well, suppose I do go to hell! I've always preferred summer to winter. And—' "

Nicole automatically handed Pierre her punch glass and rose to join the others.

"'And each to his own taste!'" quoted Victoire as her inquisitive eyes met the eyes of Pierre.

On the evening following the party Nicole de Louvenne came to borrow a book from the little colony library that was lodged at Pierre's house. M. Carles was sitting there munching cheese and sipping wine, and Frau Gresch and Victoire were weaving cloth for carpets. A thin fire was tempering the April dampness.

It irritated Victoire that Pierre often kept the company of books late into the night, and that men dropped in who were more absorbed in religion than in her own banter.

"But please, Messieurs, don't let me disturb you!" begged Nicole. "I'll just browse here at the bookshelves till I find a book to my liking."

"There's a delicious novel I just read by M. Marivaux," Victoire suggested, going back to her loom. "The blue one on the first shelf—on the right."

"Perhaps Mlle de Louvenne doesn't care for fashionable boudoir novels," said Pierre.

Victoire shot him a torrid glance, but Pierre was watching the small brown fingers flicking the pages of a volume of Edmund Burke. He had not been able to sleep last night after Mme d'Autremont's fete. And tonight even before Nicole had come she had seemed to be standing there at the books and it had been hard for him to follow M. Carles's thoughts.

M. Carles had taken it upon himself to shape Pierre's doubts into a tolerable Catholicism. He had found Pierre too often reading the sixteenth-century Frenchmen who wrote in favor of Protestantism, Jean-Claude and Pierre Viret, as well as the American Cotton Mather. And what right had anyone to read the popular ribaldry of Tom Paine to whom all Christian religion was hateful?

M. Carles had not found Pierre an easy problem, for Pierre believed in the inherent worth of the individual, along with Ramus, and in a personal God, along with Hume, only until the book was finished.

M. Carles had persuaded Pierre to come to Mass, and Pierre laughed a little to think that his being there pacified the priest. Pierre told himself he went to Mass because of Nicki. It was certainly not to keep his prestige in the colony. Religion in the colony was not rigid. The majority attended Mass; some gave time to confession. Mme d'Autremont had given to the chapel a beautiful illuminated missal, a family treasure. But few were as devout as Mme d'Autremont, and in Asylum there were Protestants and even the little Connecticut family who read the Bible on Sundays and prepared no meals and pursued no pleasure on the seventh day.

At Mass, Pierre's lips framed the conventional words but he still could not pray. Although his conscience was filled with Catherine he was thinking of Diderot who claimed that belief in God was bound up in autocracy, that man will never be free "till the last king is strangled with the entrails of the last priest." And if in Mass he was not thinking of these heresies he was looking at the soft brown curls of Nicole, wondering if she believed what her lips repeated.

He had a gnawing desire to know what Nicole believed: about God, about morals, about slavery—or music.

When Nicole arrived the two men had been arguing about Kant, the frail Prussian professor whose simplicity so appealed to Pierre. M. Carles went on now with his interrupted opinion.

"A man who teaches that prayer is useless should be guillotined!" he expounded.

"He only said prayer is useless if it 'aims at a suspension of natural laws,'" Pierre defended. "Rousseau himself declared that no God worth his salt could be swayed by the selfish desires and prayers of man."

"Rousseau, Rousseau, Rousseau!" ejaculated M. Carles, angrily snatching a crumb of cheese from his knees and popping it into his mouth. "The cause of the Revolution! He's unleashed all the animal instincts of man! Where did Robespierre's Festival of Reason stem from if not from Rousseau! Even America, across the water, has been tainted!"

Nicole turned from her books and said suddenly: "But how thrilling to live in a country where all religion is lawful! . . . Quakers, Presbyterians, Episcopalians, Anabaptists. . . . Do you know there are hardly thirty thousand Catholics in the States . . . and a Jewish synagogue in New York? Imagine!"

Victoire paused in her work and Pierre looked up in surprise. M. Carles snatched the cue at once.

"That's the very reason religion is declining in America, Mlle de Louvenne," he exclaimed. "What has the 'catch-penny materialistic morality of Franklin' done for his country, or the philosophic deism of men like Jefferson?"

Victoire smothered a smile. Let little de Louvenne struggle for an answer to this one!

"They've made us think!" said Nicole, and she looked at Pierre strangely. "Isn't this progress?"

"Is it progress when a country becomes nonreligious, confused as America—even antireligious in spots?" M. Carles demanded.

"America too must have her philosophers," Pierre said with acute enjoyment. "I think philosophy should be pursued more and more as an independent branch of learning."

"From theology to natural rights, and from natural rights to democracy?" Nicole interrogated.

"Is that a statement or a question?" M. Carles challenged.

Nicole's face turned a dark red.

"Fine talk for Christians! Worse talk for Catholics!" jibed M. Carles. "And treason for Royalists!"

There was a scuffle in the corner of the room as Frau Gresch abandoned her loom and disappeared in a state of embryo hysterics.

Nicole faced M. Carles squarely. "I can't speak for M. de Michelait," she retorted. "But *I* am a Christian, a good Catholic, and a better Royalist!"

"*Mais oui.* I am sure of that!" said M. Carles, a trifle ashamed of his outburst. "It's M. de Michelait who's been corrupted by America."

"Come, M. Carles, why blame America?" asked Pierre suavely. "Where did she get her culture and learning? Have you forgotten Rousseau? . . . With the new speed of ships and mails it's only natural that the States should swing Continental in their thinking. And just as natural that Europe should swing democratic in her politics."

"Perhaps some day, a thousand years from now, we shall be one world!" cried Nicole.

There was a burst of laughter from Victoire. It was chagrin enough that these men forgot her in their excitement, that her convent training had neglected books and ideas that seemed so important to men who were so important to her. But that another woman should help them forget her! . . .

"You've found your book, Mlle de Louvenne?" she inquired. "Something light by Plato or Aristotle? . . . Let's join the men then in some wine and biscuit."

"*Merci,* Mme de Michelait, but I must be going. I have work to do at the inn." To the volume of Burke she held in her hand Nicole added

M. Marivaux's book of blue and signed for them in the ledger on the mantel. Her hand was shaking.

"I'll see you back to the inn," said Pierre, trying to be casual.

"Non, non, non—merci beaucoup. It's not yet dark."

He lighted a flare for her at the fireplace and walked with her to the gate, leaving Victoire and M. Carles in a thorny silence.

"You've come alive tonight," said Pierre with warmth.

"Have I?" she asked a little wistfully—and wondered how gratified Dr. Buzard would be with the result of her call.

"Nicole," he said, her name slipping so easily from his lips that it seemed no license, "don't be afraid of yourself . . . don't be afraid to say what you think! These things may help you to remember the past. . . . You've read a great deal—serious things?"

She looked at him with a sort of weary accusation.

"I'm sorry," he said simply. "You see, I think of you only as I've known you. And it seems to me very natural that you'd be more interested in Burke than in Marivaux."

"Marivaux is a beautiful shade of blue!"

Pierre laughed and held her arm as she turned away.

"I want to walk back to the inn with you."

"I'm not afraid."

"The panthers are screeching."

"I'm still not afraid."

"I didn't expect you to be. It's just that I want to walk back to the inn with you."

"No, Monsieur."

There was a finality in the two words that chilled him, and he stood for a few moments after she had said good-bye and watched her pick her way over the rutted road.

M. Carles left when Pierre returned to the cabin.

"How does she know what she thinks?" Victoire exploded at once. "A woman whose mind is empty as a sack!"

"An empty mind isn't one that can't remember," said Pierre sharply, "but one that can't think."

"Thinking! Is that what you call all this drivel that goes on night after night? . . . What good will it do you? How will it help you get back your estates and your title?"

Pierre only laughed a little, and Victoire went into a rage.

How could he explain to her that these thoughts, these books, were giving him mental freedom, worth more to him than a thousand estates

—that he would find his God at last by reading all the great men who had written on the subject? What did Victoire care about God? What did she care that some day with enough birth pains he would bring to life his own peculiar religion from the chaos of other men's Gods?

"After the Duc de La Rochefoucauld-Liancourt's visit I am going to go back to Philadelphia," Victoire stormed.

"Bien," said Pierre, banking the fire for the night.

A week later Victoire asked Pierre to return to Mme de la Roué a sausage gun Victoire had borrowed.

When Pierre reached the house he found Nicole there ironing, and taking care of the baby.

"From barmaid to nursemaid!" he teased her.

"I have a passion for children—especially little boys."

"I was right then. You did grow up with a horde of brothers. . . . Why don't you put your ironing aside for a moment and rest? I'd like to know what you think of Burke."

He had the feeling once more that she would rather be alone. But she put aside her iron and went out to sit with him on the rustic bench. It was dusk, and it annoyed him that her dress faded into shadow and that although he might reach out and touch her hand, he couldn't see the shape of her fingers, which he had forgotten.

"Have you finished the *Reflections on the French Revolution?*" he asked. He was irked that he should feel ill at ease. No woman had ever embarrassed him before.

"Oui," she said. "And it has given me a mental heartburn!"

"But why? M. Burke felt that law must grow out of customs—that new power in new persons is dangerous. Surely you think the same?"

"Mais oui," she assured him hastily. "It is only that as I read I am sick with wonder at the outcome. Our beautiful France, Monsieur—what will become of it?"

"I am not afraid. Now that I have had time to think."

"You feel that the Bourbons will rule again?"

"Why not? Every fire burns itself out in time. So will the Revolution and the peasants who are making the laws. What was it Burke said about the man that 'holdeth the plough'? It is probably fresh in your mind."

"Oui, Monsieur. 'How shall he become wise that holdeth the plough?' . . . It is from the Bible, you know."

"Yes, I recall it now. But you haven't finished it: 'He will set his heart upon turning his furrows; and his wakefulness is to give his heifers their fodder.' The Bible was right. And Burke too, when he said: 'Those who always labor can have no true judgment,' or something like that. . . ."

"What will become of these peasants then? These men who have murdered to gain freedom?"

Pierre was suddenly conscious of her voice, alive in the shadows. It was the voice of the hermit thrush, low and throbbing. For a moment he struggled to revive what her voice had said so that he might make an answer.

"Men of intemperate minds can never be free!" he answered.

"They'll not be satisfied till they have gained equality—and that's freedom. They'll not be satisfied till they have destroyed the Church and the Bourbons."

"And you—and me."

"Mais oui, Monsieur."

Her voice was intense now. She was a little girl frightened in the dark, he thought. He wanted to take her hand and tell her that tomorrow would be bright.

"Because they're ploughing," he said, "they can't know the strength that still lies behind the Bourbons—the energies bent to free them—the hope of millions of rescuing one small boy from his Temple prison."

"You think there's a chance of his escape?" she asked softly. And as he made no answer she went on: "The waiting seems so endless."

They talked for a while of politics in Europe, about which she seemed surprisingly well informed.

Pierre asked her then if she remembered the royal family, if she had ever seen them. Yes, she was almost certain she must have seen them . . . or was it simply their pictures? She could not distinguish what things she had seen and what things she had read. But she had a distinct memory of Paris; perhaps Paris had been her home. Ah, if only she could go back to Paris, now, tonight! There was a room she often dreamed of. The shape of every crystal in the luster was clear as print before her eyes; there was a bust of Louis XIV and the chairs were covered in crimson Utrecht velvet. There was a green-lacquered cupboard in the corner, ornamented with porcelains. People drifted in and out of the room—a man, a child, a woman. The woman perhaps was herself. In her dreams she had tried to project herself into the woman . . . but when she strained to discern their features they became shimmery like a pond in which a pebble is thrown. Yes, she was certain the room was in Paris . . . or could it have been in Le Cap?

Pierre listened with a cold stone weighing down his heart. Here in this intimate dusk, with the whippoorwill whining and the lamps of the village beginning to sparkle, Nicole belonged to him. For this was the present and she was talking with him and no one else shared their thinking. Tomorrow might bring the truth of her. A letter might come or she might remember the faces of the room, and these would bring other faces crowding about her. And then she would be of another world, with memories excluding him, and love and pain and beauty in her heart that he could never share because they were of the past.

The baby began to whimper, and she rose and said quietly: "He would like his cradle rocked."

Pierre rose too, and he could not be sure if he reached for her hand first or if she extended it to him.

"Good night, Nicole," he said. His lips pressed the fingers he could not see; and he thought as he sauntered down the path fragrant with dew that perhaps he had kissed a shadow, though the warmth of her hand was bittersweet on his lips.

CHAPTER XXXVI

"AND NOW, M. Nicolas Claude, it's time to get ready for the picnic," said Pierre, lifting Nicki down from the handle of the plough. "And I want you to practice your bow. Remember, the Duc de La Rochefoucauld-Liancourt is a great man."

"Why?" asked Nicki, jabbing at a lush, moist worm with his stick.

"Because the Duc staked all of his fortune on a plan to get the King out of Paris. *Dieu,* it was a miracle that the Duc escaped to England! And it's an honor to have him visiting us at Asylum."

"Nicki likes worms," he said, hunting now in the endive bed.

"Come, *mon cher*. Stand straight. *Bien*. Your feet together. Your worm behind your back. . . ."

Nicki performed his bow like a small marionette. Pierre laughed, leaned over to kiss the dark curls, and tossed the child to his shoulder. "It will be a wonderful picnic, Nicki; it is such a wonderful day!"

It was true. The May day was full of wonders. Rummerfield Mountain was a soft pastel mingling of pink maple tassels, golden willows, wild plum, and cherry, laced with a green so tender that it was almost one with the sunny haze of the spring. Paris had never flaunted a more joyous profusion of flowers than the colony gardens. Pots of coral-pink oleander or flaming azalea stood at many of the doorways; tulips and lavender iris and white lilacs bordered the walks, transforming the brown cabins as a tropical bird transforms a wooden birdcage. Geraniums bloomed on window ledges which had been smothered with drifts of snow; woodbine, wild grape, and morning-glory clambered over arbors. And the birds gathered and sang out the new hope of the season. Yellowhammers attacked their anthills with cunning; the woodpecker trilled poetry of the snow escaping, free now, bounding over rocky ledges.

Pierre thought of the cage hanging from a birch-bark post at Heraud's inn, its goldfinch nipping at lettuce from Mlle de Louvenne's fingers. He wondered if Nicole would be at the picnic. She no longer avoided him when he saw her; but strangely he did not see her so often. When he stopped at the inn for a drink on his way home from the blacksmith's or the ferry, M. Heraud placed his tankard before him. She had not come of late to Victoire's dancing classes or to the cabin for books. At Mass he noticed that she was thinner and her eyes had a tired, haunted look.

Only a few days ago as he was riding home from the smithy he had come upon her beyond the lively market place. She was swinging a kettle of milk and seemed startled when he overtook her.

"Mademoiselle looks very charming today," Pierre said, dismounting and taking the kettle from her hand. "A Marie Antoinette who has just milked her cow Blanchette."

She smiled. But there was no word to describe the sudden beauty he saw in her. The cheap cotton dress of pale green was the hue of winter wheat in the lowlands, and its riot of flowers disturbed him somehow, so that now he heard the slow, rich song of the meadow lark that had been pealing over the fields as he rode along inattentive. The breeze had taken liberties with her brown curls, which had grown to her shoulders, and the late spring had already disposed a few new freckles on the saucy nose. The flame of the sunset glowed in her eyes, on the curved red lips, on the bare throat and arms, so that she seemed a trembling part of the sunset, of the rose that tinted the landscape. His eyes lingered on the miniature she wore, but it was because he was conscious of the little hard, ripe breasts beneath the flounce of her print.

He forced his eyes sheepishly from the miniature. He knew he had been looking at her as if she were naked and he knew that she had an awareness of his passion. Instinct told him that he was defeating his own purpose, that if he did not get his eyes under control he would not even be blessed with an occasional word with her. *Dieu,* how long could her muddled memory withhold from him the sweet taste of her in his arms!

"Monsieur," she said, recalling him to his senses.

"There must be a portrait of you somewhere," he said, "with the sunset in it."

"How poetic you are, Monsieur! And I thought you calculating—a man of purpose."

"Surely I'm entitled to another self, the same as you?"

She looked at him guardedly; he was kicking a stone ahead of him out of a rut bitten deep by the winter frost.

"You are still a little boy—spoiled," she said, and she waved to the tailor's wife who was shaking a tablecloth of crumbs out to the birds.

"You know nothing about me. I've never told you what I've done or what I've been. You've never asked."

"Perhaps I know enough about you, M. de Michelait. And now, *s'il vous plait,* I'll take the milk again. I've decided to stop for M. Heraud's coat which was mended. *Merci. Merci beaucoup!"*

She smiled warmly, and his heart gave a twist until he met her eyes, which were cold and gray. He watched her go down M. Charet's path with its clumps of purple violets transplanted from the woods. Then he mounted his horse and rode home at an angry canter.

The picnic for the Duc de La Rochefoucauld-Liancourt was held at Prospect Height, a ledge of the ridge behind the town site. Giant trees met overhead in a green parasol, but to the north obstructing branches had been trimmed off, so that the view of the meandering mountains and curling river lay beyond the cliff. In an opening of forest, tables were hewn of tree trunks, armchairs had been hollowed out of stumps, and there was a seesaw. The floor of the woods was rough with large

stones, laced with the spring tendrils of the exotic walking fern; but
a patch had been cleared away for battledore and shuttlecock.

When Pierre arrived in the midafternoon with Victoire and Nicki,
Talon's Julie and Wallois were preparing the meal. Wallois, in chef's
cap and apron, grilled quail and fried frogs over an open fire, and Julie
whipped the pancake batter. Coveys of helpful women in dainty muslin
aprons made a nuisance of themselves. Couldn't the cheese be cut—or
the tarts? The Duc was squeamish about only a soupçon of garlic in
his salad. Had anyone sampled it? . . . *Dieu,* why didn't someone get
the children settled to a game of darts or ball? The boys were constantly peeking under the white cloths at the oranges and marzipan
and the fifteen-layer cake that was decorated with the Duc's coat of
arms.

The slaves of the San Domingans, having dragged hampers of condi-
ments up the mountain, now gathered wood for the fire, fanned the
ladies who had been playing blindman's buff, or replenished Madeira
glasses.

The Duc himself was occupying the place of honor, a throne hewn
from a rock.

"You know I never noticed before how like he is to Louis," Pierre
mentioned in an undertone to Victoire as they approached to greet him.
"And with that absurd crown of flowers you've made for him, he looks
every inch the monarch."

"Is it his great nose that makes his chin and forehead recede? Or his
frightened chin and forehead that make his nose so long?" she whispered with a giggle.

"What?" demanded Nicki, who was shiny as new pewter.

"Shush!" ordered Victoire. "Make your bow and then go play with
your ball."

Pierre settled down in the group of men about the Duc, who was
giving his economist's view of Asylum. But his eyes roamed the woods
for a glimpse of Nicole.

"I think it a shame," the Duc was saying, "that you have so strong
a dislike for your American farmers even if many of these are ignorant
and of the low class."

"Ah, but these Hermans and Johnsons take advantage!" complained
M. Carles, patting his round stomach as the aroma of quail reached his
nose. "Such a high price they demand for their labor! And how they
putter at their work!"

"The Americans have taken a keen delight in misadvising us about our farming," said Talon, rubbing his white hands together thought-fully.

"What does it cost you to clear ground?" asked the master.

"It costs the company thirty dollars an acre. And it takes ten men three months to clear an acre of ground!"

"*Oui*, M. Talon, that *is* dear." (Obviously the flower crown pricked as spitefully as one of jewels, for the Duc now removed it.) "But what is your yield?"

"Twenty bushels of wheat an acre, or sixty bushels of Indian corn."

"M. Carles harvested three tons of hay to an acre," interposed Pierre, with enthusiasm.

"*Bien*. I am proud of you!" said Liancourt, stretching his short, fat legs. "And you prepare molasses and vinegar, and send flax and grain to Wilkes-Barre?"

"*Oui, M. le Duc,* and get four dollars a barrel for tar there."

"A good price—a good colony," he said like a lenient schoolmaster as he sipped his wine. "But only two hundred French here at the moment? You should draw more. What's wrong with your agents abroad and in the Indies? You should advertise the whole million acres. Settle the land dispute with Connecticut as soon as you can, and better your breeds of horses and cattle. Establish a school. Finish the roads you've begun. You'll soon get a new flock of sturdy, industrious families."

Perhaps M. le Duc was racing with the well-browned quail, for the meal was being announced with pomp by Wallois. M. le Duc, in his journal that night, wrote cryptically, "Have never eaten a better meal. '*Refugium Peccatorum*' will either rise or fall rapidly."

Yes, it was high time for the banquet! The supply of wine was ebbing, the flurry of skirts on the seesaw had become wilder, and rescues more frequent. Laughter had risen imperceptibly to a higher key.

Purée de petits crabes—tout le monde! (Children!—elders first, even at a picnic!) *Dieu!* did you see M. Homet drop that bottle of claret on the rock? Everything near dripping red. . . . Victoire has torn her fine cambric apron on the seesaw? Well, it took four strong men to help her! . . . Have Major Hoops and Mlle de Louvenne only been picking flowers for the table? His face is red as his beard, and how can we use the flowers she has? They're all crushed. . . . *Parbleu,* Mme de Blaçons has forgotten to bring the anchovies presented to her by the Duc. . . . Now there are other places for a dog to—it wouldn't have to be so close to the food! A whole bottle of Anisette de Hollande? But how divine!

. . . Do you think Mme Homet is *enceinte* again? . . . *Absurde!* . . .
just baby fat. How well the new family from Philadelphia seems to be
mixing! Did you notice her large garden hat with the feathers? Then
that's what they must be wearing. . . . *Pest!* Look at that caterpillar
fallen into the butter! I hate the squirming things! . . .

The feast was over. Ants came to claim the crumbs. Wilhelmine
Buzard bulged, had a stomach ache, and lay in bovine adolescence on a
large flat stone. A few of the men drifted away behind the trees. Some
of the women took out their needlepoint. Mme d'Autremont darned
the socks of her three boys. The seesaws languished. Now that they
were empty no one wanted to seesaw. Mme Homet nursed her child.
M. Carles produced some miniature chessmen, and he and Major
Hoops straddled a tree trunk and fell to pondering. One of the Negroes
back at the fireplace strummed a guitar.

The children played tag till one of them skinned a knee. After that
they were content to battle with last year's acorns. The Duc was hit by
an acorn·in the ear. He was noble about it, of course, but the game
must be stopped. Young Buzard was ingenious. Why not play guillotine? His sister looked half dead anyway. She could be Marie Antoinette.

"*Nom de Dieu!*" cried Mme Seybert, who was a widow without
children. "Can't someone amuse the little darlings?"

"I'll take them for a game in the woods," offered Mlle de Louvenne.
"*Allons!* Hide-and-seek."

"Be careful of the ravine!" warned M. Talon. "It's terribly steep."

They followed her like the rats—the Pied Piper; Pierre watched her
disappear through the trees with Nicki's hand in hers. Nicki wanted
to break away from her, wanted to romp ahead with the older children. Foolish Nicki, thought Pierre, burying his nose in a bed of pine
boughs.

"It's getting cool," said Mme Buzard, drawing a scarf over her plump
shoulders. But she let the young Negress continue her fanning. "I
should have told René to put on his coat."

"Fooh!" said Victoire, who was wearing the wilted crown of the
Duc. "The young are warm-blooded." And she lay back in a nest
of pillows she had brought with her. Her neck and bosom were bare,
and as she relaxed she smiled faintly into the dog-yellow eyes of the
middle-aged doctor. His sleek glance under the drowsy lids always
seemed angular, oblique.

"Look how red the river is!" exclaimed Mme de Blaçons, her voice rising above the others like a harp harmonic. Mme de Blaçons had been at the point of laughter or tears all day. The Duc had been obliged to bring to his hostess news of the guillotining of her sister. The Duc had brought other news, good and bad. Catherine de Michelait, it was said, had escaped into Germany to a convent there. M. Roland had committed suicide. Mme Lebrun was painting in Italy. The Vicomtesse de Noailles—what had become of her? Guillotined? And Monsieur Y and Mlle Z? *Mon Dieu!*—they too?

The group looked down at the river at Mme de Blaçons' bidding. The mountain and river were drenched with red sunset.

"*Oui, Madame,* it is very beautiful," said the sensitive little M. Heraud.

Then irrelevantly Victoire asked: "And what has become of the little dancer Mlle Violette?"

"Hyacinthe," Pierre corrected her tensely.

"Ah, Mlle Hyacinthe of the ballet?" said Liancourt. "Guillotined long ago. But gather your courage, my friends. Paris is dancing again. Not the ragged dance of the sans-culotte, but the dance of the *Bals à la Victime*. One must have lost a relative to attend, must wear a black band on the left arm. The women dress as nymphs and Minervas and Junos, they say—with Greek sandals and Mahometan flesh-colored drawers."

"Who is there left to dance?" inquired the widow d'Autremont, her black doll's eyes bent on the changing of her thread.

"A little more anisette, M. le Duc?" asked Talon tactfully.

"You're right, Mme Buzard, it *is* getting cold."

"Has anyone seen my thimble? Gold with ruby—"

"I should know better. Fowl has never agreed with me."

"But I'm afraid to let him gather raspberries alone. The bears are so fond of them."

Pierre lay there on his bed of pine boughs with the little nothings of a picnic twittering about him, and he was filled with the nothingness of his heart. He had had Maytime in Paris, the love of Silvie—which he had plucked like a carnation, worn as a boutonniere, and allowed to wilt. He had had the smile of Marie Antoinette feeding his youth, but with her had gone the passion of his purpose, leaving him only with a cooling sense of duty and hands manacled to a plough. In rare moments he had even known the excitement of knowledge, of curiosity unappeased, his thoughts reaching out beyond what he had read to what he believed. He had had the cries of Paris and her lusty *joie de vivre* and he had sickened of her and wanted freedom. Now it seemed as if the beauties and the wild freedom of Asylum were closing in about him, strangling while they charmed, and that he had nothing left in his heart but desire for a woman who would soon go out of his life too, leaving him less than nothing—unrequited love.

His reflections were pierced by a scream from the woods, and he jumped to his feet and was the first of the group to dash over the stones toward the ravine near which Nicole had taken the children. Close on his steps were Dr. Buzard and Talon. Before them were the cutting screams of the children; behind them the terrified cries of women trying to escape tangled yarn and prankish skirts.

The children hovered on the edge of the ravine, clinging to trees and to each other's hands, shouting for help for someone who had fallen down the precipice.

When Pierre reached the edge he saw Nicole clinging with one hand to a laurel tree, with the other to Nicki on a ledge of rock beneath her. Blood gushed from the boy's forehead and bleared his eyes and dribbled into his mouth. He lay limp, half conscious, whimpering.

Pierre saw that the smallest move might send Nicki down into the black gully with its stream far below.

"Quick—a chain!" cried Pierre, and he gave his hand to Dr. Buzard who in turn took Talon's. Others had arrived; Major Hoops anchored the chain with his strong arm about a tree. Pierre clambered down the rocks, reached the child at last, and gathered him up with his free arm.

"Can you hold on?" he asked Nicole, his voice trembling like a choir boy's. "I'll be back for you in a minute."

The brown curls tumbled Medusa-like over her blanched face, and the eyes that fastened onto his were black as a cavern.

When the rescue was complete Dr. Buzard ordered the hysterical group to return to the clearing. Victoire had snatched Nicki from Pierre's arms and was mopping his head wih her torn fichu. The women surrounded her, offering tears and sympathy. The men followed the women, applying smelling salts and shooing the children ahead of them.

"Rest here for a moment," Dr. Buzard said sternly, turning to Mlle de Louvenne. "I'll come back to examine you when I've bandaged him."

Then as he saw they were left alone he added: "You little fool—risking your life! Why didn't you call for help?"

"There wasn't time. . . ."

"If you had broken your neck!"

"He's such a beautiful child!"

"There's always another neck for a scarf."

"I'm tired of being a shell." The words came with a quick, tearless sob.

"That is not for you to say!"

She sank down on a bed of moss and covered her face with her hands. Dr. Buzard hurried on to examine Nicki.

Ten minutes later Nicki was bandaged and Dr. Buzard said he had no fear of a concussion. The picnic was over. People were gathering their straggled belongings.

Victoire, hugging Nicki in her arms, was telling him a stupendous story about an elephant frightened by a field mouse.

"Nicki's ball," she said in an undertone to Pierre. "He keeps crying for his ball. Back in the woods perhaps. . . ."

Pierre was glad to escape. Now that he knew Nicki was safe he felt he must pour out his gratitude to Nicole whom everyone seemed to have forgotten.

She was standing close to the ravine, quiet, looking down to the bottom. Strewn about her feet were the trampled spring beauties and mandrakes of the children.

She turned as she felt rather than heard him.

Her apron hung limp and torn and her gown was smudged with the damp loam of the ravine. There were red, ragged scratches on her arms.

"Nicole," he said softly, and he took her in his arms and brushed the damp curls from her cheeks. She made no resistance. And he held her so close that he could feel the little hard, ripe breasts warm as if their flesh had pressed to his hunger.

The blood pounded crazily in his ears—loud, like the tocsin of Paris. He bent to touch her lips. They were cold as a marble effigy he had once kissed in St. Marks, but they were soft, yielding to his madness and warming to his madness as he clung to them, so that at last when he released her, her lips were not a separate thing but a burning part of him.

"Please, Monsieur," she whispered, "don't ever do this again."

There were no words for what he felt, any more than a million years ago there had been words for the wind, the sun, the sea. There were no words for the longing stirred by the touch of her hair on his cheek, the cold lips come to life with the warmth of his own.

He held her to him quickly, with fear, with a greater urgency, but she struggled and broke away from him. She stood for a moment, her shoulders straight, her head proudly high, looking beyond him into the unresponsive blackness of the wood. Then she turned and walked ahead of him to the edge of the clearing and the debacle of the picnic.

✿✿✿✿✿✿✿✿✿✿✿✿✿✿✿✿✿✿✿✿✿✿✿✿✿

CHAPTER XXXVII

Two HOURS LATER Nicki lay sleeping in his bed. The small, red lips were shiny and puffed, and his head was swathed in bandages that Dr. Buzard had given the humorous twist of a West Indies turban.

Frau Gresch stood at his bedside, her lower lip protruding with indignation as she watched Victoire tuck in the covers he had restlessly tossed from him.

"I told you I dreamed of baking bread," cried Frau Gresch with the liberty of one who pares potatoes toward one who only garnishes the salad. "And that means illness. You should have watched him."

"He isn't ill," retorted Victoire. "He's had an accident."

She flounced out of the room to the little cubby hole that was her own bedchamber.

Only today as she had seen Nicki romp with the other children she had thought: "But he is beautiful!" And now with a stupid accident his beauty might be impaired by a hideous scar. She felt bitter toward fate as she drew the chintz curtains of her one window, and began to undress. Nicki was the apotheosis of her passion for Pierre, and she would not have him marred by a hideous scar!

Frau Gresch was cruel to blame her. One could not watch a child every minute. How could she help it that even at the age of two Nicki had the sense of adventure of his father? Besides, Mlle de Louvenne had had the responsibility of the children. The rattlepate had not even apologized for her negligence, had only touched Nicki's fat little hand with her own, accepting praise of her daring with a smug silence.

Victoire tossed her stockings across the room just as she would have liked to toss Nicole out of Asylum. For three months now Victoire had been increasingly irritated with this woman without a past. What in the name of Lucifer did the men see in her? Obviously not just a pug nose, freckles, chameleon eyes, and a mess of blowzy curls! The girl wasn't pretty and she hadn't the personality of Victoire's thumb. Men of course were always intrigued by a mystery, egoists enough to think they could solve it. Young Louis d'Autremont was head over heels in love with her; Aristide was helpless as a fly in honey; even the fresh young cabbage Homet wilted a little under her smile. And such a maddeningly effortless smile! . . . Only Dr. Buzard seemed immune, with his sleek, black glance directed another way. . . .

Victoire began to put on her night shift; then on second thought she tossed it after the stockings and brought out from the chest one trimmed lavishly with lace and blue ribbons. What would it be like, she wondered, looking at one's bare body and not knowing if it had ever been embraced! But *absurde!* . . . Sometimes one was tempted to doubt . . . except that no woman in her right mind would choose to come to Asylum, would come here unless there was a man like Pierre whom she had to follow.

Pierre and Nicole! She flung herself on the high squeaking bed, braced her chin on her crossed arms, and watched her image in the mirror. Pierre and Nicole! . . . It was no more than instinct, subtle as the breath of spring on a late March day. There had been the time he danced with her on Mme d'Autremont's fete day, and later had fallen asleep over his books in the early morning, never coming to bed at all. Then the night of the sledging party on the river. When Victoire and Pierre arrived it was dark and they had joined M. Talon for a moment beside a roaring bonfire. Groups of twos and threes melted into the darkness. As he talked Pierre's eyes were restless.

When M. Talon said: "It's a pity Mlle de Louvenne does not have M. Homet's piano down here this evening," Pierre's eyes stopped wandering, and he laughed as if this were a mighty joke, drawing Victoire's arm gaily through his own.

Then tonight. There was something about the way Pierre and Nicole had come out of the woods together. Was it that her shoulders were drawn so straight—or that they weren't walking sociably close together?

"Where is the ball?" Victoire had asked.

"The ball?"

"Nicki's ball."

"I couldn't find it."

"Ah, c'est triste. He keeps crying for it."

"I'll look again." And in a short time he had returned with the ball.

Pierre too was in love with this woman. She knew it quite suddenly with a sickening flash. Mlle Hyacinthe was dead—but the Mlles Hyacinthe never died! They were born into a man's blood as surely as syphilis, eating into his life and the lives of his wife and children.

The sound of Pierre's step coming slowly up the stairs made her burst into angry tears.

He came into the room yawning and said: "I've got to be up before the sun tomorrow to transplant those damn *légumes* and artichokes from the greenhouse—why, what's the matter?"

Try as she would she couldn't control the fury of her tears.

Pierre, with his shirt already half pulled off, came over and sat down on the bed beside her.

"Come, *ma chère,* don't worry," he said. "Nicki will be all right."

"He'll be scarred for life!"

"Every man has a scar or two."

He stroked her hair a little awkwardly. He had never known how to be tender with Victoire. And tonight he felt a distaste at the stiffness of her curls.

"I won't stay in this place any longer. It's not fair to him," she sobbed. "Bears and wolves at the very door—and a ravine or snowdrift every other step. If he's not eaten alive some day he'll freeze to death! . . . Think, Pierre, he's your son! The oldest son of a marquis! He should have luxury, and travel, and—and a governor!"

"He seems so happy with his crow and worms."

"It's male instinct to grovel. Worms—women," she sniffled, a little mollified now by Pierre's touch. (Lace and blue ribbons were irresistible, whether in Coblentz or Asylum.) "But I want *everything* for him. I want to get him out of this howling, barren place. . . . It's even made me barren. . . ."

"That's all for the best, Victoire."

"Why do you say that?" quickly.

"There are enough hardships here for a woman besides childbirth."

"I don't think you want more children! Pierre, look at me; don't stare into the corner as if you saw Louis's head there."

He turned his black eyes on her with apathy. He hated this room, which was Victoire's from the gaudiness of its curtains to the heavy

Oriental scent that smothered the senses. She had covered the puncheon walls with wicked French prints, and the toilet table he had built was a mass of beauty concoctions. The room bulged with her trunks, her clothes. He merely slept here.

"Pierre—kiss me!"

"I'm very tired, Victoire . . . Nicki frightened me so."

"Bête! I only asked you to kiss me!"

His black eyes were more piercing than steel as they came closer to her, and she felt her desire whetted by the small, physical things that coarsened him: the calluses of his fingers, the snuff on his breath, the strong smell of his armpits, the pricking hair of his chest. She would hold him like this forever, she thought frantically, as her full red mouth covered his thin passive lips. Hard, hard he was—of body and soul! The hardness of his body drawing her, the hardness of his heart enraging her.

She closed her eyes because she hated the proud quivering of his nostrils like that of an untamed Arabian steed. She had never really tamed him, but she would not surrender him now to any mystery woman, she thought passionately.

"Pierre, you *must* take me away! Me and Nicki!"

"Are you so unhappy?"

"Nom de Dieu, I am dying inside!"

"Could you be happy anywhere—with your ambition?"

"Mais oui, anywhere!" she answered artfully, but he knew that she had not misunderstood him. "It won't have to be Philadelphia, New York, or Charleston or—anywhere until we can safely return to Paris!"

"I can't leave Asylum."

"Then you *are* in love with her, aren't you!" she exploded.

"I don't know what you mean." It was the conventional answer. But it gave him time to collect his wits. He stood up and began to unbutton his breeches. He could feel the hot pressure of her fingers on his arms as if he had been branded.

"You know very well I mean Mlle de Louvenne!"

Victoire could have bitten her tongue out; she had never meant to mention Nicole. And she knew that if Nicole lived with them in this room from now on—an evil genius between them—it was she, Victoire, who had brought her here. He had never really committed himself by word or action, and from now on he would be doubly wary of doing so.

She was too mortified to cry. She lay staring at Pierre, wanting to embrace him and wanting to kill him.

"Perhaps you'll remember I refused to leave here before she came," he said coldly. "And I shall be here long after she goes."

"And what of now—*now* while she's here!"

"I'll be raising ten bushels of barley an acre!"

Dr. Buzard sat at his rosewood desk the following morning figuring what his indigo plantations would have brought him this year if a hundred thousand slaves of the island had not revolted. The Sultana in a voluminous red robe was writing a letter on a lapboard. Beside her on the table was a bottle of dandelion wine. (The doctor had recommended this and no baths for her eczema.) A bare-footed slave girl in a striped turban fanned the Sultana indolently, following with her eyes the young Negro who watered flowers. From the Grande Maison, a few lots away, came the sickly notes of Wilhelmine Buzard's practicing.

M. Heraud's troubled knock at the front door was so urgent that Dr. Buzard did not wait for the slave girl to answer, but let in the innkeeper himself.

"It's Mlle de Louvenne," said M. Heraud, rubbing his hands together. "Some of it's come back."

The great, almost popeyes of the Sultana and the small, blurry eyes of the doctor were fastened on him curiously.

"You mean—her memory?" inquired the doctor, and his eyes narrowed.

"*Oui, M. le Docteur,* and you were right—she's San Domingan."

The doctor muttered some oaths under his breath as he went off to get his coat, and M. Heraud, close to tears, babbled out details to the Sultana.

The doctor drove M. Heraud back to the inn in his phaeton, learning the outline of her story.

"It came sudden as lightning," said M. Heraud. "It gave me goose flesh. But, *M. le Docteur,* she didn't know any of us; she doesn't remember now how she came to Asylum!"

"The accident yesterday," mumbled Dr. Buzard. "Of course, the accident—the shock, you know. Her memory came back as it went—with a shock. . . . I'll drive her up the Loyalsock Road a way. It'll be better for her nerves if I talk with her in the open."

Half an hour later Nicole faced Dr. Buzard in a small glade that commanded a view of the road in both directions. Neither had spoken a word in the ten minutes since they left the inn.

He took out his snuffbox as he squatted down on a flat stone and said: "I should send you back to M. Barras without a sou's compensation. He gave you strict orders to follow my directions!"

Nicole leaned against a tree and watched the doctor's fat thumb flip the snuff up his nose. "But it was the perfect time to bring back the past; why should we wait and have to plan a shock when fate provided one?"

"I am the one to decide these things, not you. *Dieu,* working with you has been like working with a mule!"

"I think I have been superb," she said softly. And she thought what a happy little glade this was with its low-hanging roof of leaves and the stones of the brook flecked with sun.

"In the first place," he went on, "you've avoided M. de Michelait although you knew he was the key man. By this time you might have been his mistress and we might have Jean de Batz's plans at our fingertips. But what do you do? You avoid him!"

"I don't want to be M. de Michelait's mistress."

"I've told you before it's not a matter of what you want. It's a matter of what you must do. You undertook this mission because you wanted to see the Dauphin out of the way, didn't you?"

"*Oui, Monsieur.*"

"Is it too much to ask if you've changed your mind?"

She returned his sarcasm with her engaging smile. "*Vive la République!*" she said triumphantly.

"*Eh bien!* You will become M. de Michelait's mistress within the month then. If Jean de Batz ever carries out a plan of escape you'll be the first after M. de Michelait to know it on this side of the water. And every day of advance knowledge will be to our benefit in getting rid of the child after he arrives here. But these are ABC's that need hardly be repeated to a woman of your shrewdness and capacity."

"I like you better when you flatter me, *M. le Docteur.*" Nicole picked a bit of loose bark from the tree and began to toy with it.

"We understand one another then?" The doctor gave a few little gasping breaths that preceded his sneeze. "I am sure it will be a pleasant duty. If I'd recommended M. Talon instead, with his white aging flesh. . . . But M. de Michelait, one of the handsomest men of the court, with hard, brown muscles that should make any virgin's groins ache with desire and—"

"*Monsieur!*" She had tossed her head back and her eyes flashed fire. "I'm your accomplice but I demand respect!"

He raised his eyebrows in surprise. "What a little spitfire you are! I was told you had the zeal of a Jeanne d'Arc. I'm beginning to believe it, Mlle Roucault!"

"*M. le Docteur,*" said Nicole, her voice dropping as she heard horses' hoofs in the distance. "I have my very good reason for refusing intimacy with M. de Michelait."

"When you undertook this mission you vowed that you'd let nothing personal come between you and success."

"This is not personal. Or if it is, Monsieur, I am thinking first of my purpose in being here."

"If you refuse I shall ask for someone to replace you."

Nicole laughed. "It's a little late for that, Monsieur, *n'est-ce pas?* And if the reports are true, the Dauphin will die before any escape is effected. Then you and I, *M. le Docteur,* will find our partnership dissolved. . . . 'Parting is such sweet sorrow'!"

"I'll carry on here alone," he snarled at her.

"You're encumbered with a family. It would be a real sleight of hand for the four of you to disappear with the Dauphin in the wilderness and never be seen again—if those are the instructions. Or would you simply leave your—"

He held up a warning finger. The horseman was close to the phaeton and proved to be John Herman. The doctor hallooed to him and walked over to tell him the news of Nicole and that the poor girl was almost hysterical trying to fit the pieces of her life together.

When John Herman had departed there was silence until the hoofbeats were out of hearing.

"Another thing," began Dr. Buzard. "You've taken it into your hands to forget what happened since your supposed husband was lost to you in Philadelphia. This is pure madness, Mlle Roucault. It estranges everyone in Asylum, and you've worked for months to gain their sympathy and confidence."

"Again, I had my reason."

"You'll get over this last memory blank *tout de suite,* Mademoiselle . . . and before you have any more *fugues* or regain any more of the past I expect to be consulted."

"You don't realize how hard it is for me, *M. le Docteur,* never to be myself. I'm afraid to sing a snatch of a song for fear it might be the *Marseillaise.* I'm afraid I'll cry out in my sleep and reveal my dreams. I'm afraid to look at anyone lest he see my name blazing in my eyes: 'Mlle Félicie Roucault, secret agent of the Republic!' My very hands seem to shriek the things I've done. If I speak and a silence follows I'm sure that they've guessed—"

"Not so loud, Mlle Roucault!" whispered Dr. Buzard in alarm. "The trees have ears! . . ."

"And I must listen to stories of Marie Antoinette and the rotten court until I could scream my contempt of these blue bloods. Blind, they are—and proud! *They* are the murderers, Monsieur, not the poor little peasants who rose in revolt! *They* are the ones who have murdered France, with the slow rot of champagne and desecrated altars and —and adultery with their Mlles Hyacinthe!"

"For anyone who hates the blue bloods as much as you, I would say your friendship with Mme de Blaçons and a few others has been surprisingly tender."

"They've been good to me. But don't you see—I've got to forget that?"

Dr. Buzard sighed. Why was an excitable woman always indispensable in an intrigue like this—a woman who worked for ideals rather than the purse of gold at the end of a job? . . . *Dieu,* what possessed her now that she refused Pierre's advances! Was that idealism too? Of course it was hard for the girl, and she was right—it was too late to replace her. . . .

"I appreciate your position, Mlle Roucault," and his voice had a soothing honey note now. "My own is not easy. Mme Buzard would like to go to Charleston where we can rent out our slaves to plantationers and live in greater comfort. . . . Her eczema is a form of defiance, I think. . . . But who would have thought we must wait for so long for word from Paris? Ah, we must be very patient, Mademoiselle: patience is part of our stock in trade."

"I despise them so! I must have my *fugue* from them for a while if I am to keep my wits for the work ahead of me."

"You say you despise them. And yet you risked your neck for one of them yesterday—the son of a marquis! As if he were more important to you than the Dauphin!"

She flushed. "He's such a beautiful child . . . and I am still human."

"Too human for one who is helping to change the course of history! . . . But come, what have you remembered of your husband and your past? Since you've taken the liberty of choosing your own time for this revelation I trust you've changed no detail of the story plotted for you —that you've recalled nothing before your life in San Domingo?"

"*Mais non,* I am hardly such a fool!" She came toward him, her whole expression changed. Her eyebrows were arched in a frown of pain; her eyes had a look of feverish distraction. For a moment her lips quivered as she clasped and unclasped her hands nervously, and there was a droop to the straight shoulders as if someone had tossed about them a cloak of lead.

"Ah, if only God had stricken my memory from me forever! . . . It's more than I can bear—to remember those cruel years—the island like hell with fires and murder . . . everything gone at last. . . . And I had all in the world a woman could want! Love, a child, wealth. . . . He was a Creole, my husband—tall, black-eyed, so handsome that every woman turned in the streets. . . . But he was not only rich, he was loved. He was too kind . . . he was a friend of the slaves, the *gens de couleur,* the *petits blancs.* He was human."

At this point Nicole fumbled for her handkerchief, buried her face for a moment, then gathered fortitude to go on. Dr. Buzard sat quiet as a sphinx, and even a little chipmunk paused in a patch of arbutus, and seemed to be waiting for her to continue.

"The superintendent of our plantations was a mulatto, had loved M. de Louvenne from childhood. But when the revolts began he joined Sonthanax, the civil commissioner in the north. Others of our slaves joined the mulatto and colored army that took Port-au-Prince—we lived near Port-au-Prince. . . . M. de Louvenne was taken prisoner, sent to the eastern part of the island still wild from its Spanish days. Through a faithful slave I knew he was safe . . . that he spent his time writing a vocabulary of one of the native languages. . . . We had a child, Claude Christophe Jean Nicole de Louvenne, a little boy of four. . . ."

Nicole clasped the miniature (which had been bought in a second-hand shop in Paris) holding it in tense fingers. Her voice blurred as she continued.

"A beautiful child . . . he was frightened—hiding, hiding always from the madness of the blacks. . . . Years it seemed that we hid away waiting for him, scarcely eating, scarcely breathing . . . unable to escape after the fire at Le Cap—refusing to go without him. But at last he came back to us—and God knows how!—but we got to the coast, got aboard a merchant vessel of Stephen Girard's. . . .

"On the boat my little Claude took ill with the fever; I prayed to God to spare him—to take me instead. . . . *Nom de Dieu!* . . . why have I remembered? Why must I live again with a knife in my heart?"

Nicole leaned against the tree once more, her eyes closed, her brown curls swept by the soft innocence of early leaves.

The little chipmunk scampered away at the throbbing ring of her voice, and Dr. Buzard wet his lips.

"We came off the boat alone, M. de Louvenne, and I . . . I remember the house in Baltimore where we lived. I must have been ill too. I remember calling for my little Claude—certain he would be able to hear me. I remember M. de Louvenne's lips on mine. He seemed to be pleading with me . . . but I had to find my child! I must have gone off to find him, wandered away. . . ."

She crumpled to her knees, graceful as a dead rose that softly sheds its petals at a human touch. And she lay there, face hidden in the cotton folds of her skirt, without even the comfort of a sob.

Dr. Buzard stared at her in exultation. But now she had sprung to her feet and was smiling, triumphant, breathless.

The doctor pulled his fat body up from the stone with a lurch.

"And you've wasted this—this chef-d'œuvre on M. Heraud!" he exclaimed.

"M. de Michelait happened to be there also."

"*Magnifique!* If I've offended you this morning I apologize a thousand times, Mademoiselle! I am humble before a woman who can wrench tears from a stone!"

She began to walk toward the phaeton.

"Ah, but one thing more, my dear Mlle Roucault, or I should say, *Mme* de Louvenne! Now that you remember your beloved husband, naturally you think you can find him yourself. Tonight you'll attempt to leave Asylum—by this road, shortly after dark. There will be cards and music for Liancourt at la Grande Maison. I'll see to it that your walk is not too long. . . . It will be a touching episode—and very convincing. Then for several days you may indulge in any sort of hysteria you like. And I no longer have any fear that this will not be convincing too!"

CHAPTER XXXVIII

August 1795

MME REYNAUD, the new sloth-eyed San Domingan settler, lolled in the chair farthest from the windows of the French ladies' drawing-room, her petticoats bunched about her knees, a slave fanning the white-silk ankles. Another of Mme Reynaud's slaves fanned the legs of Victoire, as shockingly exposed. In a little while there would be a roomful of women, gasping for a breath of air fresh from the river, moist fingers clinging to the wool or silk of their needlework. Mme Reynaud, who had been duly called upon by the ladies of the colony, had offered them this respite: for everyone who took tea with her today at la Grande Maison she would furnish a fanning slave.

The rich Reynaud family, opulent with slaves and children, had arrived in Asylum two weeks before on the same Durham boat as Victoire's piano, and were still guests of the absent M. Talon.

Mme Reynaud, a Creole with blue-black hair and skin the tint of skimmed milk, meant to sacrifice no luxury during this annoying interlude in her life. At this moment her hands lay in her lap, ivory and quiet as a brace of lilies. From the first Victoire had appealed to her.

"I wonder if Mme de Louvenne will come," she said in a voice that hummed softly. "She intrigues me."

"I doubt it. She's inconsolable since she recalled the death of her child."

"C'est triste! . . . But how stupid of us not to arrive before the excitement! Did you say that M. Herman actually raped her the night she tried to run away, or-or . . . ?"

"I believe the searching party arrived in time," said Victoire casually. She knew every detail of Mme de Louvenne's torn clothing and exposure of virtue. Also Dr. Buzard had confided in her John Herman's frantic endeavor to accomplish his purpose before the very eyes of the men. But what had Mme Reynaud done to be deserving of such choice bits?

"They heard her screams of course?"

"But of course!" said Victoire. "She wasn't so far from the inn. Luckily the doctor had gone to give her a sedative before the party for the Duc de Liancourt."

"I understand M. Herman's broken nose is a gift from M. de Michelait," Mme Reynaud said invitingly.

"M. de Michelait always likes to be first." It was a shame, thought Victoire, that this lovely epigram had to be lost on a newcomer.

Mme Reynaud's hands disentwined and she carefully examined the hem of her handkerchief, and finding the wrong side, touched it to her nose; there was a soft sound like a baby's sigh.

"I'd like to copy her coiffure," she said. "It's original. . . . *Dieu,* Marie, tend to your fanning!"

"She used to wear her hair like a child's, in a rumpus of curls. Now that she knows she has a husband—whisk, her hair goes up and she's taken on the dignity of Maria Theresa! Except when she plays with the children. Very fond of children, it seems—especially little boys . . . she paints, too—off in the woods or fields, alone—Dreadful landscapes that look like a ragout. It was very amusing when her memory came back for San Domingo; she forgot how she came here and we all had to be introduced. . . . The men were distracted at losing Mlle de Louvenne the mystery maid for a faithful matron."

"How innocent of them!"

"Ah, but she's very conclusive. And now and then a woman prefers her husband, *n'est-ce pas*—if he's one that all the other women prefer too?"

Mme Reynaud's eyes drifted from the sparkling river with its little islands to Victoire's large, mobile lips.

"Strange that M. Reynaud and I can't remember! . . . one usually knows all the large plantations. . . . She is madly in love then with M. de Louvenne?"

"*Oui, Madame.* M. Talon has redoubled his efforts to find him."

"I insist that an absent husband only adds sauce to the goose!"

"She has already frightened away some of the ganders!" laughed Victoire. "M. du Petit-Thouars made up his mind in a moment to go to Niagara on foot, along with the Duc de Liancourt and the Marquis de Blaçons. Louis d'Autremont is in self-inflicted exile—writes morbidly in his journal all night."

It was not necessary to add that Pierre's moping was definite proof of his own failure. Even M. Talleyrand, who had come this summer in a rifleman's suit instead of his bishop's lawn and purple, had been sweetly rebuffed. It was the laugh of the colony that the "rosewater abbé," who had deflowered every bloom within reach on both sides of the water, had met his defeat at last in Mme de Louvenne.

"And I heard before I came that this was a little utopia!" Mme Reynaud came near to smiling. This was one luxury involving wrinkles that she usually denied herself.

"*C'est vrai, Madame*. It was!" declared Victoire. "A year ago when I came it was all sweetness and purity."

"And now it is a baby in its second summer—teething and irritable? . . . *Nom de Dieu,* Marie, *fan!* My thighs are sweating like those of a racing horse!"

Victoire looked up and burst into a sudden laugh. This was the open sesame.

"The second summer isn't nearly so boring," she admitted. "First, M. Herman stirs up the hornet's nest with his lust, and there's need for a village council after all, and a law or two, and judgment. . . . M. Herman is at large again, you know, after two months in the Wilkes-Barre jail. . . . Then, someone attempts to steal the jewels Mme de Louvenne remembered she had sewn into her muff. Another law is needed for thieves. . . . But what to do with Master Buzard, who let Mme de Louvenne's goldfinch out of its cage? Not theft, of course, but vandalism! Or what to do—"

"Why not let Mme de Louvenne make the laws?"

Their eyes met in a mutual dislike of Nicole, who would have to be minimized.

"If you'd been here a year you'd be grateful for the need of laws," said Victoire tensely. "You'd be suffocated with people you see every day! . . . You'd be glad to see Asylum become human as Paris; you'd be glad, for instance, to see—"

"You needn't worry, *mon ami*. They can't fan and listen at the same time."

"One of the Johnson girls is pregnant. M. Montullé has been superintending that part of the woods lately. . . . Mme de la Roué confesses herself for hours every day to Father Fromentin . . . and Wilhelmine Buzard is ripening like a plum on an espalier—thirteen now, and haunting the smithy where John Herman assists M. Aubrey. Mme Buzard is frantic trying to keep her at home—spends her whole time breaking out in more eczema and sipping dandelion wine to cure it! . . . Perhaps we'll need a law for ecze—"

Victoire lowered her head over her needlepoint as the Sultana's voice was heard in the hall. She wondered suddenly if the Sultana's calf would be formless and flabby.

"And you have had no news of your runaway slave, Madame?" Victoire inquired politely of Mme Reynaud.

"Dieu, if he's found he shall have an ear lopped off! He should have been made to wear the collar we use on new slaves on the island—iron it is, with high spikes, so escape into the forest is starvation."

The fanning increased with perceptible vigor.

The Sultana floated into the room like a soap bubble. With her were two slaves of her own—silent denunciation of a San Domingan who had presumed to offer something as common as bread and butter to another San Domingan equally affluent. The slave in the red turban began to waft her fan near Madame's perspiring neck. The slave in the yellow turban knelt at Madame's feet and concentrated on the limbs that Madame exposed with a little grunt.

Victoire saw with a shock that the Sultana's calves were thin as a bamboo pole.

"Mme de Blaçons is only a few steps behind me . . ." panted Mme Buzard.

"I hope she will tell our fortunes!" said Mme Reynaud.

"She has told us our fortunes three times over!" exclaimed Victoire. "She's never without a pack of cards in her hands lately. . . . There's always a prince in my future and the blackest of tragedy. . . . *Ah, bon jour, Madame la Marquise!"*

Mme de Blaçons entered with a mild bow, and a slave of Mme Reynaud's immediately shadowed her. Mme de Blaçon's eyes were red, but the women of the colony were used to that now. With the circumspection of an ex-canoness she inched her skirts halfway to her knees, and a flush spread over her thin, lovely features.

Victoire noted with a suppressed giggle that Madame's calves were stalwart as an aging oak. She drew her own skirts a little higher, revealing a flawless knee.

"Mme de la Roué will be a little late," said Mme de Blaçons, lowering her skirts an inch as the fan of the slave flipped them. "She is confessing to Father Fromentin. . . . He comforts her so. He says we are meeting a challenge here—that the refugee sees in the New World what he wants to see—that he reveals his philosophy of life in his reaction to—"

"M. Carles is working on his fifteenth cheese recipe," said Victoire.

"*Fromage aux amandes avec bière*. He got his inspiration for the four-teenth from you, I believe, Mme Buzard?"

"*Oui, Madame . . . fromage fondu au vin de pissenlit*." Mme Buzard reached out a curved palm to the slave in the red turban, who promptly handed her a vial from her pocket. "M. Carles is very fond of cheese. I am very fond of cheese too."

She took a draft from the bottle and handed it back to the slave.

"My eczema . . ." she said, softly licking the wine from her lips.

Pierre went to Mass the following Sunday in an obstinate mood. He and Victoire had just visited the new house they were building.

Victoire had selected property halfway between the Standing Stone, below the picnic woods, and the ferry landing. The plot overlooked the Susquehanna. Victoire chose it because she said she wanted the first glimpse of Christopher Columbus coming up the river!

The new home had been conceived as the proper setting for an Erard piano and a marquise and was financed by one of Victoire's emeralds, sent down the river with John Keating.

Pierre and Victoire argued whenever they went to see the progress of the house, which he hadn't wanted in the first place.

"If you *must* have a new house," he had said when they drew up plans, "why must you copy Mme Seybert's, which is typically San Domingan?"

"And why not? Is there anything wrong with the San Domingans? They're French too. And at least the men were shrewd enough to escape with some of their fortune!"

"If you want an *exact* replica then why must it be larger and grander?"

"*Nom de Dieu*, if I must rot here in Asylum I'll rot in style! In a little better style than anybody else but M. Talon!"

"If you call this rotting why the devil don't you pack up and go to Philadelphia?"

"Alone . . . and leave Asylum to the mercy of a *ci-devant* courtier?"

"If you mean Mme de Louvenne by 'Asylum,' you might be gratified to know she's the soul of honor."

But of course she hadn't meant Mme de Louvenne . . . nor had she meant to say what she did that night of the picnic. She had been over-wrought with Nicki's accident. And sometimes there seemed no respite from the intense blackness of the night and the intense whiteness of the snow. She knew that Pierre had been a devoted husband from the moment of their coming here, that his every thought had been for her and Nicki, that he had seemed to find something spiritual from the simpleness of his life, his books, and his deep friendship with Aristide du Petit-Thouars. . . .

The conversation had ended on a lofty note after all. It was quite necessary, she thought, that he should feel her confidence. He had not needed to tell her that Nicole was a model of honor. Victoire could have sensed that with her eyes blindfolded. It amused her, moreover, to see Pierre frustrated, his passion dwindled to a chaste idolatry. So dull! At times she even felt magnanimous enough to pity him! . . . But Mme de Louvenne deserved watching. She might be a model of virtue now, but she was a woman and a woman could not remain in love with a wraith of a husband forever. Why in the name of all that was holy didn't she strike out and look for the man if her love was so ardent?

"If it was a man *I* wanted," thought Victoire scornfully, "I'd have tracked him down as a mouse finds cheese."

But Mme de Louvenne was staying. And Victoire was as determined now to outstay her as she had been to leave Asylum when the weather permitted her traveling down the river. If it meant rotting here forever she would not lose Pierre to a sanctimonious half-wit!

Once Mme de Louvenne was disposed of, Victoire would insist on leaving, for she did not believe Pierre—that this was the only place that could give him peace of heart after the torture of the Revolution.

The house grew, as Victoire had planned it, large enough to include any male or prominent guests to Asylum. Thirty by twenty feet (Mme Seybert's was only thirty by fifteen), covered with nail shingles, it had two lower and several upper rooms with fire-places. But this was only the nucleus. On either side a one-story building was connected with the main house by a piazza. One annex was Frau Gresch's personal precinct, the kitchen; the other was the dining-room with a well-stocked cellar below.

Mrs. Bingham had been kind enough to select wallpaper for the bedchambers and salons, and a ruby had also supplied furniture from the best Philadelphia shops.

The garden, enclosed by a nailed pale fence, promised to be the Eden of the colony. The summerhouse, nestling among the poplars and weeping willows, was only a skeleton, but in another summer it would be honey-sweet with flowers and there would be espaliers and trellises and arbors. Let Pierre have his hundreds of fruit trees in the meadow

below; Victoire would have her seesaw and her rope swing, and little
Nicki his sand pile and feeding stations for the birds.

On the way to Mass this morning Pierre had said petulantly:
"There'll be plenty of added work in the new house, you know. And
you've been complaining lately of the work in the cabin!"

Victoire had laughed. "I'll sell a pearl and buy a couple of slaves
from Mme Reynaud."

The remark rankled. Although Pierre was grateful at times that Victoire had found a new vent for her energy, he found it distasteful to
live on her jewels. What could have changed him, he wondered?
Hadn't he married her so that he could live in luxury? What would
du Petit-Thouars think of the new house when he returned?

As they entered the log church a little late Pierre glanced about
quickly for Nicole. He was sure she was missing and he began at once
to indulge his moodiness.

As he knelt and rose, mechanically crossing himself, he hated the
nasty little René Buzard, busy about the altar, and still more he hated
the droning of M. Carles, whom he felt would rather be eating cheese.
He missed Aristide, who often sat with them. He knew he was abominably self-centered but what was he to do about it? He remembered
a conversation he had had with the Little Admiral at his sugar camp
in the spring. They had been talking of Nicki.

"I have an idea that before you came to Asylum you were the perfect
egotist," Aristide had said. "And now you admit you no longer matter."

Pierre had smiled. "I matter awfully; I'm still the whole world,
really. When I was born the world began. When I die the whole world
will crumble and there'll be eternal darkness."

"Fickle as a grasshopper, consistent as a weather vane! A moment
ago you wanted only security for Nicki; now he is not even of your
world!"

"My Jansenist training, perhaps. First it teaches me I have great
duties to fulfill to myself, to Nicki. Then it laughs at me and says I
can do nothing of myself unless God sanctifies me by his grace, and
that of course is predestined. Why should I bother to try when there's
no one to tell me if God has favored me with His grace? The Jansenist
God is a harsh God."

"You told me a few weeks ago you'd given him up for the Jesuit
God."

"Ah, so I did. But I'm still a little of everything. Jansenist without
grace; Jesuit without love of poverty, chastity, and obedience."

"Once a Jesuit, always a Jesuit!" Aristide repeated the well-known allegation because he liked to hear Pierre rant on the subject of religion.

"But I never was really Jesuit in spite of the Abbé Blafond and my mother. You know I've been as bitter against them as some of the famous men who've broken away—Pascal, Descartes, Voltaire. I think I really broke away when the fat little Abbé taught me I must believe everything in the church, and of course when I came to have a doubt or two, I pulled out the bottom block and the whole tower fell. . . . And yet, do you know, Aristide, I must confess it's annoyed me that Nicki was never baptized. Some day when it's convenient for Father Carles we shall have a baptism. And I want you to be godfather! . . . There's a certain security in seeing a child borne on a lace cushion by its god-mother. And in watching the urchins scramble for the sous and bon-bons strewn on the street by the godfather . . . even if one believes with Diderot that there is no God!"

"So today you are an atheist!"

"You think I'm childish, don't you!" said Pierre a little peevishly.

"No one who thinks seriously is childish . . . but Diderot is so—depressing!"

"He can be very convincing. Of course so can Rousseau—and a dozen other philosophers. But you know they're only agreed on one thing—their scorn for each other's theories. And look at them! A new theory to every great thinker—Diogenes, believing that the soul is part of the substance of God; Epicurus, that it's composed of parts the same as the body; and good old Plato, who vowed it was both corporeal and eternal."

"I prefer Father Malebranche who was certain we live wholly in God —that God is, as it were, in our soul."

"Aristide, do you really believe in God?"

The Little Admiral drew a pipe and pouch of Indian tobacco from his pocket, filled his pipe, struck a spark with flint, and blew out a cloud of smoke before he answered.

"Have you ever felt the power in a storm at sea?"

"Your God then is of the heart, the emotions, rather than of the reason."

"God remains unchanged in spite of the theories of the philosophers or those of you and me. God can't be analyzed by a frail human being, can he? That's why he's God."

Pierre stared into the smoke of the pine knots. "I know what you mean, of course. I've felt God in a clod of earth that I've crushed. That's the same as your storm at sea, I suppose. But that's only a fleeting emotion, no proof of God's existence. Now and then I have a strong belief, bright and brief as a meteor. Then there are all the days between. . . ."

"But you still believe God is worth the searching."

"There are too many Gods! Since I'm little I've been bewildered by them. The God of the Jansenist! The God of the Jesuit! Zeus, and the Indian Manito! Holbach's God of Matter! Sometimes I hate the name of God! I curse the searching. It's like a fever that racks the body and weakens one. And here in the wilderness one must be strong to earn his bread and butter, to survive."

His lips were set in a thin, hard line.

"Now you do rant like a child, *mon ami!*" said Aristide. "You've spent too much time in learning what others think instead of thinking for yourself. Who has ever found God between the covers of a book? He is another man's God. . . . You know the story of the old Brahmin priest and the *religieuse*? He saw the old woman, thinking herself the happiest of women because she lived to get some of the sacred water from the Ganges in which to make her ablutions—believing in the bottom of her heart in the metamorphosis of Vishnu."

"*Oui,* I vaguely remember the story."

"And the old priest said: 'It's a happiness I do not desire!'"

"You think he was wise?" asked Pierre.

"*Mais oui.* Why should he attain to the old woman's happiness when he had a philosophy of his own?"

"Ah, but if he was a Jesuit I'll bet he tried to convert her."

"I don't know. The story ends there."

"So you think it's wise that you have your storm at sea—I have my clod of earth?"

"Natural, rather than wise. . . . But God is not only in the storm and the earth—not only in you and me. He is in the fifth dimension, which is the storm and me, the earth and you."

For a moment Pierre had hated Aristide for his confidence, his lack of anxiety.

"Perhaps you've never really loved a woman," said Aristide.

The statement was so incongruous that Pierre stared at him and had to laugh.

"I've loved dozens of women."

"I'm speaking of love, not lust."

"I've loved my mother," Pierre said firmly. "But I don't see that this has anything to do with God."

"Then I'm right that you've never really loved a woman as you should, my young Œdipus. And love—I don't mean infatuation—has a lot to do with God."

"You're very smug!"

"Don't be angry with me, Pierre. I simply mean you've never given wholly of yourself, either to God or woman."

Pierre had brooded. He was angry because Aristide was right and the truth was a painful revelation. To love with sacrifice had always seemed pretentious, contrary to the code of the day. Why should one be deprived of his freedom by actually loving? And what was so sweet to the Frenchman as his freedom? Freedom meant happiness; it was the oldest of the quotients. . . . And yet the philandering he had done with God and woman had not given him either freedom or happiness, and he knew it.

"You *are* angry with me!" said Aristide, with a warm pleading smile.

"*Non, non, non!* You're the first human being I've ever really loved, Aristide."

"Forgive me if I've seemed to preach."

"You've only made me resolve that I'm not going to die until I've lived fully."

"*Bien!* And when you die it will be very comfortable to have a God of your own to welcome you."

"Inferring, of course, that I cannot go back to my Maker until I have found Him!"

The conversation with Aristide slipped away as the voices of the small congregation rose in the *Gloria*.

He tried earnestly to think of God, to invite God into his soul. He would like to tell Aristide when he returned that he had faith at last, that he was no different from these others. But it was no use, for now he heard the boyish voice of Nicole, not so loud, but pure and clear, like a freshet.

Holbach, Diogenes, Malebranche . . . it was not even the voices of these that he listened for now above the *Gloria*.

It was only the voice of Nicole that mattered.

CHAPTER XXXIX

NEWS OF THE DAUPHIN reached the colony the night early in September that Pierre and Victoire had invited guests to a housewarming. Nicole was ready long before the time that M. Heraud was to escort her to the new Hôtel de Michelait. She stood at the window of her bedchamber and looked out on Luzerne Avenue. Pierre would no longer be walking by to the small cabin up the road. The little log house was already occupied by a bourgeois hairdresser and his wife from Marseilles. It was symbolic of her feeling for Pierre, she thought, that the cabin which was so close that she had been able to hear the ringing of his ax at its door, was now peopled with her own class. It would be easier to forget him, since he was lodged in the greater luxury that was the principle for which he fought.

It was good to be alone here in the dark, she thought. The dark was quiet and lulled the indefinable ache in her heart over the sumac and woodbine leaves turning crimson, over the prospect of another winter of hypocrisy and suspense. Supposing one of the plots of the Chevalier de Jarjayes or Lady Atkyns might be successful and the Dauphin would be smuggled to Switzerland or England instead of the States? There was every possibility too that if the Baron de Batz got the child to America he would never reach Asylum but be abducted by one of the other agents whom Barras had stationed in the seaports.

How much longer would she have to remain in Asylum—days, months, years? And how long would she be able to deceive the doctor? To avoid telling him that if she gave herself to M. de Michelait she would have no other thought but her longing for him—that to carry on one's duty, one could not be the mistress of a man and love him, too. . . . Even the simple Félicie Roucault knew this much of the laws of nature.

Félicie Roucault . . . alone in the dark, she could be Félicie Roucault for a moment, homesick for her family who lived proudly as Protestants in the Catholic province of the Vendée. How she wanted to hear the grave, sweet voice of her father, more healing to the sick than his medicine by far! How she wanted to watch her mother don a clean white apron and add a bay leaf to the soup or wash her grandmother's cups from the *vraisselier!* Often she thought of Gabrielle, sixteen, dreaming of knights over her books, laughing at Félicie who, like Jeanne d'Arc, she said, had been born with a purpose. And a purpose was deforming as a wart on the nose and never won a Galahad!

Nicole closed her eyes to the twinkling candles of Asylum the better to see Félicie Roucault in the shabby, provincial house. It was a humble place, small, set in a tract of half-baked sand furrowed by canals and completely flooded at times like a little Holland. There was only a ground floor with its great chimney piece jutting out into the room, the pyramid hood sucking up the smoke that escaped from the dried manure; at the foot of the beds perched on high legs on either side of the fireplace were chests of coarse clothing.

How different from the lush beauty of Asylum! How different—but home! . . . Félicie and Gabrielle were haggling again over the space in the amaranth and rosewood chests; the cat was rubbing her back on the heavily turned legs of the table; Jacques, sitting stiffly on a rush-bottomed chair, declared with his eyes the love that refused to come to his lips. . . . The doctor paced the floor; the child of the cobbler had died. . . . There was a goose for dinner today instead of ragout. . . . Mme Roucault was praying on her knees at her bedside, a Huguenot prayer for the lost souls of the Catholic cardinals. . . . The firelight came and went on the heavy mahogany of the room, breeding flame and shadow, as books had bred flame and shadow in the heart of Félicie.

Tangled memories, thought Nicole, senseless and bittersweet to a Mme de Louvenne across the sea! And the smaller the memory—the more insignificant—the sharper it ate into one's loneliness and longing.

The year of 1794 had brought the first separation from her family when Aunt Ninon, whose husband was being sent to the Convention, took the broody Félicie to Paris for a "change." Félicie had been reading too much, had been thinking too much for a girl of twenty, so they said. It had been a mistake to let her study all these years with the old lawyer who had once been a secretary to Voltaire. History and Latin didn't teach a girl to bake bread. And moreover M. Flèche was a physiocrat. That was a long name for one who believed all members of society should have the same rights, that nature furnished the model to which they should conform; and that the revenue of the state should be derived from a land tax. Yes, strange thoughts for a girl old enough to be tending her own babies! Far better if she had been made to marry one of her suitors: Jacques, a capable mason; or the son of the minister; or the gamekeeper of the Baron de Toile. . . .

Nicole sank onto the bed, crushing the fresh-pressed black taffeta. The miniature of Claude de Louvenne, the unknown child for whom she was in mourning, lay heavily between her breasts, a constant reminder of her bondage, like the Catholic crucifix which hung above her bed.

She had first known what it meant to be alive, she thought, when she went to Paris. Poor Aunt Ninon, she had meant so well, planning the "change" for Félicie, planning theater parties and soirées and meetings with nice young men. M. Barras's nephew Georges Brigaud had even been Aunt Ninon's favorite, and it had been quite simple to dupe Aunt Ninon about his politics, especially when the sudden onrush of the Terror sent her to bed.

The first meeting with M. Barras had been arranged by Georges Brigaud. M. Barras, of the anti-Robespierre faction, was already of the front rank. Though it was said that he was a dissolute and shameless adventurer Félicie had seen in him only the same purpose for which Gabrielle had taunted her. M. Barras believed in a republic. He wanted the Dauphin safe, in his own hands, in order to dominate the Comte de Provence in the event of a restoration. He needed men and women of unbounded courage to help him, to bring to the little man of France eventual liberty, he said. And he was impressed with a young girl who had dared to go to secret meetings in the fiery Vendée, a young girl who proclaimed she was willing to sacrifice life itself for the man in the streets. He had a job for Félicie if she would risk it. . . .

She had remained in Paris until after the execution of Robespierre, her heart heavy with indecision. Although she had faith in M. Barras there were things about the new, struggling France in which she did not believe. The Festival of the Supreme Being had been a pagan debauch; St. Just's proposal of an ideal society in which every man would have just enough land to sustain him was in accord with her hopes, but his belief that a dictator should take over this perfect state seemed futile as a monarchy. What difference if a Robespierre or a Bourbon ruled supreme? And there were some who said M. Barras would make a worse dictator than Robespierre. . . .

Terror-stricken, she had watched the execution under the law of seventeen thousand persons in fifteen months, had watched the carnage spread to the innocent, to peasants and artisans, children, and the aged. Would this mutual hatred ever make political liberty possible? . . .

Only if the rotten spots were gouged out of the apple. Robespierre had been a rotten spot. The Bourbons were rotten spots. She could help to get rid of a Bourbon. She must not waste more time with doubts and secret meetings.

And she had fled to America on her mission that August of 1794, her spirit lighter because at last she was acting instead of thinking.

Young Georges Brigaud had been needed in Paris. She had loved him with all the fanaticism of her new life and he had been right for her, she thought now as she gazed at the twinkling candles. Together they had planned for the future of France; they believed the same things; they dreamed the same dreams. If his kiss had not started the wild beating of her heart his ideals had kindled her mind, and that was the important thing. She knew that Georges Brigaud would be waiting for her as he had sworn he would and she would go back to him. It was Georges Brigaud, not Pierre de Michelait, who was right for her. . . .

There was a hesitant tap on the door. It would be little M. Heraud ready to go to the party, his long nose shining like his party pants, his fingers eager to show the company some new sleight of hand he had been practicing.

"You are ready, Madame?" came the gentle voice through the door. *"Oui, Monsieur."*

She opened her eyes and said to the dark: "Mme Nicole de Louvenne. I am no longer Félicie Roucault. . . . But I should like to have said good-bye to them—like to have told my father that this is the right thing, that I will do my work and go back to France to raise children and bake bread."

It would be strange going back to France, but it would be thrilling and beautiful too helping to build the new France. It would be hard to forget Asylum, and Pierre de Michelait, loathing her as a traitor to his cause. It would be hard. . . .

But M. Barras had chosen her because she was strong.

When Nicole and M. Heraud arrived at the party most of the guests had assembled. The musicale had already started. Wilhelmine Buzard, as the ingénue performer, was sapping the life from a Bach prelude. Her nail-bitten fingers goaded the keys of the new piano with the precision of a slave driver.

Nicole walked softly to the second salon, though if she had tramped she could not have been heard. She sat back in the shadows behind a few other latecomers. She was glad that M. Heraud had been detained by the chatty M. Bec-de-Lièvre. More and more as the consciousness of Pierre filled her she wanted to be alone.

She began to take a mechanical census of the rooms; brocaded chairs, ivory miniatures, delicate rose Venetian lusters. She felt suddenly closed in by the orchid-striped wallpaper, like a bonbon in a candy box.

With shrewd eyes she knew the tempo of the soirée at once. And the tempo had no connection with Wilhelmine Buzard's stoic playing.

Nicole knew that Louis d'Autremont's eyes were on her folded hands, her miniature, the white of her bosom, her lips half parted in an apologetic smile. She was not looking at Louis d'Autremont, but she could feel his eyes as if they traced a dotted line from her hands, to her hair, smoothed high now in a black-bowed coil. He was a sweet boy, Louis d'Autremont. Mme Roucault would have thought him an excellent match. . . . Dr. Buzard, it seemed, would like to have a word with her alone. (He was scratching his left ear with his snuffbox.) The whites of his eyes were barely visible. And he was sitting much too straight, alert. Ah, and what was this? The new San Domingan, Mme Reynaud, must be carried away by the virtuoso or surely she would not allow her hand to lie fallow in Major Hoops's under her fan!

Was anybody listening to the music, thought Nicole. Mme de Michelait was subtly counting heads. M. Carles in a dark corner had ostensibly forgotten to clean his nails at home. René Buzard, the only child present in deference to his sister's début, was practicing knots with two bits of string. Even Mme Buzard was obviously waiting for the moment when Wilhelmine would make her bow and Maman could relax and spread her feathers.

As many types of men and women as there were small emotions of love, ennui, fear, jealousy. Men and women who wanted the old régime; men and women who wanted the Dauphin as a figurehead to a democracy; men and women who wanted the Republic; men and women who wanted security and wealth above all, and the type of government be damned! Men and women who wanted only a little peace. All of them knit together in their need for bread and butter into the doubtful unity of Asylum—drawn together at this moment by the universal language of Wilhelmine Buzard's music. The lid kept on the box by Bach. . . .

She must have applauded, Nicole thought, for now the little doll-faced Mme d'Autremont was accompanying M. de la Roué on the violin.

Moving forward only a trifle, Nicole could see Pierre. He stood leaning against the doorway that divided the salons, and his black hair caught the candlelight as the black water of a pool reflects the moon. His arms folded, his head back, he was staring at a portrait of Marie Antoinette with her hand on the Dauphin's shoulder. But his heavy brows were drawn in a frown, as if he looked beyond the painting.

Nicole had a swift longing to know what he might be thinking, to explore the deep recesses of his mind, as in France she had explored the minutiae of his life. She had come to Asylum prepared to hate him, to gather courage and impetus from her hatred. And she had known at once with the wild beating of her heart that she would be unable to hate him.

She lowered her eyes. Her heart did not beat so wildly if she looked away from him, away from his lips. She had come here tonight with a purpose and she did not mean to come again. She had come here to be stifled with the mingling of fresh paint and sawed wood and gentlewomen's scents. It was the antidote she needed for the wild beating of her heart. This was Pierre's house because Victoire's pearls and emeralds had conceived it, and at night he lay with Victoire in his embrace. Yes, coming here would help her to remember that his world was as foreign to hers as the moon to the sun, and that he had always gotten what he wanted only to scrap the old for the new. It would be easy now to forget the tall, lank figure passing by the inn in his buckskins. If she thought of him at all she would think of him winding the exquisite clock on the mantel, taking snuff from the mother-of-pearl box, touching the keys of the piano with the delicacy of a marquis. . . .

But she had no idea if he could play a note of music. Strange, she had thought she knew everything about him, but she did not know if he could play a note of music! . . . It maddened her that she did not know. She must know at once, even if it meant rushing up between valiant listeners and demanding to know in a voice loud with tears! . . . But what was coming over her? It was as if she'd been running. . . .

Pierre had seen her. He was not looking at her, but there was no longer the air of detachment. It was almost as if he had answered her about the music, as if he had sent to her a silent communication through the strong mingling of sawed wood and perfume. . . . There was a certain release of tension, an ease of bearing and expectancy as he watched the contortions of M. de la Roué.

Yes, the house was stifling. Nicole rose and slipped through the half-open doorway and out to the piazza that led to the dining-room. The two Negro servants were arranging *petits-fours* and ices and bonbons on the lace-gowned table. The Marquise, thought Nicole, would have her silver surtout on a cake of ice if she were stranded at the North Pole! And stranded at the North Pole, the Marquise would first gain the respect of the Eskimos by making whale soup a little better than the natives. Victoire de Michelait was a woman to be reckoned with, a woman of no mean stamina and astuteness.

The night was moving up fresh from the river, dispelling the softness of the late summer's dark, and the moon, like a soap bubble, paused in its flight on the top of Rummerfield Mountain. The garden had a restless look, with its stumps of newly guillotined trees. Someone had deserted a wheelbarrow filled with gravel beside an unfinished path. The summerhouse of a few weeks' standing, waited, anxious there in the gloom, holding no secrets, longing for clinging vines and lovers. Loose, upturned soil and unused lumber gave out a raw woodsy smell. In the corner of the piazza were a clutter of tools and some cans of paint.

Nicole stood at the rail, breathing deeply, recalling the night she had said good-bye in Paris to Georges Brigaud. He was right for her and she would go back to him, and she prayed to God that it might be soon. She tried to think how he looked, and felt a sense of panic that his features evaded her.

She knew Pierre's footstep, and her heart began to race again madly. But she continued to look down at the fringe of trees that bearded the river.

"You are not . . . ill, Madame?"

"No, Monsieur. Only restless," she said, trying to tame her voice. "It is very beautiful here with the view of the river. . . . Can you lie abed and see the river flowing? It must be soothing, like a cradle."

"I preferred the cabin in the woods."

"But why, Monsieur?"

"I built it with my own hands. Every board, every peg, was an old friend."

The words hurt her a little, and she turned away from him. She was angry with herself again. Now that he was beside her she knew why she had come out to the piazza, that her coming was only an invitation for him to follow. And she had supposed she was faint from the warmth of candles and people. So, she could not even be honest with herself any more! How could she ever expect to overcome this futile, dangerous emotion if she could not at least be honest with herself?

She said shortly: "You will soon make friends with the new house."

"When Nicki has laughed in it, perhaps."

"And when you've scattered your books over the tables and chairs and floors!"

"Dieu, how shall I ever find what I want! They're all in order on the book shelves, half hidden by Sèvres."

"You speak like a bourgeois, M. de Michelait. You will scarce be fit for the Château de Grenauld when they put the Dauphin on the throne."

"Poor little Dauphin! He will never come out of the Temple alive." Pierre kicked aside a curlicue of shavings.

"Non? There have been so many attempts to steal him from the Committee of Public Stafety, surely one must succeed?" she angled. *"M. le Duc* de Liancourt thinks it will not be long. . . ."

"The first gentleman of the King's bedchamber is an odd hybrid. An enthusiast of the American cause and yet willing to stake his life and fortune trying to rush the royal family to the coast and safety. . . . If *M. le Duc* had spent less time translating the American Federal Constitution of 1789 and the constitutions of the young states—"

"M. le Duc has always believed in a remodeling job, *n'est-ce pas?* But do you think, Monsieur, that one can take an old house struck by lightning and put on it a roof the wind will not blow off?"

"By the old house you mean France, no doubt. And Louis Charles is the roof?"

"Oui, Monsieur, if you like. . . ."

"Not if one uses rotting boards for the roof," he said guardedly.

"Ah, that is a great admission for a Royalist of your stamp to make. It is practically treason! . . . But we're in a maze of metaphors. As for me, M. de Michelait, I still believe in the old régime. We need loyalty to one man to be secure as a state—loyalty to the Crown."

"You *are* old-fashioned! That was all right when the state was intangible, when the feudal system started because wealth lay in the land. That was all right for the barbarians of the year 900. But this is the year 1795, with a Constitution!"

This was very funny, she thought, scarcely able to control her laughter. M. de Michelait was too smart to wear his heart on his sleeve.

He had work to be done, too. This was like an exchange of *étrennes,*
this conversation. She and Pierre were handing one another packages
fancy with paper and ribbon, concealing the nature of the gifts within.

"Marie Antoinette should have come here with her children those
early days in the Temple when it was easy to escape," she said.

"The Queen was proud—the proudest and sweetest woman who
ever lived. She would never have deserted Louis."

"But we would have had our little Prince here safe—where the eyes
of the world would never think of looking for him. Even now it would
not be too late, M. de Michelait. . . . It would be the ideal place to
hide him, *n'est-ce pas?*"

"Do you know, it has just come to me that your voice is like that
of Mme Roland? Low and clear—and mellow. . . . My father was a
Girondin. He used to frequent the Roland salons. Now and then I
went with him. . . . Deep and mellow—her voice has haunted me
through the years."

Nicole felt the wild beating of her heart again. But this time it was
not for Pierre. Why should he shift the subject—unless he had been
taken unaware? Asylum was to be the hide-out then! The ideal place
for the Dauphin! . . . But of course, they were talking of the voice of
Mme Roland.

"Perhaps it is only the voice of conviction," she said. "Even though
Mme Roland was convinced of her new republic, and I, as you said a
moment ago, am still barbaric."

"Mme Roland's voice had more than conviction. It had a spiritual
beauty, a sort of chastity. She had the fire of a Charlotte Corday and
the energy of a Marat. . . . One could hear all of these things in her
voice."

"M. de Michelait, I fear I am not very good company these days."

"You have come out here alone to dream of him again?"

"Mais oui, Monsieur."

"M. de Louvenne was good to you then, Madame?"

"He loved me and he was true to me."

"But of course."

"Why do you say of course? What does a courtier know of faithfulness?"

"If he knows nothing of faithfulness it's because he knows nothing
of the kind of woman you are, Madame."

"That was a pretty speech, Monsieur."

"It was not a speech, it was from the heart," he said curtly.

"You have no idea what kind of woman I am. I scarcely know myself."

"We have an instinct about people. It isn't the facts that matter. It seemed to me when you first came here that I had known you for a long time, perhaps always."

The night air that had felt so balmy at first was beginning to chill her. She unfolded the shawl on her arm, and Pierre helped her to draw it about her shoulders. His fingers touched the nape of her neck, and if she had not seen him fold his hands firmly on the rail she would have believed that his fingers lingered there at the nape of her neck.

"You *must* remember the times we've talked together," he said, urgently, "the times before you saved Nicki."

"I've told you I do not remember."

"I don't mean the words that were said. I mean the fullness of saying them. The way one remembers a love he has never known. The way a child knows he has lived a million years in his ancestors when he looks at a shooting star. . . ."

"You are the very *soul* of poetry, Monsieur." She was shivering now with the cold.

"Don't mock me. I couldn't bear it. . . . In those moments alone with you I found something I've never had from another woman. I want to keep it."

She struggled to think of an answer, to turn the subject away from them.

"If you can't remember that day at the picnic I am going to tell you about it—I want you to know. I went back to thank you for saving Nicki. You were alone. You were scratched and torn and there were twigs caught in your hair. I felt when you looked at me that you had done this thing for me as well as for Nicki, that—"

"Monsieur!"

"Let me finish. I've got to say this to you! . . . I had always wanted to know the touch of your hair, to feel its softness. I wanted to run my fingers through your hair the way a miser wants to run his hands through gold. . . . And then, like a miser, I wanted more. And you let me take you close, and I kissed you. And for a moment I knew you felt as I felt, that there had never been anything like this for either of us."

"Monsieur!"

"It was very sweet, Nicole."

"Your life has been full of this—sweetness!"

"You're the only woman I have ever loved!"

"You must forget this, Monsieur! But at once! I was shaken, lonely, out of my senses if I allowed you to touch me."

"Do you know," he went on in a voice so low that it was scarcely audible now that Victoire had begun to play, "it was the one moment since you came that I felt you were not alone—in your heart, I mean."

"We are always alone, Monsieur—all of us, even when we are with those we love—perhaps more when we are with those we love—because we expect them to understand. And they try, they reach out to our yearning—and fail."

"*Oui, oui, oui.* I know what you mean. I remember the first time it came to me—with a shock, the way truth often comes through the little things. . . . I was riding my horse near Passy. I passed a peasant boy and girl on the road. They were holding hands. She was just going to pick a buttercup from the roadside when he pointed out the sunset. She looked at it and smiled at him, and then she stooped and picked her buttercup and handed it to him. He was still looking at the sunset. I remember feeling a little sad. They had different ideas of beauty. They were trying to reach one another, and soon the sunset would fade and the flower would wilt. And they would only have one another's hand. And because neither had felt the vision of the other there must have been a little loneliness in each of them. . . . I don't know why I am telling you this. It was so insignificant. I have never thought of it since until now. . . ."

"It is the most significant thing in life, Monsieur. And how could it be otherwise? God has compressed a million souls of the past into every living heart—each man different—no two the same—each loneliness a little different from the other. . . . That's why men turn to God."

"But now and then one soul touches another."

"Only for a shivering instant, Monsieur. It's not enough, but it is all that we can ask."

"My poor little peasant lovers! They must have had so much hope."

"Isn't it better that youth starts out with hope? . . . It gives us courage—for the long road alone."

"You have an old philosophy for a woman who is young—and a woman in love."

She was silent.

"You *are* in love with your husband, aren't you?"

"Yes, Monsieur. But love and age aren't the only teachers."

"What then?"

"Tragedy—disillusionment."

"Disillusionment is part of age. I remember my early days at court. As long as there was gaiety and laughter I never felt alone. A pretty face, a rendezvous, were all I could want. Then a little later I began to need books."

"Oui, Monsieur?"

"I can look back at those days now with a fair perspective. I had no feeling of being immoral. I was only living like others about me. I can see now it wasn't so much that we had a greed for lust as a passion to be understood—a poignant need, never to be fulfilled. Men and women lost and wandering—with a dreadful seeking that went on day after day, hour after hour! And so we filled our days and hours with hunts and balls and *pâtés de foie gras* and nakedness. . . ."

"You were only a dog, Monsieur, that knew he existed."

"Exactement! Now at least I am a human being, for I know that I know!"

"One doesn't become a man, Monsieur, till he has learned to walk alone with dignity and courage."

"Do you always think of me with contempt?"

"Non, non, non. I think of you with pity."

He began to say something but the powerful chords of Victoire were annihilating. They filled the ears and the valley and the soul with thunder. Nicole felt her body trembling. She had no desire now to lie to herself. She knew that she trembled because she loved Pierre and because he was so close that the hem of his coat moved the folds of her gown.

Although she was unable to see the sharp black eyes she knew that they embraced her and that he trembled even as she did. It seemed that the thunder of the music engulfed them like a storm, and she wanted to cry out that she had need of him, that she would not sacrifice this moment although it would mean to her a life of despair and humiliation. For while they talked of lonelines she had not been alone. It was as if her hands had been locked with Pierre's and their hearts had beat hard, one for the other. And if they were only the peasants of Passy, one with his sunset, one with her flower—there was the illusion of the moment.

The applause began as thunderous as the chords, then dwindled suddenly as if by a signal. The voice of M. Talon was soft, mechanical, like the ticking of a clock.

"*Mes amis,*" he said, "news has just come with the post. News of the death of our Dauphin in the Temple. June the eighth . . . long live the King!"

There was no sound in the valley now, no sound in her heart. There was only the stillness of fog. She gripped the rail for support.

Then Pierre said tautly: "*Après-vous, Madame,*" and he stepped back to make way for her so that she might return to the salon.

❁❁❁❁❁❁❁❁❁❁❁❁❁❁❁❁❁❁❁❁❁❁

CHAPTER XL

M. TALON was the last to leave the party. There had been little thought of food, the Buzard children taking on almost the entire burden of the *petits-fours*. What effect would the death of the Dauphin have on the politics of France? Would the Comte de Provence, now Louis XVIII, renew his efforts to consolidate Royalist France? Was home a little closer?

During the general excitement M. Talon whispered to Pierre, who filled his wineglass: "He's safe; more—later."

Pierre offered to walk down the road with Talon. Perhaps a bit of exercise would help him sleep, he told Victoire, who was as grateful to the Dauphin for enlivening her party as she had been to the truculent sheep at the fete at Passy.

As they walked through the moonlight Pierre and M. Talon talked impersonally of farms. When they were once behind the closed door of Talon's study, when Wallois had been dismissed for the night, the windows closed and the curtains drawn, Talon faced Pierre with an air of triumph.

"He is safe," whispered Talon softly. "It was a miracle! . . . I have a letter here, in code of course, from—the walls so often have ears! Read it yourself and then burn it. It came today in the same post as—"

Pierre was embracing him, his eyes blinded with tears.

"*Dieu Merci,*" he returned in a whisper, "I had almost given up hope!"

They settled themselves in two *bergères* before the high carved fireplace. The study was polished as M. Talon himself, with walls of walnut reflecting the candlelight, a huge secretary—its books and papers methodically arranged—and a grandfather's clock that thumped out a joyous eleven.

Talon reached into his pocket and drew out a letter ostensibly from his attorney in Paris, reporting in detail on family affairs and properties. The handwriting was that of the secretary of the Baron de Batz. Pierre deciphered it slowly:

26 Prairial an 3

Monsieur,

First, I want to inform you that in spite of the official report of the Dauphin's death on June 8th, the escape of the Dauphin has at last been effected!

I hope that my letter will reach you before any public announcement which would occasion you shock and pain.

I have informed you that during October of last year, it seemed likely to me that there had been a substitution for Louis Charles on the third floor of the Tower, and that the Dauphin was still in the Temple. As you know, the Jacobin faction has kept close surveillance of the child, especially since M. Barras appointed Christophe Laurent as the boy's guardian in July of last year.

From October on, there have been reports that the Dauphin refused to talk at any time, and I could conclude that a dumb child had been substituted for Louis Charles. Doctors who saw him reported that the child suffered from a tumor on the wrist, and tumors on both knees. Caron, the pantry boy whom I have managed to place in the Temple, was never able to see the child, but knowing the Dauphin's tastes in food, deduced that the Dauphin had been supplanted by some little bourgeois.

In May of this year, the Convention found itself definitely embarrassed by the child's existence. (As I have not communicated with you for several months, and do not know what facts you may be in possession of through the public news, I will go into detail, to be certain your information is reliable.) Negotations were being made in the spring with the violent Vendée, which was still eloquent on the boy's behalf; peace with Spain did not seem possible without surrendering the person of the child to that country; in England, a French Royalist expedition was preparing to embark in British warships for descent on France in the name of Louis Charles

In May, a Doctor Desault who had never seen the Dauphin, was called in by the Convention to attend him, and being considered the source of rumors spread throughout the city that this child was not really the Dauphin, it seems M. le Docteur found himself mysteriously ill and died suddenly in June.

Only two weeks ago, I had another report from Caron that a second substitute had been smuggled in by M. Barras and his cohorts to replace the first substitute. This second substitute was a child who was ill enough that he could be expected to die soon. Caron also reported to me at that time that he felt almost certain he knew in what portion of the Temple the Dauphin had been hidden.

M. Pelletan, a doctor, a scoundrel, and rabid partisan of the Revolution, was called in to the Temple about June 6th, and finding the supposed Dauphin suffering from dysentery, he prescribed for him. On June 7th, at eleven in the evening, Pelletan was sent for, but did not come as he claimed that night time was "not favorable for any kind of remedy." When Pelletan arrived on the morning of the eighth with a colleague, the boy was in a critical condition, with discolored and bloated belly, and by the afternoon, the Committee of General Security was notified that he was having a violent spasm following a dose of potion ordered for him. Although summoned again, M. Pelletan did not arrive until after the death of the child in midafternoon.

Paris, of course, whispered poison. The Convention seemed indifferent. The Vendée rose in arms at once, but the expedition from England was forestalled, and it looks even now as if peace with Spain will be effected.

An autopsy of the child was made in the utmost secret, and the doctors recorded the fact that they had found "the corpse of a child who appeared to us to be about ten years old, which the Commissioners stated to us to be that of the son of Louis Capet." Burial in the Temple Parish grave-yard was ignominious and furtive, and Mme Royale has still not been informed of the death of her brother, though she may now use the Temple garden.

Naturally you are not so eager for these details as for those of the escape of the Dauphin himself. I apologize for my procrastination. On June fifth Caron was able to chloro-form and gag the Dauphin's warden and the boy was smuggled out of the Temple in a hamper of wash. Caron's brother was the accomplice, and escorted the cart full of dirty line through the streets to his home. During the night the Dauphin was transferred to the house of one of my agents, and in due time, when the first excitement dies down, will be traveled to the Vendée, thence to England by water, and finally to America. Naturally his arrival in America may be many months hence, but you will be in-formed upon his arrival in Philadelphia by a Mrs. Williams, who will nurse him. I grieve to report that the Dauphin is in lamentable condition, but I think that good care will re-store him to health.

If plans do not evolve smoothly, I shall notify you in the usual manner. I know that you and the Marquis de Miche-lait rejoice with me on your long-awaited success, and in the name of Louis XVII I salute you for your loyalty and faithfulness.

I have the honor to be with great respect and esteem, dear sir,

> *Your most obedient*
> *and most humble servant,*
> *Jean de Batz.*

"Incredible!" whispered Pierre, and the letter shook in his hands. "Incredible, but true!"

Their eyes met in mutual restraint and caution. Then Talon's hand made a motion toward the fire.

Pierre sank to his knees on the great bearskin rug, took a half-burn-ing ember from the hearth and lighted the corner of the letter, watch-ing the brown scallops eat into the fine handwriting. He wanted to

shout with joy and victory, and he must do his work here as if he
mourned, a dark bottle of effervescing wine tightly corked.

"I shall want you to go to Philadelphia when the time comes. You
were intimate . . . you would know any fallacy at once. . . ."

"I would know my little Prince with my eyes closed! . . . Born
gay! But under what pretext will you bring him here?"

"My widowed niece will die crossing the ocean. It will behoove me
to take her son as my ward."

"But how can you deceive others who knew him?"

"The years change a child. You forget how long he has been in
the Temple. And there is the official word of his death."

"Somehow I am a little frightened. Has it occured to you, M. Talon,
that there might be others here who know—who might be spies?"

Talon's small mouth turned up quizzically, and he smoothed the
threadlike wrinkles of his brow.

"*Mais oui,* it has occurred to me. Not likely, but possible," he said in
a voice so low that Pierre had to strain to hear it. "The Reynauds
from San Domingo . . . what did we know of them? I think it best
to discourage newcomers from now on, in spite of the advice of the
Duc de Liancourt."

"You've had no suspicions?" asked Pierre tensely.

"*Non, non, non!* Or I would have shared them with you at once.
But it won't hurt to suspect everybody. And now I think it is better
that you go, *mon ami*—with a proper look of melancholy for Louis
XVII, and a faint trace of rejoicing for His Majesty, Louis XVIII. . . .
What do you say to our fishing tomorrow in some very remote spot
without echoes?"

Some weeks later Victoire and Nicki and Mme Reynaud took a
stroll to the shop of M. Bec-de-Lièvre, near the ferry landing.

It was a tiny one-floor cabin boasting a fancy sign "Bec-de-Lièvre, *Épi-
cier.*" No one was there, but a fire busied itself in the fireplace. Running
over and about the small casement windows were smooth, sanded
shelves; on these, helter-skelter and friendly as M. Bec-de-Lièvre's chatter, were medicine bottles, herbs, snuff, copper pans, bonbons. There
were lightning rods and nails and window panes for new house; there
were scissors and needles and bolts for the seamstress; there were
cordials and tea and chocolate for the salon. Nicki was always as entranced with its wares as an Indian with his first glimpse of Paris.

Victoire fingered everything and chided Nicki for not keeping his hands to himself. Mme Reynaud, matching a skein of silk to a bit of material, went to the window for better light and saw Nicole coming down the road.

"Here comes the Queen," she whispered to Victoire, and with her sloth eyes on the entrance by which M. Bec-de-Lièvre might enter: "I'm convinced she doesn't know Le Cap. . . . Twice I've asked her very pointed questions about places and she's evaded me. And one night Dr. Buzard answered my question as if I'd been talking to him instead of Mme de Louvenne. . . . But why would she lie? . . . Do you know, sometimes I think she's Dr. Buzard's mistress and her story is just a ruse to fool the Sultana."

Victoire laughed. She had reasons to know that the doctor was not in love with Nicole.

"How I'd love to be the one to trip her!" she exclaimed, and as Nicole entered the shop she added: "I think the silk's a very good match, Mme Reynaud, don't you?"

The three women chatted with frozen cordiality, waiting for M. Bec-de-Lièvre to answer the tinkle of bells on the door.

Nicki, his small cherry nose running from the sudden heat of the cabin, was forgotten and happily explored the maple-sugar barrel.

"Ah, Mme de Louvenne, how I miss our beautiful shops at Le Cap," said Mme Reynaud, slyly languorous. "At times like this, for instance, when I want silk for a new scarf. . . . Don't you long for our famous M. Troupe and his marvelous stock of skeins?"

"I was better acquainted with the shops of Port-au-Prince," answered Nicole, suavely.

"*Naturellement,*" said Mme Reynaud. "You must have dealt then at the shop of M. Morget—just as fine as M. Troupe's—Famous all over the island."

Nicole nodded absently, and Mme Reynaud, approaching her with a sort of triumphant stealth, went on with her vivisection.

"M. Morget's mustache was the talk of the colony—*wasn't it,* Mme de Louvenne?"

"*Mais oui! . . .*" Nicole's hesitation had been no more than the flick of a hummingbird's wing. She was examining a copper kettle.

"Of course you know, Mme de Michelait, that Port-au-Prince has shops as fine as those of Paris," said Mme Reynaud, shooting a brief glance of triumph at Victoire. "For instance, there's nothing to com-

pete with the patisserie on the rue de Vrons, *is there*, Mme de Louvenne?"

"Nothing," said Nicole, not raising her eyes.

Mme Reynaud straightened and almost smiled as M. Bec-de-Lièvre
bustled into the shop.

When the two friends had made their purchases and drifted out
into the fall sunshine, Mme Reynaud said avidly: "I've caught her!
There's no M. Troupe—no M. Morget—no mustache! . . . I never
heard of a rue de Vrons!"

"So we've got the little fly in the web at last!" Victoire ejaculated.
"Now all we have to do is eat her! . . . What is she? Who is she?
Why is she here? I knew I was right! . . . Not knowing at first if
she was married! Fooh!"

Victoire hadn't felt such intense pleasure since coming to Asylum.

They returned to Mme Reynaud's and sent Nicki to play with the
children while they considered every possibility but the right one.

When she arrived home, Victoire found Dr. Buzard at the house
bandaging a burn on Frau Gresch's hand.

It took no cajoling to get him out to the summerhouse when he
had finished.

"Mme Reynaud and I have made a most exciting discovery!" she
whispered. "Mme de Louvenne is a fake!"

There was a spark of life in the tired yellow dog eyes that Victoire
had never seen as the doctor demanded an explanation.

Victoire elaborated and made a great deal of the mustache. She had
never told the story of the Duc de Menneville with as great a relish.
Doctor Buzard's answer, his lack of excitement, were like a shower
of hailstones.

"Only part of her illness," he said, mopping his face. "A fuzzy mind
. . . can't even remember sometimes the things she's known best. She
cried the other day when she told me she couldn't remember the face
of her husband."

"But why should she lie to us? Mme Reynaud thinks—"

"So you won't think she's stupid—natural pride! . . . I'm beginning
to think myself that the case is hopeless. Likely a brain tumor or—"

"You really feel she's worse?" asked Victoire. Dr. Buzard's hand was
on hers, and she was gratified that it shook with passion.

"But of course! . . . She'll end by swallowing poison or tossing herself into the river. . . ."

He cast aside the subject by taking Victoire in his arms. She forgot Nicole, for his large gleaming smile was flattering and possessive.

"You little witch!" he whispered, backing her into a screen of morning-glories. "How long are you going to keep me waiting?"

The next morning there was fresh news for the colony. Imagine— Mme du Louvenne had had another *fugue!* This time she remembered nothing of her life before the death of her child on the ocean. Dr. Buzard, it seemed, was not surprised. For a long time he had seen her memory for San Domingo slipping. . . .

❁❁❁❁❁❁❁❁❁❁❁❁❁❁❁❁❁❁❁❁❁❁❁

CHAPTER XLI

Spring 1796

THE FOLLOWING SPRING M. Talon had a brief note from Mrs. Williams, who was lodged in a Philadelphia pension with her "charge."

Pierre prepared at once to leave on the next Durham boat from Tioga Point. For months he had lived under the greatest tension. The winter had been a successful fury, with stubborn snows and a dearth of food. A pair of oxen he had bought for seventy dollars died of some strange malady. And as if the fury were not satisfied by spring, a heavy frost had returned to raid the fruit trees in bloom.

In March an epidemic had swept the valley, bringing chills and fever followed by a chest ailment that lingered and wasted the victim. Dr. Buzard had worked day and night, baffled by its tenacity. He had even resorted to primitive treatment: sweat baths in blankets in the Indian style followed by a dip in an icy creek. John Herman's mother had pounded herbs into a hot brewed drink, and muttered spells over the sick. She herself had been the first to die. Two of the farmers' children had died also, and the bourgeois hairdresser from Marseilles who had tenanted Pierre's cabin. One of the Reynaud children had succumbed. The whole de Michelait household had had its turn, leaving everyone irritable and enervated.

Victoire, Mme d'Autremont, Nicole, and others who had fearlessly nursed the sick were thin and haggard. By spring it seemed that the colony was living on nerves. There was unrest among the slaves, and several disappeared when news reached the colony that the Negro Toussaint had been promoted to Brigadier General by the French Directory and was now recognized as the foremost black man in Haiti —indeed in the world. News from France was no more sanguine: although Mme Royale had been released from the Temple and sent to Austria, the few *émigrés* who had returned to France were watched with the strictest surveillance by the Directory, who feared their intrigue and excluded them and all their relatives from any sort of office. The power of France lay in the hands of five men including a fiery little Corsican named Bonaparte, who even had the brashness to fall in love with Barras's mistress, Joséphine de Beauharnais.

Cards and music were neglected for talk of politics; since the Dauphin's death all hope was pinned on subversive movements in France to bring Louis XVIII to the throne. The subject was bandied about like an old rubber ball that grows limp and cracked with the playing.

Victoire, who spent a great deal of time with Mme Reynaud, stated that she would never live here another winter, and Pierre knew that this time she meant it. Often he wondered how their problem must eventually be solved. Nicki adored her more as time went on, for she was inordinately proud of him. His lively green eyes sparkled with her outrageous stories; she had become adept at drawing caricatures of the colonists; she read him fairy tales with lavish gestures; and although she even went coasting with him in the winter she never for a moment let him forget that he was the son of a marquis. Pierre marveled at her maternity, and yet it was not so much that, he thought, as an instinct to bewitch every male within sight. Sometimes he was frankly jealous, but he told himself that as the years went on, Nicki would necessarily belong to him. As the years went on . . . would he and Victoire and Nicki be living together?

Aristide had been forced to stay in New York with the return of an old tropical fever caused by the fatigue and exposure of the Niagara trip. Pierre missed him keenly. With Aristide gone, the problems of the colony and his own personal qualms seemed paramount. The Little Admiral would return with the warm weather, but summer seemed a long way off.

And the summer—what might it bring? What would there be to plan for with the Dauphin safe in the valley? Would it be two years, five years, twenty years, before Louis Charles sat on the throne? Now that this first moment of triumph was at hand why should it seem to bring with it a melancholy? Or did this dismal outlook derive from frustration—from passion for Nicole unfulfilled? What was there about her that kept him in tow like a chained puppy? A few years ago if he had felt this passion for a woman he would have left no stone unturned till he had won her for his mistress. He tried to understand himself. Thinking led him round in a circle. Books became vacuous.

The night before Pierre was to leave he went to Heraud's inn. He wanted to say good-bye to Nicole, and he wanted to see her alone, though he knew that this would be difficult.

M. Heraud had lately gone into the haberdashery business with a newcomer, Barthelémi Laporte. A small one-story cabin had been added to the *auberge*. M. Laporte's brother, being a captain in the East India trade, had already sent his first shipment of shawls, hand-worked *mouchoirs,* tortoise-shell combs and bolts of silk. The new wares had made M. Bec-de-Lièvre's shop near the landing seem primitive.

It was a warm May night and there was a chorus of lively singing issuing from the open door of the taproom. But also there was a light in the shop, which was usually closed after dark. Pierre walked up to one of the small-paned windows and looked in. The shop was cluttered with finery newly arrived, and Nicole was on her knees unpacking some delicate china from the Orient. He watched her for a few moments and wondered if this was how he would remember her while he was gone and if he would ever see her again after tonight. Better perhaps not to pour out the things that crowded into his mind at thought of a permanent separation; better not to touch her hand and know that it was for the last time.

Her eyes, which had never seemed large, were huge and dark in the pallor of her face. Now and then she brushed a strand of hair from her cheek with the back of her hand. A fit of coughing struck her and she rested a moment, leaning wearily back against a packing case.

Pierre knocked on the window with a sudden instinct to rescue her from some unknown fate. Alarmed, she peered at the darkness then recognized his voice. He thought that she hesitated a second before she unbolted the door. A tinkle of mocking sleigh bells ushered him in.

He stood there looking at her, wordless, smiling, and then she began to smile too as she rubbed her smudgy hands on her apron.

"A woman's work is never done," he said.

"No, Monsieur." And she went down on her knees again, unpacked another cup of fine porcelain, and held it to the candlelight to test its perfection.

"You're not going to be polite and ask me to sit down?" he said.

"I thought you were going through to the inn."

"I've come to say good-bye to you."

Her eyes met his briefly, and she waved her hand grandly toward a small chest on which was a music box. He put the music box on the floor and squatted down on the chest.

"You're tired," he said. "Why don't you stop?"

"If I stop, I think."

Once more he silently cursed M. de Louvenne. It seemed improbable that love for a man she hadn't seen for almost two years could so obsess her. And yet it wasn't impossible. He would never forget Nicole.

"I hate him," he said quickly. "I hate him for giving you anguish. . . . Why can't he find you? Unless—"

"Please, Monsieur! We have said these same things before."

"And if he is dead you will go on loving him!"

"*Oui, Monsieur . . . Ah, c'est triste!*—here is one with a nick!"

I am going back to Georges Brigaud, she thought. I've promised to go back when my work is done. I loved him once; I can love him again. But I mustn't look up—I shall burst into tears. Tomorrow and the next day he won't be here . . . I've always been able to think of him somewhere in the village. If he's gone a day or a month or a year it won't really matter. . . . After tomorrow a day will be long as a month, a year. . . . If only he'd go—leave me alone!"

Pierre had started the music box.

"Don't!" she cried.

He looked up in surprise, snapping off the music.

"It's such a gay little tune I thought—"

"I've always hated it!"

"If you *must* finish this work tonight I'm going to help you," he said, and he began to delve into the chest for a piece of china.

"I'd rather do it alone."

"Can't you be civil to me? I'll be gone tomorrow . . . I may never see you again. Do you know what that means to me?"

"I'll be here when you return."

"If you haven't found him—if he hasn't found you."

He's an aristocrat, she thought. I despise him and all of his kind. He wants one thing, and I want another. He is going to bring the Dauphin here, and I am going to abduct him. . . . Can he hear my heart? I should have let him play the music. . . .

"I may be gone a long time." Pierre was not concentrating very well on the unwrapping. "If I ever see you again I want to feel that I've told you a few things about myself. . . . Won't you come into the garden where we can sit down and talk?"

"We can talk here."

He wet his fingers and put out the candles. There was an outburst of laughter from the taproom as if from an unseen audience.

Without a word she led the way to the little garden behind the shop, where there was a rustic bench under a lilac shrub. They were enveloped by darkness, for the moon had just waned.

"I want you to know what I am from myself, not from what you've heard of me or what you think of me," he said. "Often I have the feeling that you despised me—because I was of the court and its corruption—that you're too pure to understand the temptation of the life there."

"I believe in the old régime."

"*Oui*, Nicole, I know. But in an old régime bathed and scrubbed and dressed in a new suit. . . . Again, I think you hate me because we've had a few moments together of—of desire. And you hate yourself for being weak, for forgetting a vow. So you hate me too. . . . Won't you be honest with me? It'll be good for both of us—if this is the last time we're together."

"I can't be honest with you."

Pierre was silent a moment, depressed, conscious that she was far away from him although he could feel the warmth of her nearness.

"I won't urge you then. You must have your good reason. But I want you to see me as I really am. I'm not really rotten at heart. I was a sensitive little boy—cried when Mme Dulange's cow had its calf. Wrote a poem to a dewdrop when I was ten. . . ." He began to talk of his growing up: how he had prayed with his mother, awed by her saintliness; how she had told him of her visions, so that he was frightened in the dark at night and found it a relief to be bad, running away from something he could neither see nor understand. He told her of his affairs at court, of his adoration of Silvie; he even told her of the freakish passion he and Victoire had known, born of their hatred of one another. And then he related the story of his escape from France, only omitting his purpose in coming to Asylum.

Nicole listened intently, a woman in love—hungry to glean anything new of her lover.

"I want you to know something else," he said. "Something I can't account for. If I wanted a woman nothing ever stood in my way. I've wanted you—more than you'll ever know. You've never been out of my mind since the first night I saw you at Homet's inn. I go insane with the thought that you'll go from my life, that I'll never possess you. But I feel closer to you than any woman I've known, any woman who's been a physical part of me . . . I love you, Nicole!"

He groped for her hand, which was cold as it had been the night of Mme d'Autremont's fete.

"Why won't you answer me!"

"You know that I love my husband."

"He's only a myth standing between us. I try to think of him—but he hasn't blood or bones! If he had he'd have found you. If I'd lost you I'd be covering every inch of every desert and iceberg till I found you. And God knows it wouldn't have taken me so long!"

"I think you're very cruel, Monsieur." Her voice trembled and she felt a wild rush of tears.

"I can't leave like this. I've tried to be gallant. But I'm only human. I've tried to remember that you belong to someone else, that you don't even want me. And in spite of your words, I know that you do! I won't ask you. You'd only lie to me. . . . You're weak, not for loving me, but for lying to yourself—for giving up what's real for a shadow."

She pulled her hand away from him and jumped up. He caught her in his arms, forcing her lips to his own. And he held her so fiercely that she couldn't escape, his lips on her hair, her wet cheeks, his heart pounding against her bosom.

"I love you! . . . And if you're gone when I come back I'm going to find you. I've got to see you with him—got to see the truth with my own eyes. I won't live without you if you love me!"

"You rave like a madman!" she cried desperately.

"I'm not drunk with lilacs!"

"You're drunk with vanity!"

"*Oh, chérie*—don't you understand what's happened to us? Don't you know what you feel when you tremble and weep? You're not so young—a woman married who's had a child! Don't you know love?

Haven't you known it before? Haven't you felt closer to me than to God—just for a moment? The way I've felt close to you. . . ."

He kissed her again, knowing her answers in the soft submission of her body.

It was John Herman who had first released his passion. It was now the guffaw of John Herman that restrained him. His head was burning, but his hands seemed to him stiff, ugly claws apart from him. He managed to drop his hands from her so that he wouldn't crush her.

"Bravo!" came the booming voice of Major Hoops from the laughter of the taproom.

It doubled and trebled like the sound of a voice in the cave at St.-Émilion, and reverberated through him as he stumbled away from the garden.

❀❀❀❀❀❀❀❀❀❀❀❀❀❀❀❀❀❀❀❀❀❀❀

CHAPTER XLII

LATE ONE AFTERNOON Pierre arrived in Philadelphia. It was a day unseasonably hot, with the sun struggling to penetrate the fog. He went at once to the lodgings of the Vicomte de Noailles on Third Street. He was glad not to find the Vicomte there. In the first place, he felt in no mood to condole with Noailles who had lost five of his family by the guillotine the summer before. Moreover, he wanted to waste no time in getting the address of Mrs. Williams, a private home in a section of the city remote from the French settlement.

Until he began to change his clothing he supposed he was in a hurry. Now his fingers faltered as he put on fresh linen. His fingers did not want him to see the Dauphin quite yet.

Since he had left Asylum the nights had been filled with restless dreams. Although it was Nicole he thought of despondently throughout the day, Marie Antoinette came to him at night, rousing in him a carnal passion he had never once felt for her in his waking hours.

The dreams lingered into the bright daylight, puzzling and shaming him as well as taunting him with their brief ecstasy. But the dreams were never of Versailles. The Queen came to him in the cave of St.-Émilion, and they crept into the recesses of the cavern for their amours. Louis watched them. He was headless, but one knew it was Louis by the bulk and the hands and the untidiness; and one knew that he watched, as if there were eyes in his hands. Again, they lay in one another's arms in the damp dungeon at Grenauld. Louis Charles, it seemed, was their son. But Louis Charles was Nicki, weeping over the death of his pet crow.

Wherever he went in his dreams Marie Antoinette pursued him, now with her ludicrous towering feathers, now with her simple milk-maid's garb. And always someone was there to watch them: Silvie, humming little snatches of song as she danced, or Victoire, laughing at the nudity of the Queen.

Sometimes his dreams were more grim. He was tangled in a mesh of bats; he was jumping from the battlements at Grenauld; he had cut off the head of Annette's baby at birth, and he held it in his hands, a tenuous blue soap bubble. . . . He often wakened wet with sweat, and he told himself that if the fever that had swept Asylum left him fairly strong of limb, it had taken an insidious toll of his nerves.

Wasn't he filled with joy at the thought of seeing Louis Charles? Of holding the boy in his arms and comforting him as if he had been his father? Wasn't the moment of triumph at hand, if there could be a moment of triumph in a world that lay fallow in blood?

He walked slowly to the address of Mrs. Williams, and now happy memories of the boy began to crowd into his mind. The Dauphin was in "lamentable condition" at the time of his escape, but that was many months ago—nearly a year. By now he must be returned almost to normal. Normal . . . what would that mean now that the boy was past eleven? Tall? Boys didn't grow fast so early as girls, and Louis Charles had never been tall for his age. Plump, as he had been in early child-hood? But not really plump, of course, if he had been ill.

It never occurred to Pierre that the Dauphin would not remember him, that it was four years since the child had seen him. He would talk to Louis Charles of the flowers he had gathered and taken to his mother; they would laugh at the pictures Pierre drew for him behind Mme de Tourzel's back; there was the little de Soucy girl with whom Louis Charles used to play wedding; and Jean Legros, child of one of the royal grooms, with whom he baked pies in his sandpile. The

Dauphin had so insisted one day that Pierre ride one of the eight little black ponies his aunts had given him. The ponies no bigger than large Spanish sheep—and Pierre really twice their size! There was the day the Queen had caught the boy whistling during a lesson, chiding him for a scatterbrain, and he said with his quick wit: "I was reciting so badly, Mama, I was making catcalls at myself!" Pierre would remind Louis Charles of that and they would laugh together. And how the boy had stormed when his mother let him work at her embroidery frame and the wool became tangled! Oh, and the day the Dauphin had jumped out of the clothes closet cabinet next to Louis's private bedroom and had said "Boo" to Papa King! Heinous disrespect on the part of the little Duc de Normandie and the sort of thing Mme de Polignac should have been dismissed for allowing! But everybody laughed. Born gay! Some day he would make a gay monarch, but a wise and understanding one, for Marie Antoinette had allowed no tantrums and the child loved everyone.

Pierre quickened his steps, wanting to see Louis Charles at this very instant and yet wanting to postpone a joy he had nursed in his heart for so many years. It was frightening to have a moment at hand that one had longed for, wept for, clung to in the direst hours of grief. It was like the first hour of rapture with a woman one wooed, never quite to be equaled again, always to be a little mourned for.

He passed a shop filled with imported novelties and, on second thought, retraced his steps. He would buy a toy for Louis Charles. What did boys of eleven like, he asked the young man who waited on him?

What kind of a boy?

A very bright little boy, but a boy who had everything in the world.

A jeweled dagger from the Orient? A tiny Swiss clock with gnomes that played tag? A copy of Chaucer, illuminated by an Italian monk?

No, preferably a game. He was a lonely little boy.

Ah, like most of the little boys who have everything. . . . Then what of a new chess set of lapis lazuli, just arrived from China?

Pierre bought the chess set. He could borrow money from de Noailles if he had to stay in Philadelphia longer than a week. The orchard would never pay for the chess set, but Victoire was generous. It was so easy to sell another of the gems of the asthmatic deceased.

The house of which he had the address was only a stone's throw from the Pennypot Inn where he had talked with the French sailor. An old mansion, it now had a dirty façade, and in spots the marble had turned green and dank. A half-dead geranium plant sulked in a window box. On the top step blocking his path lay a large, long-haired dog, thin and mangy, and pestered with fleas. The dog paid no attention to him or to the fleas. Pierre reached over him for the knocker, a couchant lion turned black with two half-rubbed spots showing brass. He laughed at himself because his hands were trembling, and he found himself looking up at the windows, half expecting to see the face of Louis Charles pressed against a pane. But the child would be kept out of sight of course—possibly even disguised again as a girl . . . not even allowed to look out at the busy street leading to the wharf until dark had engulfed the house and there was nothing to see but a street lamp and occasional lantern.

The door opened cautiously, just enough for Pierre to see the face of a very old woman. A birthmark covered her mouth, making her lips seem purple and swollen.

"Is Mme Williams at home?" he asked.

"Who are you?"

There was a stale smell from the house now, as of old people and old food and old dark. It seeped out into the dampness.

"Pierre de Michelait."

The door opened wider, and he stepped over the languid dog and entered. It was dark and airless within, and he thought suddenly of the catacombs.

"Can you identify yourself?" said the old woman.

Pierre gave her the letter in code that mentioned that Mrs. Williams would be at this address. She took it down the long hall and examined it carefully at the light of a Betty lamp. Then she returned and began to mount a flight of stairs step by step like a little child. He found himself counting each shuffle of her feet. She was gone a long time. He stood in the same spot between the stairs and the door and he began to think of what he should do when he saw the Dauphin. Louis Charles would be too old to run into his arms; Louis Charles had full realization now of who he was, would expect the obeisance due a king. Pierre would fall on his knees, wait for the boy to extend his hand. . . . *Mou Dieu,* what had he expected—that they would romp together, turn back the formidable years to the carefree days of Versailles?

"*Monsieur le Marquis . . .*" said a voice from the top of the stairs, an English voice. "*Montez ici, s'il vous plait.*"

He climbed the stairs. At the top was a fresh-looking middle-aged woman holding a candle over his letter. Her arms were strong and ruddy, as if she had just finished a family wash. She looked at him shrewdly, out of small blue eyes.

"*Je suis Mme Williams,*" she said in her wretched French; and to the old woman: "*Allez vous en!*"

Pierre attempted to bow. The three of them were crowded together. He had the feeling of being glued to these others.

"Have you told him? Does he know that I've come?" Pierre said softly as the old woman clung to the rail and the stairway swallowed her.

Mrs. Williams held the candle to Pierre's face. He felt that he had shrunken to a very little boy. He almost felt that he had been impudent. The moment was more than he could bear. Waiting, waiting, waiting . . . there was no end to waiting even when waiting was at an end!

"Where is he?" he demanded testily.

She nodded and he followed her to the end of the hall. She held the candle low so that she could open a door with the key from her petticoat pocket.

At first Pierre could see nothing in the room, but Mrs. Williams held the candle over a child in bed asleep.

It was not the Dauphin. Pierre stared at the child half stupefied. It was a clever substitute, with the same high, receding forehead, prominent cheekbones, Habsburg nose. Even the dark arched eyebrows were like those he remembered, but the hair that had been live yellow was a dull-straw color, spread thin on the pillow. The child was emaciated, his skin the hue of the tenuous blue soap bubble Pierre had held last night in his dreams.

There was an odor coming from the bed, and Pierre thought with a shock that this child had just died. But the child moved.

Mrs. Williams drew the covers from the boy and pulled back his night shift, exposing the whole ugly body to Pierre. The belly sank below the framework of ribs, and the thighs ended in swollen knobs of knees. Half a dozen sores were moist with pus, and the flies of the room hovered close. The stench was overwhelming now, a mingling of pus and green fetid bowel movement.

"Ah," said Mrs. Williams in cockney English, "he has had another accident—dysentery he contracted on the ship. But he's better. In another few weeks, the doctor thinks. . . ."

"This is not Louis Charles!" cried Pierre, snatching the covers from her hand and tossing them back on the child. "He's an impostor! You're an impostor!"

Mrs. Williams set the candle down on a table calmly. Then she slipped off the child's sleeves and pointed to a vaccination scar on each arm. The boy half opened his eyes and whined a little.

"This is a ruse!" Pierre exclaimed. "I knew him as well as my own child. I lived with him. I read to him . . . I. . . ."

The boy's eyes were on him now with no more expression than those of a fish. Pierre leaned over, swept the thin locks from the child's right ear. The lobe hung like a fat pendant, a bulbous pearl.

"Louis Charles . . ." whispered Pierre, crumpling to his knees. "Look at me, Louis Charles . . . M. de Michelait—don't you remember? The little black ponies—the—*the little black ponies!*"

He could seem to think of nothing but the little black ponies with their long hair and crimson and gold harness.

Louis Charles kept staring at him as a baby stares at a red apple.

"Four years in the Temple is a long time, Monsieur," said Mrs. Williams. "And now perhaps I had better change his bedding. . . ."

Pierre reached impulsively for the boy's hand to kiss it. It was not much bigger than Nicki's. When he saw the ulcer he dropped the hand as if it had been dung.

The boy and the room slipped out of focus.

"Come tomorrow, Monsieur," said Mrs. Williams kindly. "And we will talk over plans. . . . Tomorrow, perhaps, he will know you. . . ."

She took the candle from the table again and held it discreetly low now so that it wouldn't expose the tears on Pierre's cheeks.

"Oh, M. de Michelait . . ." she said as he fumbled with the latch of the door. "You have forgotten your package."

Pierre rambled along the waterfront. He was not sure that this last half hour was not phantasy, only a part of the nightmare of these last few nights. There was nothing real about the moment he was living. The fog swept in from the water, clinging to him with warm, wet fingers, and yet his linen was cold against his skin. He was glad for the fog. It closed out the city. The smug Quaker warehouses behind him retreated in the grayness, leaving him alone with his pain. The ships, blurring with the oncoming dark, were blending with sky and water. Voices came and went, and now and then he was conscious of a sailor's curse that had been shouted long moments before. Shreds of laughter came from the hull of a West Indies freighter. He remembered the laughter from the inn as he and Nicole talked in the garden. There was something final about laughter.

He was exhausted as if he had walked the whole way from Asylum, and he sat on a barrel beside a huge lading of rum. He tried to give some order to his thoughts: he was responsible here for Louis Charles. Tomorrow he would go back to the house. Tomorrow the fog would be gone. Tomorrow Louis Charles would know him. In Asylum the boy would get well. Born gay. . . . For five years he had lived for this moment. He had touched the hand of Louis Charles who had lain in the womb of Marie Antoinette. Marie Antoinette was France. The future of France was in his keeping. . . .

Was it tar and fish rot that filled his nostrils or the stench of pus and feces?

A lantern swung beside him and a bare-chested sailor with black pigtails said: "What the devil you doing here—tapping the barrel?"

"Waiting," Pierre answered.

The sailor laughed and gave Pierre a clap on the shoulder.

"Oh, that!" he said. "There'll be one around in a minute."

The lantern jogged away.

Waiting! That's what these five years had been. There had seemed nothing worse than waiting—waiting in the Abbaye; waiting at Grenauld; waiting in St.-Émilion; waiting in Asylum. Waiting filled one as dripping water fills a jar, and finally there is a last drop and the water spills over. . . . He had thought there was nothing worse than waiting.

He was filled with a sense of drowning, of pressure from without and within. He moved away from the lading of rum but the drowning moved along with him. Like a drowning man he relived his life swiftly . . . there had been moments of beauty in it that he wanted to grasp and hold secure. He tried to hold them as they flowed over and escaped him, tried feverishly to grip them, to hold them firm in the desperation that engulfed him. There was the meadow shimmering red with poppies beyond the Dulange barn; there was the smile of the little girl with the apple; there was Grégoire's voice, deep, fondling, as he read: "To thine own self be true, and it must follow as the night the day, thou canst not then be false to any man." Once the words had seemed poignant as altar music; they had filled a hollow as the vibrations of an organ fill an empty cathedral.

At Versailles there had been the sparkle of fountains by moonlight, an ecstatic union of heaven and water; and the hour he lay wounded in Marie Antoinette's bedchamber, proud in the thought that he had given his life for his Queen. Silvie too, chirping with her canaries, had offered him the essence of springtime and youth. Until it was too late he had not wanted to look into her heart, had not wanted to see beyond the elixir of lilting toes as he accepted the beauty of a love freely given. There had been something of formidable beauty in the night that Annette's child had been born, when he had breathed life into its mouth, not because he was frightened but because Annette's suffering had wrung his very entrails, because her weakness had made him human enough to be traitor to his Dauphin and to his class. He could not think now why this seemed to him to be a moment of beauty. . . .

Then too there was du Petit-Thouars and the thoughts Pierre had shared with him like a confessor. At first Asylum had been only beauty —primitive, grand, challenging the steel in a man with its bitter snows and its rugged trees. If he had weakened now he had met the challenge at first, stirred with a new hope and a craving to meet the challenge even to the very God that had created it. One met the resistance, the awful power and glory of God in the forest. One only knew His might when he tried to chain the elements, to harness God to man's purpose.

Now as he tried to run away from himself in the shifting fog two drunken sailors collided with him, reeling over with the neatness of tenpins so that Pierre stumbled and almost fell into the common heap. He left them floundering there, heading for the Market Street oil lamp that looked like a watery, clouded moon. Their sprawling filled him anew with a sense of drowning, of conclusion; and the beauty was gone.

As he came to the lamppost he saw a woman. She was young, and a few dark locks framed her pretty face under its shawl. When she reached out her hand and detained him he had the feeling that she had come alive from a statue.

"Monsieur?" she said softly.

He looked into her face. She was younger than he thought—too young for this. She hadn't the look of total disillusionment; she had almost the look of a bewildered child. Her hand drifted into his and it was warm and heartening, easing the sense of drowning.

"You needn't be afraid of the yellow fever, Monsieur," she said. "I've had it. . . ."

He hesitated, and in a brief second her hands had slipped up to his shoulders and locked behind his neck. "You are very beautiful, Monsieur . . . and very sad."

He stood looking down at her, tempted.

"What's your name?" he asked.

"Silvie."

"Silvie!" He began to laugh huskily.

"It's a pretty name," she said, pouting briefly.

He put his arms about her and kissed her, finding the warmth of her body a comfort.

"I live only a few doors from the Pennypot Inn," she coaxed.

"All right . . . Silvie," he answered, and he found her hand in his again. She led him over the cobblestones from clouded moon to clouded moon, and he was grateful that she didn't chatter.

The room she took him to was clean and simple. An old and battered doll sat on a chair. Later that was all of the room he could remember.

He watched her undress: she still seemed little more than a child when she came over and slipped her arms around him, but he found that she had the passion of a woman. He was drowning and she was drowning, and tonight it seemed good that they drown together.

In the early morning just before dawn Marie Antoinette came to him again. In her arms she carried a cadaver. It was small with legs and arms that hung limp like those of a marionette. Pierre saw at once that it was Nicki. He gave out a frightful cry; his heart was shredded with pain as if clawed by a beast. He tried to back away, to escape the pain and the child, but he was in a corner and she came closer and closer with the charming smile of her early youth.

"No—no, I won't have him!" he screamed. "I won't touch him!"

The small body of Nicki was covered with oozing sores; they began to multiply, to run together. As Marie Antoinette pressed the hand of the boy to his mouth she threw back her head and laughed. Pierre writhed with the horror of the pus on his lips, the thick, wet, putrid jelly of pus on his tongue.

"Suck the pus!" she commanded. "Suck the pus like St. John of God and save him! . . . Once a Jesuit always a Jesuit!"

Retching, he sucked, the dry hollow of his mouth filling with the pustules so that he choked at last with the putrefaction and the cries of his soul were muffled.

"Monsieur—Monsieur!" Marie Antoinette was saying. *"Monsieur—* wake up!"

He was shaking violently and the cold sweat dripped from his cheek to his lips. He stared at the girl Silvie who lay in his arm like a kitten, one hand on his quivering breast.

"You were dreaming, Monsieur," she said softly. "You have been dreaming all night. Lie back—I will sing you to sleep."

The room and the girl and the fog came back to him slowly. They were hardly better than the dream.

He staggered to his feet fumbling for his clothes, the nightmare clinging to him like a barnacle.

"Monsieur . . ." the girl pleaded, sitting up now. "You will come back? . . . I . . . like you so much, Monsieur."

She was sitting up in bed now, her eyes fixed on him with a mixture of solicitude and hope. A small cherry bow was askew on her curls, and with one hand she held together the night shift so that her small, pink breasts were hidden.

He still had no voice to answer, to tell her that the Vicomte de Noailles would be waiting, that Louis Charles would be waiting—that the things one ran away from would always be there waiting.

Nor would she have understood, he thought with a surge of pity and envy. She was so very young.

He took her in his arms before he left, stroking her tangled hair for a moment, and kissed her as he would have kissed Nicki.

CHAPTER XLIII

June 1796

NICOLE had gone to bed early. Now that the moment of the child's arrival was imminent all of the waiting of the sixteen months seemed trivial. There was an inward trembling that never left her, the excitement of one who has watched a fire out of hand. She had to guide her fingers with the absorption of a baby so that a cup would not slip from them and break. She had to guard her words with renewed intent, for now that the Dauphin's coming was an actuality, success might depend on the smallest word or action. Often she looked into a mirror to see if her eyes belied her. If they had once revealed a new passion for Pierre de Michelait, how much more must they shout the old, trenchant hope of years!

News had come from Pierre that "Charles Vivet" was unable to make the trip to Asylum at once. The child was recovering from dysentery after a harrowing ocean voyage; he had been hidden for months in a deserted monastery with his mother near Marseilles; lack of food had caused sores; the shock of his widowed mother's death had further enfeebled him so that he scarcely spoke. His nurse, who had escaped with them out of love and loyalty for her mistress, now felt obliged to return to her own needy family in France, knowing that Charles would be in the capable hands of M. Talon. Pierre would make the trip as soon as it was feasible for the boy to endure its hardships.

It was Victoire who began the charitable movement, evoking promises from everyone for the child's comfort and amusement. As a personal gift she had a sandbox and seesaw erected on M. Talon's lawn and directed the preparation of the room next to M. Talon's that had originally been intended for the Dauphin. The drapes must be changed from a royal blue with their mocking fleurs-de-lis to a brighter chintz. The bed must be placed so that the boy could see the boats on the river. All boys loved boats. Nicki at three and a half had a passion for them. There must be books and games at hand. She herself would come over and read to him often.

Mme d'Autremont offered to nurse him till he recovered from the journey and was able to play normally around the garden; Mme de Blaçons knitted socks for the winter; M. de la Roué took up an odd collection of books and toys, though the bedchamber still retained the exquisite music box and games that had originally been furnished for the luckless Dauphin. The Little Admiral, who had just returned from New York and was carving a ship model for Nicki, began one also for Charles Vivet. Mme Buzard said she would prevail on René to sit still now and then and play a game of chess with him. Dr. Buzard, not to be outdone, quietly arranged with his Iroquois agent never to leave the island cabin one mile down the river.

Nicole wondered how ill the Dauphin would be. She and Dr. Buzard had marveled at the fact that M. Talon allowed the child's coming to be common knowledge. Granted that secrecy would only arouse suspicion among the colonists later on, still weren't there more than a few in Asylum who would recognize Charles Vivet as Louis Charles? She herself who had never laid eyes on the Dauphin would know him at once. What did M. Talon and Pierre have in mind? Did they think Asylum still as remote and safe a hiding place as it had been several years ago when it was established for Marie Antoinette? And were they so trusting of everyone in it? Obviously not, if Louis Charles were arriving in the guise of a sick, bereaved cousin.

In the six weeks of Pierre's absence she had reasoned her passion for him into subordination. The process had not been easy. But he had not been there to upset the process. There had been the first nights after his leaving when she wanted to run away into the woods and never see another human being. There had been the memories of his touch, of his eyes upon her, and the wild beating of her heart even at the sound of his voice. The first peach trees he had planted near the cabin were beginning to bear. He had loved them and so she loved them. The mention of his name had given her a quick stab of pain, as if poison were suddenly taking hold in her blood. Often Nicole had walked out of her way to have a glimpse of Nicki, for he looked so much like Pierre in spite of the green eyes of his mother.

He was never still for a moment, filled with questions, too curious even to wait for an answer. He kept Frau Gresch panting. His pudgy legs were too young to attempt a tree, but he climbed it. Running away was almost a daily event; he wanted to know how bolting cloth was made, how a horse was shod, how the osprey dove into the river for its fish. Usually he returned with a battle scar: a cut finger, a burn from the anvil, a bloody nose. Victoire, who had no nerves, was proud of his mettle, predicting that some day he would be leading the Royal army of France.

There was the day Nicole had thought him alone in the de Michelait garden and had held him to her with such hunger that in spite of his early adoration of her he had fretted. Victoire, it seemed, was watching from the arbor and had said lightly: "*Nom de Dieu,* Mme de Louvenne, what a passion you have for the cradle!"

There had been a slow-growing, subtle hatred between the two women for months, since Pierre lived with one and loved the other. •

Night after night in the dark Nicole had pitted Pierre de Michelait against Georges Brigaud. Granted that Pierre had his moments of vision and humanitarianism, he was still an aristocrat. He had been born with a gold spoon in his mouth; she and Georges Brigaud had been born with a wooden ladle. Pierre was handsome; Georges Brigaud was only the average Frenchman. Short, slight, swarthy with an aquiline nose, he was a Marseillais that any woman would pass by without notice. Pierre had a suave mastery over his gestures, his emotions; Georges Brigaud was uninhibited—fireworks touched off by a flare. Aristocrat—bourgeois! Pierre had only bewitched her with his touch; Georges Brigaud had enslaved her with his ideals. The choking passion she had felt for Pierre was unreal—simply born of the nearness of a man too attractive. What had some writer said? "When one once tastes love he must continue his diet?" She had been lonely here—so lonely that she had almost given herself to Pierre in her desperation. She often wondered how this might have changed her life. She knew that when she returned to Georges Brigaud—and she would go back to France— Pierre would return with her in the core of her being. But Pierre, living in her heart alone, was someone she could at last eject; Pierre in her very flesh would have stayed with her forever. It was the other way for a man, she thought, who never forgets a woman who doesn't surrender. . . .

At last with a sense of triumph she had reduced her love to a cold, mathematical formula. Like anyone else she wanted long happiness. For her that would consist in nursing the new nation, in joining her life to a man whose motives were her own.

She thought of the hours she had spent struggling with a geometry problem for her old tutor M. Flèche. Sometimes she had worked late into the night, tense, exhausted, determined, as if her very life had depended on its solution. The victory had been so very sweet, a moment calm and lucid like the victory over harrowing fever. A moral victory like the victory Georges Brigaud had won over Pierre. It was good to be done with the fever, to see it for what it was.

And in a few more weeks the Greek drama would be played and over. She and Pierre and Louis Charles would be dispersed—a weary lot of actors gone home their different ways. The audience, properly thrilled, would settle back to its banal daily living. If the heroine carried with her a scar it was because she had been foolish enough to forget this tragedy was only before the footlights and had given to her part more emotion than it called for.

Pierre had said that he would follow her even if she found her husband, that he must see them together to know if she loved him. She

had reason to believe that he would carry out his threat if she weakened
in so much as a glance. When Pierre returned, above all things she
must convince him she had no feeling for him since receiving M. de
Louvenne's letter.

Shortly after news of the Dauphin's death Dr. Buzard had remembered a friend from San Domingo now in New Orleans. As a last
resort, he told M. Talon, since the consuls had failed Nicole the friend
might be able to help her. M. Talon had written at once. The answer
had just arrived. It had come direct from M. de Louvenne to Nicole.
The colony had rejoiced at the happy ending and Victoire had given a
fete for Nicole in her garden.

She knew the letter by heart, the letter that had been flaunted with
joy among the colonists:

> *Beloved:*
>
> *My hand trembles so that I can scarce write, and my tears
> of unbelief almost blind me. I felt that I knew suffering
> when we lost our child, but what greater suffering to lose
> you, my very soul!*
>
> *For months I have prayed God to give me understanding
> of the fate that separated us, to give me some meager faith
> in the future. In the blackest moments it has seemed impos-
> sible that such love as ours could be gone forever. . . .*
>
> *Oh my beloved, believe me that God was kind to strike
> from you your memory, if only for a little time! My greatest
> anguish was that you were suffering in the thought that I
> was indifferent! I, at least, had the comfort of holding you
> to my heart every waking moment, holding you in my
> dreams with infinite longing. Ah, if only there had been the
> grave of our son to weep over, we would soon have met
> there in our mutual sorrow!*
>
> *I have looked for you from the moment that you wan-
> dered from home in your delirium. I have gone from door
> to door on the streets of Baltimore and Philadelphia. I was
> told at last that you'd gone to the Scioto Colony in Ohio. I
> traveled there only to return desperate. I had written every-
> where, describing you, pleading for help. I had written to
> Asylum but this must have been before your arrival. People
> have tried to be kind but they have their separate sorrows.
> . . . When I heard of the many French just arrived in New*

Orleans I was so hopeful I'd find you here. . . . Oh, my darling, the dreadful pain of ever searching and not finding!

M. Strageaux, the friend of M. Buzard, has been more than kind, making it possible for me to eat and to hope, for I have been ill and poverty-stricken. . . . I shall leave at once for Philadelphia, awaiting you at the pension of Mrs. Phillips on Pine Street.

Tears prevent my writing more. But I promise that some day you shall have your home again at Port-au-Prince, my dearest wife, and God willing, we shall once more hold a child of our own to our aching hearts. Bless you and keep you until the hour of our joy.

The letter had brought with it a sense of stark reality and danger. It was the signal to go.

"How long would it take my mythical husband to make the trip from New Orleans to Philadelphia?" Nicole had asked Dr. Buzard.

"Six weeks perhaps."

"And if M. de Michelait hasn't returned with the child?"

"You'll have to feign illness. I have a drug to produce fever."

"When will you leave here, Monsieur?"

"A week, perhaps, after you. I've also received a letter from our convenient M. Strageaux. He writes glowingly of New Orleans, the little Paris. Mme Buzard plagues me to go there now—she's forgotten Charleston. Haven't you heard me airing the possibility of our departure? Everyone but you is properly sad."

Dr. Buzard's tired yellow eyes narrowed with malice.

"If God is just," said Nicole, with her bewitching smile, "you and I will not meet again until the Judgment Day!"

"And then," Dr. Buzard retorted, not to be outdone, "perhaps at last you will obey orders from your Superior!"

Nicole was in her first sound sleep when there was a knock at the door.

"Who is it?" she called with a premonition that the hour had come.

"M. Heraud . . . M. *le Docteur* is here. It is very important, Madame!"

"Un moment. . . ."

She slipped on her peignoir, the ribbons tangling in her fingers. Then she folded her hands briefly and said to the darkness: "Dear God! . . ."

M. Heraud was holding a candle, and beside him was Dr. Buzard.

"M. Talon's nephew has arrived. The child is very ill," Dr. Buzard said. "We need a woman to nurse him through the night."

Unflinching, she met the eyes of the doctor. Now that the first moment of challenge was over she was exhilarated.

"Mme d'Autremont has already offered to nurse him," she said.

"Mme d'Autremont has a family. M. Talon asked for you. He knows you are fond of children."

She hesitated for an artful moment.

"Surely you cannot refuse M. Talon, Madame?" urged M. Heraud. "I can spare your help."

It came to her that M. Heraud, with his pathetic legerdemain, was no more than a child.

She drove off with the doctor in his phaeton. On second thought she had put M. de Louvenne's letter in the bosom of her gown.

"You must brace yourself for a shock," he whispered as they reached a long, dark stretch between houses. "I never would have known him."

"How do you know it is he?"

"*Bête!*" he laughed shortly. "Haven't we had reports from a dozen people since the day he escaped?"

"Is he very ill?"

"Not ill enough! But there'll be strict orders for no one to see him. And perhaps he's ill enough that a little medicine to encourage the dysentery. . . . We will have to see. We can't afford to dawdle."

She wanted to ask if M. de Michelait was still with him but she couldn't bring herself to form the words. Before they arrived at la Grande Maison Dr. Buzard said softly: "I didn't even have to suggest you. That's how indispensable you have been to little boys during the epidemic . . . to little boys in general. If you are here tonight it will be natural M. Talon will want you to stay on."

"Do they have the child pledged to secrecy, do you think?"

"He seems not to care or know if he's Charles Vivet or Louis Capet."

He drew the horse to the hitching-post and took her hand to help her down.

"Are you frightened?" he asked in a sharp whisper, holding her hand so tightly that it pained.

"Not any more. . . ."

Louis Charles lay in a large, regal bed lighted by candelabra, and M.

Talon sat beside him motionless, his hands folded on the counterpane. Nicole was at once conscious of Pierre who stood in the shadows, leaning against the mantel. She looked at the Dauphin whom she had never seen before and who had filled her mind for the last two years. Her first emotion was a grim satisfaction that he had come to this state of debility. She studied the thin pale face with its high cheekbones and the lashes too lush for the delicate skin. His lips, full, dry, cracked, were petulant. They were not the laughing lips of Mme Lebrun's painting, of all the paintings she had so carefully studied. Indeed, Dr. Buzard was right; there was nothing about the boy that she might recognize, and the quick fear returned to her that the stories of the Dauphin's exchange in the Temple were true.

Why the two deep lines between the arched eyebrows gave her a feeling of pity, she did not know, unless it was that the lines were old and the body was small. She reached out and touched his forehead for a moment almost with a sense of guilt, recalling the day when all France had thrilled at the boy's birth, even herself, and knowing that her gesture belied her now.

Dr. Buzard was taking his pulse again.

"It's a little stronger," he said. "Could we have a warming pan for his feet, M. Talon? And an extra cover? . . . He bears a marked resemblance to you, M. Talon—the high forehead, the same fine texture of skin. . . . We will have him well and playing on Mme de Michelait's seesaw in no time. . . . Now, I think, it is better to leave him. Oh, and one thing more, Monsieur, he is to see no one—absolutely no one but you and M. de Michelait, perhaps."

M. Talon tiptoed from the room.

"If he has pain during the night you will give him a teaspoon of this mixture with a glass of water, Mme de Louvenne . . . And now I think I shall get some sleep. I'll be back the first thing in the morning."

Nicole put on the apron she had hurriedly slung over her arm. Pierre didn't move though she could feel the black eyes piercing her. It was as if they fixed her to the spot like the sharp point of a lance. The moment became so long, so intensely unbearable that she turned and looked at him at last.

She could not see him too well for the shadows, but she knew at once that he had changed. He seemed disheveled. She had seen him disheveled before: with a week's beard in the hunting season, with his black locks dangling over his forehead as he wielded an ax, with his linen wilted from the blazing sun of an Asylum summer. Tonight he was well enough groomed. It was only that he gave the appearance of dishevelment as he never had in actuality. He was not even so tall as she remembered him, or quite so young, but surely the shadows were playing tricks. Perhaps his lingering there leaning against the mantel had something to do with the deception. All along she had dreaded that he would come to her impetuously when they were alone, that he would make it harder for her. She felt a swift pang for the impalpable something that had escaped him, and the feeling of wanting to comfort him was so dangerous to her well-thought-out equanimity that she smiled and said briskly: *"Ah, bon soir, M. de Michelait,* and welcome home again!"

Her words had a metallic note. They were so aloof from her thoughts that she wondered at once if she had said them. She sat down in the chair M. Talon had vacated.

"Why didn't you want to see me when you came into the room?" he asked.

"But how absurd! I didn't see you." She straightened the coverlet over Louis Charles.

"Not with your eyes, perhaps. . . . You are still lying to yourself?"

"Monsieur! . . . The trip hasn't improved your manners!"

"I was so sure you'd be gone when I returned . . . the conviction haunted me. I saw you a hundred times on the streets of Philadelphia."

She made a supreme effort to look up to him, to force a jubilance into her voice, for he had come over to her and stood with his hand resting on the chair back.

"Oh, Monsieur, haven't you heard the news? Haven't you heard I've found him at last—that in a few shorts weeks we'll be together?"

"M. Talon told me about the letter. . . . Are you really happy, Nicole?"

"Oui, oui, oui, Monsieur . . . I'm so happy I cry and sing all at once."

"I want you to be happy. But I want to be sure you're happy."

"You have only to read his letter, Monsieur. . . ." She groped for it in the folds of her fichu.

"I don't want to read his letter . . . Wouldn't that be a sort of sacrilege?"

She felt a hot flush spreading over her face. All of Asylum had seen the letter.

"It's a beautiful letter," she retorted, and now there were tears in her voice.

"I shall take your word for it."

Her thoughts began to collide. She couldn't go on lying! It was too much for her to see him again, to know that he wanted to take her in his arms, to remember the pain of his touch. . . . She would go off with him. She would have her hour of ecstasy if she must spend the rest of her life bleeding to death. . . . The only important thing was what one wanted with one's heart and body . . . The little ugly Dauphin, holding them apart, holding her to her vows, with his weak, scrofulous hands! . . . Cold, cold years ahead . . . emotions frozen . . . brain like steel, alert . . . a victory of the brain . . . an emptiness! . . .

They were both staring at the Dauphin. His lashes moved with the soft quiver of a butterfly's wings. The bright blue eyes, confused, looked at Nicole, and then up at Pierre, who leaned forward and touched his hand.

"*J'ai soif,*" he whispered thickly.

The spell was broken. Nicole reached for the carafe on the bedside table. Pierre went around to the other side of the bed and lifted the boy's head gently from the pillow so that Nicole might hold the glass of water to his lips. He sucked a few swallows.

As he released the boy Pierre's fingers brushed those of Nicole. He hadn't meant to touch her. They looked into one another's eyes for a long moment.

He had expected to find a softness behind her tears, but her eyes had never seemed so gray, so pure and hard.

At the sound of M. Talon's footstep the mantel clock began to tick again.

"Wallois is a thoughtful soul," said M. Talon softly. "He thought of the warming pan himself and had it ready."

CHAPTER XLIV

By the first of August the colony was in a delicious turmoil. The three d'Orléans princes, sons of *Égalité,* were coming for a two-weeks' visit. Details of the princes' lives formed the only conversation. The ward of M. Talon, whom one could not see anyway, and who from reports was hardly worth the seeing, was relegated to oblivion.

But the princes! What more succulent fare for jaded appetites! Louis-Philippe Bourbon d'Orléans, the oldest, was in direct line for the throne. During the Revolution he had distinguished himself as a colonel of the dragoons in the National Guard and had fought against Austria and Prussia, welcomed, as some one said, "by the old soldiers as a prince, by the new ones as a Patriot." When the Bourbons were expelled from France Louis-Philippe had gone to Coblentz, had then taught in Switzerland, an impoverished schoolmaster, and later had wandered through Denmark, Sweden, Norway, and Lapland. His brothers, the Duc de Montpensier and the Comte de Beaujolais, arrested at the Palais-Royal, had been imprisoned in Fort St.-Jean, the citadel of Marseilles. Finally the Duchesse d'Orléans had been informed by the Directory that if she might prevail upon her eldest son to go to the United States, her other sons would be released to join him and her own property would no longer be under sequestration.

More intimate news of the princes had been drifting to Asylum through letters from Philadelphia. Louis-Philippe had had the most humble of lodgings in Prune Street over a barbershop, rooms so small that his guests were obliged to sit on the bed! On the arrival of his brothers he had moved into the spacious house of the Spanish consul on Sixth Street. Rumor had it that Louis-Philippe had wooed Abigail Willing without success. For, as Mr. Willing had sagely reckoned, if the Duc should never arrive at the throne Abigail would not have the luxury to which she was accustomed; if the Duc ever did fall heir to the throne Abigail would have luxury to which she never could become accustomed!

Even Mme Buzard was secretly aflutter at the prospect of the visit.

Wilhelmine was beginning to thin out a little, and if only she could be coaxed to care for her nails! Dr. Buzard was no less pleased at the princes' coming.

"Providence is playing into our hands!" he told Nicole. "Louis-Philippe will of course want to pay his respects to a sick ward of M. Talon's. One can't refuse a prince. We will see that he recognizes the Dauphin if we must nail a crown on the child's head. With d'Orléans in line for the throne it'll be hard to convince Asylum later when the boy disappears that Louis-Philippe didn't want him out of the way!"

"Perfect!" Nicole had exclaimed, but without her usual vigor.

Tending the child for so many weeks straight had tended to dull her spirit, thought Dr. Buzard.

"The most subtle kind of poison," he said with relish.

"It was never to have been anything else, Monsieur."

"Sometimes I suspect you are almost fond of the boy!"

"But absurd!" she retaliated. "I've hated him long before he was born!"

"I'm not normally given to praise," he said with a slow motion of his fingers over his oily whiskers, "but you've played your part like a virtuoso . . . the child never wants you out of his sight for a minute. And the little toys you make for him out of rags! And the dandelion chains for his scrawny ribs . . . superb, *ma chère!*"

"Doesn't one always feed the prisoner a good meal before his execution?"

He laughed. Dr. Buzard never made any sound when he laughed. One only knew he laughed by the sudden expanse of white teeth and the tilt of his head.

"He still never drops a hint of his identity?"

"No, Monsieur. And I never pry. You see I am one to obey orders after all."

"*Bien* . . . but the medicine bottle is still full."

"Nature is a great healer, Monsieur," she answered obtusely.

It was true, the child's health had made strides. The dysentery had ceased and the flesh was less taut over his bones. The faint lavender of his skin had turned to ivory as a few of the sores had stopped running. There was not even the stench about him that there had been. During the last week Charles Vivet had been able to walk a little and sat many hours propped by pillows in a chair in the sunshine of the window. M. Talon was so encouraged by his small nephew's progress that he had been willing to go on a business trip.

Now that M. Talon was gone Pierre relieved Nicole occasionally so that she might have a little exercise in the fresh air or a visit with one of the women. He came one evening as she was feeding Louis Charles his supper. The boy sat at the window, and the red of the sun encompassed him and Nicole so that Pierre paused in the doorway with a sudden ache in his throat. In the red of the sun there was almost a glow of health about Louis Charles, like the bloom of Nicki. Nicole looked up and smiled warmly, impersonally.

"You are just in time to help Charles with his sweet," she said. "Tomorrow I think he will try to eat alone."

"I want *you* to help me with my sweet," Charles said to Nicole.

She wiped a bit of gravy from his lips.

"M. de Michelait will tell you about Nicki while he helps you," she answered. "I've promised to go to Mme d'Autremont's. She's made some soup for you. The *potage au ris* that you love."

"I know about Nicki," said Louis Charles, "and I want to hear the rest of your story."

Nicole handed Pierre the tray and he took her place. There was the look on his face she had seen the night he returned, but it was not so much an expression as an absence of expression. It had hurt her then and it hurt her now. It made a little boy of him, somehow, a little boy who wanted to burst into tears but was being very brave. . . . How awkward men were about feminine jobs! The very stiffness of his knees that braced the tray, the distorted angle at which he held the spoon to the boy's mouth! . . .

She took off her apron and hung it in the wardrobe. Then she brought washcloth and towel from the lavabo, all dampened and ready to use on Louis Charles's hands and lips. The pillows had settled into a hump, and she fluffed them up, delicately avoiding the sores on his back.

"I *must* cut your hair!" she said, as she straightened it with a few soft strokes of the brush. "You are beginning to look like a little girl, *chéri.*"

Louis Charles didn't smile as she hoped he would.

"When are you coming back, Madame?" he asked with the first mouthful of sweet he had been chewing all this time.

"In an hour, M. Vivet! . . . a very little hour, almost as small as an elf!"

He raised one thin hand to restrain her, holding onto the folds of her sleeve. The bright blue eyes lifted in reproach. The one bit of tenacious life and beauty about the boy, the amazing blue of his eyes! . . .

She took his hand from her sleeve with a little pat, laid it back on the pillow, and said: *"Au revoir, Messieurs!"*

Somehow she had not wanted to meet Pierre's eyes, or the eyes of the child, or the eyes of anybody. She wanted swiftly to be out in the open where the breeze would sweep over her from miles of woodland, healing for a moment the indefinable ache with which she awoke and went to sleep. Of late she had the sensation that she grew larger, even as the four walls of the Dauphin's bedchamber shrank.

Pierre and Louis Charles watched her as she crossed the terrace garden and disappeared around the side of the house. Louis Charles pushed the spoon away from him.

"You haven't breathed a word of our secret, have you, Louis Charles?" Pierre asked anxiously. "You've given me your word as a Bourbon!"

"Mais non!" And he winced a little with pain as Pierre's arm brushed a sore under his sleeve when he removed the tray.

"When you are crowned you must make a great lady of Mme de Louvenne," Pierre said. "A title, and château and—diamonds!"

"She would rather have a garden, I think. Some day she wants a blue garden—all blue but the grass and the leaves."

"Blue is her favorite color then?"

"She wants a garden the same color as my eyes."

"Your mother had eyes that color too, Louis Charles! Oh, you *must* remember her. Beautiful, sweet, always smelling of roses . . . don't you remember her roses? How she loved them? In her boudoir, in her hair, in the pattern of her gown? . . . You were always bringing her roses. . . . When you laughed she used to hug you to her and say that you laughed like rose petals scampering in a breeze. . . . She used to call you her little Charlot. . . . You *do* remember, don't you?"

Louis Charles picked at the wool of his comforter and said patiently, *"Mais oui, Monsieur."*

"How she used to laugh at your jokes! . . . You were smart, you know. . . . One day she came in to your lessons. Mme Royale couldn't remember the name of the Queen of Carthage. I could see you wanted to cry out Didon, but Mama Queen wouldn't have liked that . . . and you knew it. So you tried to hint. 'But *say* the name then! . . . *Mais dis donc le nom!'* . . . Everybody caught on but Mme Royale."

Pierre looked for a glimmer of memory in the boy's eyes, which were fastened curiously on him as he talked. Day after day alone with the child he had tried to coax him back to the small, bright boy who had been "born gay." Reminding him of black ponies, the tiny sister Sophie, Papa King's thermometer, the *marcassin* of Mlle de Varionnet, the wondrous mechanical clock in the clock cabinet (with planets revolving around the sun), the procession of the Order of the Holy Ghost in the Big Gallery. But of course in his four and a half short years at Versailles he might not remember. . . . Pierre had tried larger canvases then and later memories: St. Cloud, Marly, Fontainebleau with their parks; the gaunt, barren hag of a Tuileries, the Royal Dauphin Regiment of which he was colonel; the flight to Varennes.

"Mais oui, Monsieur," Louis Charles always said. But Pierre knew that he did not remember. That if he recalled any of that early panorama before the Tower, it was the recollection of a child who has been shown many pictures, read many stories before a fever.

"There was the day Papa King brought you the lock he made for the safe where you kept your shell collection," Pierre went on doggedly. "It was shaped like a butterfly . . . really exquisite."

"Papa King must have been very clever."

"Yes—yes he was—and good, too. He never wanted to hurt anyone, least of all—"

"He was like M. Simon then. Do you know M. Simon?"

Pierre stared at the boy in silence.

"M. Simon let me play with the dog. He gave me birds too—real ones—and a cage with little birds that hopped like real—all silver gilt and crystal. And when the birds hopped there were little bells and whistles . . . I wish I had my bird cage."

"I'll buy you another bird cage, Charlot . . . just like the one you had, with even more—"

"M. Simon went away. I wonder where he went."

"You must forget M. Simon. He was a beast!" Pierre exploded angrily. "He taught you filthy songs and let you forget your prayers. He and the guards got you drunk with brandy, and showed you nasty pictures . . . you must forget M. Simon. He lied to you about your mother, and Aunt Babet, and Mme Royale. He—"

"But they were stupid aristocrats, Monsieur!"

"Louis Charles!"

"Are you an aristocrat, Monsieur?"

"Oh, Charlot," cried Pierre, hiding his face in his hands. The room was closing in upon him too.

There was nothing of the young Louis Charles in the boy who sat peevish before him. Shrunken frame, swollen knees, mind dulled with drink and prostitution, the filth of imprisonment oozing from the very pores of his body . . . rotting flesh, its smell mingling putrid with the midsummer fragrance of petunias from the parterre below! Could the blood that flowed in his sluggish veins be the royal blood that Marie Antoinette had given him in her travail?

"When is Mme de Louvenne coming back?" whined Louis Charles.

Mme de Louvenne, it seemed, was back. She stood in the doorway, unable to retreat, unable to advance. Louis Charles saw her even as he spoke, and called a welcome. It was the first time he smiled.

Pierre's hands dropped slowly from his face.

"I've forgotten the book for Mme d'Autremont," she said lightly, and Pierre rose and walked out to the hall where he stood at a window looking out on the river. She thought of the time in the Vendée when she had gone to a funeral. She had not been able to look in the face of the mother whose child had died. The expression there had seemed to be meant for no human eyes—for God alone.

"Nicole . . ." Pierre called, and she went out into the hall to join him. "I know you have heard. . . ."

"I had already guessed, Monsieur," she said gently. "The boy dreams. Now and then he calls for his mother."

"I can trust you then not to talk—for his safety—for the future of France?"

"You can trust me—not to talk."

"You've been like a mother to him—"

"I find I am human, Monsieur."

"I will always be grateful to you."

"When I am gone, Monsieur, will you remember that I was human?"

He turned to her, his fingers locked in a hard knot behind him.

"You had a soft look then," he said, "like a madonna."

She smiled at him.

"You were thinking of your own child, perhaps . . . I often forget that you were a mother."

She still did not answer. The days were too few until her leaving to make words important. Ten, twenty days . . . and they would never again stand like this facing one another. She had a clean feeling, as if for a moment he knew her without artifice, or hidden motive, or even passion. She had no desire for anything further, willing to talk without touching hands, because there was an emotion even greater than passion.

At last she said: "It's been good to be needed."

"Mme de Louvenne," called Louis Charles. "I will eat my sweet if you feed it to me."

"Why don't you go, Monsieur, and I shall stay," she said softly. "There are times when it's best to be alone."

He walked away from her slowly without answering, and his tread was heavy on the stairs.

※※※※※※※※※※※※※※※※※※※※※※

CHAPTER XLV

THE DUC DE MONTPENSIER had begun a water color of Victoire the morning after his arrival. She sat to him each morning, vivid against her background of orchid striped wallpaper and Grecian urn of white flowers. Marie Antoinette with her hand on the Dauphin's shoulder looked down on her with a regal understanding; the Queen had endured this sort of tedium so often!

The three princes were Victoire's guests. With M. Talon in Ohio it would be nonsense, she had claimed, for them to stay at la Grande Maison; the house had become a morgue anyway, with the servants tiptoeing and a spoiled, sick child demanding the constant attention of Mme de Louvenne. The boy was so nervous, it seemed, that he still was forbidden all company, and if the Duc de Montpensier should so much as whistle at his shaving the dysentery would be released like a turgid spring brook. No, la Grande Maison was no better than Fort St.-Jean!

The Duc de Montpensier had laughed gaily. It was this early remark that had determined him to paint Victoire. She had the same éclat as the women who had made his father's dinners the scandal of a Paris not easily shocked. He had not been too young in those days to sense what Mme de Genlis, his *gouverneur,* was hiding from him; if Mme de Genlis had educated the d'Orléans sons in the modern manner, with not only foreign languages and dramatics but even vocational training, why had she detoured them from this still more animating branch of knowledge?

In a short week Victoire and Montpensier had come to a subtle understanding, and while he tried to yoke her impulsiveness to paper with his indifferent talent she amused and analyzed him.

She had used her usual formula of classification on the princes when they arrived. Louis-Philippe, Duc de Chartres, *Indifferent*. Rather tall and well formed, with fine dark hair and eyes, he spoke in a pleasing voice without the condescension for which his father had been noted. From his moments of melancholy absorption it was easy to see, however, that his heart remained in Philadelphia, entwined with Abigail Willing's. Yes, Chartres was engagingly dull, talking of the trip they had made equipped as Western traders, on horseback to Pittsburgh, on foot to Niagara Falls, from Chenung to Asylum by Durham boat. What did she care of his vast knowledge and cunning of mind when he dwelt on details of his journey? What did she care that they had often slept on the "soft side of a plank," or had eaten salt beef, corn bread, and pumpkin butter in the woods? Only a man of cold efficiency would carry a lancet and bleed himself!

As to Beaujolais, he was definitely *Bad*. Seventeen, delicate, with a handsome face having nothing behind it but thoughts of fencing and pastry. He had not even yet grown up to his manly hands and feet!

But the Duc de Montpensier . . . *Good!* In fact, *Excellent!* The least attractive physically of the brothers, he was by far the liveliest. At twenty-one, he had neither the dull balance of the older Chartres nor the stuffy naïveté of the sapling Beaujolais. He was just old enough, she thought, to relish the sophistication of a woman a trifle older. No mundane talk of saddlebags or moth collections—Montpensier was interested in life!

This morning they were alone in the salon. Louis Philippe had gone to confer with an agent of Mathias Hollenback who was to arrange for the princes a permanent American home, if such should be their fate. Young Beaujolais had gone to fence with one of the d'Autremonts, his pockets stuffed with bonbons.

Victoire absently watched the Duc paint, her head busy with plans for the coming fete on the island. She had assumed charge of it and she intended it to be far grander than anything given for Talleyrand or the Duc de Liancourt. Rumor had it that the princes traveled with white satin suits in their saddlebags, and this fete would be worthy of white satin!

A small pseudo-marble temple was being erected on the island, and would serve as a musicians' gallery. Victoire had composed verses in the Greek style which had already been distributed among the colonists. Assembled at an early hour, they would await the signal from the perron of a flying Mercury (Louis d'Autremont, winged), who would interrupt their singing to announce the arrival of the three princes. At this point attention would center on Victoire in a flowing Greek gown, her hair banded à la Sappho (*Mon Dieu*—what if it should rain!) . . . She would extend a chaplet of flowers to each prince, singing out in a strophe of exultation: "We welcome thee, princes of *Égalité*—" and the guests would answer in an anti-strophe. (Certainly no one would remember that the whole show was stolen from Mme d'Houdetot's fete for Benjamin Franklin.) Then there would be wine and songs—and songs and wine. And when the libretto ran out the guests could improvise. No fete could be successful if it ran too long on schedule, she thought. With the lighting of the Japanese lanterns at twilight and the serving of supper, she hoped the whole stuffy thing would go bacchanalian. In front of the mirror she was really magnificent singing: "We welcome—"

"Do you know, Madame, you defy the brush?" said Montpensier. "This is our fifth sitting and what do I have but a feeble likeness? The eyes aren't bad. The mouth is fair. But *you* . . . *you* elude me!"

They laughed together. They had laughed a great deal together over the smallest nuance. Their laughter met like two aimless winds, seeming to interlock without purpose and yet not without effect.

Montpensier laid down his brush, took a speck of snuff in his fingers, and toyed with it. There was a careless elegance about him, neither the foppishness of M. de Tuite nor the masculine grace of Pierre de Michelait. It was an inviting medium.

The sandy-haired Montpensier was hardly handsome. Once florid, he had lost his bloom in prison, much as grass compressed by a stone turns pale. Fort St.-Jean had robbed him of a robustness due his height. The small full mouth and the long straight nose were typically Bourbon, the sensuousness of the one belying the dignity of the other. One knew that the thin white fingers had too long been idle, that the large brown eyes had too long been dreaming. He looked to be a man of thirty with a provoking charm neither too intimate nor too impersonal.

It was as if on meeting they continued a friendship begun in the cradle; as if long ago they had passed the stage of stilted communication.

"And yet, nothing eludes *you,* Madame . . ." he went on. "The men grovel. The women wince. The children salute. The colony genuflects . . . even Paris is waiting for the time when you will return and lead it by the leash!"

"And—M. de Michelait?" she asked, waiting curiously for his answer.

"There's an air of defeat about him, *n'est-ce pas?* . . . He talks when he ought to be silent; forgets to laugh at your wit."

She leaned back in her chair suddenly, and the white urn of flowers wavered as her hand jogged the table. She caught the base of the urn firmly with a gesture quicker than the first.

"And yet it is M. de Michelait who has defeated me."

He looked into her eyes, the color of green gage plums.

"Non, non, non," confidently . . . "or else I should be able to paint you."

He dropped the bit of unused snuff into a Chinese bowl and picked up his brush again. She resumed her pose.

It was true: she had vanquished Asylum. It was so thoroughly vanquished that it lay flat, breathless under her tread. There was no longer the fear that it might revive and attack her. Nicole de Louvenne was leaving. A second letter had come from her husband who awaited her in Philadelphia. With the next Durham boat she would drift slowly, irrevocably out of Pierre's life. Slowly because he was so stupidly in love with her; irrevocably because Nicole de Louvenne, it seemed, loved her husband. If her going was a negative sort of victory it was nonetheless assured, thought Victoire.

Pierre's utter indifference to her since his return from the city was galling. It was useless to comfort one's self with the fact that he was indifferent toward everything. His books lay unopened, his gun and fishing rod neglected. To the new orchard he gave such scant attention that the American farmers who worked it were on continual holiday. He had made no attempt as yet to see Aristide, although Nicki was to be baptized before the princes left and du Petit-Thouars would be godfather. Only Nicki seemed to divert him, and M. Talon's ward with whom he spent part of every day.

"Chartres and I both thought it curious," Montpensier was saying, "about Charles Vivet."

Victoire smiled. This was not the first time Montpensier had begun to talk on the subject of which she was thinking.

"You have paid your respects then?"

"*Oui, Madame,* only an hour ago while you were primping."

"How do you mean, curious?" she asked.

"He is so like a Hapsburg, the little skeleton. Yet scarcely a chip of the old block! Perhaps just a wrinkled shaving! . . ." He looked up at the portrait of Marie Antoinette and the Dauphin. "He never had our flabby Bourbon chin."

Victoire stared at him for a moment. The truth jumped at her, like a night landscape in a flash of lightning. *Charles Vivet was the Dauphin!* Swift as a black snake, she slipped to the window that looked out upon Pierre and Nicki. They lay on their bellies, under an oak in the meadow. Her first instinct was to rush out to Pierre, shouting to him that she knew, that she had known all along. If the Duc de Montpensier had not been there she would have done this. But a moment ago he had handed her laurels of victory; she would have to flaunt them for his benefit.

The last hope of leaving Asylum soon with Pierre and Nicki died at once with the revelation. Pierre would stay here with this imbecile as long as need be, as long as France refused the throne to a Bourbon. Years—long, futile years perhaps. Now that she knew there was no solution her infinite patience and fidelity rose up to mock her. She had given Pierre the best that she had; he had not even given her his confidence in return!

"I won't stay here another month!" she thought wildly. "I'll take Nicki and fly. I'll have the last word. I'll have Nicki! Let Pierre rot here with his Dauphin—with his memories of Nicole . . . dregs, both of them!"

"Have I said something to offend you, Madame?" asked Montpensier, and he put down his brush and came over to her at the window.

"The little chip, the little shaving!" she repeated frantically, turning to him eyes that were too enraged for tears. *"Ah, mais vous êtes drôle!"*

She began to laugh, and Montpensier began to laugh so suddenly that he ended in a fit of coughing.

"But if I am droll," he gasped, "you are—bewitching!"

The words fell away. There was a heaviness to the moment that followed, and yet a lightness, a giddiness.

Montpensier looked intense now, his slim white fingers on her arm, on her throat.

"Your eyes swallow me!" he whispered. "I used to dream of them at

Fort St.-Jean before I even knew you. . . . I knew them at once when
I came here. . . ."

She met his lips, thinking of Pierre in the meadow, thinking of
Pierre in a frenzy of desire as her life with him crashed before her.

❀❀❀❀❀❀❀❀❀❀❀❀❀❀❀❀❀❀❀❀❀❀❀❀

CHAPTER XLVI

THE NIGHT of the fete la Grande Maison was deserted except for
Nicole and the Dauphin. In a fit of magnanimity Dr. Buzard had
given his slaves money for a brawl of rum and dancing. Julie and
Wallois had been invited.

It was just turning dark. Nicole stood at the window of the bedchamber that looked down upon the festive island. In another hour,
she thought, her work would be over. The long process of hoping and
waiting and suffering was something akin to childbirth; a brief, agonizing struggle at the end, and then freedom. In the event of either
failure or success there would no longer be the tension, the strain of
wondering, tortured, at the outcome. . . .

In an hour, the Iroquois would await the boy at the river. She would
have to carry Louis Charles for several hundred yards. That would not
be easy, though she had accustomed herself to his weight by carrying
him to his chair and back or by holding him in her arms for a long
period while he watched the dog romping on the lawn, or Wallois
hoeing. If she were intercepted she would say that she had decided to
take Charles rowing, to see the lights and festivity on the island. It was
not a convincing alibi but who could refute it?

"Mme de Louvenne," said Louis Charles from his chair, "I am getting sleepy. I would like to go to my bed. Just till the lanterns go on.
Then you will call me."

"But of course," she said, and made him walk to his bed. She had
given him a sleeping potion with his supper. Tonight too she had

bathed him with special care, dressing the sores with fresh bandages, putting on him a clean night shift.

She sat on the bed beside him and held his hand.

"Tell me a story," he said with a plaintive yawn.

She considered a moment. "I'll tell you a story about a bird. He was a wild bird and very beautiful. Full of color—purple and white with a golden crest and blue eyes. A hunter saw him one day and trapped him for his mistress. It was a wonderful gift, a wonderful find. But the bird was used to the woods and the sun, and he stopped singing and beat himself against the sides of the cage. His lovely feathers molted and he didn't eat and his bright color faded. His mistress was worried. She really wanted to let him go free. . . . After a while the bird got used to the cage. He wasn't happy and he didn't sing, but he'd forgotten the woods and the sun. Well, the conscience of the lady still hurt her. In fact it hurt her so much that one day when her lover was gone she opened the cage and let the bird out. He fluttered out to a tree, but the sun blinded him and his wings had lost their strength. He wanted to go back to his cage and couldn't find it. Then a storm came with a wild wind and rain. He was very frightened. He had no home. And so— the wind and the rain beat him to death. But back in the house the mistress was happy for she had given the bird his freedom."

The blue eyes of the Dauphin clouded.

"I don't like that story."

"No, *bien-aimé,* I shouldn't have told it . . . we'll talk about something happier."

"When you came from your walk you said you had a present for me."

"*Mais oui*—to be sure. I'd forgotten." She groped in the pocket of her gown and found a four-leaf clover. Putting it in the palm of his hand, she closed his fingers over it. "This is for good luck, my little Dauphin."

His blue eyes opened wide and surprised as those of a china doll.

"Who told you the secret?"

"I guessed it."

His eyes filled suddenly with tears. "I don't want to be king. I just want to stay with you always, Mme de Louvenne."

She gripped his hand tightly.

"I don't want to be a filthy aristocrat!" He broke out into a tirade of swearing and obscenity.

"Louis Charles!" she reprimanded sternly. "Do you want your mouth washed with soap? I thought I'd taught you that you are a gentleman —not a guard in the Temple!"

He hid his face with his arm, sobbing, and she continued to hold his hand. At last she felt his fingers relax a little.

"Louis Charles," she whispered, leaning close to him. "You won't have to be king. But you mustn't be frightened when you waken. . . . Will you be sure to remember? . . ." His eyes flickered a little and closed.

"Louis Charles, I love you."

She was not certain he heard. He was lying so still and was breathing deeply. She waited. She had always heard of time standing still, had never known what it meant. The twilight hung pregnant, refusing to deepen, while her heart fought like the bird to be free of its cage.

At last she was unable to see the oak tree outside the window. She gathered Louis Charles in her arms, tossing about him a cover from the bed. He hung limp on her shoulder, so heavy in his deep, drugged sleep that her every step was an effort.

The house was black, and the moon not yet up over Rummerfield. But the night was alive with life that frightened her. There was a strange mixture of violins from the island and voodoo tomtoms from the Negro quarters. Crickets chirped. An owl hooted. The stones of the rutted road rolled with her impact—all of them thundering in her ear like the rumble of a boulder down a mountain.

Twice she stopped, kneeling in the underbrush, dizzy with the weight of the Dauphin. She couldn't go on with her breath coming so short and fast . . . but she must go on! Waiting only made her conscious of breathing . . . and yet the child had turned to iron. How to lift him again with arms that had turned to thistledown?

Was that the voice of *M. le Docteur* singing above the others, urgent, insistent?

Fear began to fill her. What if the Iroquois would not be there? What if she should sprain her ankle and sink under her burden? What if a pair of lovers from the island should be drifting into the shelter of the inlet?

She remembered suddenly a talk she had had with her father when she was only seven. She had been crying because her dog was dead. Until then she had not known the meaning of "dead." He had stroked her hair, wisely waiting until she had had her tears. Then he had said: "There is no death but the fear of death." She had not understood the words then, but they had given her comfort. And she had come to know in time what they meant.

She went stumbling on, her arms stronger.

The damp of the river was close, the fresh-smelling fern and water-lapped weeds, the stinging of gnats and mosquitoes. The red of a lantern at the end of the dock blinked like a Cyclops' eye. She turned right toward the clump of buttonwood trees, burrowing through the lush growth of skunk cabbage. The dark pressed her body like strangling hands.

She could sense rather than see the bronze, squat figure before her.

"Le Petit," he whispered, clipping the syllables sharply.

"Le Petit," she repeated huskily.

She felt the large hands that groped for her burden, and she leaned over swiftly and kissed the cold cheek of the boy.

For a moment she waited, dizzy, reeling with lightness. There was a crackling of undergrowth, soft scuffling, and then the lap of oars in the water.

As she probed her way back to the house the lap of water persisted above the violins and the dance of the chica. Tears were streaming down her face.

The empty room was chill as a mausoleum. She moved quickly, lighting a candle and placing it on the Dauphin's bedside table. Then she took a vial of ether from her pocket, opened it, and laid it on the floor near the bed. From a chiffonier she took one of the Dauphin's bedsocks and tangled it in the sheet so that it would be seen at once; the mate to it was on the trail of Rummerfield Mountain.

Her work was not over. As the party broke up on the island she would have to rush breathless into its midst to report that the child was missing. In the meantime she must wait again—one, two, three hours. She tossed a shawl over her shoulders and went down to the garden; there were iron chairs there about a bird bath, and the shrubs and flowers were beginning to take form in the moonlight. She sat down, exhausted, her eyes focused on the lights twinkling through the trees at the river's edge.

She had a distinct feeling of being two people. Part of her—the physical part—was a conflagration of nerves that made sitting still a crucifixion. Within, she felt cold, hollow of triumph. In a few hours she would have to say good-bye to Pierre.

She began to think of her life cut in two by a knife, like a loaf of bread. Her purpose was accomplished. All of her bitterness, all of her fire of patriotism lay in that stroke of the knife that divided the bread. Now that her work was done none of it seemed to matter. She tried to rouse herself with thoughts of her return to France, how much there

376 Asylum FOR THE QUEEN

would be for her to do there. M. Paul-François Barras would secretly commend her, give her gold in return for tears. Married to Georges Brigaud, she would have a life of ferment, of zealous *Liberté, Égalité, Fraternité.*

Married to Georges Brigaud—listening to his excitable, high-pitched voice, day after day—watching his short, stocky hands gesticulate—following the swagger of his stride. But that would not be all. She would belong to Georges Brigaud, her body as well as her soul. She would have to lie with him, quivering under his touch, loathing him as she submitted to his passion, loathing herself even more as a whore.

She would not marry Georges Brigaud!

The decision was like cool, sweet water to a fever. She need never see him again, never taste of the seething of the sewer of Paris. She would go back to the Vendée, where she would have to neither think nor feel—feel nothing beyond the cool, sticky dough as she kneaded it, or the soft patina of the rosewood chest as she dusted. It would be good to let the fire die down to a bed of ashes. . . .

The hours lagged. Then lanterns began to go out on the island. There were snatches of singing again as the boats plied back and forth —no longer verses of Greek pomp but risqué tunes of café and brothels. The fete was over.

Nicole paced the gravel path, rehearsing the last act of her drama. . . . She would say that she had put Charles Vivet to bed, and, going out for a bit of air in the garden, she had fallen asleep there; the lustiness of the singing at last had wakened her. When she returned to the bedchamber the boy was gone. Only half an hour before she had been up to cover him. . . . That was all except her tears and abject remorse. That was all, that is, to her part in the life of the Dauphin. There would be the good-bye to Pierre: no more perhaps than a meeting of her eyes with his own.

An hour later Nicole followed the silent Pierre from his house to la Grande Maison. She could hardly keep up with his stride, and might have been his dog Neige trotting at his heels. She knew he was considering possible places of hiding: St. Louis, the tribe of the Oneidas, the Moravians, Vincennes on the Wabash—figuring who should go up the river, who down; which of the men should take the Sullivan Trail, the road to Homet's, the woods of Rummerfield.

Her part had been easy to play. She had almost collapsed now that the strain was over, and the tears had come again without effort. Dr. Buzard, who had returned with the princes for a nightcap, administered smelling salts, giving her an ecstatic look of congratulation.

The Dauphin's identity was revealed at once, and various men had rushed home to change clothes and get their guns and horses, neglecting hysterical women. While Pierre hastened to la Grande Maison for possible clues the others would organize.

When Pierre and Nicole reached the house it was still deserted and the voodoo music wailed on in the Negro quarters. Dr. Buzard had not only been generous but munificent.

Pierre glanced about the bedchamber, tossed open the wardrobe of untouched clothes, and seized the vial of ether that dribbled onto the floor. The smell of ether was sweet, cloying. He searched in the sheets for the mate to the bedsock, which he'd stuffed in his belt. Then he saw the wad of half-dried mud that might have fallen from the heel of a boot. He snatched it up, fingering a bit of squashed wild flower that was imbedded in it. It was a rare white violet.

"They've come by Rummerfield!" he cried. "That's the only place this grows!"

Nicole leaned back against the wardrobe. Here was the moment she had worked for, and now that it had come she no longer believed in it. Here was her moment of victory filling her with sordidness and desolation. It came to her as she looked at the pitiful hope in his face that she could not do this one more thing to deceive him—that she was no longer strong enough for deceit. Facing his disillusionment too would take less courage than going through life knowing that he still loved her. She must tell him the truth now. She must stand naked before him. If she must go on through the years bearing each day as it came, she must hear from his lips that he loathed her.

"You will never find him," she said.

He turned to her, suddenly startled. It was the way she had said the words with a quiet confidence.

"What do you mean?"

"He's gone—quite safe, but forever."

It took him a stupid moment to penetrate the truth; she was staring at him with shining eyes, with shoulders back, with the look of a crazy, triumphant murderess.

He seized her by the arms.

"You know where he is!"

"I only know who took him."

"Where has he gone?"

"I don't know, I tell you."

His grip tightened. "You *must* know!"

"*Non, non, non* . . . Pierre, you're hurting me!"

"Who took him from you?"

"I will never tell!"

"You can be made to tell!"

"*Non, non, non*—you can cut out my tongue, burn me at the stake, but I'll never tell you!"

Her voice rang out like a tocsin as his fingers dug into her flesh.

"You may have to die for this!"

"I would rather die!"

"I could easily kill you!"

Her eyes were filled with terror, for his nails bored into her like the nails of a crucifix.

"I had to tell you!" she exclaimed wildly. "I'll never see you again—"

"You wanted to torture me."

"Oh no, *mon Pierre* . . . I love you! I've always loved you!"

"If you lie to me now I'll strangle you!"

"I'll never lie again—never, never!"

He released her with the suddenness of a spring, afraid of the rage in his hands.

She began to cry out the truth to him: what she believed, why she was here, how she had always known their love was hopeless. She was not even certain he heard her, until at last he stopped pacing up and down the room and crushed her hands in his.

"You have an accomplice!"

"*Oui*—"

"M. Heraud—"

"I won't tell you!"

"You think that because I love you I won't denounce you—that you can stand and laugh at me and mock me!"

"*Non, non, non, mon Pierre* . . . please, believe me."

"I don't love you. I hate you as I've never hated another human being! Right down to the rotten, lying core—"

She stared at him blankly, as a widow stares for the last time on the face of her husband. Haunting, sharp black eyes; thin, quivering nostrils; tight, white lips, too angry to curse her. She would carry this death mask in her heart through life like the widow; and her heart would weep at the cold here close to her lips that had known his passion.

"Don't go for him!" she whispered at last. "You don't really want him! . . . I've watched you loathing him and his sores—loathing the France he stood for. I've watched you fighting yourself—afraid to give in to something new you've believed in!"

"I no longer believe in anything." His hands became iron clamps.

"Oh but you did, *mon Pierre,* you did!"

There was the canter of Major Hoops's horse in the distance, and the sound unleashed her thoughts, the dreadful sound that seemed to press all time to an atom.

"You believed in freedom here—for yourself—for the little tailor. . . . You ate with him, hunted with him, made laws with him on the council. Nicki played with his children . . . you loved him and wanted to help him . . . he loved you, believed in your goodness—"

"I made a vow to Marie Antoinette!"

"A stupid vow! A curse to you if you keep it! Look into your heart, *mon Pierre,* before it's too late. . . . Don't be afraid of the truth, I beg of you! . . . They're the same people here and in France. I had to learn it too. . . . I came here loathing you—and I love you! I wanted to hate Louis Charles and his royal blood—and I loved him!"

"You've kept your vow!"

"God help me! . . ."

The tears came like burning acid, and she stood there, trembling, desperate, praying for she knew not what—praying perhaps for some miracle that would take away the pain of living.

The hoofbeats were close, icy, inexorable as the gash of a great steel blade. Pierre snatched her suddenly in his arms, like a savage, crushing the breath from her lips, crushing the strength from her body.

Along with the heavy tread of Major Hoops on the stairs, came the sound of other hoofbeats, other horses.

Pierre thrust her from him and sank down on the *bergère,* his face in his hands.

The Major bristled in, his red beard braided in three small plaits by the facetious Mme Reynaud. He stood gripping the bedpost, swaying like a catkin in an eddy.

"*Allons—à la Dauphin!*" he cried with drunken relish.

Pierre stumbled to his feet. His eyes seemed to cut the shadows. Nicole waited for the words to come—words that would expose her to the drunken Hoops and the colony. Words that would bring in-

quisition and the punishment of a heinous crime. Words that would
keep her here till Pierre returned. Words to forestall good-bye. Oh
God! Why didn't he say them?

"*Allons!*" cried the Major again.

Pierre was swallowed up by the blackness of the hall.

Seeing Nicole, the Major made a mighty, sweeping bow. As he followed Pierre, the three red spears of his beard caught the light like a
bloody trident.

CHAPTER XLVII

SEVERAL DAYS had passed. A few of the searching party had returned
despondent. The fat M. Carles had the hungry look of a cat that has
lost its mouse; Dr. Buzard had vowed that he would find the little
King if he must live on berries the rest of his life; M. de la Roué had
quite frankly said he was interested only in his razor, and to hell with
the Dauphin!—he was legally dead anyway, and one king was as good
as another.

The colony itself had gone into a desultory mourning. Everyone had
been to the Dauphin's room to see the rumpled bedclothes, the shriveled violet, the stains eaten into the carpet by the ether. It was said *sotto
voce* that Louis-Philippe had recognized the Dauphin, and that since
the Comte de Provence was apoplectic and the Comte d'Artois, next in
line, must certainly die young of love and acrobatics, Louis-Philippe
might very easily . . . *sotto voce* . . . *sotto voce.* . . .

Yes, thought Victoire as she finished writing in her journal one
morning, Louis-Philippe might easily become king. He was young and
vigorous and court life had eaten voraciously of Louis's brothers. Next
in line after Louis-Philippe would be the Duc de Montpensier. And although Louis-Philippe was rugged with lancing himself and a careful
diet, there was always the possibility of a fall from a horse or an onslaught of yellow fever. . . . Victoire, Queen of France!

Every woman in court would have a pet *marcassin!* M. de Tuite the eunuch would be delegated to lace her girdle. Pierre de Michelait would be chamberlain of the radish garden! Nicki of course would make a royal alliance. The fleur-de-lis would be changed to the skunk cabbage in fond memory of her meeting with the Duc at Asylum. And if she were bored she would build a new Trianon and pick raspberries, like Marie Antoinette. Except that these raspberries would be hand-embroidered!

She was laughing briskly as the Duc de Montpensier entered the open doorway of her boudoir. He laughed too as he came over and stood behind her chair. But his laughter was not as carefree as in the beginning. It had a subtle note of urgency; it was like the basic thread of an embroidery, which if pulled would quickly unravel the pattern.

"Bon jour, Madame!" he said, his hands on the chair back close to her shoulders. "And a moment ago I thought it was raining!"

She leaned back and stretched, brushing his chin lightly with the quill of her feather. He stooped quickly to kiss her and found the feather between their lips.

"How hungry your eyes are, Monsieur!" she taunted. "That lazy Frau Gresch hasn't sent up your chocolate."

He made no answer and sauntered to the window. Nibbling at the end of her quill, she watched him. The dressing gown she had given Pierre on his last fete day was vastly becoming to the Duc, a dark green with autumn leaves that made his hair a shining russet. There was a flush of color now on his cheekbones, two little angry patches of frustration. The Bourbon lips were pouting. She was beginning to think he was quite handsome . . . or was it the invisible crown that so enhanced him? How would she ever know since she would never meet him as a tailor or a sawyer? The fact remained there was an air about him *faire venir l'eau à la bouche,* making each rainy day a delicious abstraction.

And it was raining again. For three days the ground had sopped up the dismal downpour, and the river had begun to swirl angrily around its rocks. *M. le Duc,* too, had felt the tide rising within him. . . .

She glanced at the last words she had written:

"The search seems to be hopeless, *Dieu merci!* In a few days Pierre should be back. In a few weeks Mme Bingham will be inviting us to one of her soggy teas. Civilization! Philadelphia, London, Paris!"

She clapped the journal shut.

"Will we finish the portrait this morning?" she asked.

"N'importe. The light is still poor."

"There's a streak of blue. Perhaps it will clear. Get your chocolate, *mon cher.* You'll feel better."

"I've had my chocolate. . . . And Frau Gresch, it seems, has done nothing but slide down banisters all night."

"Banisters . . . she dreamed of them, you mean! Banisters . . . drowning! Well, no wonder. The rain's beginning to make me feel too as if I were going down for the third time."

He didn't answer.

She went to her wardrobe, slipping off the negligee (not the green peignoir that made her maternal); and she felt the Duc's eyes on her back as she took down the gown she wore for her sittings. Even Pierre had once told her she had a beautiful back. . . .

He came over and stood leaning against the door frame, his hands stuffed in his pockets, his brown eyes sulky.

"You know very well what you're doing to me," he said.

"M. le Duc! I beg of you . . . let's get down to business. The business of painting!" she added hastily.

"Tout à l'heure!" he exclaimed, and went off for his paints and brushes.

When he returned it was agreed that he could finish the portrait in her boudoir. There were only a few details of dress and hands to be done. Victoire settled herself in the pillows of her chaise longue, watching him work in silence. She was a trifle puzzled. She had handled the sullen type as well as every other, but *M. le Duc* was a little out of hand a little too soon. . . .

She was not even sure what she wanted from *M. le Duc.* Conquest of course! But conquest meant one thing to a man, another to a woman. And it often ended in an awkward problem. She would have to wheedle him back to good humor with some of her spicy stories . . . and, *Nom de Dieu!* what wheedling she would have to do when Pierre came! For Mme de Louvenne was gone. Victoire herself had presented Nicole with a bouquet of roses as the Durham boat left the dock— every rose she could find with enough thorns. Mme de Louvenne's eyes were red with weeping, and she looked strangely like a little lost waif who has dropped his bun in the gutter. Yes, Pierre would be spleeny for a while, but after all he was a man and a Frenchman.

"Did you ever hear about the night at Trianon when Marie Antoinette was playing Colette in the *Devin du village?"* she asked. "Of course the Queen never permitted the officers of the bodyguards of the princes to attend, but there was one of them in love with her, a certain Gougenot—"

Yes, he was smiling in spite of himself, thought Victoire, as she gabbled on to her astounding climax.

"Oh, and that reminds me of the time Mme de Polignac's garter was found in the pocket of Louis's hunting jacket . . . Louis the chaste, *imagine!* Some wit, of course, put it—"

"*Maman!*" cried Nicki, bolting in and clambering up on the chaise, "*Maman!* The sun's out and it's stopped raining! And M. Aubrey is going to shoe his white horse. What are you and *M. le Duc* laughing at?"

"Life, *mon petit chou!* Ah, sometimes you're such a pink bonbon I could eat you!"

She caught him in her arms and kissed him, running her fingers through the thick black curls. "Cherry nose," Pierre called him. A little gamin of a gentleman who exulted in mud and squirming bugs and adventure! The one really strong tie between herself and Pierre, she thought, the one human being he loved more than his Hyacinthes and Nicoles!

Nicki's boot left a smudge on her skirt. It was obvious he had already been out to sample the sunshine. He was clutching the little ship model Aristide had made for him.

"Ah, you are never without your *Nina!*" Victoire exclaimed.

"Not the *Nina, Maman*. The *Pinta,*" he said patiently. "May I go out to sail her? The rain's stopped."

"A ship is a ship to a woman!" laughed Victoire, and drew one of his curls over the scar on his forehead from the picnic. "Why don't you see what Henri is doing today? Be sure to wear your galoshes."

"Henri has his throat in a flannel. I would rather sail—"

"Are you going to paint the mud on my skirt, Monsieur?" asked Victoire, half in amusement, half in annoyance.

"Why not? . . . I've put the dross in your eyes, you wicked creature!"

Nicki slithered down from the chaise longue.

"Why do you laugh at things that aren't funny?" he said.

"Ah, *mignon,* when you grow up you'll see!"

"When I grow up I'm going to be a sailor like M. de Petit-Thouars. And now I'm—"

"Tilt your thumb a little—so . . ." said the Duc.

Nicki hopped from the room like a kite tacking into the wind.

"He has the energy of a Talleyrand," she said.

"What do you know of Talleyrand's energy?"

"What every woman knows who has ever met him! . . . He was often at Passy. He married us, you know."

"A juring priest? You are not really married then!" taunted the Duc. "You are only M. de Michelait's mistress!"

"That's what the Marquise de Bussac thought! *Dieu,* what a time we had! Juring, nonjuring; juring, nonjuring! We haggled over it like the menu of a party. What shall we serve? Mme A. spews after caviar; M. B. gets a gallstone from sherry trifle—"

"And divorce has come to cure all indigestion in France—all that the guillotine didn't cure!"

"And why not? In Coblentz divorce was all the fashion. No cuckolds there!"

"You're delightfully modern, Madame."

"Et vous?"

"I am simply a man: wanting what I want—with the quickest method."

Victoire laughed, and the painting went on with more casual talk for a little while. Finally Montpensier laid down his brushes and began to fuss with his snuff, his paints—righting a chair, talking of rainbows, Nicki, chocolate.

Victoire watched him with narrowing eyes. She was not taken by surprise. She had known too many men, and the aimlessness of the talk did not deceive her. They were all alike. When not quite certain if their advances would be welcome they approached them with the stealth of a sneak thief.

She let him flounder like a fish on a hook—a kingfish, she thought with huge enjoyment. And she noted that he remembered to latch the door in spite of his abstraction.

Now he was sitting on the chaise beside her, stroking the folds of her skirt with an exquisite softness. She looked down on the disturbed fingers so long imprisoned, then at his lips, the sensuous Bourbon lips. Lying back on the pillows, suddenly tense, she knew it was what she had wanted all along. She could tell now by the fast running of her blood, the inviting whiteness of his skin, the long drought her passion had fought with the cold Pierre. It was quite funny—really funny—that the Duc had known it before her, and she had duped herself, evasive as a virgin.

She looked into his eyes and laughed, and he laughed with her, the old easy laugh of understanding they had shared in the beginning.

An hour had passed—or perhaps two—when there was a knock at the door.

"Un moment!" cried Victoire, and the Duc held her with a lingering kiss to tease her. She made a *moue* at him and hastily brushed back her curls as she passed the dressing-table. By the time she opened the door Montpensier was standing at his easel trying to steady his fingers on the brush.

Frau Gresch was not in the least duped. There had been the click of the latch, and barred doors were no boding of good—nor were Victoire's flushed cheeks and sparkling eyes.

"Nicki's gone again!" she panted. "He's not at Henri's nor in Mme d'Autremont's cooky jar. And all last night I dreamed—"

"He was here a few minutes ago," said Victoire, repressing a desire to straighten her fichu.

"Ach, Himmel, he'll be soaked!"

Victoire turned to the window in faint surprise. It was raining again. The rain dripped through the trees with a soft, slow sound, like the sobbing of a child.

"He'll be all right. He's at the forge. He went to see M. Aubrey shoe the red roan."

Frau Gresch stood there like a collapsing balloon, her eyes damp with tears, her hair sprouting, her warts like a peppering of mustard seeds against the frightened pallor of her face.

"When it's time for dinner send Sophie to fetch him."

Frau Gresch shot a cantankerous look at Montpensier, and Victoire said brightly: "Come see the portrait, Frau Gresch. It's almost finished."

"I've seen it," muttered Frau Gresch, and waddled down the hall.

Victoire gave the door an irritable push.

"I thought he said he was going to sail his boat," said the Duc, tossing the brush among some others.

"Non, non, non—he said he was going to the forge. . . . It's the same every day since he's been able to toddle. . . . Ah, *mon cher,* what a raving beauty you've made of me!"

He took her into his arms again, resenting the moments of interruption.

"I'm not going to let you go, you know. Never again—for a minute!"

"You're really in love with me, Monsieur?"

"Can you ask after what you've taught me?"

"But you're going away—"

"And you're coming with me!"

She had never seriously considered this possibility. The princes had come for a two weeks' visit. She had meant of course, to deflate Montpensier's spirits, nothing more. In the last few hours everything had changed. She had scarcely remembered that life could be so exciting. What was wrong with becoming a duchess if Pierre didn't want her—of becoming the Queen, perhaps, of this debonair madcap? Wasn't it all inevitable from the very moment of their meeting?

Her lips widened in a smile and he kissed her again—insanely. Having enough of her, he had not gone to his hoeing like Pierre, but he wanted more of her—all of her—again and again! It was very flattering, very bewildering. . . .

They lolled on the chaise longue together, bantering one moment, caressing the next. The Duc was filled with plans of utter madness. Victoire would go with them to New York, New Orleans, Havana, Spain. Eventually they would settle along the Thames, and Victoire would be the toast of London. . . . It was the whistling of young Beaujolais on the stairs that finally roused them to the present. Could it really be time to dress for dinner?

Before Victoire had finished her toilette she heard Montpensier at the piano. His rich tenor pealed out in a folk song, jubilant, she thought, as a parrot that had just glutted himself with sunflower seed. She dressed with meticulous care, getting out some antique jewelry worn by her grandmother, a gift to Mme de Varionnet from Montpensier's grandfather the Duc d'Orléans. Exceedingly ftting. . . .

As she opened her door blithely it struck her as strange that Montpensier had stopped singing in the middle of a measure. The jubilee of his voice had made the silence twice as empty. Even the rain had stopped its murmuring.

She began to descend the stairs with a regal bearing. She had never looked more lovely, more worthy the adoration of a prince. . . . At the foot of the steps in the salon there were rain-drenched people. Dr. Buzard, Mme d'Autremont, a strange man, and M. Bec-de-Lièvre. They looked up at her, and she saw that M. Bec-de-Lièvre held the *Pinta* and that its sails were gone.

"Madame . . ." murmured the Duc, coming up the stairs to meet her. But the lightness of his touch had turned to lead.

"Qu'est-ce que c'est?" she asked quickly, and the group shuffled a little.

Then she saw Nicki lying on the sofa. He lay very still, one fat bare leg dangling to the floor. He seemed to be staring out of the window toward the river. He was soaked, as Frau Gresch said he—

"Nicki!" cried Victoire, rushing to him. Her hands chilled with the sogginess of his clothes, his blue stillness. "Nicki—speak to me . . . *Mon Dieu!* Cover him, someone! He's cold—he's . . . Holy Virgin, *Mother of God!"*

Mme d'Autremont laid a comforting hand on her shoulder, and Victoire thrust it off.

"I won't let him die!" she screamed with a pitiful triumph, clutching the small, wet body to her.

They drifted away one by one.

M. Bec-de-Lièvre paused a moment before he left, and placed the wreck of the *Pinta* at the foot of the Little Admiral.

Victoire was left alone. The child was sodden in her arms, a weight that grew to iron. Even as she laid him down the weight remained.

She couldn't bear it—this immutable defeat of death. The tears came, burning, violent.

"Oh, my darling!" she moaned to the stark green eyes that looked into her own and yet beyond her. "Why didn't you tell me you were going down to the river!"

❁❁❁❁❁❁❁❁❁❁❁❁❁❁❁❁❁❁❁❁

CHAPTER XLVIII

Pierre returned too late to see the child.

He had been gone almost a week when Victoire and the Duc de Montpensier in the summer house heard hoofbeats turning in at the river road and recognized Pierre and d'Orléans. Victoire laid down

her American sampler with its flag and "United We Stand," and the
Duc gave her hand a reassuring clasp.

She was dressed in black with an ebony cross nestled in the folds
of her crisp white fichu.

"Courage, *mignonne,*" he comforted. "Remember, it is you who
suffer most. You're the mother."

"I couldn't have lived without your—understanding," she whispered,
submitting to his quick embrace.

The Duc waved to Pierre and d'Orléans from the door of the summer house, and as the men approached, Victoire could see that Pierre
knew about Nicki. Aristide had found him then before Pierre reached
the village. Aristide, who took all the blame, because he had been the
one to carve the model of the *Pinta!* . . .

Her heart ached for Pierre with the only pure emotion she had ever
felt for him. And he looked totally beaten. His shoulders sagged, his
step was heavy. The search of a week through the woods had given
him a haunted, sleepless look, and his clothes were disheveled and
dirty. His beard made him old—a stranger. . . .

After a second of hesitation she ran out to him. He put his arm
about her and looked down into her eyes with a sharp searching. It
was as if he would not believe the truth until her eyes reaffirmed it.

"You know then? . . ."

"Aristide—" His arm dropped and he took a few steps away from
them. They watched him stoop to pick a weed from a patch of mari-
golds.

"*Mme la Marquise* . . ." said d'Orléans, taking Victoire's hand and
kissing it. "*Je suis affligé. . . .*"

His fine, dark eyes beckoned those of Montpensier, and the two
princes strolled away.

Pierre followed Victoire into the summer house, and he stood looking down at the river.

Victoire began her story, the story of the last few hours of the dead
which so obsesses the living. Montpensier was finishing the portrait;
Nicki ran in. He was going to see the bay roan shod. . . . If he had
only even mentioned the river or sailing they might have found him
soon enough. . . .

The story, abridged, had been repeated to all the women of the
colony. Victoire herself believed it.

Pierre, silent, was watching the river—the river, still turgid from the
rain, shining pink from the sky and the dropping sun.

"It *is* a beautiful river," said Pierre when she finished. But his voice was weary.

"*Beautiful!* It's ugly. It's always been ugly—like an old hag, with its rocks like warts . . . I can't bear to look at it. If you'd only listened to me! I've begged you to leave—begged you to make it safe for him—"

"Victoire!"

"I wanted the best for him always! But the Dauphin meant more to you than your son. . . . The filthy little cesspool! I hope he rots in the woods! . . . You chose between them. Now you haven't either!"

He turned to her, and she faltered at the dreadful pain in his eyes.

"You must know it's true—that I'm not just trying to be cruel!" she whispered.

"Yes, I know it's true."

He watched her outburst of tears with an apathy that surprised him. There was no more room in him for emotion. He sat down beside her with a sense of duty, and took her hand.

"Oh, *mon Pierre*," she sobbed, her head on his breast, "if only you could bring him back to me! I loved him so! He was all I had of you!"

"He was all you've ever wanted of me."

"*Non, non, non.* I've always loved you—but you would never let me. Mlle Violette, Marie Antoinette, Aristide, books, Mme de Louvenne! Everything came before me!"

"You'll never know what love is, Victoire."

"How can you say that! I've given you all the passion that was in me! I've waited and waited for you to love me till I thought I would die! . . . Oh, it's not too late, *mon Pierre!* . . . We'll go away, far away, where we can be gay again. Where we can forget—"

"Nicki's the one thing in my life I want to remember," he said sharply.

"You wouldn't stay here *now?* . . ."

"I am very tired, Victoire. I can only seem to think of sleep."

The princes were to leave by Durham boat on Monday. On Sunday, the day Nicki was to have been baptized, M. Heraud came after Mass with a letter for Pierre.

"I promised her I'd deliver it to you myself," said M. Heraud, looking down his long shiny nose in embarrassment. "I thought every day that you'd come to the inn. . . ."

"She left—alone?" asked Pierre. He had been unable to face any man in the colony without suspicion.

"*Oui, Monsieur*—alone. She took it very hard, being responsible for the child when it happened."

"Is that what she said?"

"Not in so many words, Monsieur. . . . But she seemed to—to crumple."

Pierre put the letter in his pocket. Callers were drifting in and out to pay their respects to the princes and to make calls of condolence on himself and Victoire. Pierre began to wonder if he could endure Victoire's story once more. It grew in detail each time she told it: there was only the thumb to be finished on the portrait; Nicki had been wearing the suit that made his eyes green as a Luna moth; the Duc de Montpensier had been like a father, a great comfort in the hours she had had to undergo without her husband. . . .

Oh, God, thought Pierre, why can't the dead be left to rest in peace! The flowers had been left whole on Nicki's grave—not snatched and plucked to pieces! Or was the child in a place where he couldn't rest? Nicki had never been baptized, given to God in the eyes of man. Was his soul condemned then by the negligence of his parents? Such a little, innocent soul for eternal darkness. . . . Was there a God who would do this thing to Nicki?

"Oh, Mme de la Roué—if only I'd listened to what Frau Gresch told me! . . . She'd dreamed of drowning—but she is always dreaming. And half the time her dreams—"

"If you will excuse me," said Pierre, "I must go on an errand."

He took his horse and rode out into the woods. There was a cool fragrance here, like the hand of his mother. Tying his horse to a tree, he walked on until he could see the river between the sturdy pine trunks. He lay the letter on the ground before him, looking at the hasty scrawl of his name, watching an ant with a bee's wing stagger across it. For a long time he lay there wondering why he was unable to read what she had written.

Was he afraid of the truth? How could he be afraid when there was no truth beyond the loss of Nicki?

He opened the letter at last. It was very long. It began:

> *Mon Pierre:*
>
> *Is it true that you are gone? The clock still ticks—the fire still moves. And another day is breaking. I think of so many things I wanted to say to you—big things and little things.*

*I think the little things hurt the most, because I will never
be able to say them to another. I wanted to tell you about
the double lily that grew once in my garden, the pictures I
painted, and the shooting star that looked just like a bear.
Don't laugh, mon Pierre! But try to understand. . . .*

She wrote of her early days, how she had never been a happy child
like Gabrielle. It had hurt her to clean the bloody instruments of her
father, to see a wild flower ripped from its roots. There was something
in the summer dusk she couldn't bear. . . . Had he ever felt it?

Did he believe that there was tragedy in beauty? . . . When she was
five she had been called an ugly duckling. Her hair had been straight
then (it was the fever made it curl). Her eyes had no special color;
Gabrielle's were sapphire. The small pug nose with its freckles, Jacques
said, had looked like a speckled bird's egg. She had grown up knowing
she was an ugly duckling, wanting to be beautiful like Marie Antoinette

M. Flèche had seemed to guess her need, had said that the beauty
of books could be drunk into the soul, the eyes. . . . She had forgotten
her face then. It was so good to learn, to grapple with the facts of history, the stirring thoughts of genius. One day Jacques had blurted out:
"But you are beautiful, Félicie!" And by that time it had made no difference.

There was the memorable night then of the visit. Aunt Ninon's husband had returned from San Domingo with its million African slaves.
There was trouble brewing in San Domingo, along with the trouble
that brewed in France. Slaves were sometimes thrown into a flaming
furnace, her uncle said; their bodies were rubbed with sugar, and spoon-
fuls of ants poured into the body cavities; human excrements were
stuffed down their throats; or gunpowder forced into the rectum and
set afire . . . Her father, the doctor, had shaken his head in distress; the
women had exclaimed with horror. But they had *continued to sip their
wine!* Félicie had stolen away, ill, walking for hours over the hard,
cracked sand in the darkness.

In that one night it seemed she had become a woman, sensitive to
the world about her, aching, praying to do something to relieve humanity of its suffering. Oh surely Pierre must understand! . . . Had
he ever watched the sunrise alone on Easter morning?

The Vendée had risen then, against the Revolution. Its people were
simple—believed in their duty to God and King . . . they were willing
to shed their blood for Louis, for the old régime. They were willing to

let the slaves of San Domingo be thrown into a flaming furnace, willing
to let the peasant in France starve while the nobles glutted . . . because this was the way it had always been. Félicie had loved the people
of the Vendée, but M. Flèche said they were little children. Félicie believed one thing with her heart, another with her mind.

It had been kind of Aunt Ninon to take her to Paris. She would
never forget the budding chestnuts, the beauty of the boulevards in
May. One forgets the guillotine at last, but never the rich, live glow
of cathedral windows. . . .

> *What is it we dream of, mon Pierre? Isn't it very much
> the same? Isn't our tragedy not that we have parted, but
> that we stumble along different paths to the same mountain
> top? Catholic, Protestant; nobleman, peasant. Isn't it cour-
> age and truth and a vestige of beauty that we want to save?
> And humanity for those we love? Oh how tragic, my be-
> loved, that we must go by different paths—Mme Roland,
> Louis Capet, M. Voltaire, you and I! Even Robespierre had
> his faith and his Goddess of Reason! . . .*
>
> *My hand is cold and cramped. I have said so much, mon
> cher, and yet it's nothing. . . . I hear a kildee, very sleepy
> still. Strange. I am so wide awake. I have never seen so
> clear. I feel I am looking down into a pool with crystal
> water, and I can see the bottom, the emerald weeds, and
> golden sand.*
>
> *When you come back, mon Pierre, I will be gone. It is
> better so, and you've been wise. And yet tonight it is not
> good-bye. In another life, a resurrection, I will live with you
> in the fields of France. We will till the soil; we will eat our
> bread together in the hot noon sun. At night I'll lie with
> you on a mat of straw, touching your face, your lips, the
> roughness of your hands. I'll give you all the passion of my
> soul—all the passion of France. I'll bear your children, sons
> to work with us in the fields. A hundred sons, mon Pierre,
> so our beauty born in one another will go on and build the
> strength of France again. We'll live immortal in another
> life. Each day alike. Each day too sweet—unbearable be-
> cause it has to end. Work, and wine, and bread and love—
> and work again. And then always the warmth of one an-
> other's love. . . .*
>
> Nicole.

There was another page, a last page, with just one line.

"*It's no use,* mon Pierre. *I want you desperately. I want
you now.*"

Pierre stared at the little ant that crossed the page again, busy with
his bee wing and his future. As if life had not stopped forever! . . .

When Pierre returned to the house Victoire was alone with the
princes. Louis-Philippe and Beaujolais were playing chess, d'Orléans
studying a map while the young sapling divided his attention between
the pawns and some sweetmeats. Victoire toyed with her snuffbox as
the Duc de Montpensier read *Romeo and Juliet* to her.

"I'm afraid it's checkmate," d'Orléans was saying. "If you had moved
your queen instead of that last bonbon—"

"Where have you been, *mon cher?*" cried Victoire. "We kept the
dinner waiting an hour, till our little Beaujolais almost fainted. And
Frau Gresch said the chicken was dry as—"

"I've been in the woods."

"Communing with God?" God was another thing that had stood
between them.

"Is there a God?" said Pierre.

It was plain that nobody had an answer. Chartres's eyes rested on
Victoire without their usual bonhomie; Beaujolais stopped chewing;
and Montpensier repressed a smile and nervously flipped the pages.

Victoire snapped her snuffbox on the table and walked majestically
up the stairs.

"She has been through so much," murmured Montpensier, "the poor
little mother!"

Pierre followed Victoire to their room, glad to be rid of the stifling
scent of flowers in the salon.

"Are you going to stay in this fortress?" she demanded at once as he
closed the door behind him. "I've got to know. I've got to know tonight!"

"Yes, I'm going to stay here."

"Then I am going away!"

"With the Duc de Montpensier?"

"*Oui.*"

He felt a little ill. He had forgotten their room would be drenched
with her Oriental perfume.

"You want me to go!" she cried. "You always hated me—ever since
you manured your lands with my money."

"There's no use pretending any more, Victoire," he said, and he walked to the window and looked down on Nicki's river. "You're right —we're finished."

She burst into tears, throwing herself on the chaise longue. It occurred to him that perhaps she had only been bluffing, and the sense of relief he had felt gave way to apprehension.

"What have I done?" she sobbed. "I've tried everything in my power to keep you! What more could I do—what more could I be? . . ."

For once, he thought, Victoire's soul was naked. He was silent with pity and a real embarrassment.

"Why don't you answer! Why don't you tell me!" she demanded.

"Perhaps the fault was mine," he said by way of comfort.

"Or hers! . . . She held you like a leech and bled you!"

"She loved me too." His voice was like a knife.

"I don't believe it!"

"What does it matter?"

"You did love her then! She was your mistress!"

"Oh, Victoire, in the name of God—"

"You love her now!"

"I'll always love her!"

"Is that what you call love—letting a woman go out of your life as if she were a broken gewgaw?"

"I'm the broken gewgaw."

"*Parbleu!* What do you want of life, you—you—"

"I'm trying to find out."

"You'll never find it in this hell!"

"I want the snows to close me in. I only want to feel the cold and heat—"

"You want death!" she laughed with scorn. "I want life! I want to laugh and love. I want people and things. And beauty and—"

"A crown?" said Pierre.

"Why not! What's wrong with a crown!" She dashed the tears from her eyes.

"You'll get a divorce then?"

"Of course. Though why should I bother—we were never really married!"

Pierre stared at her in a second of unbelief. Then he laughed so long and so brashly that she jumped to her feet in rage.

"You know we weren't married!" she stormed. "You begged me to make it legal. . . . Ask any good Catholic if a marriage by Talleyrand is legal—ask the Pope!"

Pierre thought of Nicki. It was good the boy was dead.

"You should be overjoyed!" she cried. "You'll be free! Maybe now you can marry her!"

He was already at the door of the room. She ran after him, clutching his sleeve, frantic.

"Pierre—Pierre listen to me, *chéri!* If I stay here I'll be driven to murder . . . but I'll go with you anywhere else you say—anywhere under heaven!"

"You wouldn't disappoint the Duc?"

"Pierre!"

"How Mme Reynaud will love the scandal!"

His ultimatum was a crushing blow. But she must smile, must toss her curls, must never let him see it.

"I'll say I am going to visit the Binghams—to protect you."

He wrenched her hand from his arm.

"Has even your courage failed you then, Mme la Duchesse?"

Half of the village stood in the blazing sun to wave adieu to the princes. The polemen were lifting the hawsers, and the Durham boat shivered with the current of the river. Everyone was on board but Victoire. There was the Buzard family, the doctor mopping his face as if he had finished a race, and young René tossing a stone at an eel in the wood fern. Frau Gresch was perched on a trunk like a lump of dough. In their weathered buckskins the three princes might have been simply traders.

The Duc de Montpensier was laden with flowers that had been brought to Victoire. His eyes avoided Pierre, and he was seized with a fit of nervous coughing.

Mme d'Autremont put her arm about Pierre and said sweetly: "I'll mother him while you're gone, *Mme la Marquise."*

Pierre and Victoire looked at one another. The polemen were waiting. The group on shore was anxious to be rid of the buzzing flies and the sun blaze.

The last moment would belong to her, thought Victoire—if it were only a moment of triumph out of a lifetime. She locked her arms about Pierre's neck, held his lips with a crazy longing.

His lips, his eyes were cold—as cold as Nicki's the last hour she had held him. . . .

She tried to scream out her shame but her voice was frozen.

The spell was broken. Someone sneezed. Someone whispered that Pierre was stiff as a Maypole . . . there were the words "Nicki" and "lover" . . . and a general commotion. The adieus started again. The poles shuddered with the mud of the river. Montpensier, dripping flowers, was helping Victoire into the boat.

"Wait!" cried Pierre, pushing his way toward her, and the cheering ceased and Victoire's dull eyes glistened.

He would not let her go then—knew that life would be empty without her! He was coming to snatch her from the silly Duc de Montpensier—to make fervent promises for tomorrow and tomorrow. . . . But why did he look at her as if she were dead—his black eyes softening?

Pierre passed over to her the red velvet case he'd been holding.

"Your jewels," he said with compassion. "You'll need them, Victoire."

A wreath of goldenrod slipped from the Duc de Montpensier's arms, and he recovered it and pressed it merrily over Victoire's curls.

As the boat lurched away she tore off the wreath and tossed it into the river.

❀❀❀❀❀❀❀❀❀❀❀❀❀❀❀❀❀❀❀

CHAPTER XLIX

March 1798

"I'LL PEEL THE ONIONS; you can gouge the eyes out of the potatoes," said Aristide.

The sugaring-off was over; Pierre had remained another few days with du Petit-Thouars to help him repair his granary. In Pierre's bark and puncheon house in the village there was no one waiting.

Pierre squatted beside the stump of a table, attacking a potato with his hunting knife. Aristide shoved aside his manuscript and quill and *Robinson Crusoe* to make room for the onions. The fire blazed under a kettle of herbs and rabbit, neither soup, said Aristide, nor stew, but the specialty of the house.

"We can finish the granary tomorrow," said the Little Admiral. "No doubt you'll be glad to pull up anchor."

"In order to go back and plant my sweet peas?" chaffed Pierre.

"You're getting restless, aren't you?"

"Shouldn't we hear from Talleyrand with any post? It was in September that we wrote him."

"Minister of Foreign Affairs . . . a ministry better suited to him than the Church!" Aristide's pure Touraine accent was always more pronounced when he was indignant.

"In spite of his morals," said Pierre, aiming a potato at the pot, "he's had his ideals—reform of criminal law, free education, study of the elements of religion instead of dogma."

"They say he's asked a pretty penny from every *émigré* he's gotten back into France."

"Won't it be worth it, with your name struck from the list of traitors and your estates and revenues restored?"

"Why should I pay to be where I belong?" growled Aristide. "At the helm of a French ship!"

In the fall the two men had decided to return to France. The French were no longer welcome in America. With the Jay Treaty of a few years past they felt themselves deserted by the States, although French ships were attacking American vessels sailing to England. There was talk of an alien and sedition act, affecting the security of French exiles and other immigrants; there was talk too of President Adams's sending a commission to France in the summer to abrogate all treaties and suspend all commerce. A Federalist leader came out openly and predicted that France and Napoleon, having conquered Italy, would likely make their next objective the Mississippi River.

The colony at Asylum languished. Land titles were still jeopardized by the state disputes between Connecticut and Pennsylvania claimants. Bué de Boulogne had been tragically drowned in the Loyalsock Creek, and Talon had left the previous spring. For several years there had been constant reorganization (with no one housekeeper to guard the keys to the wine and sugar). Pierre had struggled to help the village maintain some unity, form some laws. Most of the farms had long ago been let to the American farmers. M. Carles complained—between bites of cheese—that the colony had lost its spirit with the departure of Victoire and Dr. Buzard.

Whatever the disposition of France with its feeble Directory and worthless *assignats,* it was still *la patrie* to those whose family had shed blood there. Only a few talked of remaining at Asylum: M. Homet; Barthelémi Laporte, Heraud's partner; Antoine Lefèvre, Mme d'Autremont's brother-in-law; Pierre's friend, the little shoemaker.

At first Pierre had determined to stay on with them. His change of mind had been gradual, influenced by loneliness, heat and cold, the death of Nicki, his love of Nicole.

"What are you thinking of, *mon ami?*" asked Aristide, wiping the onion tears on his sleeve.

"I was thinking of Victoire."

"She must have fought death like a hero."

"Yes, the way she fought life. . . . Have you ever seen anyone die of the yellow fever?"

"Many. It's not a—pleasant death."

"She always wanted to get to New York. Why they ever went there during the epidemic. . . . There are so many things I wish the Duc de Montpensier would have told me when he wrote. . . ."

"Victoire wasn't afraid of the fever."

"No. Being ill was dull, she always said. . . . How she'd have loved taking Europe by storm as the mistress of the Duc de Montpensier! Or returning to France some day as his duchesse!"

"You're sorry for Victoire, aren't you?"

"Aren't we always sorry for the fallen proud?"

Aristide kept on peeling though one of the wasps climbed over his fingers at a leisurely gait.

"What do you want of France when you go back?" he asked then.

"The smell of roasting chestnuts, the smell of damp on the quays. I want to hear the bells of St.-Germain L'Auxerrois and stand in the garden where Maurice is buried. I want the sounds and the smells and the sights I knew . . . it must be a thousand years ago!"

"A little dangerous, *n'est-ce pas?*"

"Why?"

"We all want to live in the past, we French—want to rebuild our houses on the old foundations. We've never learned what evolution means. . . . How else could the radicals of the Revolution have thought to overthrow everything old in a trice?"

"I'm willing to accept the new. What's good of it, I mean. I've lived through my tragedy, and so has France. We have new needs, both of us."

"What will you do after you have smelled the chestnuts and listened to the bells of St.-Germain L'Auxerrois?"

Pierre paused. "Why do you ask me that?"

"Isn't it a natural question? . . . Why do you hesitate? Surely you must have asked yourself what you want of France."

"Peace, I suppose. I want to find my mother and—Félicie Roucault."

"And what does she want of you?"

"Félicie?"

"France and Félicie—both."

Pierre frowned. "I hadn't thought of that . . . I'd only thought of what I'll do. Study law, perhaps—become nobility of the robe!"

"You'd make a good lawyer."

"Yes, I think I would . . . And yet, do you know—it sounds a little childish, Aristide—sometimes I'm frightened!"

"What frightens you?"

"I wish I knew. I feel like a little boy going into the dark. There's nothing gruesome there—and yet the danger's very real. . . . But enough of me! What do you want of France?"

"Challenge," said Aristide. "Does life have any zest without it? I'll be going off to sea as soon as I can get there. I have a new score to settle with the water."

Aristide flung the potatoes and onions into the kettle with the vehemence of a cannoneer. There was hot grog waiting on the hearth, and he poured it into a couple of tankards, handing one to Pierre. The Little Admiral raised his tankard in the American fashion.

"To France!" he cried, his soft brown eyes hard with the glint of purpose.

Their eyes met earnest and understanding as Pierre repeated the toast. His heart ached for the Little Admiral who had never forgiven himself for carving the *Pinta* for Nicki. For a while they were silent, absorbed in poignant memories.

Finally Pierre said in a husky voice: "I have never been able to understand it . . . why his dying has given me the will to live!"

"The debt you owe him; you must do his work in the world, as well as your own."

"I can remember thinking once when I believed that I was dying . . . strength passes from mother to son, from son to father . . . never lost, it seems, like hatred."

"Strength is a comprehensive thing. . . ."

"Maybe it's faith I mean. . . . I've had to believe in God to keep
Nicki."

The Little Admiral waited. He had known for months that Pierre
wanted to make confession, that there would come this moment of
confidence between them.

"When you've loved someone who's gone you can't be an atheist!"
said Pierre almost fiercely. "If you've loved him enough you can't believe he's eternally damned to limbo, unbaptized. You want to be with
him again somewhere, somehow, in spirit—in a place that's good—
with a God that's good. It's as simple as that."

"And as beautiful. You still want security for Nicki."

"Yes!"

"Who was it said that the heart has reasons that the mind can never
understand?"

"Rousseau perhaps . . . no matter. What matters is that I have found
a sort of peace—in a primitive God outside of theories and abstractions."

"You doubted me once when I said God was in the storm at sea."

"I remember. I was still feeling with my mind."

"God is easy enough to know," said Aristide, "if you don't force
yourself to define him."

"It's been a painful lesson. There've been moments—one in particular
. . . how can I put it into words, even for you, Aristide?"

"Try, *mon ami.*"

"It was back in November. I was walking home from the village. . . ."

The sky had been softly blue and pink, Pierre said, softly starred,
with the moon clear and lime-colored through the crazed, bare
branches. It was so subtle a coloring, so indefinable that he had had
a swift desire to define it. It was like a bit of dream that escapes one
on wakening—a joyous, fleet sensation, too thrilling to lose. The hue
was the delicacy of a sea shell—the haze of bluebells in a summer twilight; he had felt he must hold it with something, never let it fade.
Hold it with words, perhaps, in an ode or sonnet. And then as he had
struggled for words the beauty faded.

Pierre laughed shortly. "Why must we always use words against the
reality of God? Wanting to cheapen Nature . . . saying the grass fresh
from the rain is like the emerald green of a stage set? That the grandeur of a mountain is like a master's painting? The twigs of elm and
oak against the sky—a scarf of Spanish lace? Why can't we drink in
the beauty of a sunset through our pores without thought? Why must

we try to share it with ourselves, the mortal in us? Pack it into the port-manteau of the mind, like lavender—all crushed? . . ."

"Man wants to create in the likeness of God."

"Why?"

"To help him reach perfection."

"Then why must he use his puny little mind and not his heart? . . . I don't know why I've told you this, Aristide. . . . It seems so insignificant now—with words. . . ."

"Not to me, *mon Pierre*. It's helped me to understand the sort of faith you've found, and how you've found it."

"Poor God! No one ever seeks Him till He's needed."

"You did, I know. But we seldom eat unless we're hungry—animal instinct."

"At least tragedy teaches a man that he can't stand alone."

"You never found your God in France. Your life there was filled with tragedy."

"Not really. It's only through Nicki that I've suffered beneath the surface. . . . You know, this standing alone is a curious thing—a paradox. All my life until now I've leaned on someone human—Marie Antoinette, my father, my mother, the philosophers. Even here I leaned on Nicki though he was little . . . yet I thought I stood alone. Now, with a faith that belongs to me and no one else, I am not actually standing alone, and yet I feel that I am. . . . Plato would think me very gauche!"

"Plato would be proud of you! . . . But there's another paradox. I wonder if you've thought of it. It's this: a man finds his own peculiar religion and is ready to walk alone, as you say. It's only then that he's ready to walk with his Church. . . . Why does the Church totter now and then, have its years of success and failure? It's human, like a government, like you and me. And it needs the man like you who has learned to feel after he has learned to think."

"You confuse me, Aristide . . . I don't want a Church. There are things in the Church I never could believe."

"One usually stands by a friend he has known all his life though he doesn't always agree with his friend!"

"But the creeds—"

"They're for the man who has learned to feel before he has learned to think. . . . Is there any church, I wonder, in which every man believes everything he's taught?"

"I don't want to live by rote." Pierre frowned.

"I've often thought that religion is like an art. To be expert one must know his technique and then forget it. . . . When one forgets himself he is really working for himself."

"You want me to be an artist in faith!" Pierre smiled.

"Why not? Every fine artist is a man of prayer, as my *gouverneur* used to say. . . . Pray and the portrait paints itself; pray and the Church will come to you with its faith."

"I am still not able to pray. . . . "

"You have only begun, *mon Pierre,* to live. There'll come a time of fullness, of illumination, of a storm at sea. And when it comes—like love, you will know it."

※※※※※※※※※※※※※※※※※※※※※

CHAPTER L

"GREEN WALNUTS! Green walnuts!"

"The list of the winners in the lottery!"

"Carpe vive!"

"Portugaises! Portugaises!"

The cries of all Paris were in Pierre's ears. Here were the sounds and sights and smells he had longed for. Here were the bells of St.-Germain L'Auxerrois—more hollow, somehow, than he had remembered them.

Theater bills crowded one another in a riot of color and insistence: *Athalie* was being played tonight; come and see the marionettes, the tightrope walkers! Here, in a booth for a trifle one might see the girl who gave birth to rabbits. There were blind men's dogs and beggars' crutches; thieves and poets; saucy urchins, street singers, fortunetellers. The Pont-Neuf was still a screaming Hydra. There was spoiled fish for sale—and spoiled beauty. Cats, dogs, canaries; meowing, barking, singing. There were mud and the white footprint of the plasterer; soapy water trickling from a barber shop; straw on a walk to dull the noise of traffic for the dying. Bosoms higher—but bosoms; ankles laced—but ankles. The pungence of horse dung, perfume, roasted coffee; the whinny of horses, the kiss of a lover, the lament of funeral mourners. Flowers bloomed everywhere as if springtime had playfully tossed an armful over the city: a tiny plum tree in a window box; roses on hats; pinks in the half of a packing case, in buttonholes, crushed in the gutter, over the ear of a stallion. Carriages, still, with their gentlemen. What if the faces had changed and the blood was not so blue in the hand that waved directions!

Pierre drifted slowly through the confusion. He was on his way to see Talleyrand, who had taken a splendid mansion, formerly Hôtel Créquy, in the rue d'Anjou. Pierre realized that he was frightened. He had been in Paris for several days, and in spite of the sounds and the sights and the smells Paris had not come alive for him.

What was there in France that would give him the peace and happiness he longed for? Why had he left America if it was freedom and progress he wanted? He wondered what he had really wanted of Paris; he had not wanted her to be changed, and yet he had not wanted her to fling back at him memories of blood and hiding. Once in Paris, he had not dared to visit the Tuileries, the Palais-Royal Gardens, or go to the grave of Maurice. Yet Dominique seemed to follow him in the streets; the thought of Marie Antoinette rotting in the Madeleine haunted him; he expected to see Angélique skulking in every shadow. He had been tormented from the moment of his coming, each day a greater trial than the one before it.

Why had he supposed that the smell of damp on the quays, the bells of St.-Germain L'Auxerrois would bring to him a fulfillment he had never found anywhere—that there was any escape from this searching?

Even now, coming to the rue d'Anjou, he avoided the doll's house where he had lived with Silvie. After his interview with Talleyrand he would go on to the Vendée, would find Félicie Roucault. But what would he tell her? It would not be enough to tell her that he loved her. Could he tell her that he was frightened, a little boy alone in the dark —that he had a feeling of belonging nowhere?

He longed for Aristide; he wanted to tell him that freedom has nothing to do with a place, that freedom is in one's thinking, and that he, Pierre, was cursed without it. Aristide had always had an answer. But Aristide had already left for Toulon to join Napoleon and set sail for Egypt.

Pierre was alone.

He found the house and was shown into Talleyrand's study. M. Talleyrand would be with him directly.

The room was crowded with books, portfolios, framed maps of foreign countries; above a cabinet of liqueurs hung the coat of arms of the Périgords. It bore the motto *"Ré que Dieu"*—God Only Above Us. Also over the mantel hung a solid gold crucifix set with sapphires. But on the mantel was a Patriot clock. The dial was in the middle of two pyramids; inscribed at the top was the name of Thomas Paine, and below, the names of Republican authors and heroes. The clock ticked with a loud assurance.

In a few moments Pierre heard the Abbé's footsteps—light, heavy, light—as he limped to the study door and entered.

One never knew what to expect of this man, thought Pierre, as they greeted one another with a mild profusion. The buckskins of a backwoodsman—the embroidered lounging robe of a minister. He wondered if in all the years of Talleyrand's church life he had ever really prayed. . . .

Pierre would never be able to express his gratitude. . . .

Ah, yes, but he would. . . .

In words, that is. Gratitude from the heart. . . .

Asylum had become so unbearable then?

Talleyrand eased himself into an elegant Roman armchair. The folds of his robe seemed to flow with an elegance over his knees. His hands had no need of snuffbox or pen to toy with. There had even been something of elegance and grace in the dragging of his foot. As he talked now about Pierre's ocean voyage he spoke slowly and selected his words with delicacy. They were the rich, melodious phrases of a priest who had conducted Mass with an unctuous rhythm. He was a man who knew where he was going.

Pierre hated him. Talleyrand was old France and new France, even as Pierre, and yet with a doubt he knew where he was going.

Pierre wanted to leave at once. After the amenities were over he asked Talleyrand the amount of gratuity expected.

"Fifty thousand francs," said Talleyrand.

"Fifty thousand francs!" Pierre exclaimed.

"Mais oui, M. le Marquis. When your estates are returned to you it will seem the barest trifle. Perhaps you haven't noticed that France is having an inflation."

Pierre gazed with scorn into the blue, shrewd eyes—at the soft, cynical smile.

"It was not simple, you know, *M. le Marquis,* to arrange your papers. There were few more active than you against the Revolution. It was known of course that you went to America to receive the Dauphin. If I had not seen you personally at Asylum I could hardly have convinced the Directory that you'd changed—that you were no longer Royalist—that in fact when the time came it was you who helped to abduct the Dauphin."

"*Monsieur!* . . ." stammered Pierre, jumping to his feet and staring at the rosewater Abbé with loathing and incredulity.

Talleyrand shrugged a little and smiled.

"I was happy to do you the favor," he said. "No one has ever amused me more—by her wit alone of course—than the unfortunate *Mme la Marquise.*"

Pierre began to laugh. Like the night Annette had given birth to her baby he was unable to stop the laughter. Out in the street people turned to stare at him, mistaking the tears of shame and humiliation. All of Paris seemed to be laughing—a hard, brittle laughter that fell like splinters of glass about him.

"Rabbit skins!"

"Scissors, knives, and combs!"

"Violets!"

Even the bells of St.-Germain l'Auxerrois were laughing, mocking. The damned jangling bells that clung to him like a nest of barnacles!

So this was the kind of France he had come to—the new France, of the people! The France of Talleyrand, and Nicole, and Napoleon. A France bled of every trace of decency and idealism. He would leave it forever to the vultures—would go on to a clean land, a Sweden or a Switzerland. . . .

But where was it all to end, he thought, as he rambled, frantic, about the city. There was no running away from one's self; he had learned that lesson the night of the fog in Philadelphia. There was no running away from fear, or shame, or loneliness, or desperation. One had to meet these things with something stronger. What did he have that was stronger? The simple God that Nicki had given him? What power had this simple God compared with the faith of Maurice, the trust of an Aristide du Petit-Thouars?

Jostled by a group of youths, he drifted with them into a small café. They settled noisily at a table and banged for service. Pierre sank back into a corner where it was dark. It was a habit that remained to him from the Revolution.

He had no idea why he had come to this place. He wanted to think, if he could collect his emotions, and he was exhausted. It had been the wrong place to come to—hot, bustling, cheap, with the reek of spirits to distract him. He would go on somewhere else. It was a church perhaps that he needed—the coolness of a church with its hush and aged incense. He began to push away from the table and he had the strange sensation that there were two of him.

"You're running away again," one of him said. "It's here and now that you must face your problem!"

"I can't stand the din!" cried the other.

. "You can't stand yourself!" cried the first. "Where can you go to get away from Pierre de Michelait?"

Pierre fell back into his seat, gripping at the sides of the table.

The doubts of the years had caught up with him at last. What did he believe? What did he expect of the years before him? He had never been taught to face facts squarely . . . that was the Abbé Blafond and his infernal Jesuitism. And if the Jansenist God denied him the will for good what was the use of all this agony?

"But I don't believe in the Jansenist God," he cried out to himself. "I believe in a juster God who's hiding. Where is he if I believe in him? Why doesn't he come forth and help me? Isn't that what God's for? . . . If Aristide were here, he'd help me . . . but why do I want Aristide? I am going to have to live my life without him! I told him that I'd learned to stand alone. Now that I'm alone I know I haven't. . . .

"What do I believe? What do I believe in for the future? Do I believe I wanted the Dauphin on the throne, or do I believe in government by the people? Do I want to keep what is old and decadent, or do I want something new and better?

"Answer—*answer*, you coward! Do you want to keep on knowing the tailor and shoemaker, working together with them, as you did in America? Do you want Liberty, Equality, and Fraternity—and aren't you willing to fight for them? Why do you sweat, you fool? Why don't you come out with the truth as you see it? In your youth you weren't a coward; you believed in Marie Antoinette and you fought for her. Now you believe in the tailor, don't you—and the little shoemaker back in Asylum? Aren't you man enough to fight for them too? They're not strong enough to live without you. They need your help in their struggles. All of the guillotines they can build are not so strong as your understanding and intelligence. Well, why are you waiting—waiting

. . . I thought you'd learned that waiting makes you desperate! Why don't you say what you believe? Grégoire and Shakespeare . . . 'To thine own self be true, and it must follow as the night the day—'

"Claret, Monsieur, or brandy?"

Pierre looked up at M. Heraud. But it wasn't M. Heraud. And it wasn't Asylum. It was Paris—a new, broken Paris. He nodded.

"Brandy?"

Pierre nodded again, tugging at the cravat that had become damp and limp and insufferable.

Asylum . . . he longed for Asylum. It was there he'd found deep beauty—the silence of the winter nights, the majesty of the hemlocks, the peace of friendship, the love of Nicki. There too he had learned what it meant to love a woman—to look beyond little hard, ripe breasts into a soul more satisfying than a body. . . . "Have you ever really loved a woman?" Aristide had asked him. "That has nothing to do with God." . . . "Then you've never given yourself wholly to God or woman." . . . It was after he'd known that he loved Nicole that his greatest moment of beauty had come to him. But he hadn't left it behind. He would always carry it with him. . . .

One noon as he lay in the field he had seemed to escape entirely from his body. He had been alone and his muscles ached from ploughing. There had been a small insect climbing up a blade of grass. His first impulse was to flick it away, for no reason perhaps except that he was strong and the insect weak. But he had paused to look at it, watching the quick antennae working on some unseen substance. Then he had studied the gossamer wings webbed so finely with veins, little threads of energy that gave color and movement to the tiny thing. The blade of grass suddenly became alive too. It was greener than green, liver than the life that flowed through his own tired body. It was so small— and yet so mighty. A blade of grass—and then infinite blades of grass about him. They seemed to accumulate might, and he had almost a feeling of terror that he had never seen a blade of grass in this way before. The power he felt around him extended to the gnarled root of the tree, to the loftiness of its branches, and then to the dazzling blue of the sky. The truth of this power struck him with such force that he began to breathe fast as if he had been running, and he had no power to move for the larger power all about him. The whir of a dragonfly, the rustle of leaves, the pulse of the river—all swept into a melodic symphony growing in volume until the ineffable momentum of it was more than he could bear. Color and sound blinded and deafened him;

the smell of the earth and its lusty weeds stupefied him. And yet it was the first time he had ever felt completely out of himself, and it was as if his body lay there dead and all the ecstasy he had known had left him to unite with what was beyond him. There was no body left, only pure emotion, swept into a greater magnitude than he had ever known existed. He had no idea later how long he had lain there. Eternities had come and gone, sweeping his consciousness before them. He had never known such rapture in his wildest dreaming, for there had always been the dreams and his body to make it finite.

He remembered the shock of finding that he had a body. He had felt desolate, bewildered, staring at his hands grimed with earth. He had not even told Aristide what had happened. There are no words for the time when the soul leaves the body.

He had been close—so close—to something he wanted. He knew now that if he'd reached out his hand he might have touched it.

Now too, even in this squalid café, if he reached out his hand. . . .

There was a violent pop at the young men's table. The cork of a bottle of champagne had flown to the ceiling. The proprietor raved. His beautiful ceiling! It had just been painted. Now look! Ugly with wine marks! Pigs shouldn't drink champagne—only gentlemen who knew how to open bottles!

Pierre found that his hands were trembling as he shoved aside his glass of untouched brandy and listened to the bickering.

"A ladder!" shouted the youth with brushes bulging from his pocket. "Bring me a ladder."

The proprietor sputtered.

"A ladder!" shouted the others in chorus. "Our kingdom for a ladder!"

One of the youths emptied his pockets on the table. The rest followed suit. It was a miserable total they thrust into the mollified hand of the proprietor. The youth with the brushes bulging from his pocket hadn't a sou. He was thin and flushed with the high color of a consumptive. The coat he wore was too large for him.

When the ladder arrived he climbed it with his glass of champagne and pulled from his pocket one of the brushes and some fresh tubes of oil. Wetting the brush in his wine, he began to paint while his friends kept vigil with their singing. Others in the café gathered round to watch him. The amorphous stain was disappearing, and in its place there flew a swallow. His comrades cheered as the artist finished with a flourish and downed the remainder of his wine.

"To the spirit of France!" cried one, and the whole café joined in the uproar. "To the spirit that's never conquered!"

It was a little thing—no more than the work of the insect's antennae on the blade of grass. But to Pierre the incident was a miracle. He raised his glass with the others and shouted. "To the spirit of France!" And he knew that he had reached out his hand and touched what he wanted. The knowledge was overwhelming.

The spirit of France was in him—even as it was in the artist! France belonged to him: a deformed France in need of transfiguration. He wanted to take France in his two hands like a ball of clay and mold into her the hard-won strength of his fingers; he wanted to mold into her the cleanness and sweetness of ancient American forests; he would fashion of her a new figure of beauty, wise with the tragedy he had endured but sweet with the hope that was born of suffering. He would lift her brave hands to the heavens, her eyes to the stars. There would be a fresh purity, a litheness in the ancient, fertile limbs—a quickening of the soul that had given her birth.

His eyes clouded and he had a pain in his throat. But he felt light as the new-born swallow. He dashed his glass to the floor and hurried out to the blinding sun of the street. The Maytime of the Paris afternoon became muddled and swam before him gaudily, like the oils of a landscape too close to the vision. For a brief second, he felt ashamed . . . felt that the tears and ecstasy were maudlin.

Then suddenly he knew that he had been praying.

It was not the prayer of the Jansenist, or the prayer of the Jesuit. It had no words to give it form, no benefit of bended knee or rosary. It was a labored thing—a struggling, mighty, desperate thing like the genesis of time. It was a prayer peculiarly his own, the prayer of a man who knew where he was going.

Paris magically became alive. Every sound and smell became a part of him. Every church bell echoed his freedom. The hawkers' cries were molten music. He wanted to sing out with them all like a drunken gypsy.

"Green walnuts! Green walnuts!"

"The list of the winners in the lottery!"

"Death to the rats!"

"*La Vie! La Vie!*"